MARVEL-VERSE
KRAVEN THE HUNTER

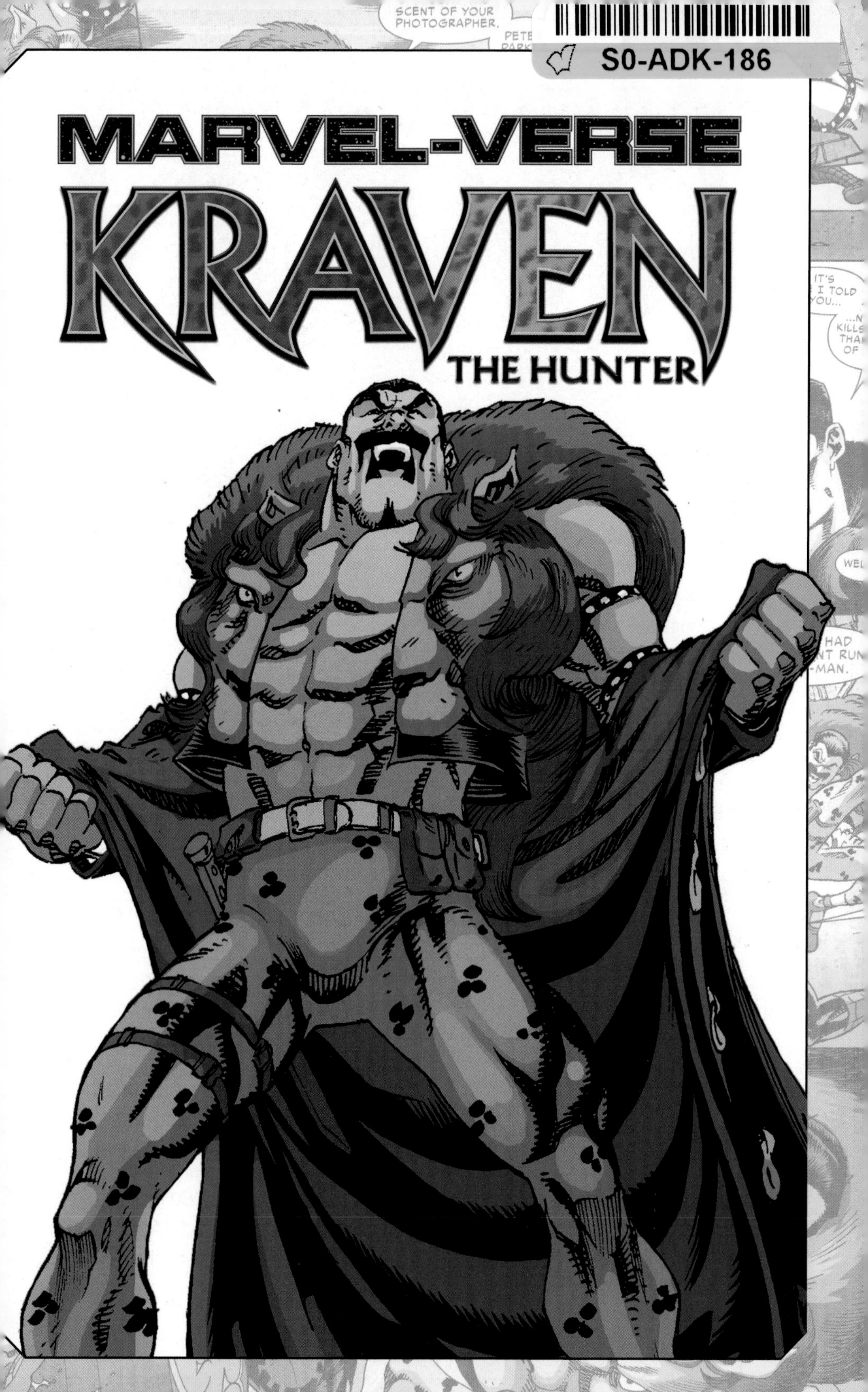

MARVEL-VERSE
KRAVEN
THE HUNTER

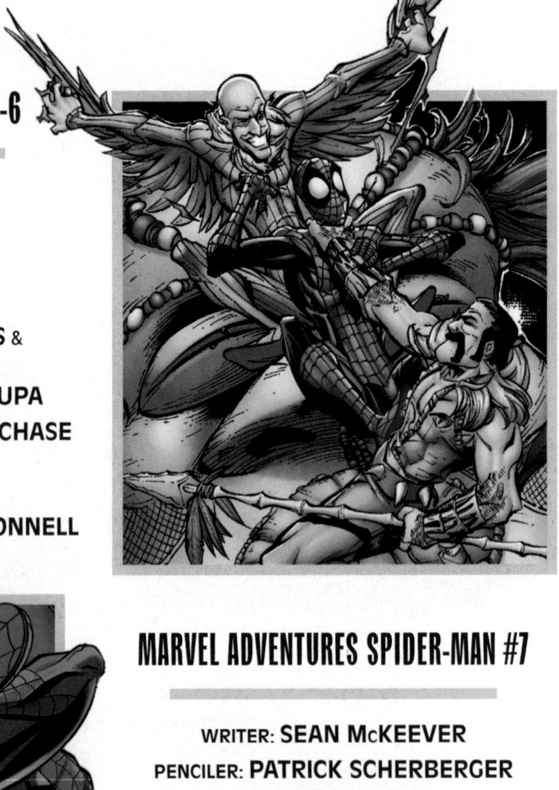

MARVEL ACTION SPIDER-MAN #5-6

WRITER: **ERIK BURNHAM**

ARTIST: **CHRISTOPHER JONES**

COLOR ARTIST: **ZAC ATKINSON**

LETTERER: **SHAWN LEE**

COVER ART: **CHRISTOPHER JONES** & **ZAC ATKINSON**

ASSISTANT EDITOR: **ANNI PERHEENTUPA**

ASSOCIATE EDITORS: **ELIZABETH BREI** & **CHASE MAROTZ**

EDITOR: **DENTON J. TIPTON**

ASSISTANT EDITOR, MARVEL: **CAITLIN O'CONNELL**

SPECIAL THANKS TO **NICK LOWE**

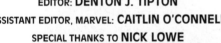

MARVEL ADVENTURES SPIDER-MAN #7

WRITER: **SEAN McKEEVER**

PENCILER: **PATRICK SCHERBERGER**

INKER: **NORMAN LEE**

COLOR ARTISTS: **GURU-eFX's HARTMAN** & **BEVARD**

LETTERER: **DAVE SHARPE**

COVER ART: **TONY S. DANIEL** & SOTOCOLOR's **J. RAUCH**

ASSISTANT EDITOR: **NATHAN COSBY**

EDITOR: **MacKENZIE CADENHEAD**

CONSULTING EDITOR: **MARK PANICCIA**

MARVEL ADVENTURES SUPER HEROES #4

WRITER: **PAUL TOBIN**

PENCILER: **RONAN CLIQUET**

INKER: **AMILTON SANTOS**

COLOR ARTIST: **SOTOCOLOR**

LETTERER: **DAVE SHARPE**

COVER ART: **CLAYTON HENRY** &
BRAD ANDERSON

ASSISTANT EDITOR: **MICHAEL HORWITZ**

EDITOR: **NATHAN COSBY**

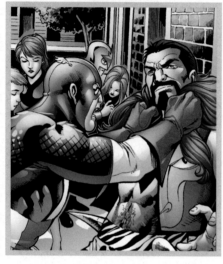

SPIDEY #9

WRITER: **ROBBIE THOMPSON**

ARTIST: **NATHAN STOCKMAN**

ORIGIN ARTIST: **NICK BRADSHAW**

COLOR ARTIST: **JIM CAMPBELL**

LETTERER: VC's **TRAVIS LANHAM**

COVER ART: **KHARY RANDOLPH** &
EMILIO LOPEZ

EDITOR: **DARREN SHAN**

EXECUTIVE EDITOR: **NICK LOWE**

KRAVEN CREATED BY STAN LEE & STEVE DITKO

COLLECTION EDITOR: **JENNIFER GRÜNWALD** ASSISTANT EDITOR: **DANIEL KIRCHHOFFER**

ASSOCIATE MANAGER, TALENT RELATIONS: **LISA MONTALBANO** VP PRODUCTION & SPECIAL PROJECTS: **JEFF YOUNGQUIST**

RESEARCH: **JESS HARROLD** BOOK DESIGNER: **STACIE ZUCKER** MANAGER & SENIOR DESIGNER: **ADAM DEL RE** LEAD DESIGNER: **JAY BOWEN**

SVP PRINT, SALES & MARKETING: **DAVID GABRIEL** EDITOR IN CHIEF: **C.B. CEBULSKI**

MARVEL-VERSE: KRAVEN THE HUNTER. Contains material originally published in magazine form as MARVEL ACTION SPIDER-MAN (2018) #5-6, MARVEL ADVENTURES SPIDER-MAN (2005) #7, MARVEL ADVENTURES SUPER HEROES (2010) #4 and SPIDEY (2015) #9. First printing 2023. ISBN 978-1-302-95064-4. Published by MARVEL WORLDWIDE, INC., a subsidiary of MARVEL ENTERTAINMENT, LLC. OFFICE OF PUBLICATION: 1290 Avenue of the Americas, New York, NY 10104. © 2023 MARVEL No similarity between any of the names, characters, persons, and/or institutions in this book with those of any living or dead person or institution is intended, and any such similarity which may exist is purely coincidental. **Printed in Canada.** KEVIN FEIGE, Chief Creative Officer; DAN BUCKLEY, President, Marvel Entertainment; DAVID BOGART, Associate Publisher & SVP of Talent Affairs; TOM BREVOORT, VP, Executive Editor; NICK LOWE, Executive Editor, VP of Content, Digital Publishing; DAVID GABRIEL, VP of Print & Digital Publishing; SVEN LARSEN, VP of Licensed Publishing; MARK ANNUNZIATO, VP of Planning & Forecasting; JEFF YOUNGQUIST, VP of Production & Special Projects; ALEX MORALES, Director of Publishing Operations; DAN EDINGTON, Director of Editorial Operations; RICKEY PURDIN, Director of Talent Relations; JENNIFER GRÜNWALD, Director of Production & Special Projects; SUSAN CRESPI, Production Manager; STAN LEE, Chairman Emeritus. For information regarding advertising in Marvel Comics or on Marvel.com, please contact Vit DeBellis, Custom Solutions & Integrated Advertising Manager, at vdebellis@marvel.com. For Marvel subscription inquiries, please call 888-511-5480. **Manufactured between 6/23/2023 and 8/1/2023 by SOLISCO PRINTERS, SCOTT, QC, CANADA.**

10 9 8 7 6 5 4 3 2 1

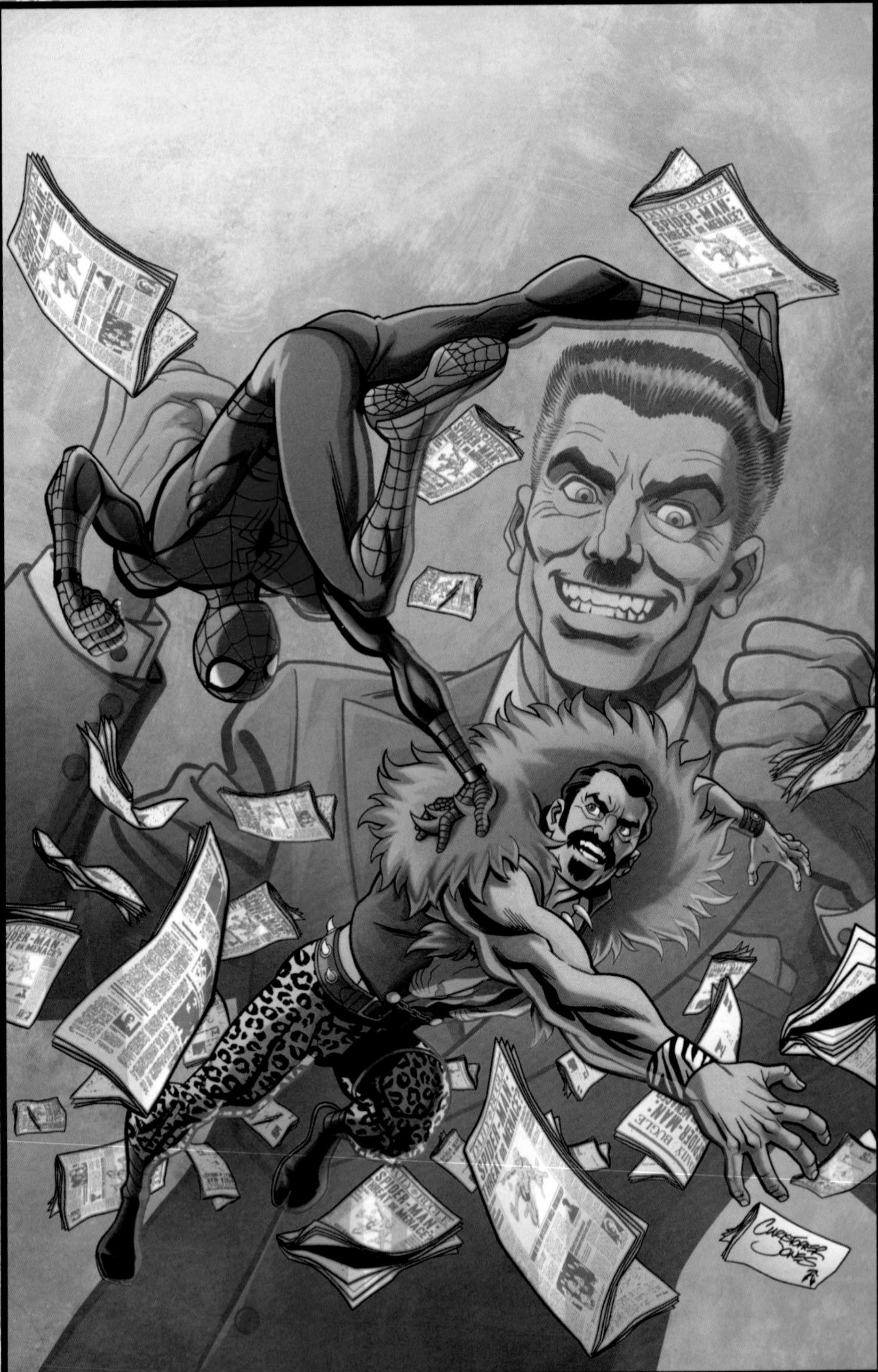
DAILY BUGLE
SPIDER-MAN: THREAT OR MENACE?

MARVEL ACTION SPIDER-MAN #5

PETER PARKER AND FELLOW SPIDER-HEROES MILES MORALES AND GWEN STACY HAVE JOINED FORCES! UNFORTUNATELY, THEY'RE ALL BEING STALKED BY A DANGEROUS NEW FOE: KRAVEN THE HUNTER!

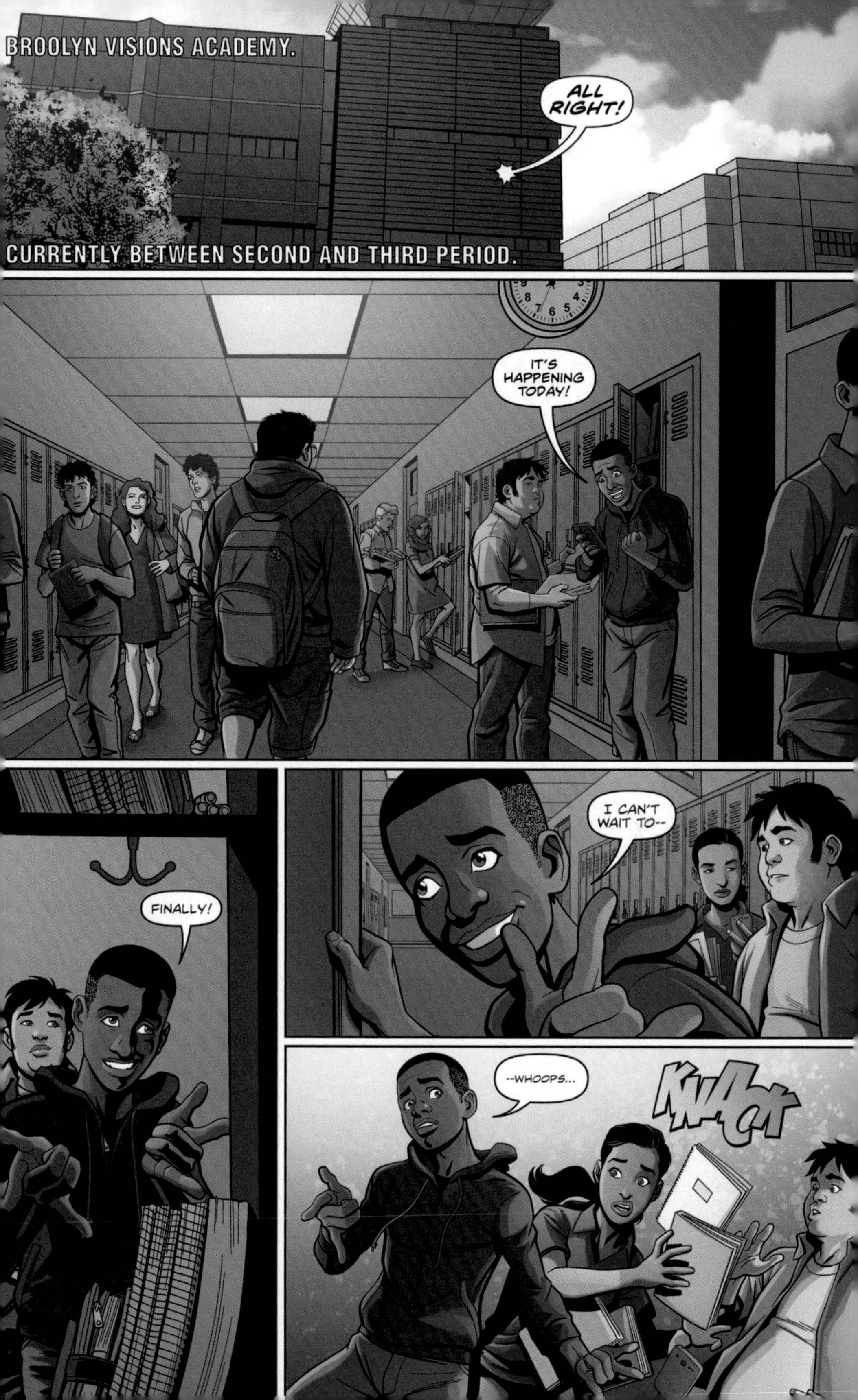
BROOLYN VISIONS ACADEMY.
ALL RIGHT!
CURRENTLY BETWEEN SECOND AND THIRD PERIOD.
IT'S HAPPENING TODAY!
FINALLY!
I CAN'T WAIT TO--
--WHOOPS...
KWACK

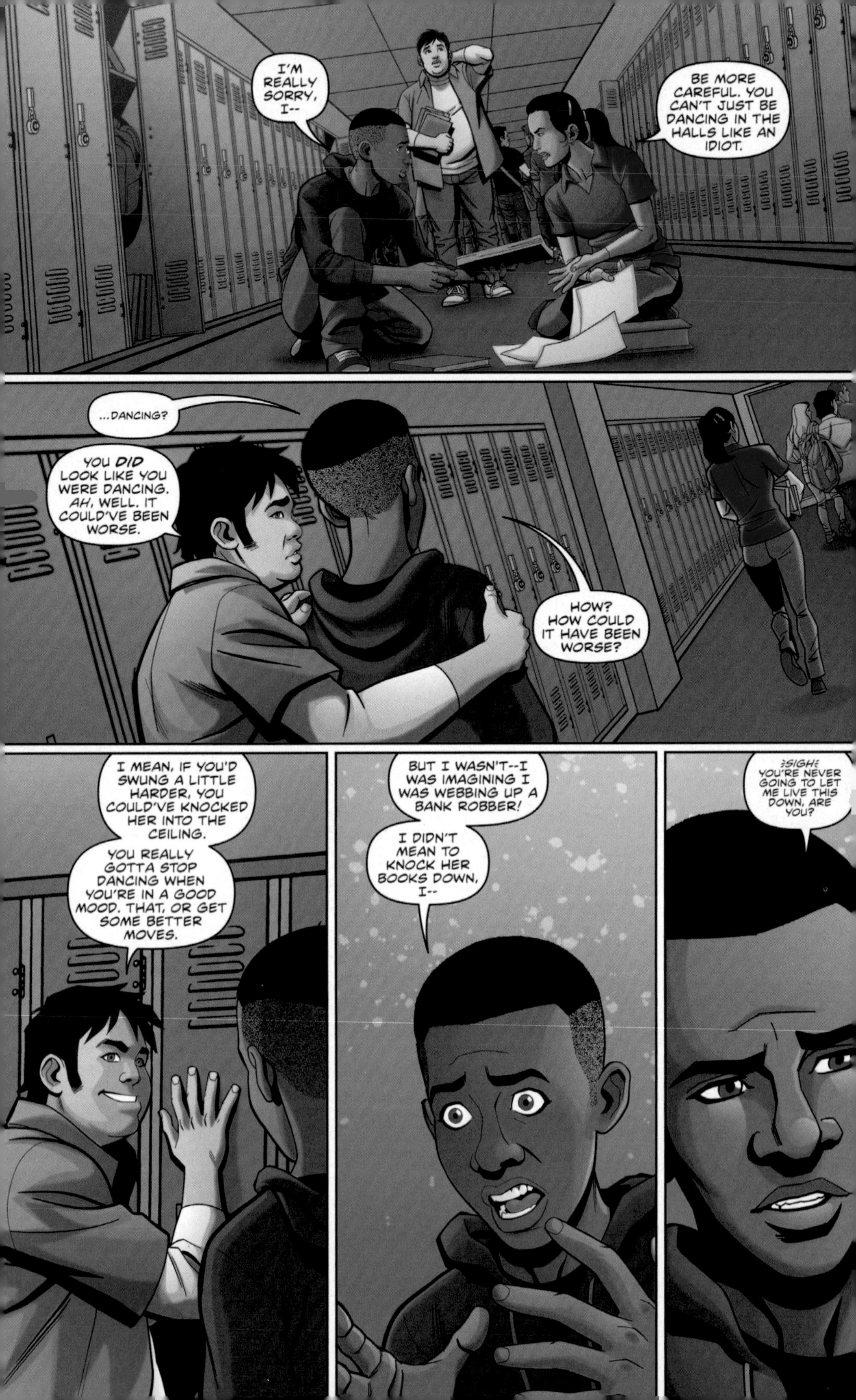
I'M REALLY SORRY, I--
BE MORE CAREFUL. YOU CAN'T JUST BE DANCING IN THE HALLS LIKE AN IDIOT.
...DANCING?
YOU DID LOOK LIKE YOU WERE DANCING. AH, WELL. IT COULD'VE BEEN WORSE.
HOW? HOW COULD IT HAVE BEEN WORSE?
I MEAN, IF YOU'D SWUNG A LITTLE HARDER, YOU COULD'VE KNOCKED HER INTO THE CEILING.
YOU REALLY GOTTA STOP DANCING WHEN YOU'RE IN A GOOD MOOD. THAT, OR GET SOME BETTER MOVES.
BUT I WASN'T--I WAS IMAGINING I WAS WEBBING UP A BANK ROBBER!
I DIDN'T MEAN TO KNOCK HER BOOKS DOWN, I--
SIGH
YOU'RE NEVER GOING TO LET ME LIVE THIS DOWN, ARE YOU?

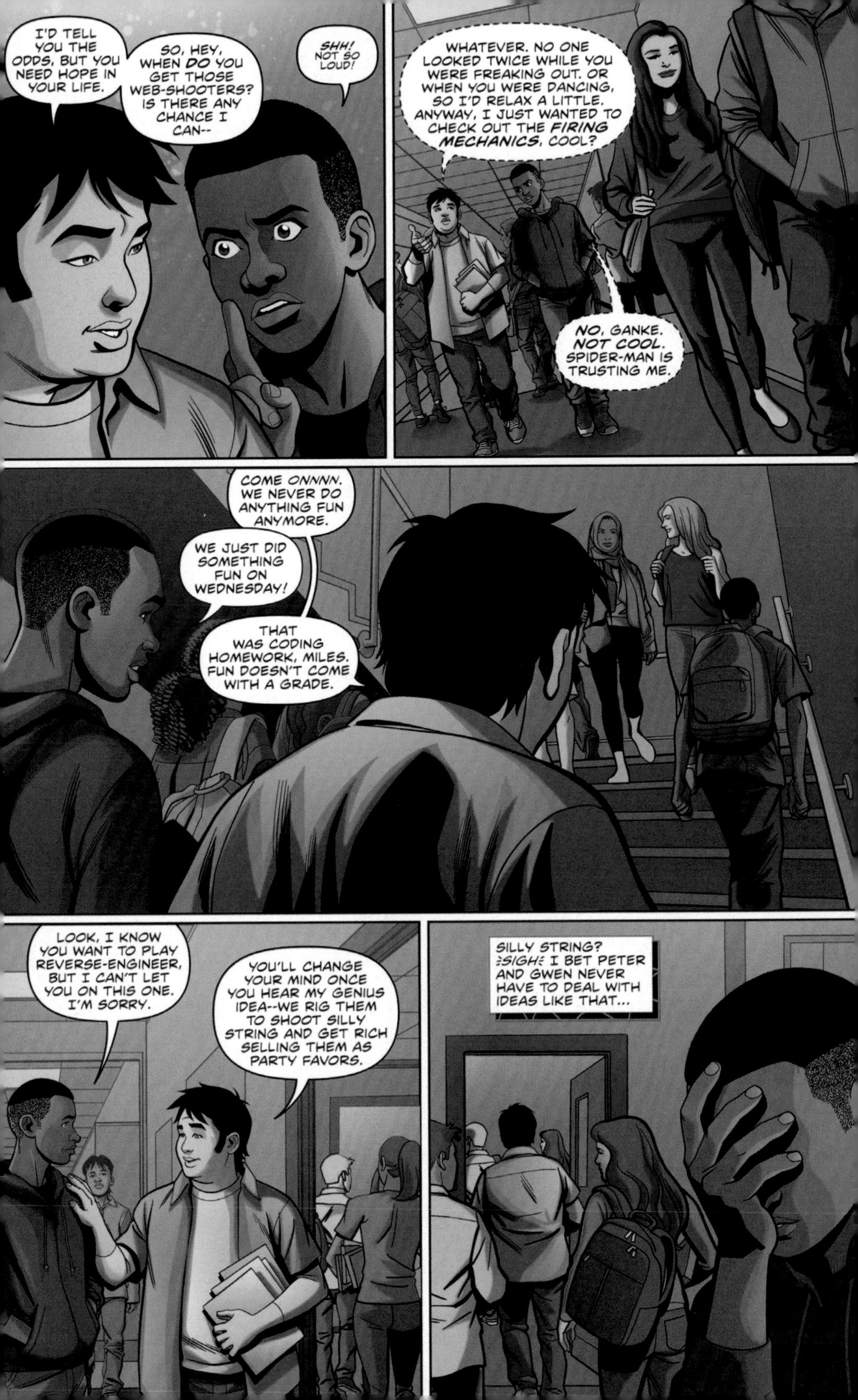
I'D TELL YOU THE ODDS, BUT YOU NEED HOPE IN YOUR LIFE.
SO, HEY, WHEN DO YOU GET THOSE WEB-SHOOTERS? IS THERE ANY CHANCE I CAN--
SHH! NOT SO LOUD!
WHATEVER. NO ONE LOOKED TWICE WHILE YOU WERE FREAKING OUT. OR WHEN YOU WERE DANCING, SO I'D RELAX A LITTLE. ANYWAY, I JUST WANTED TO CHECK OUT THE FIRING MECHANICS, COOL?
NO, GANKE. NOT COOL. SPIDER-MAN IS TRUSTING ME.
COME ONNNN. WE NEVER DO ANYTHING FUN ANYMORE.
WE JUST DID SOMETHING FUN ON WEDNESDAY!
THAT WAS CODING HOMEWORK, MILES. FUN DOESN'T COME WITH A GRADE.
LOOK, I KNOW YOU WANT TO PLAY REVERSE-ENGINEER, BUT I CAN'T LET YOU ON THIS ONE. I'M SORRY.
YOU'LL CHANGE YOUR MIND ONCE YOU HEAR MY GENIUS IDEA--WE RIG THEM TO SHOOT SILLY STRING AND GET RICH SELLING THEM AS PARTY FAVORS.
SILLY STRING? SIGH I BET PETER AND GWEN NEVER HAVE TO DEAL WITH IDEAS LIKE THAT...

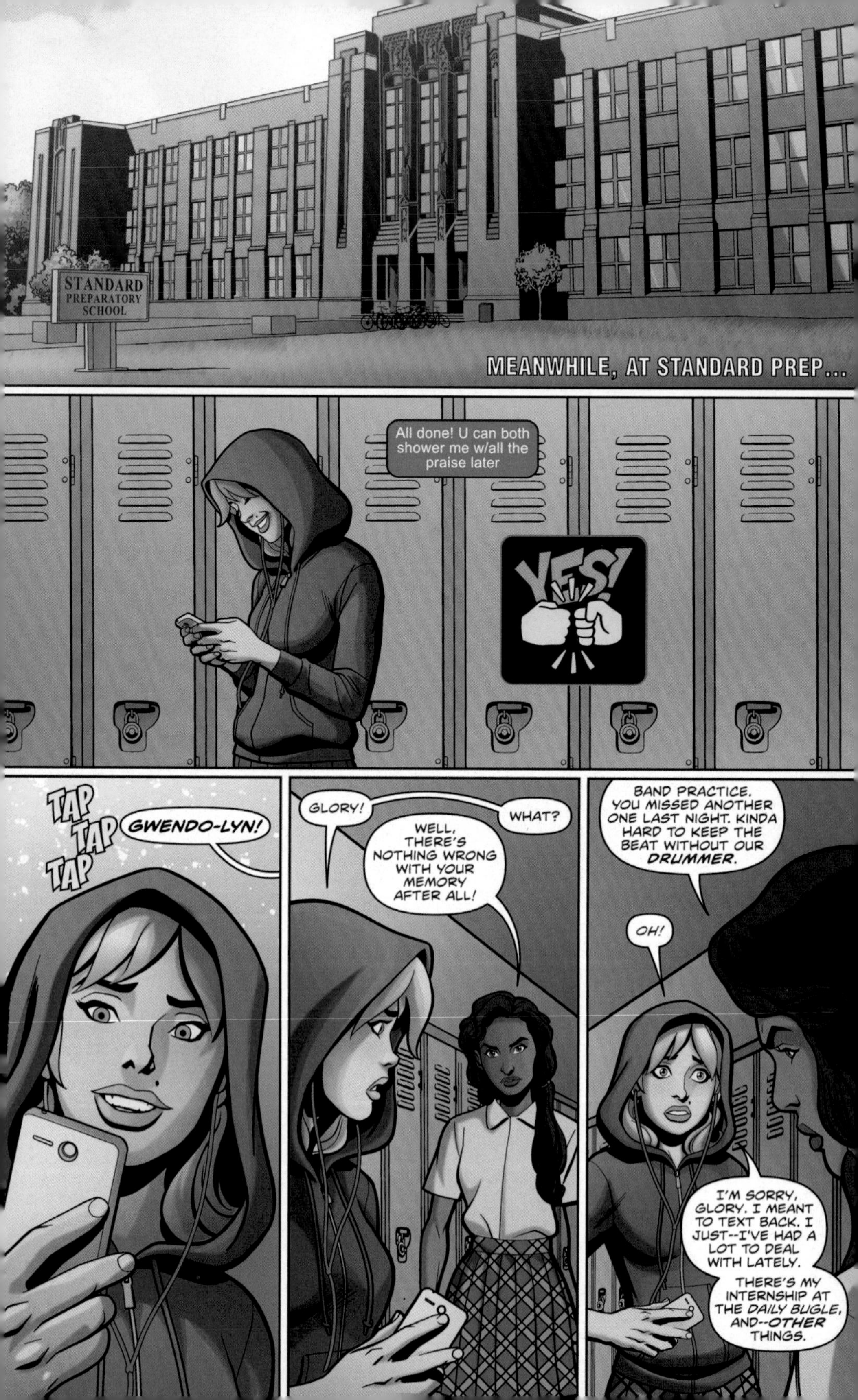
STANDARD PREPARATORY SCHOOL
MEANWHILE, AT STANDARD PREP...
All done! U can both shower me w/all the praise later
YES!
TAP TAP TAP
GWENDO-LYN!
GLORY!
WHAT?
WELL, THERE'S NOTHING WRONG WITH YOUR MEMORY AFTER ALL!
BAND PRACTICE. YOU MISSED ANOTHER ONE LAST NIGHT. KINDA HARD TO KEEP THE BEAT WITHOUT OUR DRUMMER.
OH!
I'M SORRY, GLORY. I MEANT TO TEXT BACK. I JUST--I'VE HAD A LOT TO DEAL WITH LATELY.
THERE'S MY INTERNSHIP AT THE DAILY BUGLE, AND--OTHER THINGS.

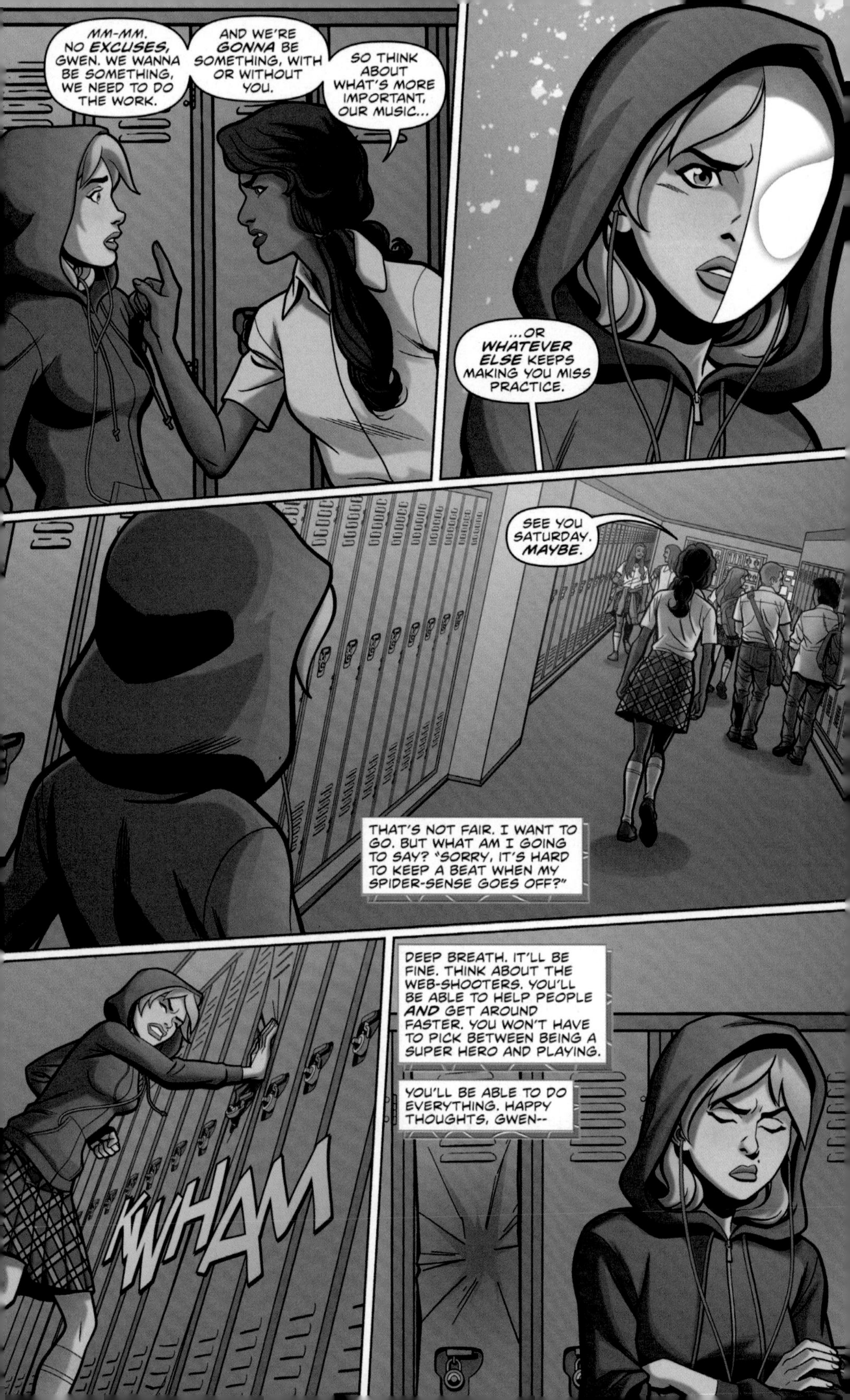
MM-MM. NO *EXCUSES*, GWEN. WE WANNA BE SOMETHING, WE NEED TO DO THE WORK.
AND WE'RE *GONNA* BE SOMETHING, WITH OR WITHOUT YOU.
SO THINK ABOUT WHAT'S MORE IMPORTANT, OUR MUSIC...
...OR *WHATEVER ELSE* KEEPS MAKING YOU MISS PRACTICE.
SEE YOU SATURDAY. *MAYBE*.
THAT'S NOT FAIR. I WANT TO GO. BUT WHAT AM I GOING TO SAY? "SORRY, IT'S HARD TO KEEP A BEAT WHEN MY SPIDER-SENSE GOES OFF?"
WHAM
DEEP BREATH. IT'LL BE FINE. THINK ABOUT THE WEB-SHOOTERS. YOU'LL BE ABLE TO HELP PEOPLE *AND* GET AROUND FASTER. YOU WON'T HAVE TO PICK BETWEEN BEING A SUPER HERO AND PLAYING.
YOU'LL BE ABLE TO DO EVERYTHING. HAPPY THOUGHTS, GWEN--

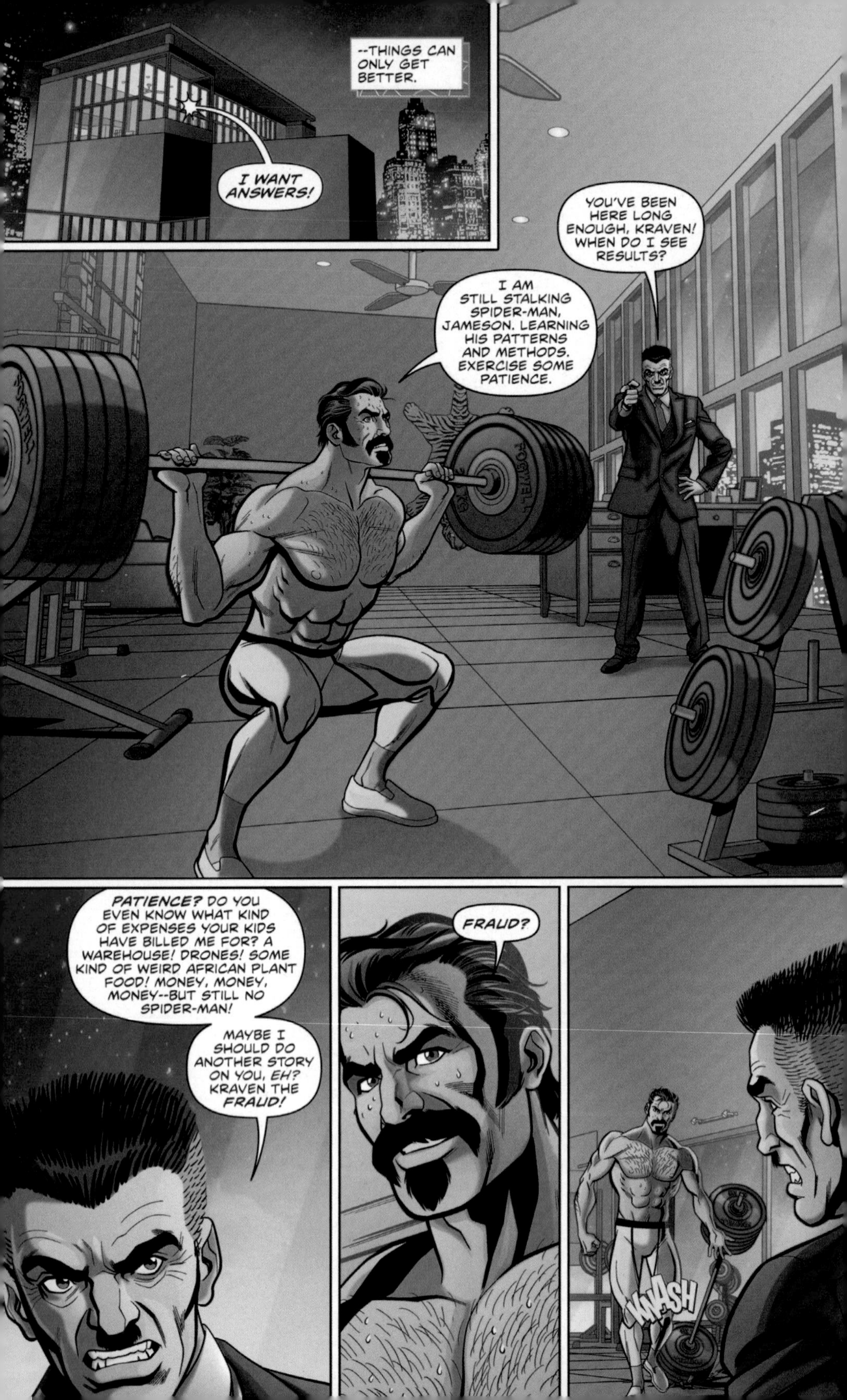

--THINGS CAN ONLY GET BETTER.
I WANT ANSWERS!
YOU'VE BEEN HERE LONG ENOUGH, KRAVEN! WHEN DO I SEE RESULTS?
I AM STILL STALKING SPIDER-MAN, JAMESON. LEARNING HIS PATTERNS AND METHODS. EXERCISE SOME PATIENCE.
PATIENCE? DO YOU EVEN KNOW WHAT KIND OF EXPENSES YOUR KIDS HAVE BILLED ME FOR? A WAREHOUSE! DRONES! SOME KIND OF WEIRD AFRICAN PLANT FOOD! MONEY, MONEY, MONEY--BUT STILL NO SPIDER-MAN!
MAYBE I SHOULD DO ANOTHER STORY ON YOU, EH? KRAVEN THE FRAUD!
FRAUD?
KKASH

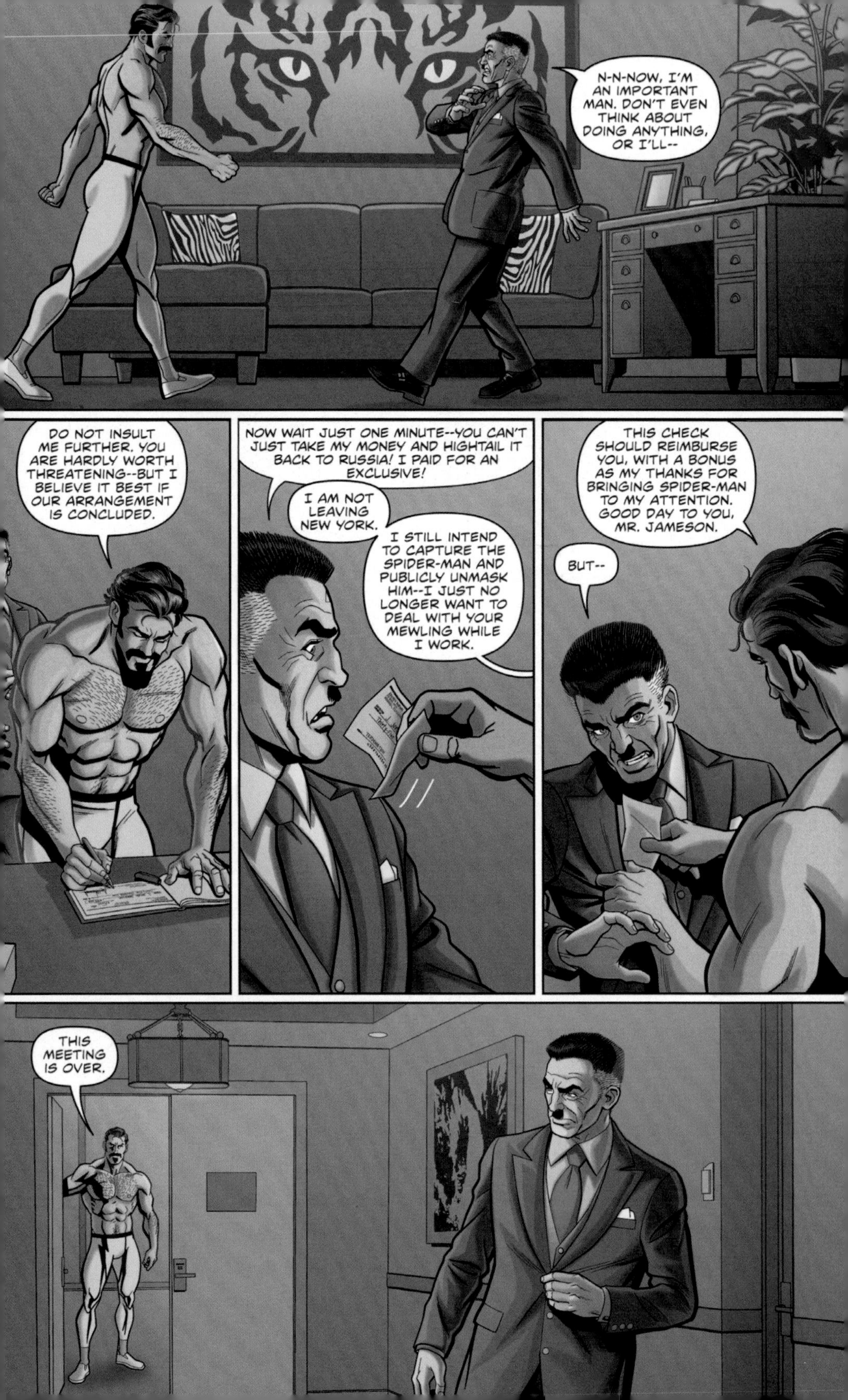
N-N-NOW, I'M AN IMPORTANT MAN. DON'T EVEN THINK ABOUT DOING ANYTHING, OR I'LL--
DO NOT INSULT ME FURTHER. YOU ARE HARDLY WORTH THREATENING--BUT I BELIEVE IT BEST IF OUR ARRANGEMENT IS CONCLUDED.
NOW WAIT JUST ONE MINUTE--YOU CAN'T JUST TAKE MY MONEY AND HIGHTAIL IT BACK TO RUSSIA! I PAID FOR AN EXCLUSIVE!
I AM NOT LEAVING NEW YORK.
I STILL INTEND TO CAPTURE THE SPIDER-MAN AND PUBLICLY UNMASK HIM--I JUST NO LONGER WANT TO DEAL WITH YOUR MEWLING WHILE I WORK.
THIS CHECK SHOULD REIMBURSE YOU, WITH A BONUS AS MY THANKS FOR BRINGING SPIDER-MAN TO MY ATTENTION. GOOD DAY TO YOU, MR. JAMESON.
BUT--
THIS MEETING IS OVER.

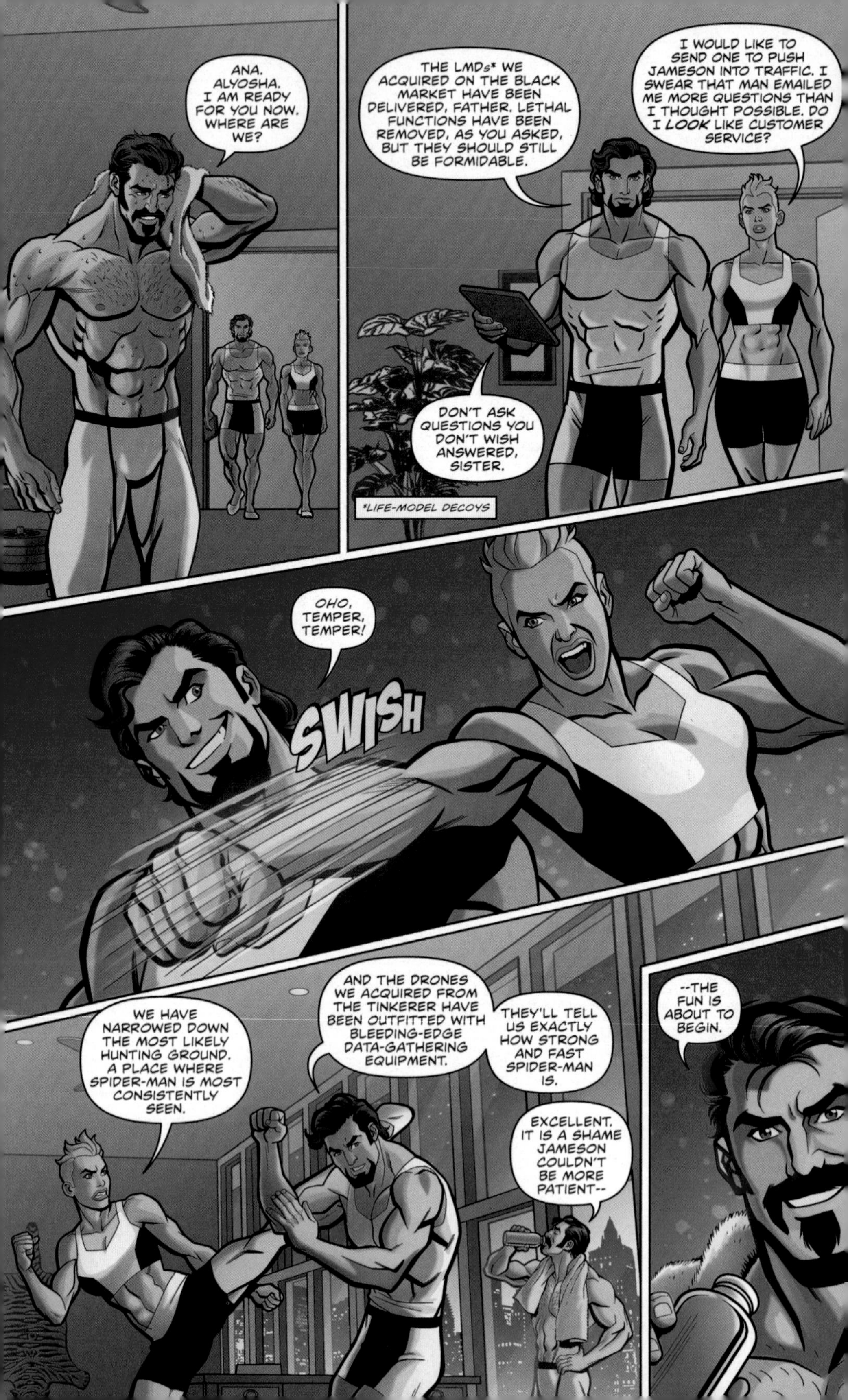
ANA. ALYOSHA. I AM READY FOR YOU NOW. WHERE ARE WE?
THE LMDs* WE ACQUIRED ON THE BLACK MARKET HAVE BEEN DELIVERED, FATHER. LETHAL FUNCTIONS HAVE BEEN REMOVED, AS YOU ASKED, BUT THEY SHOULD STILL BE FORMIDABLE.
I WOULD LIKE TO SEND ONE TO PUSH JAMESON INTO TRAFFIC. I SWEAR THAT MAN EMAILED ME MORE QUESTIONS THAN I THOUGHT POSSIBLE. DO I LOOK LIKE CUSTOMER SERVICE?
DON'T ASK QUESTIONS YOU DON'T WISH ANSWERED, SISTER.
*LIFE-MODEL DECOYS
OHO, TEMPER, TEMPER!
SWISH
WE HAVE NARROWED DOWN THE MOST LIKELY HUNTING GROUND. A PLACE WHERE SPIDER-MAN IS MOST CONSISTENTLY SEEN.
AND THE DRONES WE ACQUIRED FROM THE TINKERER HAVE BEEN OUTFITTED WITH BLEEDING-EDGE DATA-GATHERING EQUIPMENT.
THEY'LL TELL US EXACTLY HOW STRONG AND FAST SPIDER-MAN IS.
EXCELLENT. IT IS A SHAME JAMESON COULDN'T BE MORE PATIENT--
--THE FUN IS ABOUT TO BEGIN.

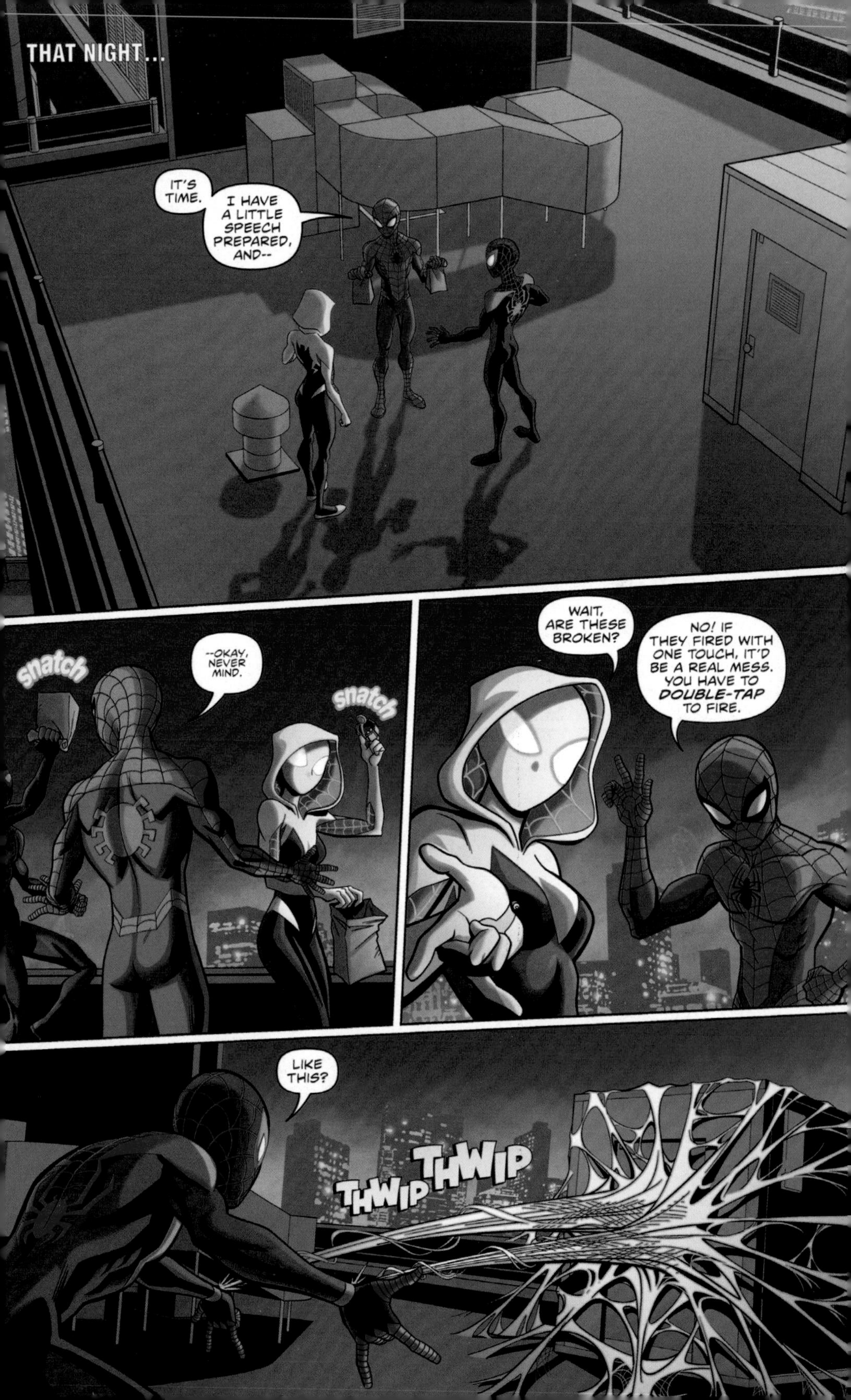

THAT NIGHT...
IT'S TIME.
I HAVE A LITTLE SPEECH PREPARED, AND--
snatch
--OKAY, NEVER MIND.
snatch
WAIT, ARE THESE BROKEN?
NO! IF THEY FIRED WITH ONE TOUCH, IT'D BE A REAL MESS. YOU HAVE TO DOUBLE-TAP TO FIRE.
LIKE THIS?
THWIP THWIP

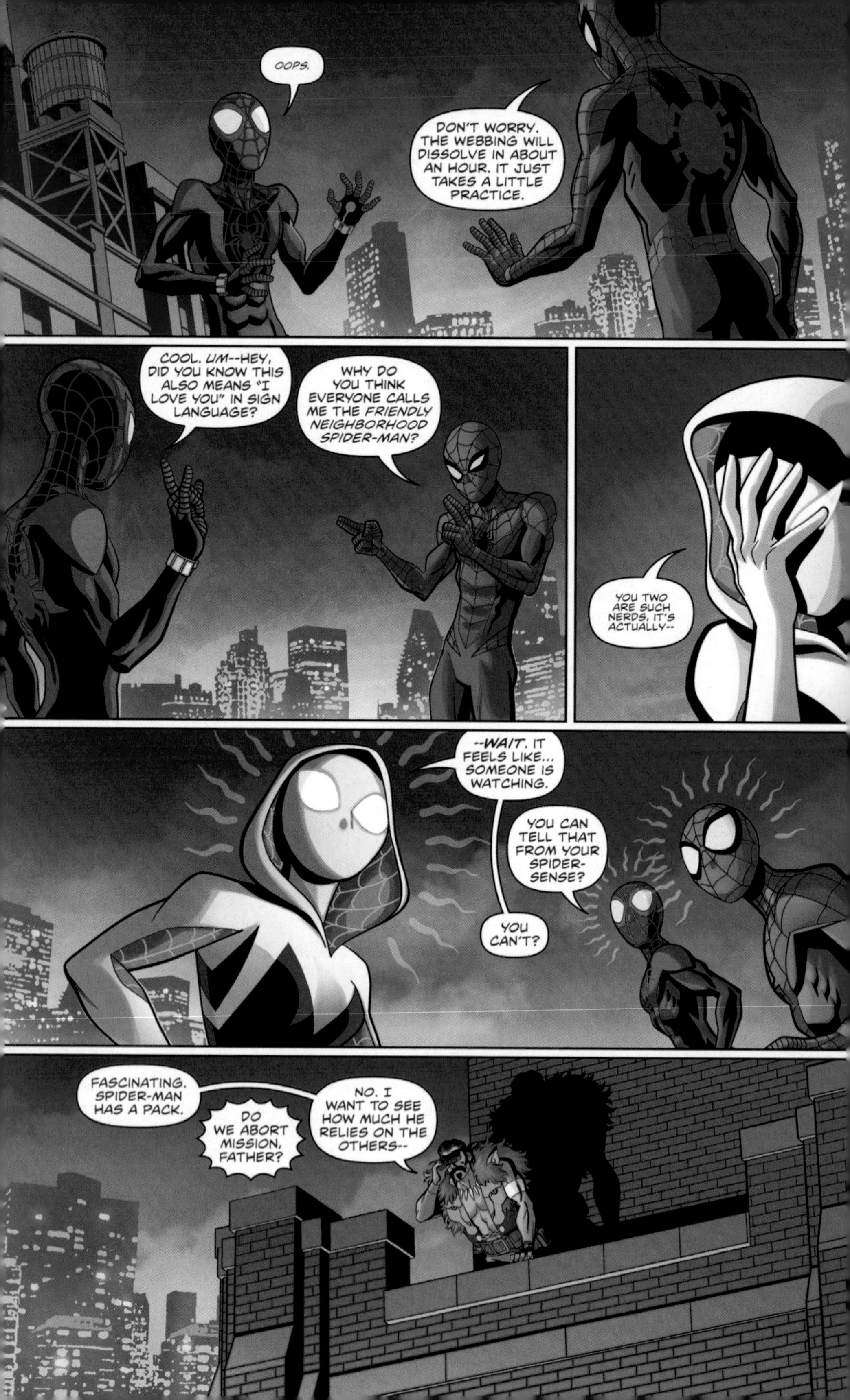
OOPS.
DON'T WORRY. THE WEBBING WILL DISSOLVE IN ABOUT AN HOUR. IT JUST TAKES A LITTLE PRACTICE.
COOL. UM--HEY, DID YOU KNOW THIS ALSO MEANS "I LOVE YOU" IN SIGN LANGUAGE?
WHY DO YOU THINK EVERYONE CALLS ME THE FRIENDLY NEIGHBORHOOD SPIDER-MAN?
YOU TWO ARE SUCH NERDS, IT'S ACTUALLY--
--WAIT. IT FEELS LIKE... SOMEONE IS WATCHING.
YOU CAN TELL THAT FROM YOUR SPIDER-SENSE?
YOU CAN'T?
FASCINATING. SPIDER-MAN HAS A PACK.
DO WE ABORT MISSION, FATHER?
NO. I WANT TO SEE HOW MUCH HE RELIES ON THE OTHERS--

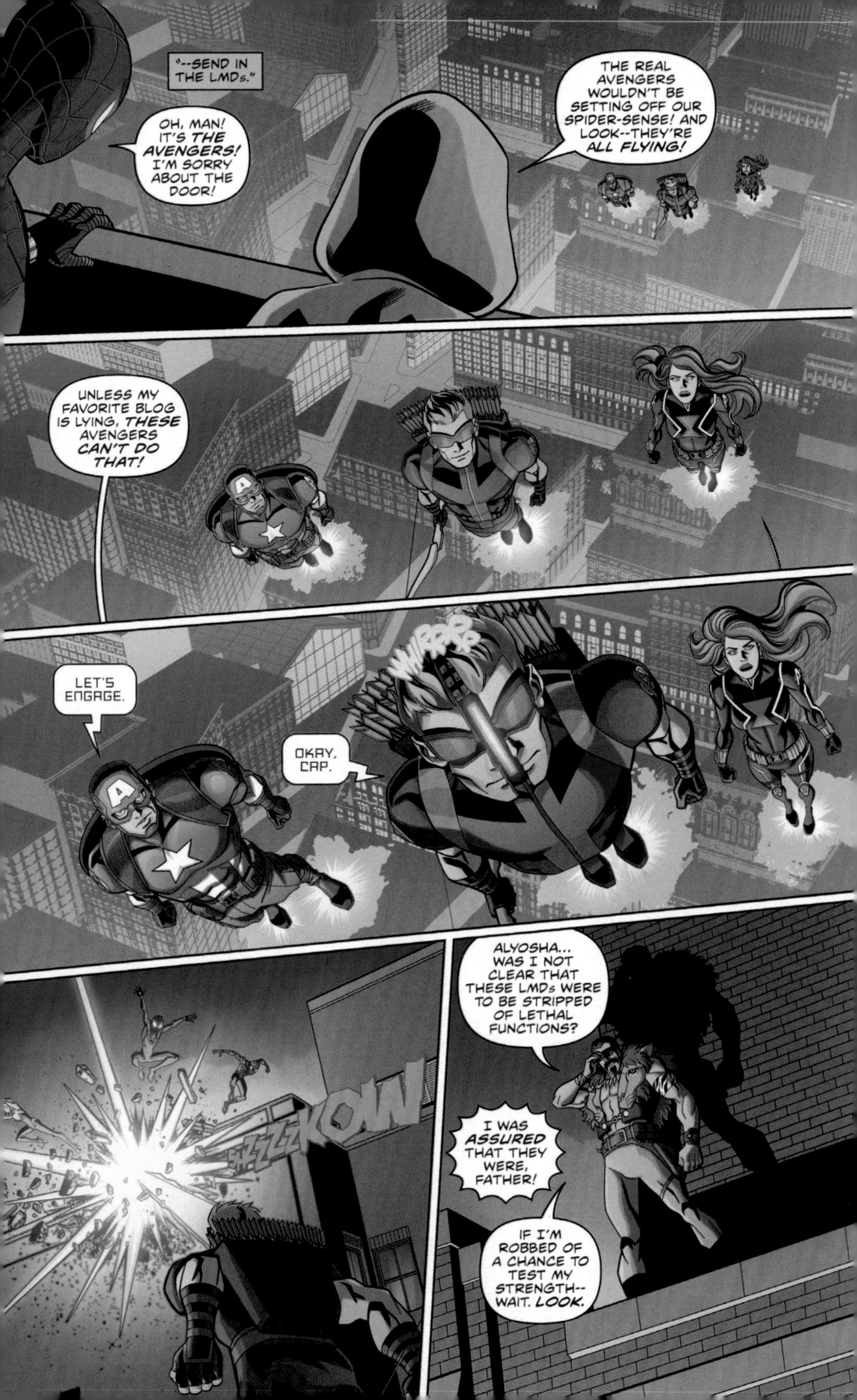
"--SEND IN THE LMDs."
OH, MAN! IT'S THE AVENGERS! I'M SORRY ABOUT THE DOOR!
THE REAL AVENGERS WOULDN'T BE SETTING OFF OUR SPIDER-SENSE! AND LOOK--THEY'RE ALL FLYING!
UNLESS MY FAVORITE BLOG IS LYING, THESE AVENGERS CAN'T DO THAT!
LET'S ENGAGE.
OKAY, CAP.
WHIRRR
SHZZZ
KOW
ALYOSHA... WAS I NOT CLEAR THAT THESE LMDs WERE TO BE STRIPPED OF LETHAL FUNCTIONS?
I WAS ASSURED THAT THEY WERE, FATHER!
IF I'M ROBBED OF A CHANCE TO TEST MY STRENGTH-- WAIT. LOOK.

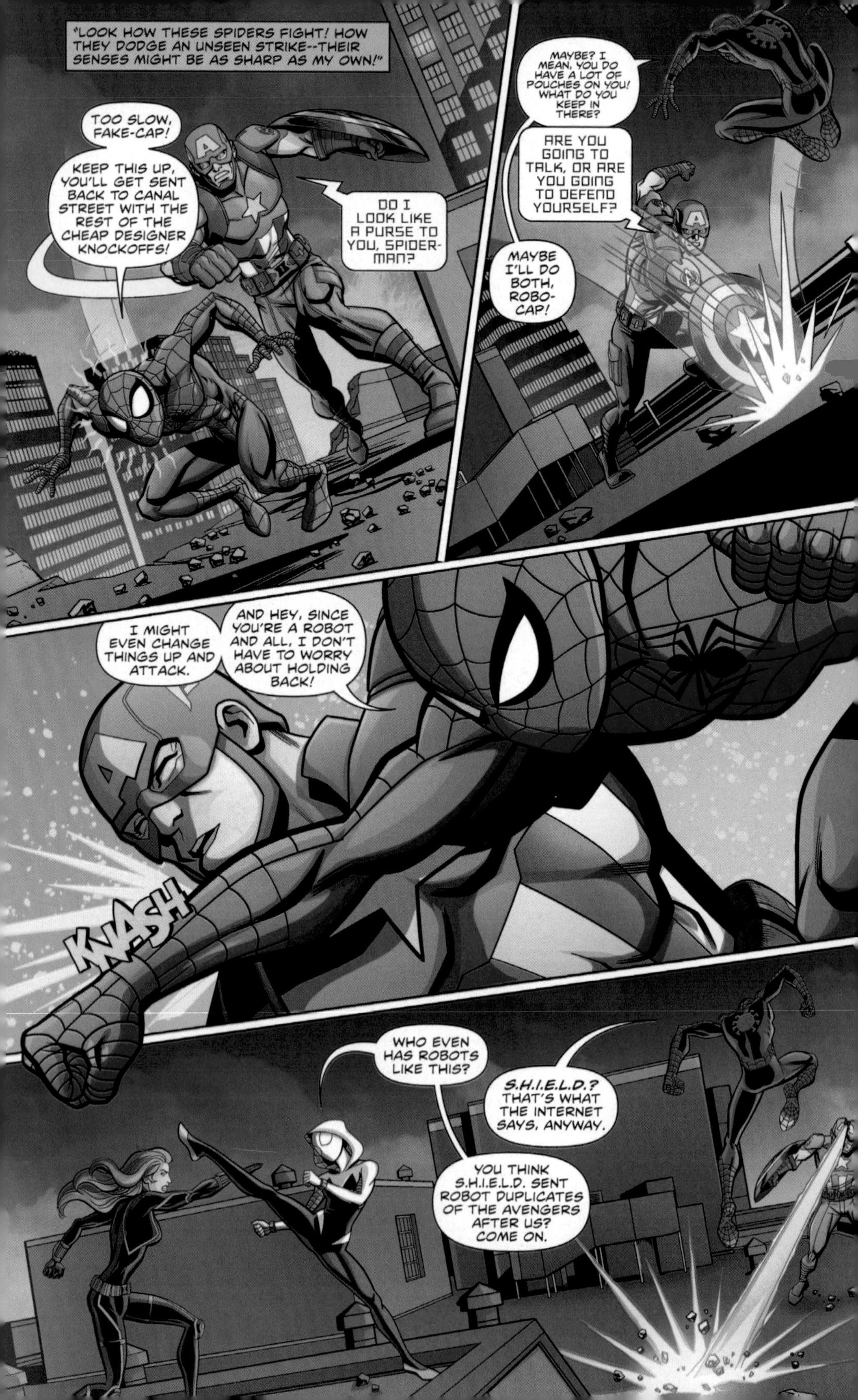
"LOOK HOW THESE SPIDERS FIGHT! HOW THEY DODGE AN UNSEEN STRIKE--THEIR SENSES MIGHT BE AS SHARP AS MY OWN!"
TOO SLOW, FAKE-CAP!
KEEP THIS UP, YOU'LL GET SENT BACK TO CANAL STREET WITH THE REST OF THE CHEAP DESIGNER KNOCKOFFS!
DO I LOOK LIKE A PURSE TO YOU, SPIDER-MAN?
MAYBE? I MEAN, YOU DO HAVE A LOT OF POUCHES ON YOU! WHAT DO YOU KEEP IN THERE?
ARE YOU GOING TO TALK, OR ARE YOU GOING TO DEFEND YOURSELF?
MAYBE I'LL DO BOTH, ROBO-CAP!
I MIGHT EVEN CHANGE THINGS UP AND ATTACK.
AND HEY, SINCE YOU'RE A ROBOT AND ALL, I DON'T HAVE TO WORRY ABOUT HOLDING BACK!
KNASH
WHO EVEN HAS ROBOTS LIKE THIS?
S.H.I.E.L.D.? THAT'S WHAT THE INTERNET SAYS, ANYWAY.
YOU THINK S.H.I.E.L.D. SENT ROBOT DUPLICATES OF THE AVENGERS AFTER US? COME ON.

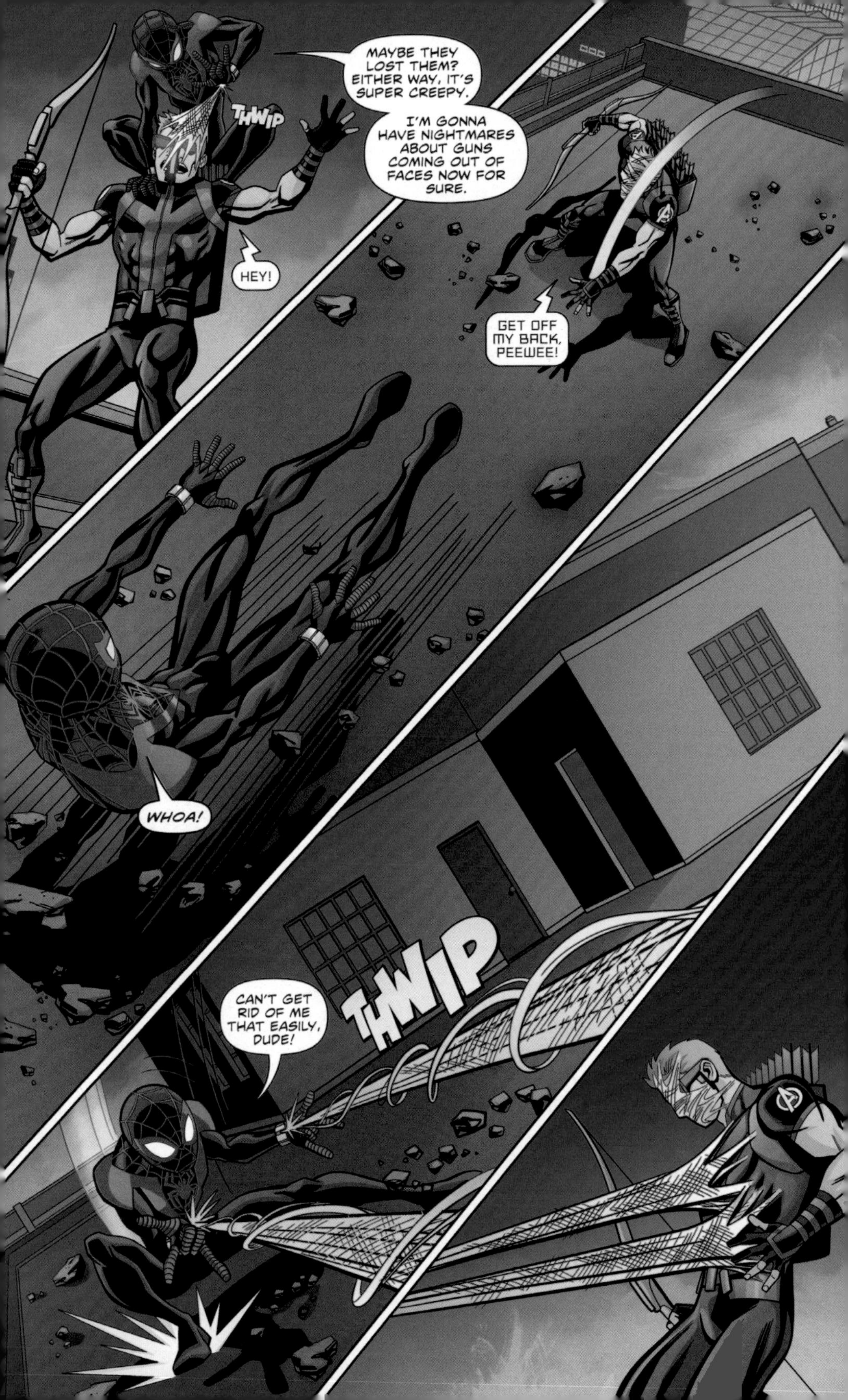
MAYBE THEY LOST THEM? EITHER WAY, IT'S SUPER CREEPY.
I'M GONNA HAVE NIGHTMARES ABOUT GUNS COMING OUT OF FACES NOW FOR SURE.
THWIP
HEY!
GET OFF MY BACK, PEEWEE!
WHOA!
CAN'T GET RID OF ME THAT EASILY, DUDE!
THWIP

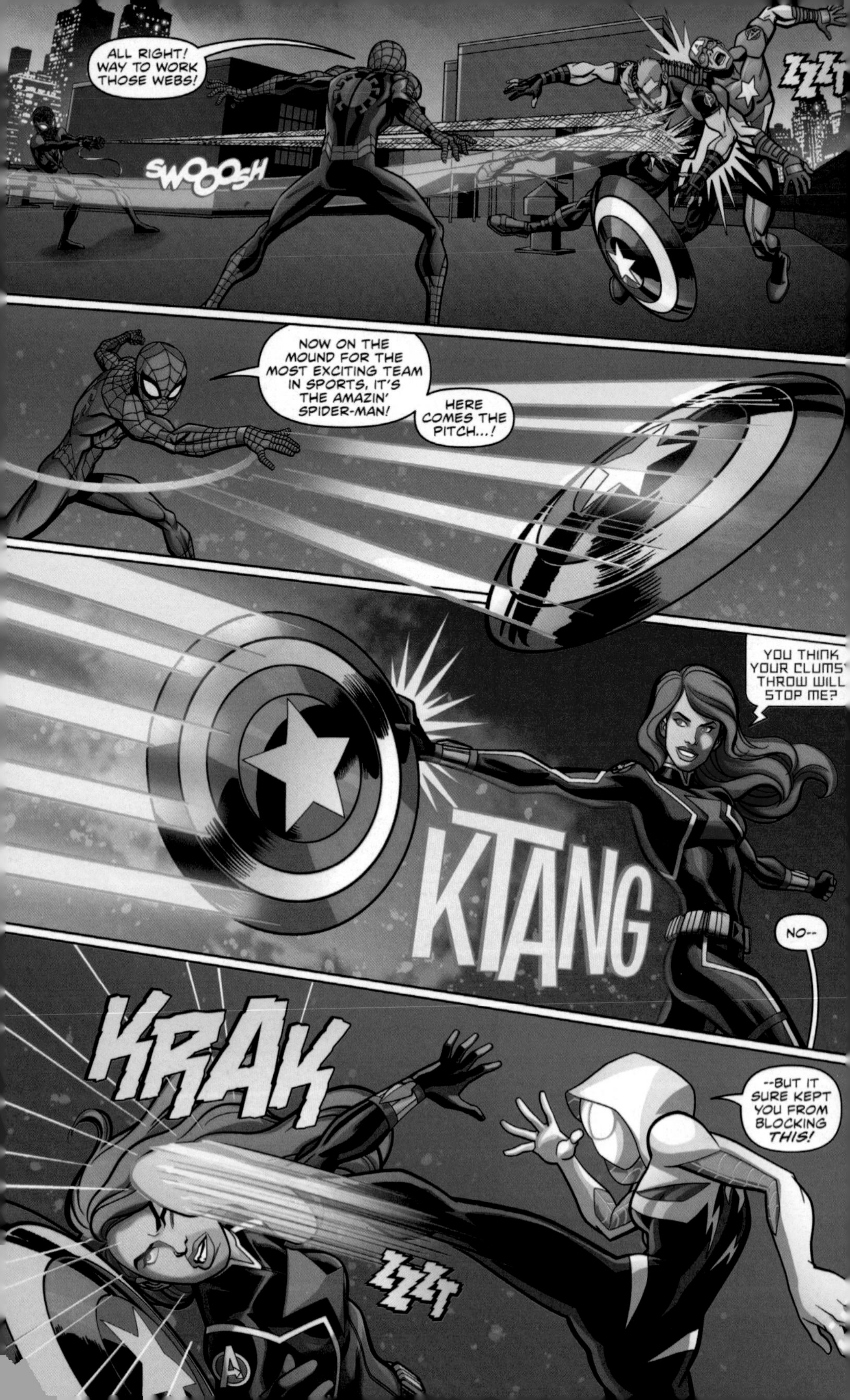
ALL RIGHT! WAY TO WORK THOSE WEBS!
ZZZT
SWOOOSH
NOW ON THE MOUND FOR THE MOST EXCITING TEAM IN SPORTS, IT'S THE AMAZIN' SPIDER-MAN!
HERE COMES THE PITCH...!
YOU THINK YOUR CLUMSY THROW WILL STOP ME?
KTANG
NO--
KRAK
--BUT IT SURE KEPT YOU FROM BLOCKING THIS!
ZZZT

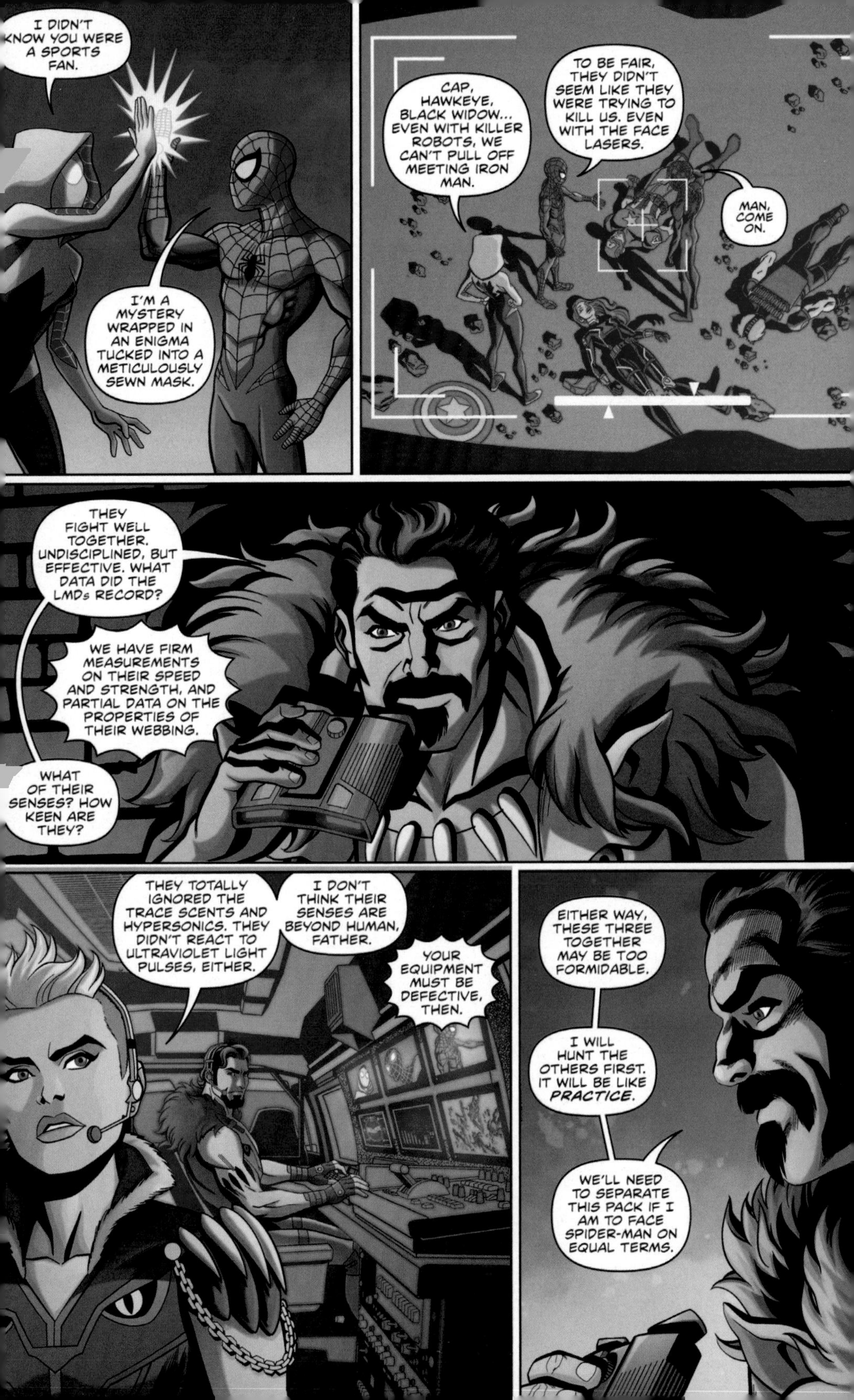
I DIDN'T KNOW YOU WERE A SPORTS FAN.
I'M A MYSTERY WRAPPED IN AN ENIGMA TUCKED INTO A METICULOUSLY SEWN MASK.
CAP, HAWKEYE, BLACK WIDOW... EVEN WITH KILLER ROBOTS, WE CAN'T PULL OFF MEETING IRON MAN.
TO BE FAIR, THEY DIDN'T SEEM LIKE THEY WERE TRYING TO KILL US. EVEN WITH THE FACE LASERS.
MAN, COME ON.
THEY FIGHT WELL TOGETHER. UNDISCIPLINED, BUT EFFECTIVE. WHAT DATA DID THE LMDs RECORD?
WE HAVE FIRM MEASUREMENTS ON THEIR SPEED AND STRENGTH, AND PARTIAL DATA ON THE PROPERTIES OF THEIR WEBBING.
WHAT OF THEIR SENSES? HOW KEEN ARE THEY?
THEY TOTALLY IGNORED THE TRACE SCENTS AND HYPERSONICS. THEY DIDN'T REACT TO ULTRAVIOLET LIGHT PULSES, EITHER.
I DON'T THINK THEIR SENSES ARE BEYOND HUMAN, FATHER.
YOUR EQUIPMENT MUST BE DEFECTIVE, THEN.
EITHER WAY, THESE THREE TOGETHER MAY BE TOO FORMIDABLE.
I WILL HUNT THE OTHERS FIRST. IT WILL BE LIKE *PRACTICE*.
WE'LL NEED TO SEPARATE THIS PACK IF I AM TO FACE SPIDER-MAN ON EQUAL TERMS.

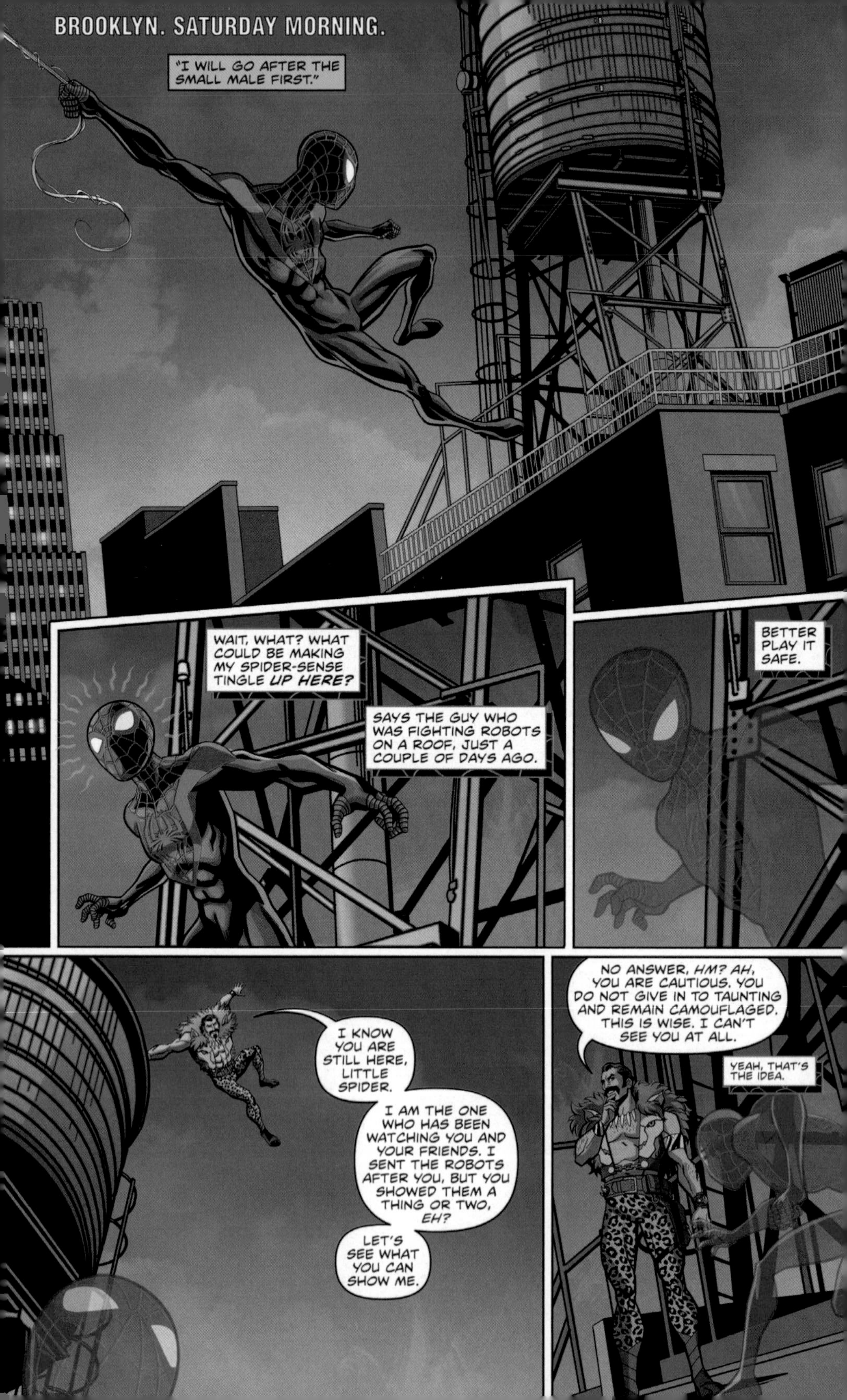
BROOKLYN. SATURDAY MORNING.
"I WILL GO AFTER THE SMALL MALE FIRST."
WAIT, WHAT? WHAT COULD BE MAKING MY SPIDER-SENSE TINGLE *UP HERE?*
SAYS THE GUY WHO WAS FIGHTING ROBOTS ON A ROOF, JUST A COUPLE OF DAYS AGO.
BETTER PLAY IT SAFE.
I KNOW YOU ARE STILL HERE, LITTLE SPIDER.
I AM THE ONE WHO HAS BEEN WATCHING YOU AND YOUR FRIENDS. I SENT THE ROBOTS AFTER YOU, BUT YOU SHOWED THEM A THING OR TWO, *EH?*
LET'S SEE WHAT YOU CAN SHOW ME.
NO ANSWER, *HM? AH,* YOU ARE CAUTIOUS. YOU DO NOT GIVE IN TO TAUNTING AND REMAIN CAMOUFLAGED. THIS IS WISE. I CAN'T SEE YOU AT ALL.
YEAH, THAT'S THE IDEA.

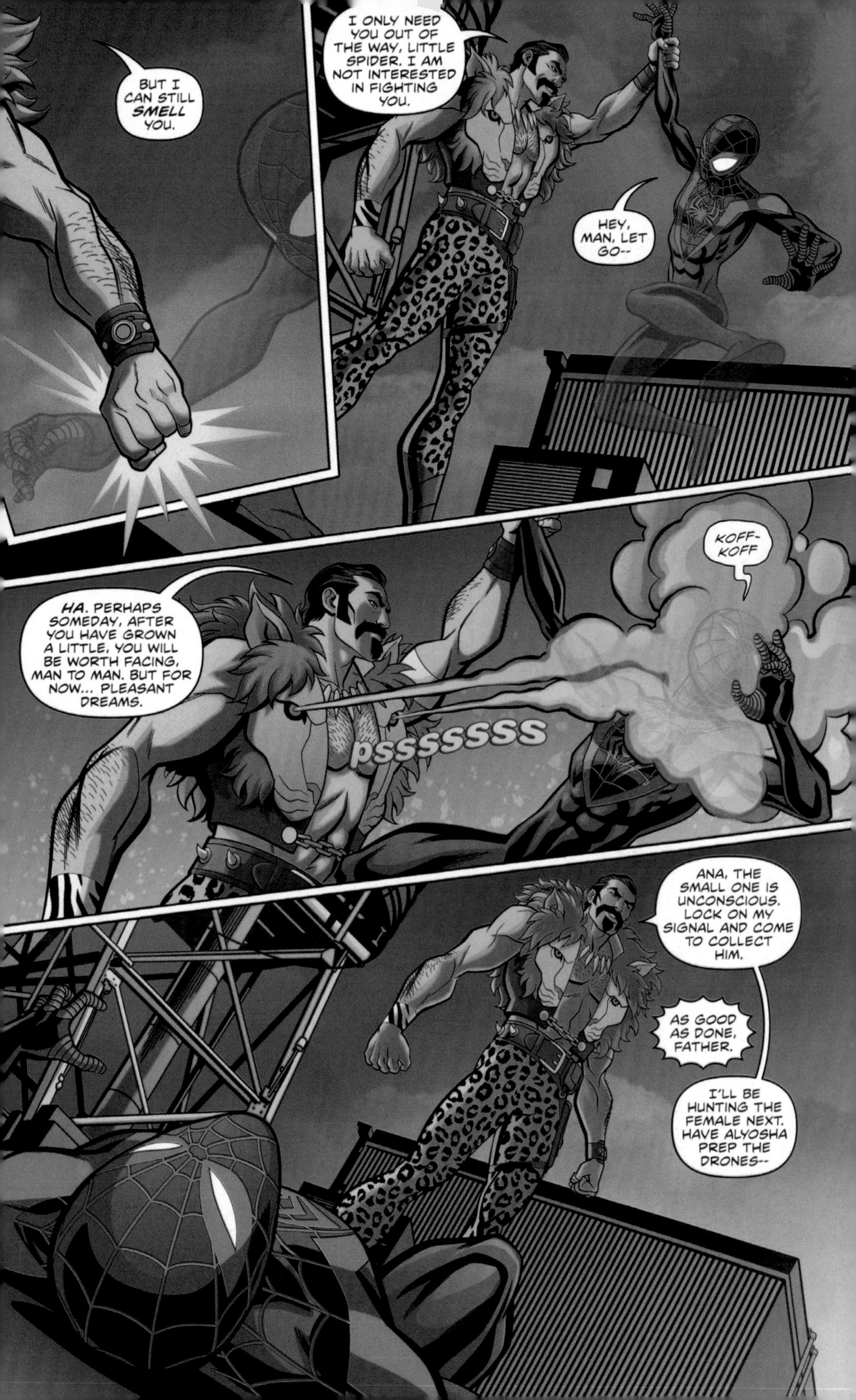
BUT I CAN STILL SMELL YOU.
I ONLY NEED YOU OUT OF THE WAY, LITTLE SPIDER. I AM NOT INTERESTED IN FIGHTING YOU.
HEY, MAN, LET GO--
KOFF-KOFF
HA. PERHAPS SOMEDAY, AFTER YOU HAVE GROWN A LITTLE, YOU WILL BE WORTH FACING, MAN TO MAN. BUT FOR NOW... PLEASANT DREAMS.
PSSSSSSS
ANA, THE SMALL ONE IS UNCONSCIOUS. LOCK ON MY SIGNAL AND COME TO COLLECT HIM.
AS GOOD AS DONE, FATHER.
I'LL BE HUNTING THE FEMALE NEXT. HAVE ALYOSHA PREP THE DRONES--

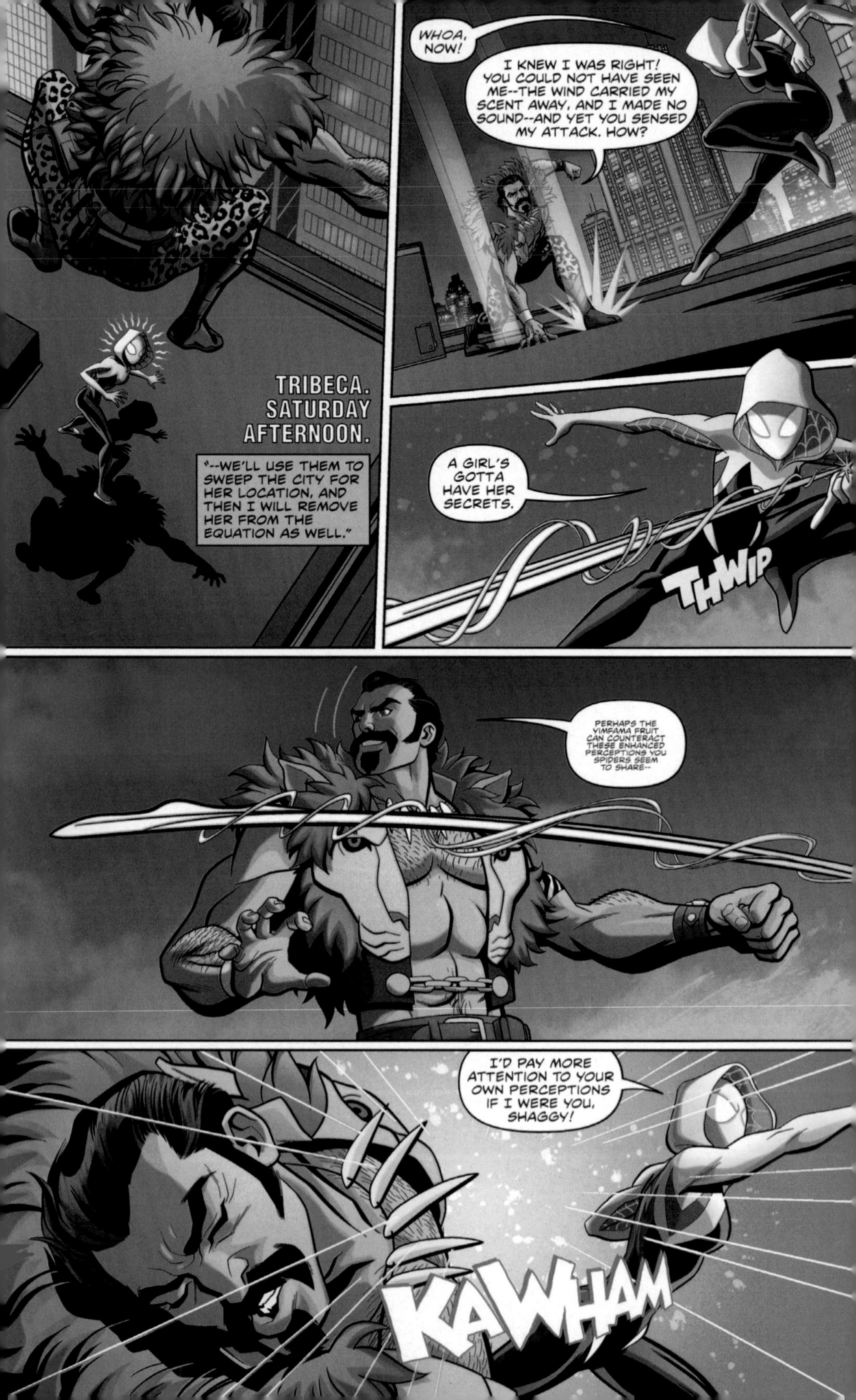
TRIBECA. SATURDAY AFTERNOON.
"--WE'LL USE THEM TO SWEEP THE CITY FOR HER LOCATION, AND THEN I WILL REMOVE HER FROM THE EQUATION AS WELL."
WHOA, NOW!
I KNEW I WAS RIGHT! YOU COULD NOT HAVE SEEN ME--THE WIND CARRIED MY SCENT AWAY, AND I MADE NO SOUND--AND YET YOU SENSED MY ATTACK. HOW?
A GIRL'S GOTTA HAVE HER SECRETS.
THWIP
PERHAPS THE YIMFAMA FRUIT CAN COUNTERACT THESE ENHANCED PERCEPTIONS YOU SPIDERS SEEM TO SHARE--
I'D PAY MORE ATTENTION TO YOUR OWN PERCEPTIONS IF I WERE YOU, SHAGGY!
KAWHAM

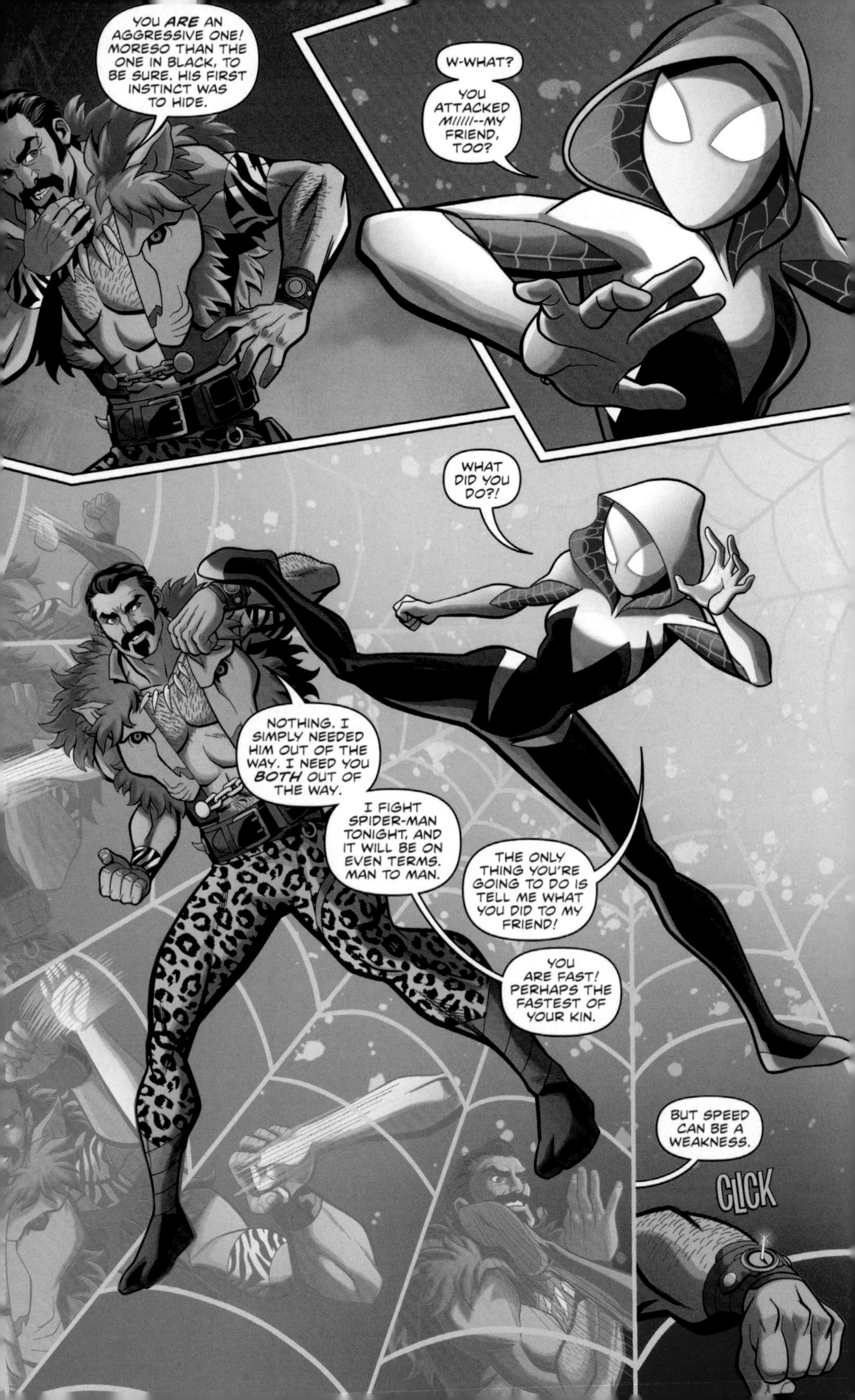
YOU *ARE* AN AGGRESSIVE ONE! MORESO THAN THE ONE IN BLACK, TO BE SURE. HIS FIRST INSTINCT WAS TO HIDE.
W-WHAT?
YOU ATTACKED M//////--MY FRIEND, TOO?
WHAT DID YOU DO?!
NOTHING. I SIMPLY NEEDED HIM OUT OF THE WAY. I NEED YOU *BOTH* OUT OF THE WAY.
I FIGHT SPIDER-MAN TONIGHT, AND IT WILL BE ON EVEN TERMS. MAN TO MAN.
THE ONLY THING YOU'RE GOING TO DO IS TELL ME WHAT YOU DID TO MY FRIEND!
YOU ARE FAST! PERHAPS THE FASTEST OF YOUR KIN.
BUT SPEED CAN BE A WEAKNESS.
CLICK

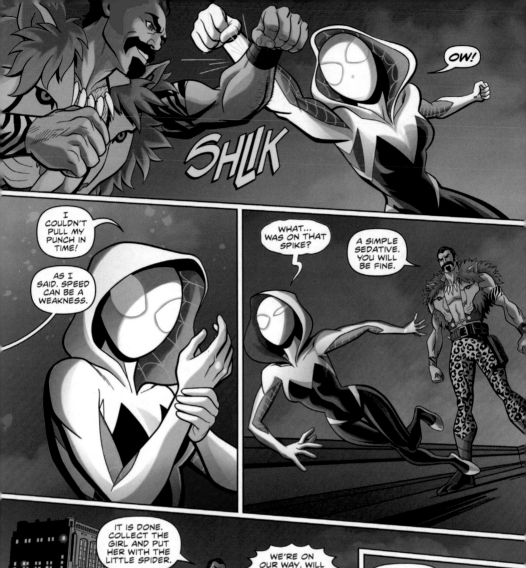

OW!

SHLLK

I COULDN'T PULL MY PUNCH IN TIME!

AS I SAID. SPEED CAN BE A WEAKNESS.

WHAT... WAS ON THAT SPIKE?

A SIMPLE SEDATIVE. YOU WILL BE FINE.

IT IS DONE. COLLECT THE GIRL AND PUT HER WITH THE LITTLE SPIDER.

WE'RE ON OUR WAY. WILL YOU NEED MORE SEDATIVE?

NO. SPIDER-MAN IS THE MOST EXPERIENCED, THE STRONGEST. THERE WILL BE NO SEDATIVES FOR HIM.

HE WILL BE DEFEATED AND UNMASKED...

...WHATEVER IT TAKES.

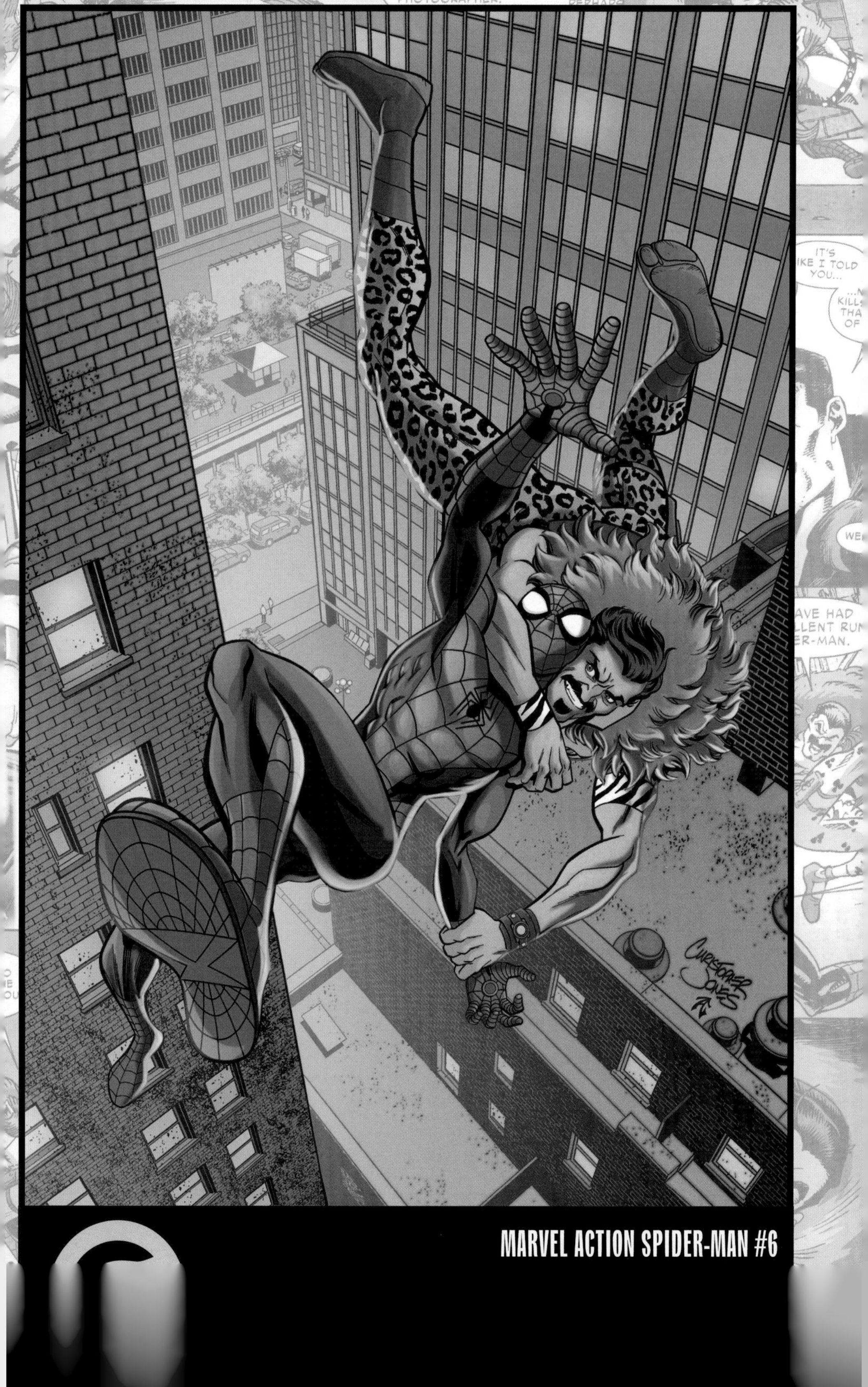
CHRISTOPHER JONES

MARVEL ACTION SPIDER-MAN #6

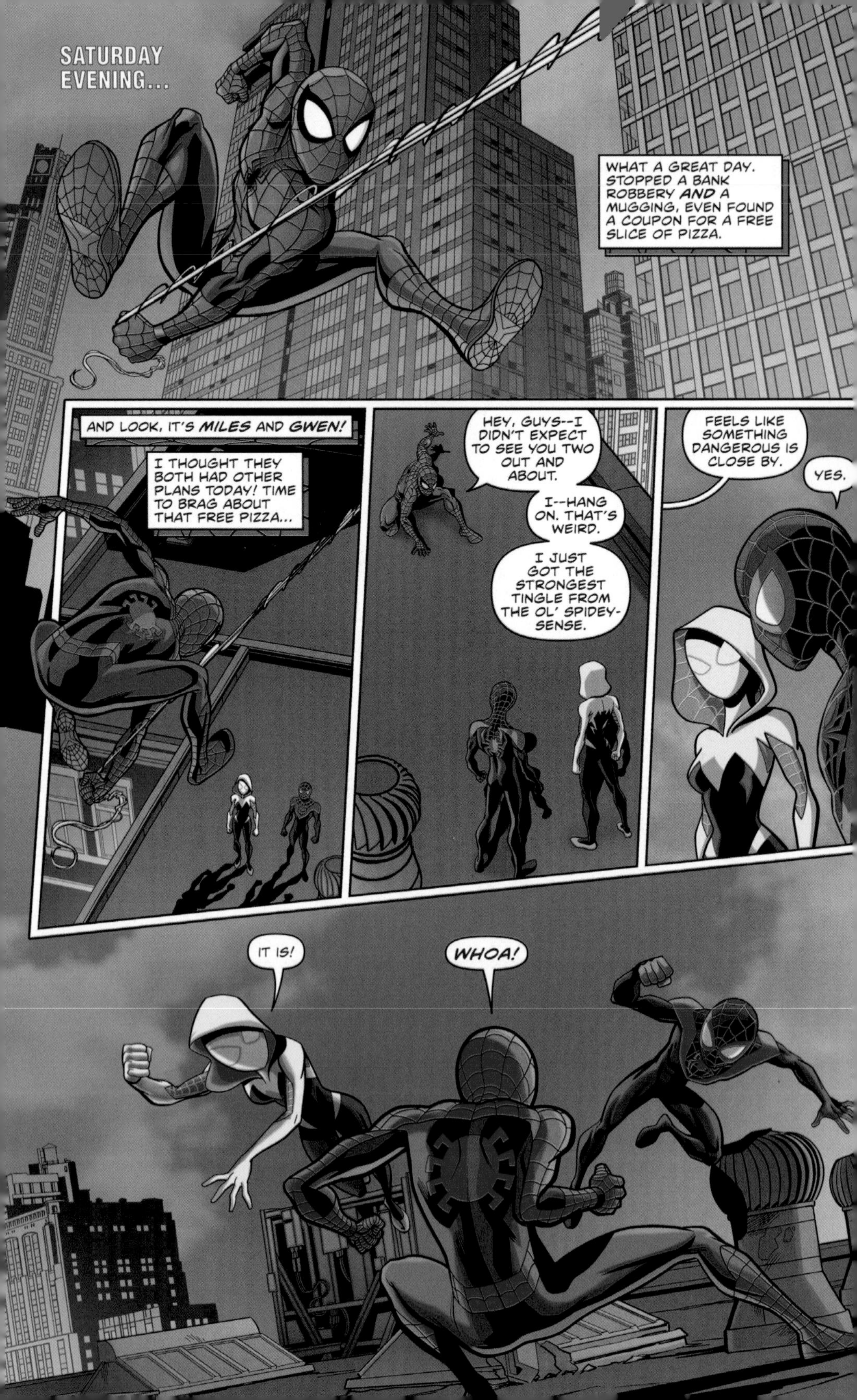
SATURDAY EVENING...
WHAT A GREAT DAY. STOPPED A BANK ROBBERY AND A MUGGING, EVEN FOUND A COUPON FOR A FREE SLICE OF PIZZA.
AND LOOK, IT'S MILES AND GWEN!
I THOUGHT THEY BOTH HAD OTHER PLANS TODAY! TIME TO BRAG ABOUT THAT FREE PIZZA...
HEY, GUYS--I DIDN'T EXPECT TO SEE YOU TWO OUT AND ABOUT.
I--HANG ON. THAT'S WEIRD.
I JUST GOT THE STRONGEST TINGLE FROM THE OL' SPIDEY-SENSE.
FEELS LIKE SOMETHING DANGEROUS IS CLOSE BY.
YES.
IT IS!
WHOA!

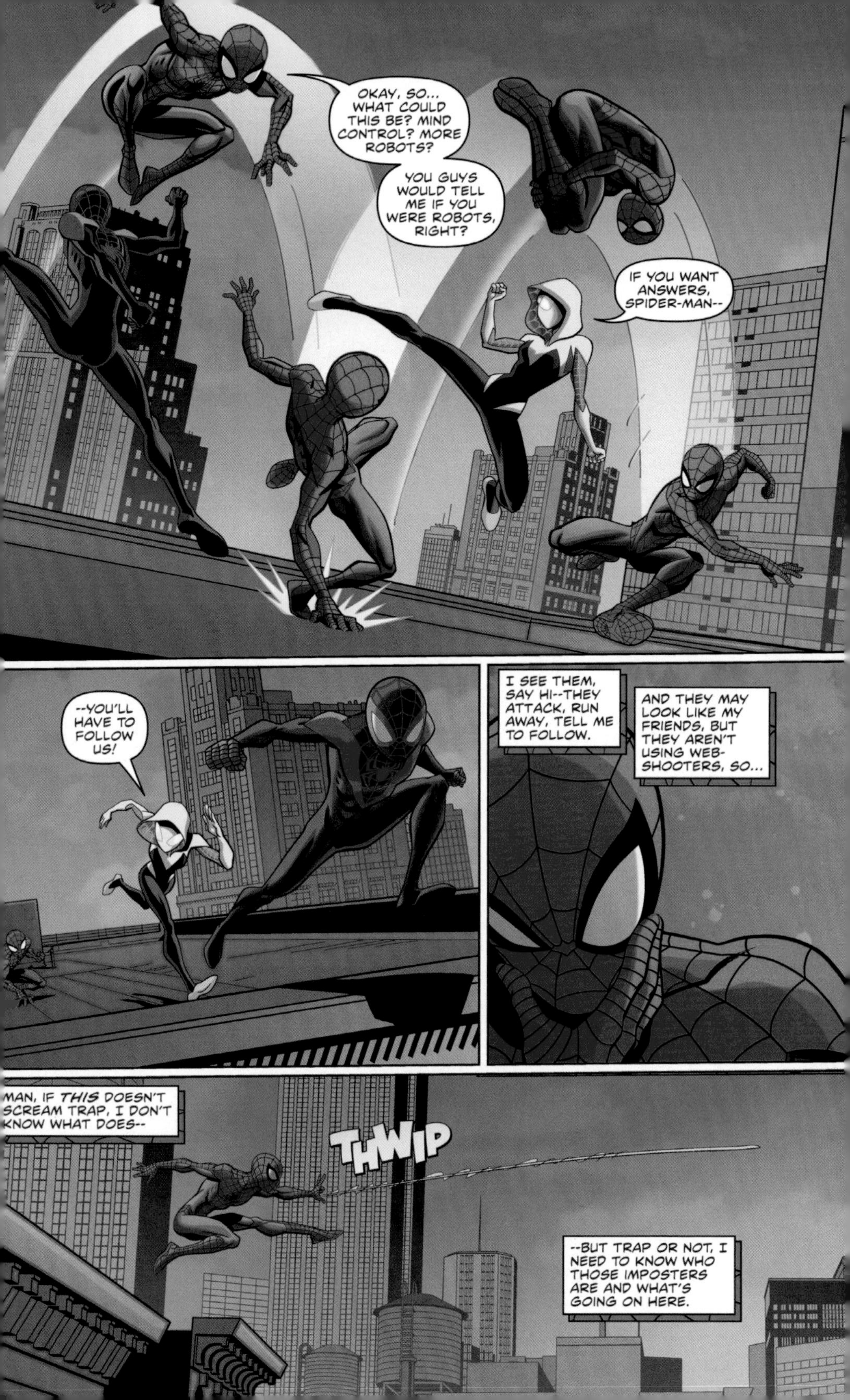
OKAY, SO... WHAT COULD THIS BE? MIND CONTROL? MORE ROBOTS?
YOU GUYS WOULD TELL ME IF YOU WERE ROBOTS, RIGHT?
IF YOU WANT ANSWERS, SPIDER-MAN--
--YOU'LL HAVE TO FOLLOW US!
I SEE THEM, SAY HI--THEY ATTACK, RUN AWAY, TELL ME TO FOLLOW.
AND THEY MAY LOOK LIKE MY FRIENDS, BUT THEY AREN'T USING WEB-SHOOTERS, SO...
MAN, IF *THIS* DOESN'T SCREAM TRAP, I DON'T KNOW WHAT DOES--
THWIP
--BUT TRAP OR NOT, I NEED TO KNOW WHO THOSE IMPOSTERS ARE AND WHAT'S GOING ON HERE.

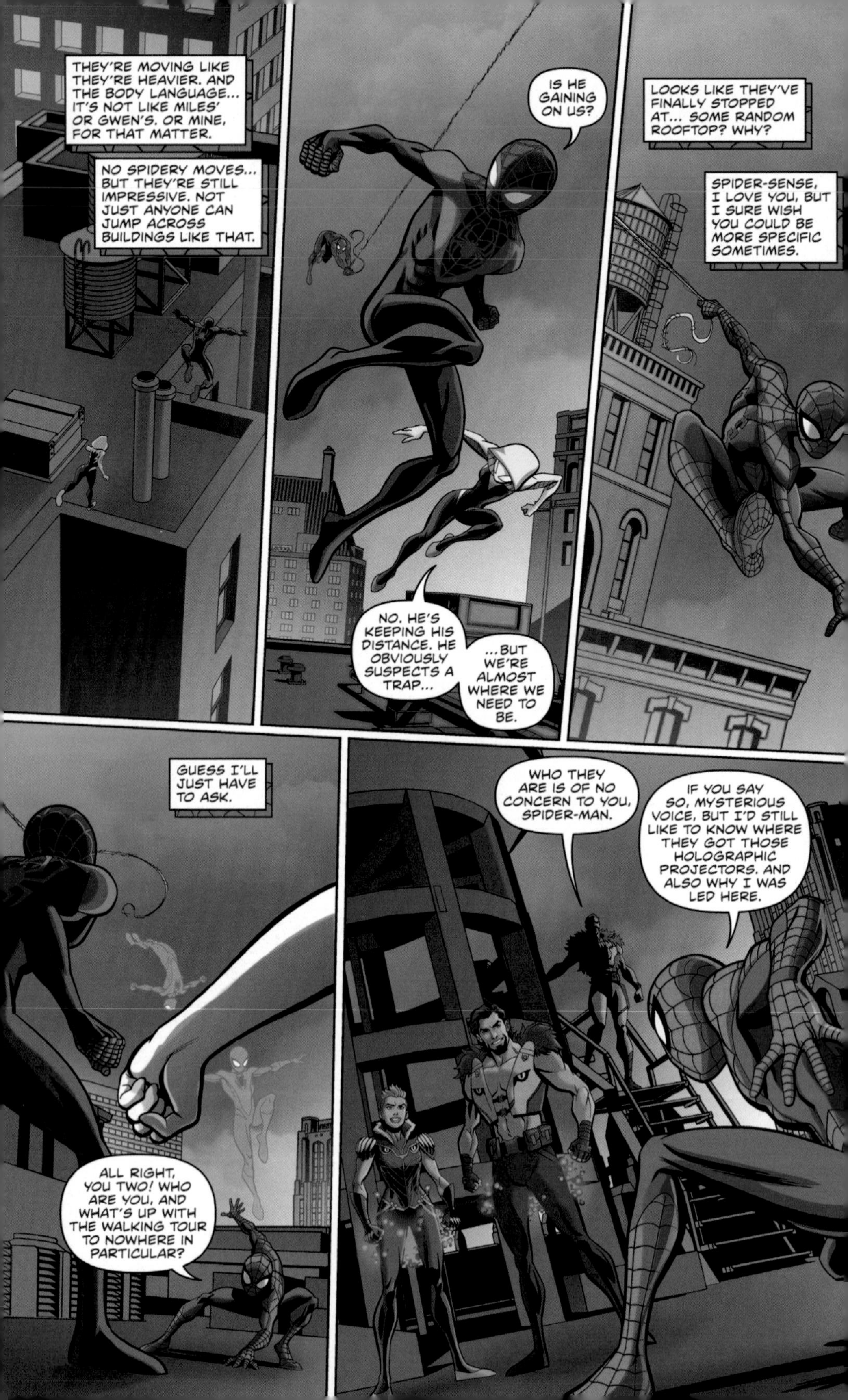
THEY'RE MOVING LIKE THEY'RE HEAVIER. AND THE BODY LANGUAGE... IT'S NOT LIKE MILES' OR GWEN'S. OR MINE, FOR THAT MATTER.
NO SPIDERY MOVES... BUT THEY'RE STILL IMPRESSIVE. NOT JUST ANYONE CAN JUMP ACROSS BUILDINGS LIKE THAT.
IS HE GAINING ON US?
NO. HE'S KEEPING HIS DISTANCE. HE OBVIOUSLY SUSPECTS A TRAP...
...BUT WE'RE ALMOST WHERE WE NEED TO BE.
LOOKS LIKE THEY'VE FINALLY STOPPED AT... SOME RANDOM ROOFTOP? WHY?
SPIDER-SENSE, I LOVE YOU, BUT I SURE WISH YOU COULD BE MORE SPECIFIC SOMETIMES.
GUESS I'LL JUST HAVE TO ASK.
ALL RIGHT, YOU TWO! WHO ARE YOU, AND WHAT'S UP WITH THE WALKING TOUR TO NOWHERE IN PARTICULAR?
WHO THEY ARE IS OF NO CONCERN TO YOU, SPIDER-MAN.
IF YOU SAY SO, MYSTERIOUS VOICE, BUT I'D STILL LIKE TO KNOW WHERE THEY GOT THOSE HOLOGRAPHIC PROJECTORS. AND ALSO WHY I WAS LED HERE.

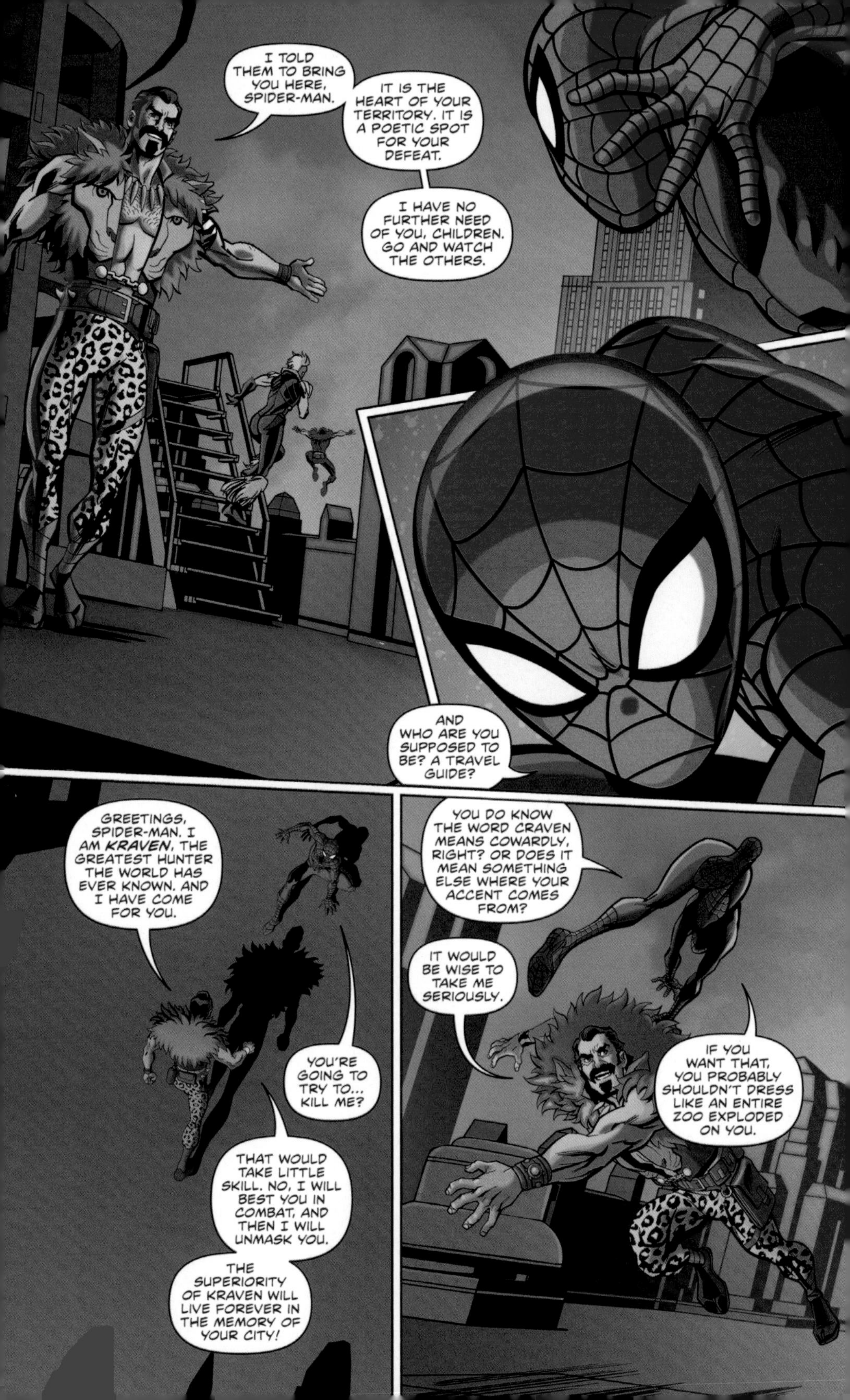
I TOLD THEM TO BRING YOU HERE, SPIDER-MAN.
IT IS THE HEART OF YOUR TERRITORY. IT IS A POETIC SPOT FOR YOUR DEFEAT.
I HAVE NO FURTHER NEED OF YOU, CHILDREN. GO AND WATCH THE OTHERS.
AND WHO ARE YOU SUPPOSED TO BE? A TRAVEL GUIDE?
GREETINGS, SPIDER-MAN. I AM KRAVEN, THE GREATEST HUNTER THE WORLD HAS EVER KNOWN. AND I HAVE COME FOR YOU.
YOU'RE GOING TO TRY TO... KILL ME?
THAT WOULD TAKE LITTLE SKILL. NO, I WILL BEST YOU IN COMBAT, AND THEN I WILL UNMASK YOU.
THE SUPERIORITY OF KRAVEN WILL LIVE FOREVER IN THE MEMORY OF YOUR CITY!
YOU DO KNOW THE WORD CRAVEN MEANS COWARDLY, RIGHT? OR DOES IT MEAN SOMETHING ELSE WHERE YOUR ACCENT COMES FROM?
IT WOULD BE WISE TO TAKE ME SERIOUSLY.
IF YOU WANT THAT, YOU PROBABLY SHOULDN'T DRESS LIKE AN ENTIRE ZOO EXPLODED ON YOU.

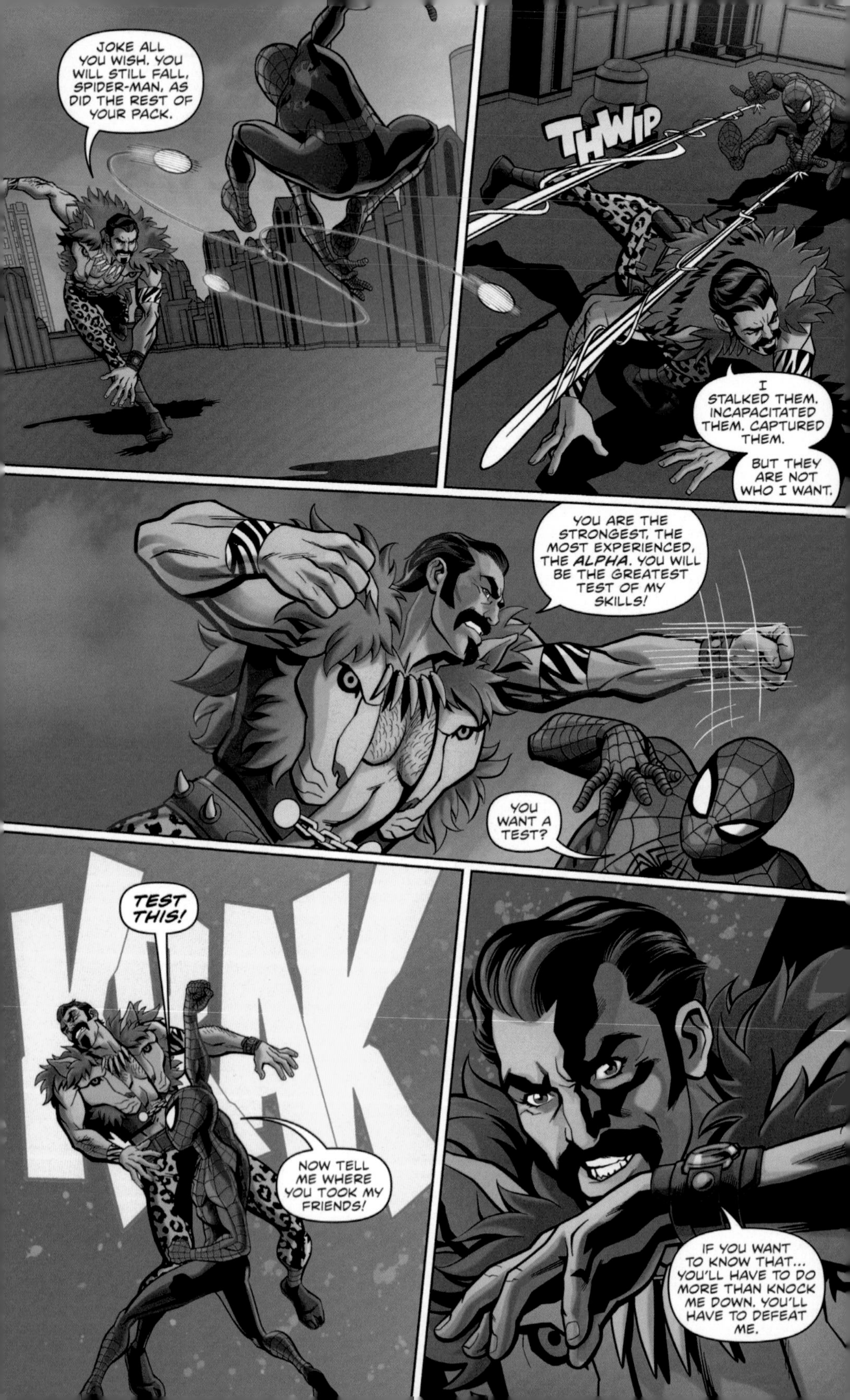
JOKE ALL YOU WISH. YOU WILL STILL FALL, SPIDER-MAN, AS DID THE REST OF YOUR PACK.
THWIP
I STALKED THEM. INCAPACITATED THEM. CAPTURED THEM.
BUT THEY ARE NOT WHO I WANT.
YOU ARE THE STRONGEST, THE MOST EXPERIENCED, THE *ALPHA*. YOU WILL BE THE GREATEST TEST OF MY SKILLS!
YOU WANT A TEST?
TEST THIS!
NOW TELL ME WHERE YOU TOOK MY FRIENDS!
IF YOU WANT TO KNOW THAT... YOU'LL HAVE TO DO MORE THAN KNOCK ME DOWN. YOU'LL HAVE TO DEFEAT ME.

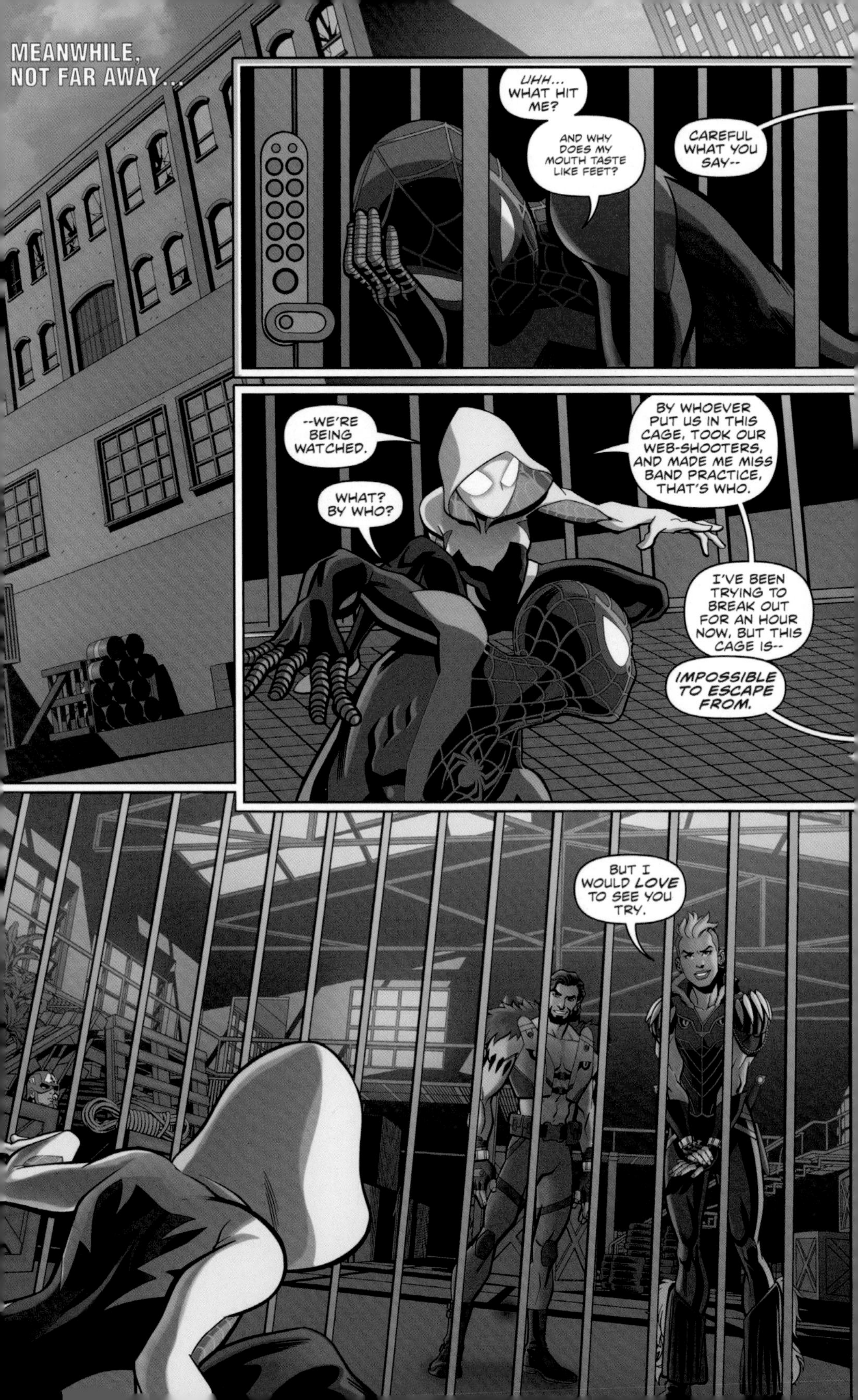
MEANWHILE, NOT FAR AWAY...
UHH... WHAT HIT ME?
AND WHY DOES MY MOUTH TASTE LIKE FEET?
CAREFUL WHAT YOU SAY--
--WE'RE BEING WATCHED.
WHAT? BY WHO?
BY WHOEVER PUT US IN THIS CAGE, TOOK OUR WEB-SHOOTERS, AND MADE ME MISS BAND PRACTICE, THAT'S WHO.
I'VE BEEN TRYING TO BREAK OUT FOR AN HOUR NOW, BUT THIS CAGE IS--
IMPOSSIBLE TO ESCAPE FROM.
BUT I WOULD LOVE TO SEE YOU TRY.

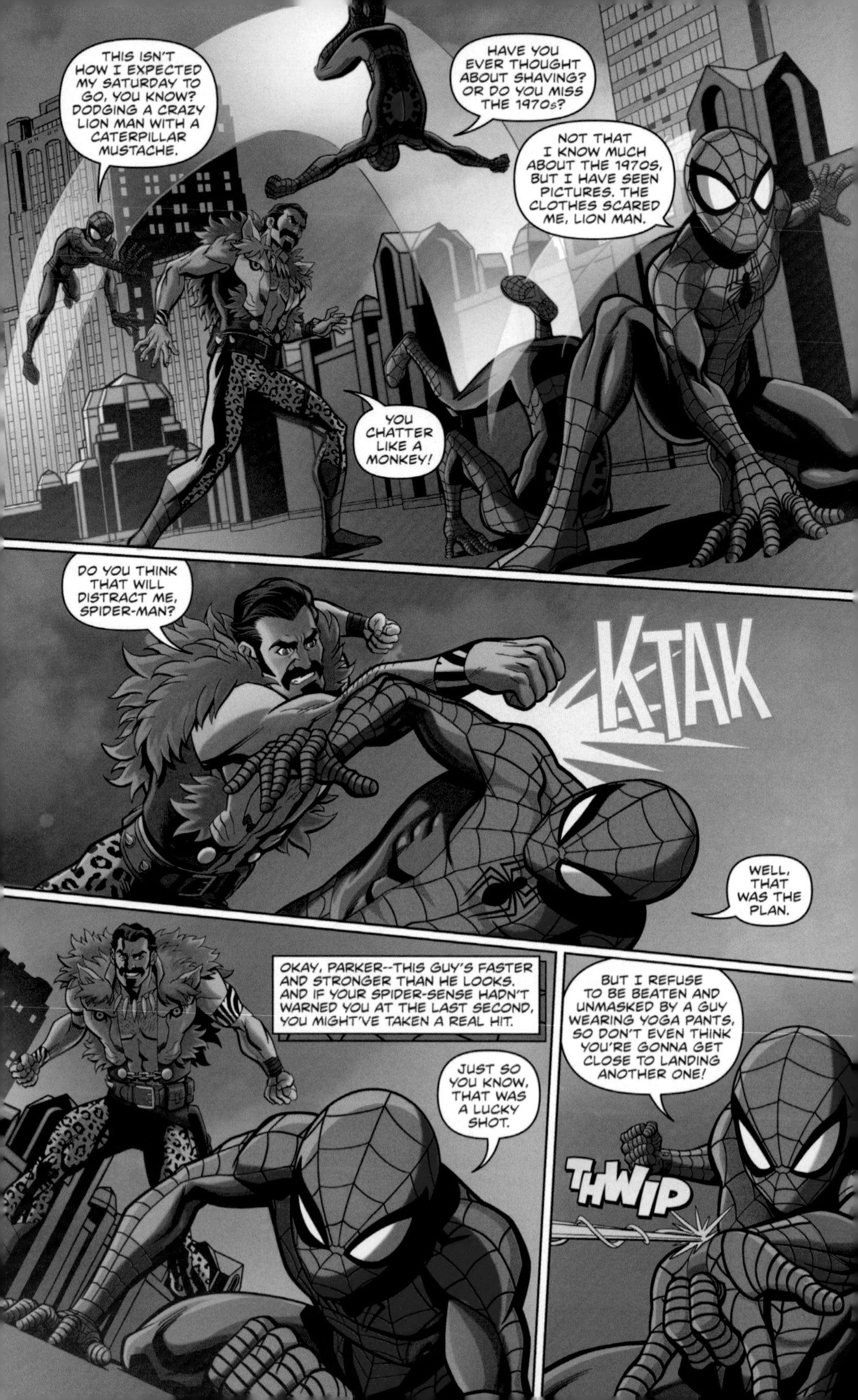
THIS ISN'T HOW I EXPECTED MY SATURDAY TO GO, YOU KNOW? DODGING A CRAZY LION MAN WITH A CATERPILLAR MUSTACHE.
HAVE YOU EVER THOUGHT ABOUT SHAVING? OR DO YOU MISS THE 1970s?
NOT THAT I KNOW MUCH ABOUT THE 1970S, BUT I HAVE SEEN PICTURES. THE CLOTHES SCARED ME, LION MAN.
YOU CHATTER LIKE A MONKEY!
DO YOU THINK THAT WILL DISTRACT ME, SPIDER-MAN?
K-TAK
WELL, THAT WAS THE PLAN.
OKAY, PARKER--THIS GUY'S FASTER AND STRONGER THAN HE LOOKS. AND IF YOUR SPIDER-SENSE HADN'T WARNED YOU AT THE LAST SECOND, YOU MIGHT'VE TAKEN A REAL HIT.
JUST SO YOU KNOW, THAT WAS A LUCKY SHOT.
BUT I REFUSE TO BE BEATEN AND UNMASKED BY A GUY WEARING YOGA PANTS, SO DON'T EVEN THINK YOU'RE GONNA GET CLOSE TO LANDING ANOTHER ONE!
THWIP

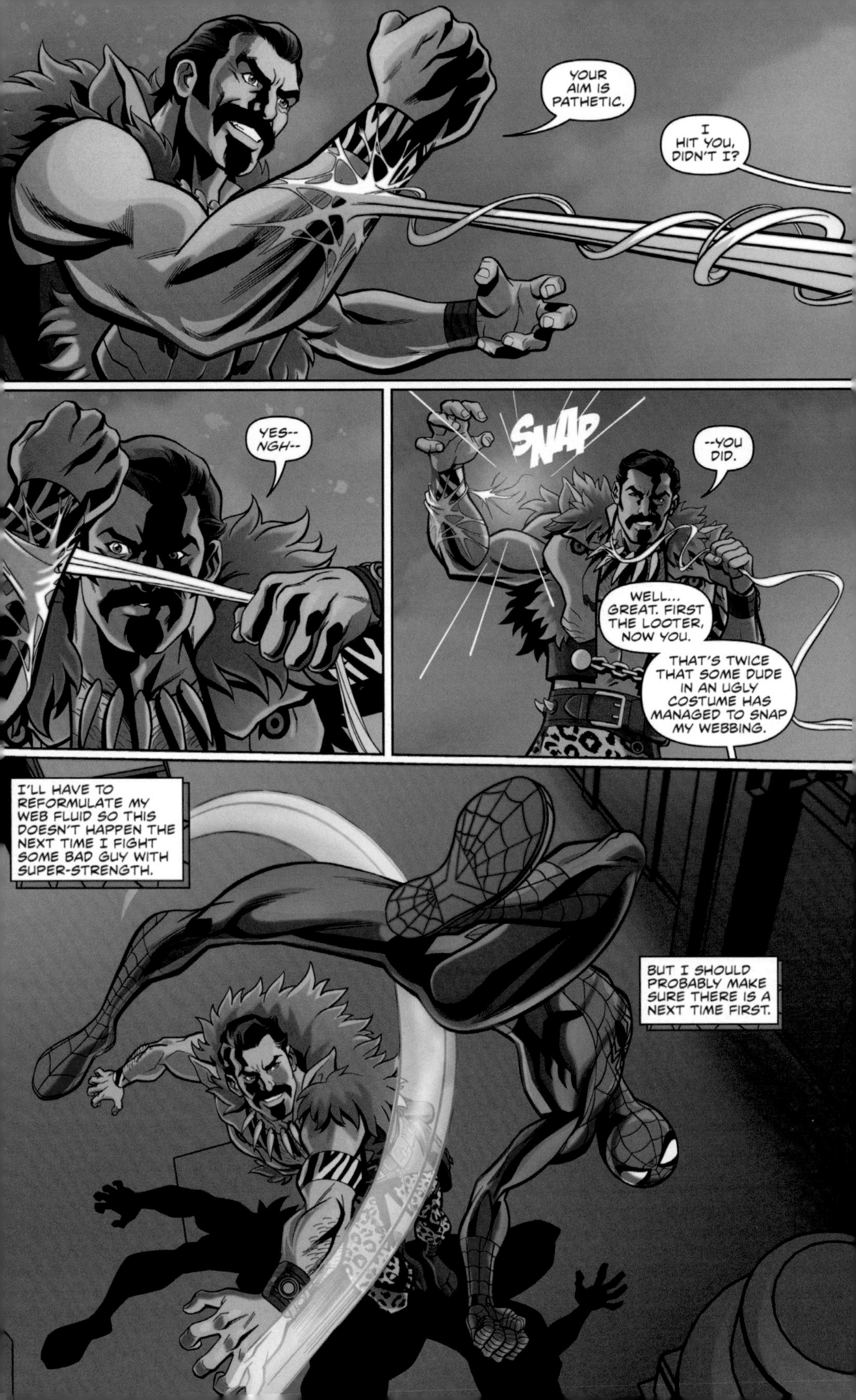
YOUR AIM IS PATHETIC.
I HIT YOU, DIDN'T I?
YES-- NGH--
SNAP
--YOU DID.
WELL... GREAT. FIRST THE LOOTER, NOW YOU.
THAT'S TWICE THAT SOME DUDE IN AN UGLY COSTUME HAS MANAGED TO SNAP MY WEBBING.
I'LL HAVE TO REFORMULATE MY WEB FLUID SO THIS DOESN'T HAPPEN THE NEXT TIME I FIGHT SOME BAD GUY WITH SUPER-STRENGTH.
BUT I SHOULD PROBABLY MAKE SURE THERE IS A NEXT TIME FIRST.

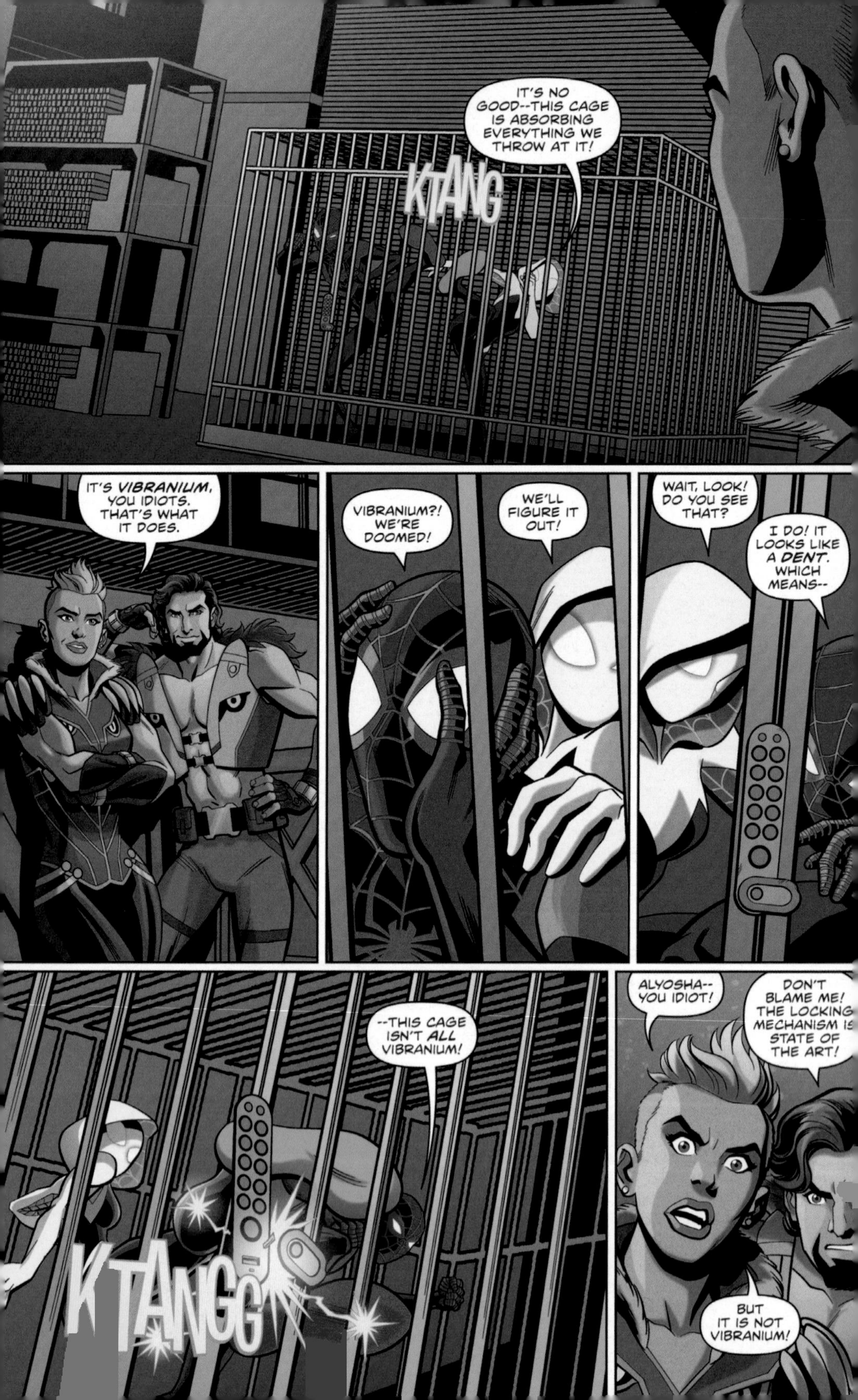
IT'S NO GOOD--THIS CAGE IS ABSORBING EVERYTHING WE THROW AT IT!
KTANG
IT'S VIBRANIUM, YOU IDIOTS. THAT'S WHAT IT DOES.
VIBRANIUM?! WE'RE DOOMED!
WE'LL FIGURE IT OUT!
WAIT, LOOK! DO YOU SEE THAT?
I DO! IT LOOKS LIKE A DENT. WHICH MEANS--
--THIS CAGE ISN'T ALL VIBRANIUM!
KTANGG
ALYOSHA-- YOU IDIOT!
DON'T BLAME ME! THE LOCKING MECHANISM IS STATE OF THE ART!
BUT IT IS NOT VIBRANIUM!

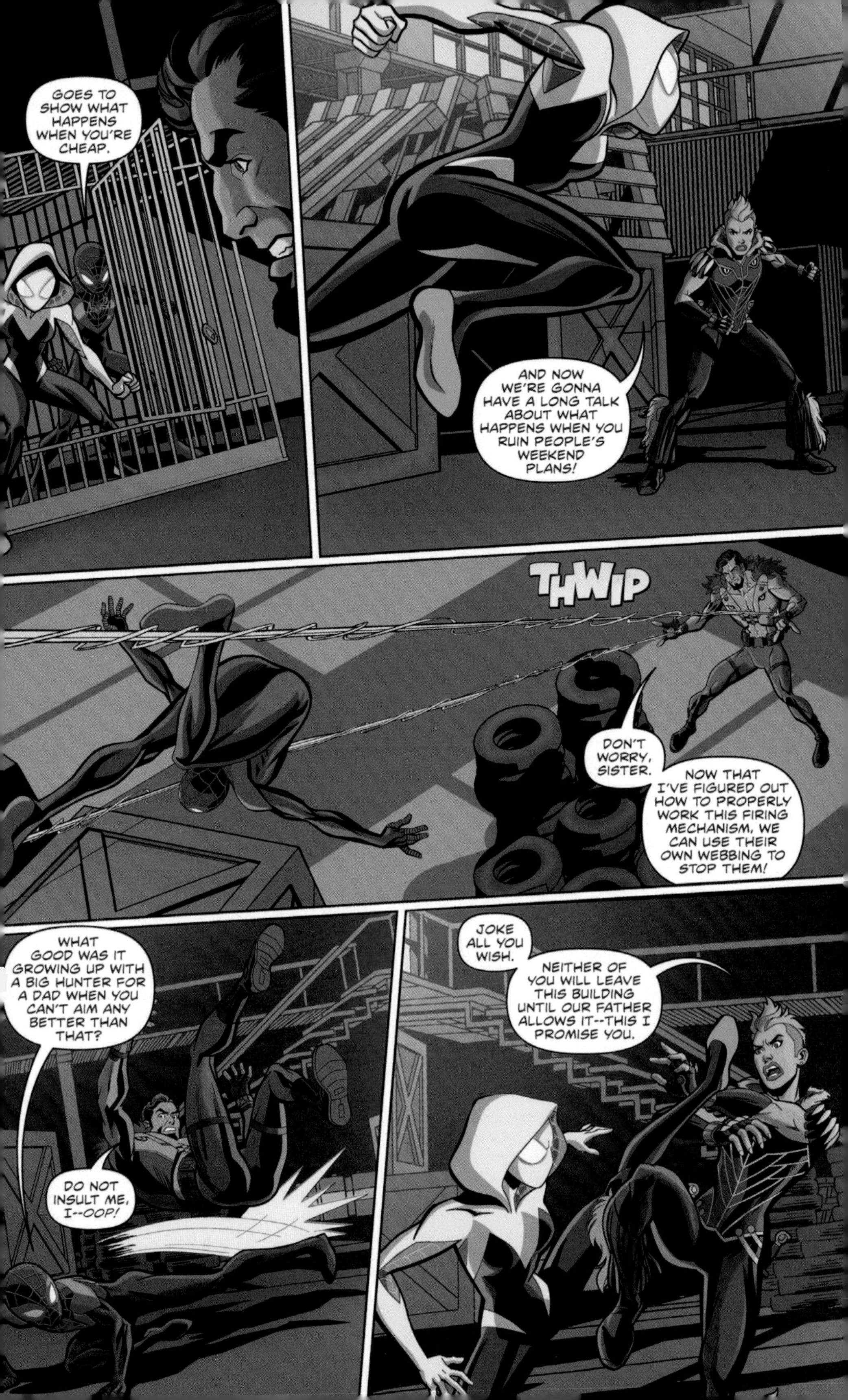
GOES TO SHOW WHAT HAPPENS WHEN YOU'RE CHEAP.
AND NOW WE'RE GONNA HAVE A LONG TALK ABOUT WHAT HAPPENS WHEN YOU RUIN PEOPLE'S WEEKEND PLANS!
THWIP
DON'T WORRY, SISTER.
NOW THAT I'VE FIGURED OUT HOW TO PROPERLY WORK THIS FIRING MECHANISM, WE CAN USE THEIR OWN WEBBING TO STOP THEM!
WHAT GOOD WAS IT GROWING UP WITH A BIG HUNTER FOR A DAD WHEN YOU CAN'T AIM ANY BETTER THAN THAT?
DO NOT INSULT ME, I--OOP!
JOKE ALL YOU WISH.
NEITHER OF YOU WILL LEAVE THIS BUILDING UNTIL OUR FATHER ALLOWS IT--THIS I PROMISE YOU.

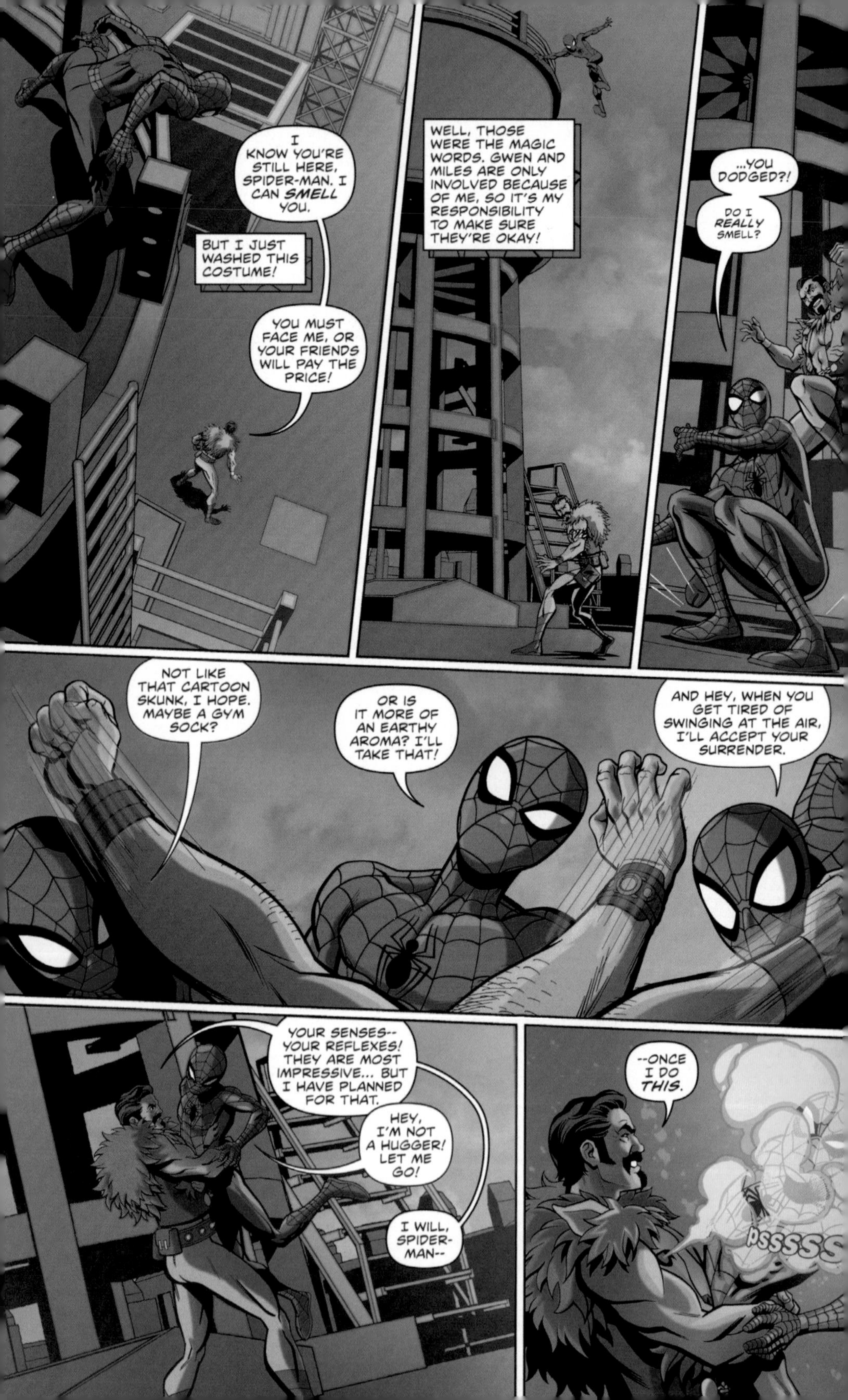
I KNOW YOU'RE STILL HERE, SPIDER-MAN. I CAN *SMELL* YOU.
BUT I JUST WASHED THIS COSTUME!
YOU MUST FACE ME, OR YOUR FRIENDS WILL PAY THE PRICE!
WELL, THOSE WERE THE MAGIC WORDS. GWEN AND MILES ARE ONLY INVOLVED BECAUSE OF ME, SO IT'S MY RESPONSIBILITY TO MAKE SURE THEY'RE OKAY!
...YOU DODGED?!
DO I *REALLY* SMELL?
NOT LIKE THAT CARTOON SKUNK, I HOPE. MAYBE A GYM SOCK?
OR IS IT MORE OF AN EARTHY AROMA? I'LL TAKE THAT!
AND HEY, WHEN YOU GET TIRED OF SWINGING AT THE AIR, I'LL ACCEPT YOUR SURRENDER.
YOUR SENSES-- YOUR REFLEXES! THEY ARE MOST IMPRESSIVE... BUT I HAVE PLANNED FOR THAT.
HEY, I'M NOT A HUGGER! LET ME GO!
I WILL, SPIDER-MAN--
--ONCE I DO *THIS*.
PSSSSS

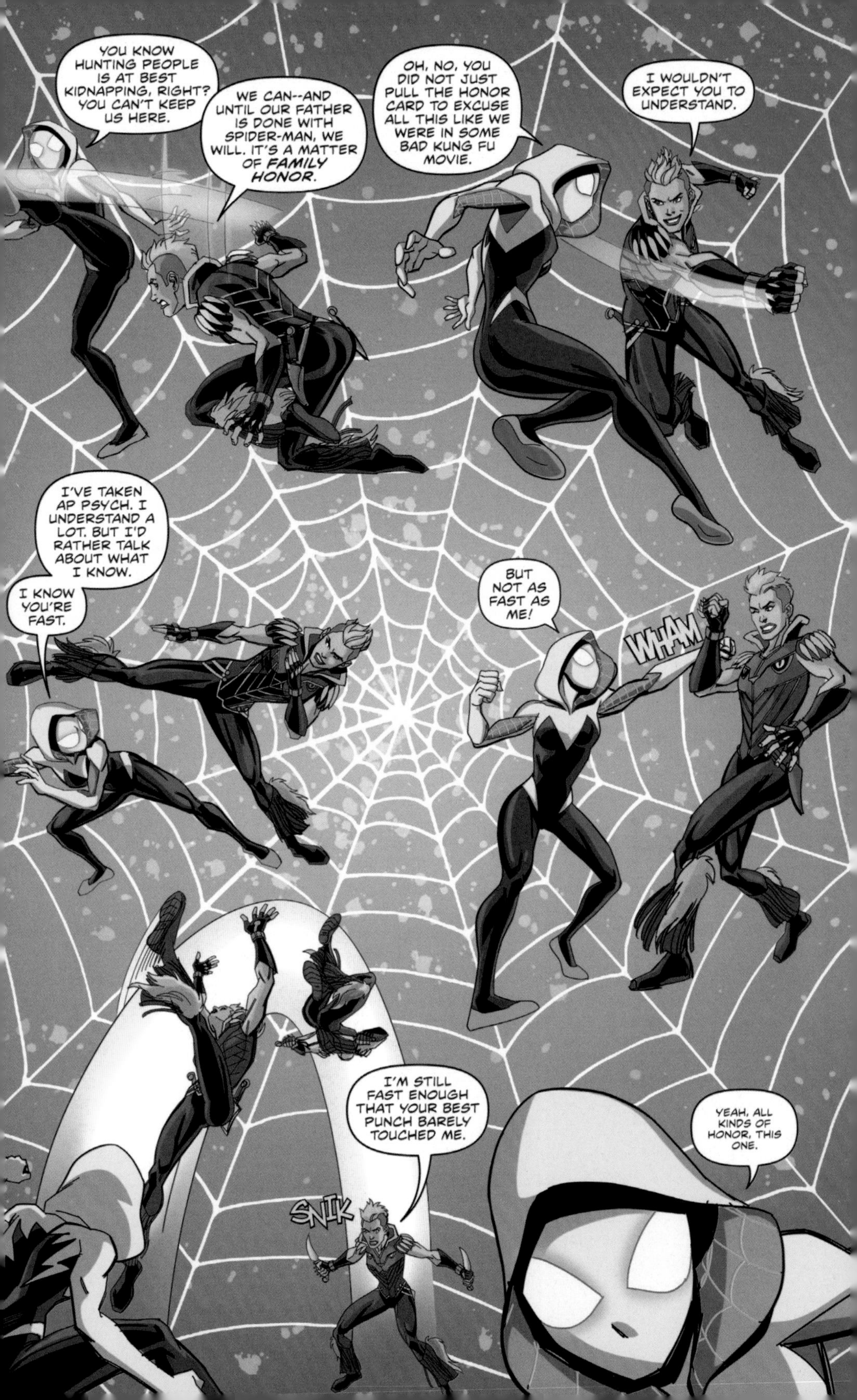
YOU KNOW HUNTING PEOPLE IS AT BEST KIDNAPPING, RIGHT? YOU CAN'T KEEP US HERE.
WE CAN--AND UNTIL OUR FATHER IS DONE WITH SPIDER-MAN, WE WILL. IT'S A MATTER OF *FAMILY HONOR*.
OH, NO, YOU DID NOT JUST PULL THE HONOR CARD TO EXCUSE ALL THIS LIKE WE WERE IN SOME BAD KUNG FU MOVIE.
I WOULDN'T EXPECT YOU TO UNDERSTAND.
I'VE TAKEN AP PSYCH. I UNDERSTAND A LOT. BUT I'D RATHER TALK ABOUT WHAT I KNOW.
I KNOW YOU'RE FAST.
BUT NOT AS FAST AS ME!
WHAM
I'M STILL FAST ENOUGH THAT YOUR BEST PUNCH BARELY TOUCHED ME.
SNIK
YEAH, ALL KINDS OF HONOR, THIS ONE.

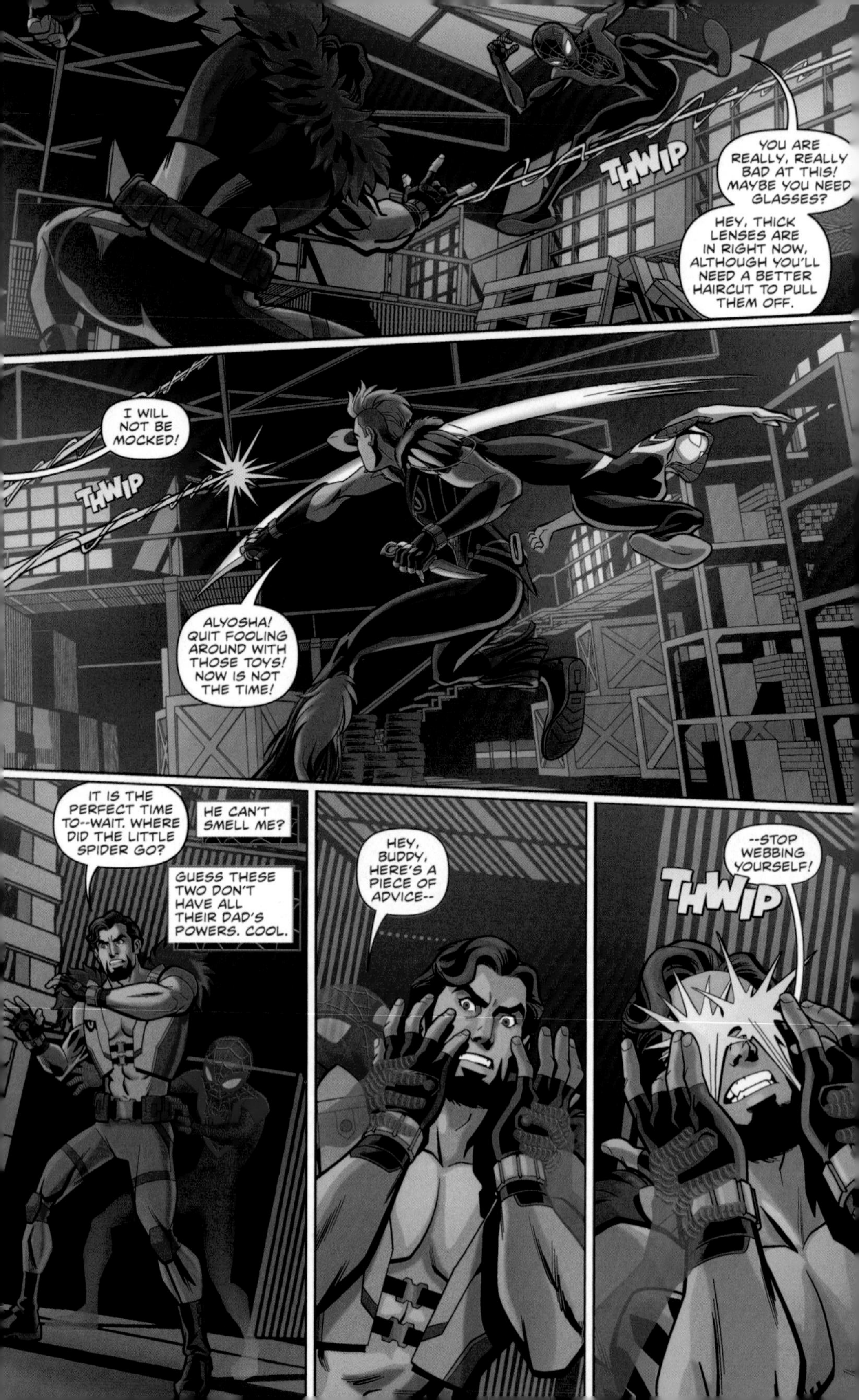
THWIP
YOU ARE REALLY, REALLY BAD AT THIS! MAYBE YOU NEED GLASSES?
HEY, THICK LENSES ARE IN RIGHT NOW, ALTHOUGH YOU'LL NEED A BETTER HAIRCUT TO PULL THEM OFF.
I WILL NOT BE MOCKED!
THWIP
ALYOSHA! QUIT FOOLING AROUND WITH THOSE TOYS! NOW IS NOT THE TIME!
IT IS THE PERFECT TIME TO--WAIT. WHERE DID THE LITTLE SPIDER GO?
HE CAN'T SMELL ME?
GUESS THESE TWO DON'T HAVE ALL THEIR DAD'S POWERS. COOL.
HEY, BUDDY, HERE'S A PIECE OF ADVICE--
THWIP
--STOP WEBBING YOURSELF!

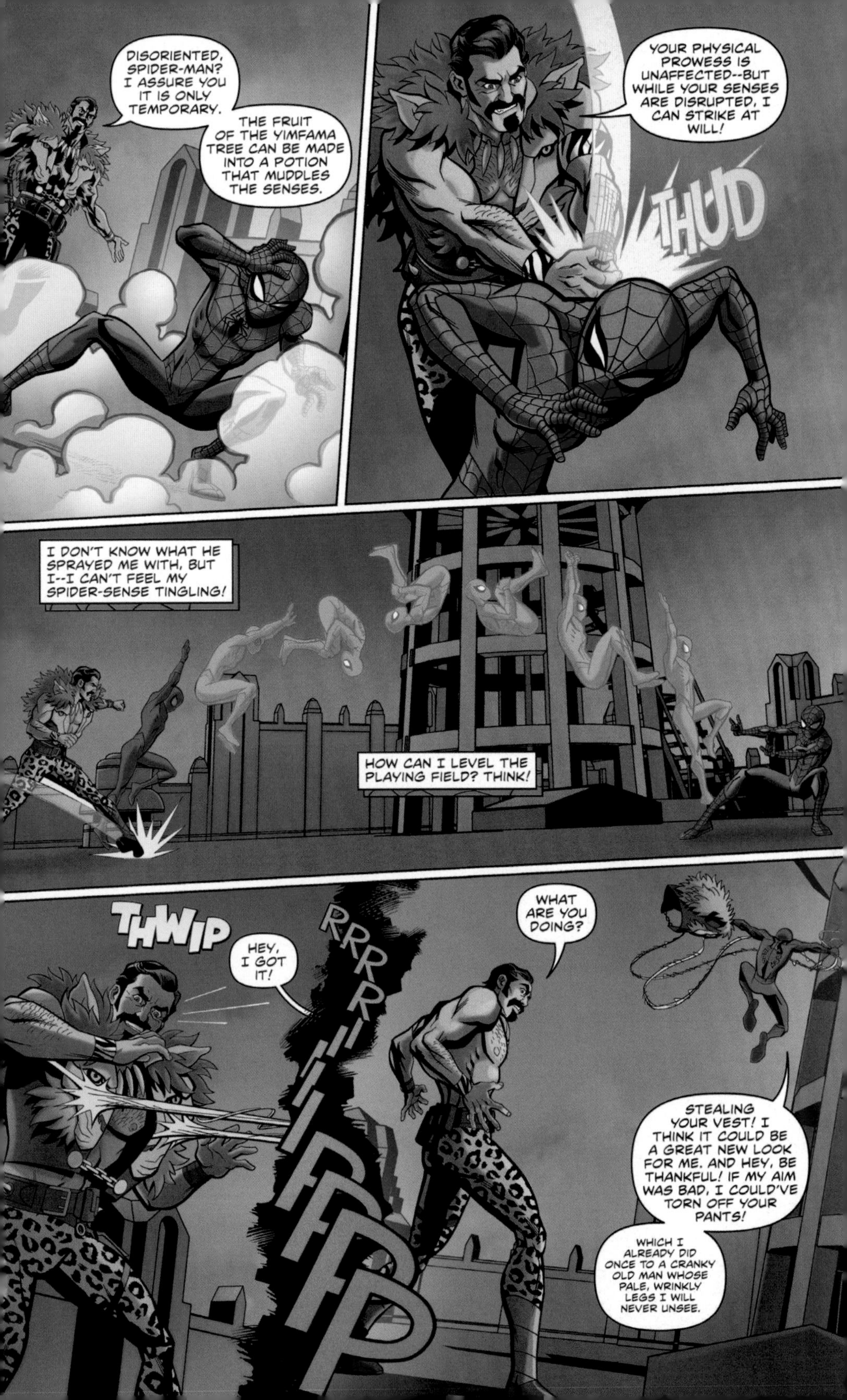
DISORIENTED, SPIDER-MAN? I ASSURE YOU IT IS ONLY TEMPORARY.
THE FRUIT OF THE YIMFAMA TREE CAN BE MADE INTO A POTION THAT MUDDLES THE SENSES.
YOUR PHYSICAL PROWESS IS UNAFFECTED--BUT WHILE YOUR SENSES ARE DISRUPTED, I CAN STRIKE AT WILL!
THUD
I DON'T KNOW WHAT HE SPRAYED ME WITH, BUT I--I CAN'T FEEL MY SPIDER-SENSE TINGLING!
HOW CAN I LEVEL THE PLAYING FIELD? THINK!
THWIP
HEY, I GOT IT!
RRRRIIIIIPPP
WHAT ARE YOU DOING?
STEALING YOUR VEST! I THINK IT COULD BE A GREAT NEW LOOK FOR ME. AND HEY, BE THANKFUL! IF MY AIM WAS BAD, I COULD'VE TORN OFF YOUR PANTS!
WHICH I ALREADY DID ONCE TO A CRANKY OLD MAN WHOSE PALE, WRINKLY LEGS I WILL NEVER UNSEE.

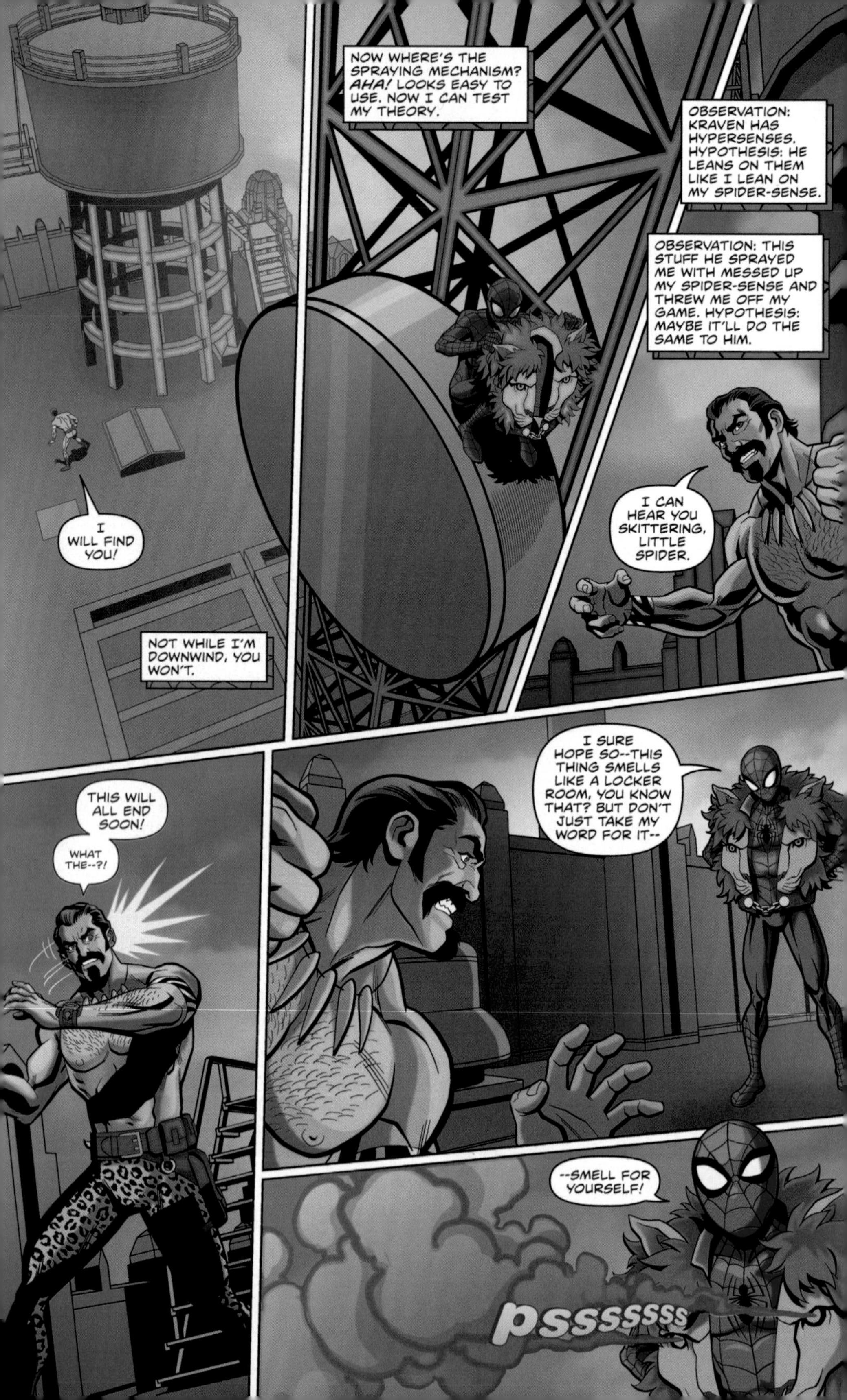
I WILL FIND YOU!
NOT WHILE I'M DOWNWIND, YOU WON'T.
NOW WHERE'S THE SPRAYING MECHANISM? AHA! LOOKS EASY TO USE. NOW I CAN TEST MY THEORY.
OBSERVATION: KRAVEN HAS HYPERSENSES. HYPOTHESIS: HE LEANS ON THEM LIKE I LEAN ON MY SPIDER-SENSE.
OBSERVATION: THIS STUFF HE SPRAYED ME WITH MESSED UP MY SPIDER-SENSE AND THREW ME OFF MY GAME. HYPOTHESIS: MAYBE IT'LL DO THE SAME TO HIM.
I CAN HEAR YOU SKITTERING, LITTLE SPIDER.
THIS WILL ALL END SOON!
WHAT THE--?!
I SURE HOPE SO--THIS THING SMELLS LIKE A LOCKER ROOM, YOU KNOW THAT? BUT DON'T JUST TAKE MY WORD FOR IT--
--SMELL FOR YOURSELF!
PSSSSSSS

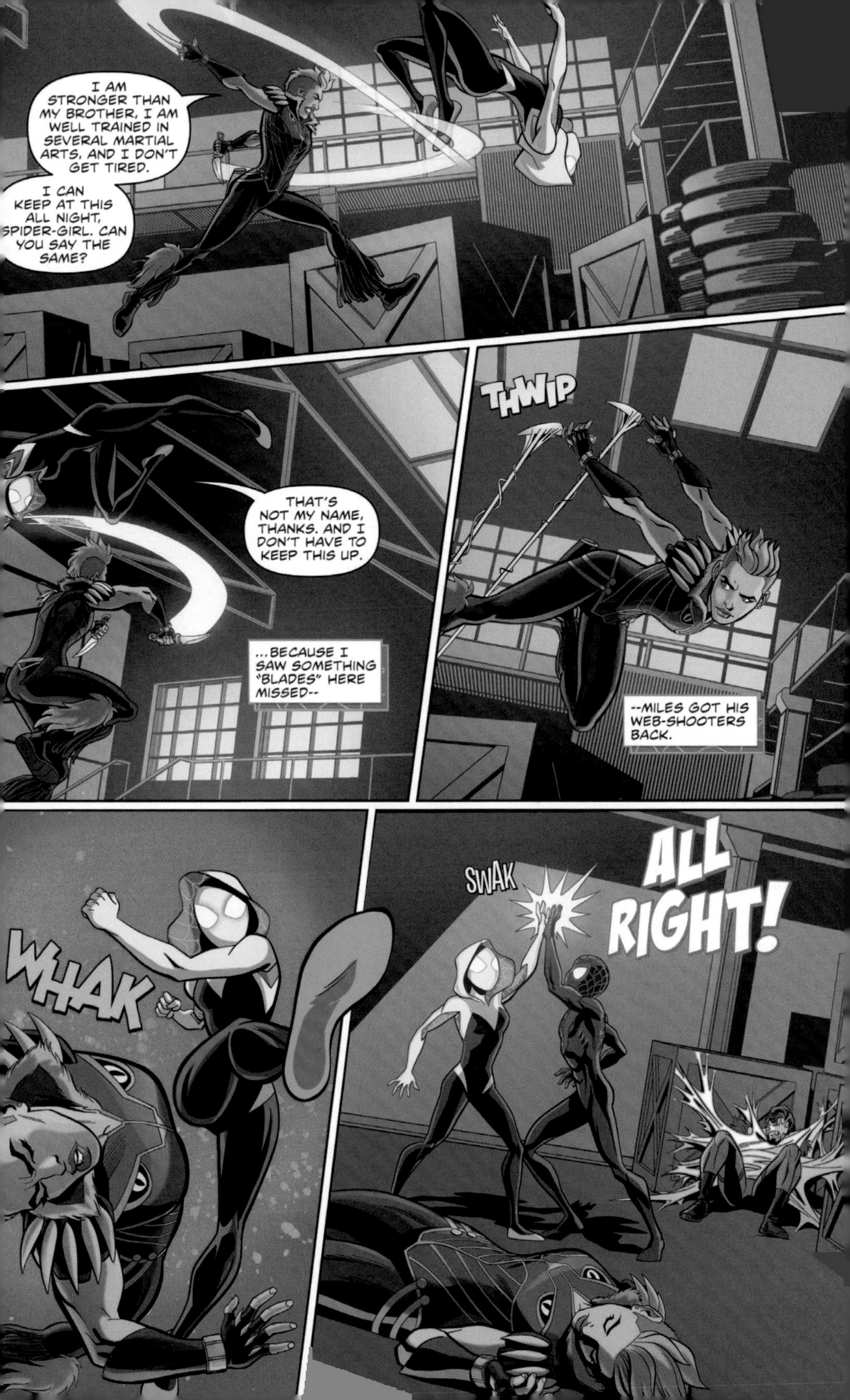

I AM STRONGER THAN MY BROTHER, I AM WELL TRAINED IN SEVERAL MARTIAL ARTS, AND I DON'T GET TIRED.
I CAN KEEP AT THIS ALL NIGHT, SPIDER-GIRL. CAN YOU SAY THE SAME?
THAT'S NOT MY NAME, THANKS. AND I DON'T HAVE TO KEEP THIS UP.
...BECAUSE I SAW SOMETHING "BLADES" HERE MISSED--
THWIP
--MILES GOT HIS WEB-SHOOTERS BACK.
WHAK
SWAK
ALL RIGHT!

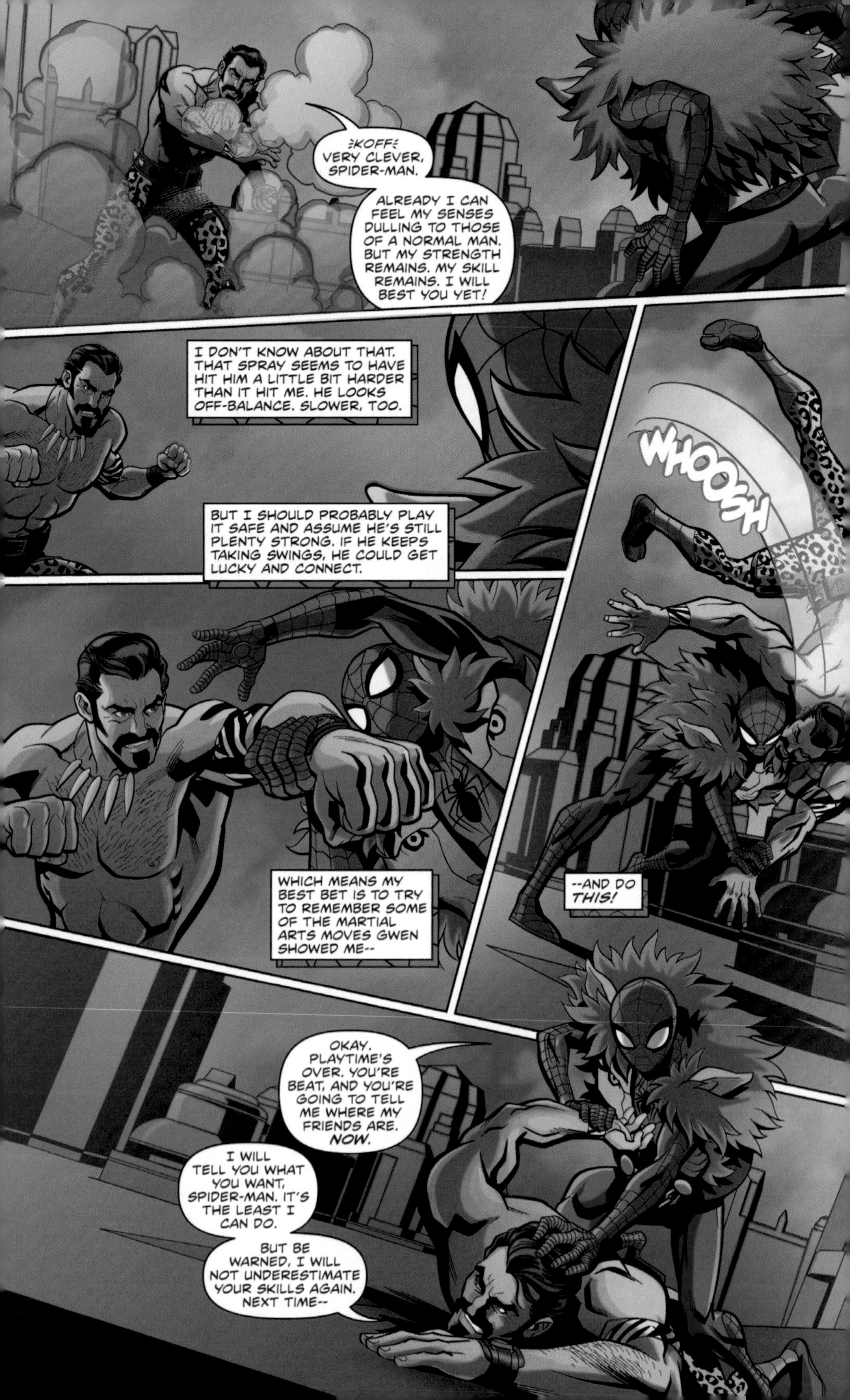

KOFF VERY CLEVER, SPIDER-MAN.
ALREADY I CAN FEEL MY SENSES DULLING TO THOSE OF A NORMAL MAN. BUT MY STRENGTH REMAINS. MY SKILL REMAINS. I WILL BEST YOU YET!
I DON'T KNOW ABOUT THAT. THAT SPRAY SEEMS TO HAVE HIT HIM A LITTLE BIT HARDER THAN IT HIT ME. HE LOOKS OFF-BALANCE. SLOWER, TOO.
BUT I SHOULD PROBABLY PLAY IT SAFE AND ASSUME HE'S STILL PLENTY STRONG. IF HE KEEPS TAKING SWINGS, HE COULD GET LUCKY AND CONNECT.
WHICH MEANS MY BEST BET IS TO TRY TO REMEMBER SOME OF THE MARTIAL ARTS MOVES GWEN SHOWED ME--
WHOOSH
--AND DO *THIS!*
OKAY. PLAYTIME'S OVER. YOU'RE BEAT, AND YOU'RE GOING TO TELL ME WHERE MY FRIENDS ARE. **NOW.**
I WILL TELL YOU WHAT YOU WANT, SPIDER-MAN. IT'S THE LEAST I CAN DO.
BUT BE WARNED, I WILL NOT UNDERESTIMATE YOUR SKILLS AGAIN. NEXT TIME--

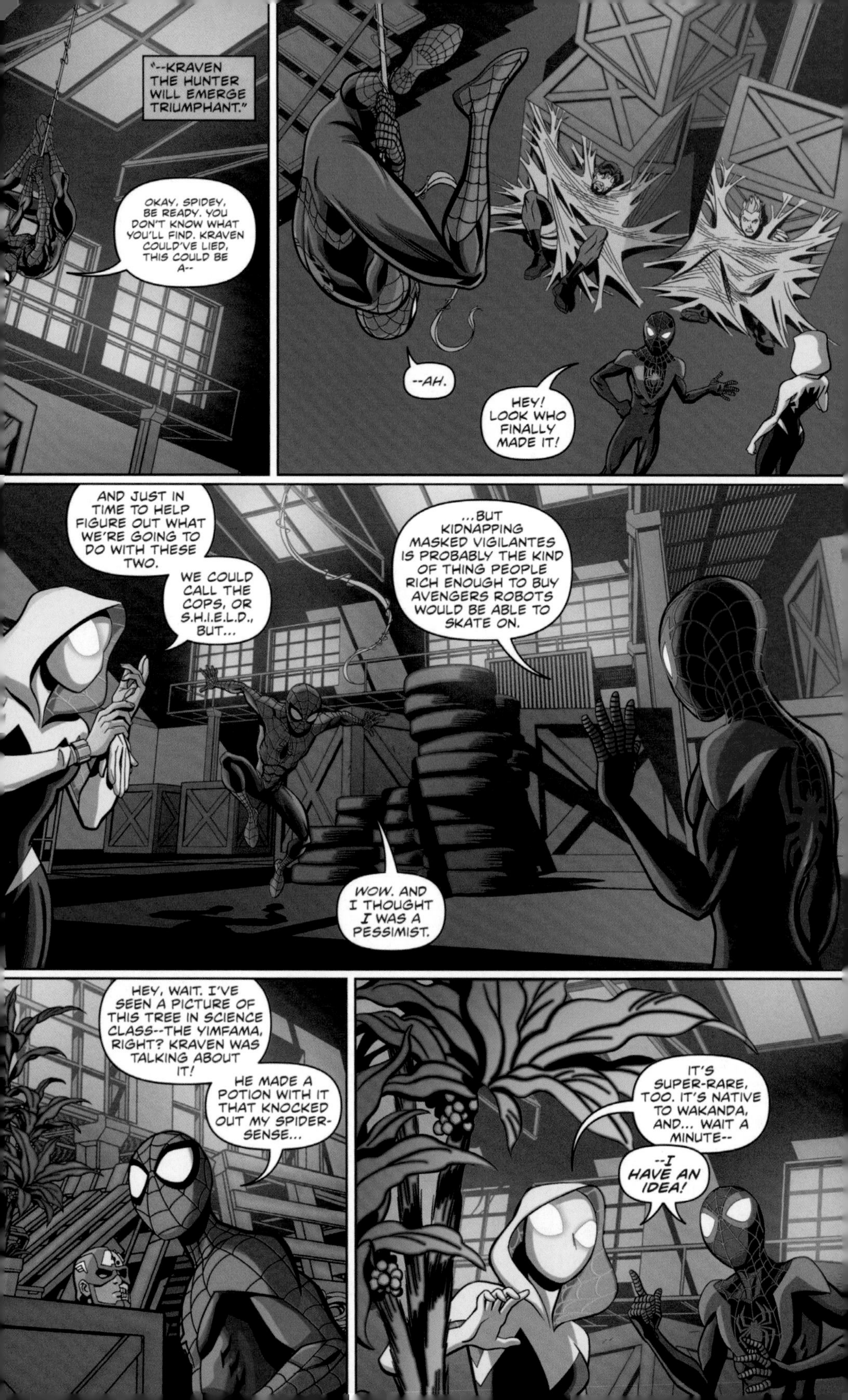
"--KRAVEN THE HUNTER WILL EMERGE TRIUMPHANT."
OKAY, SPIDEY, BE READY. YOU DON'T KNOW WHAT YOU'LL FIND. KRAVEN COULD'VE LIED, THIS COULD BE A--
--AH.
HEY! LOOK WHO FINALLY MADE IT!
AND JUST IN TIME TO HELP FIGURE OUT WHAT WE'RE GOING TO DO WITH THESE TWO.
WE COULD CALL THE COPS, OR S.H.I.E.L.D., BUT...
...BUT KIDNAPPING MASKED VIGILANTES IS PROBABLY THE KIND OF THING PEOPLE RICH ENOUGH TO BUY AVENGERS ROBOTS WOULD BE ABLE TO SKATE ON.
WOW. AND I THOUGHT *I* WAS A PESSIMIST.
HEY, WAIT. I'VE SEEN A PICTURE OF THIS TREE IN SCIENCE CLASS--THE YIMFAMA, RIGHT? KRAVEN WAS TALKING ABOUT IT!
HE MADE A POTION WITH IT THAT KNOCKED OUT MY SPIDER-SENSE...
IT'S SUPER-RARE, TOO. IT'S NATIVE TO WAKANDA, AND... WAIT A MINUTE--
--I HAVE AN IDEA!

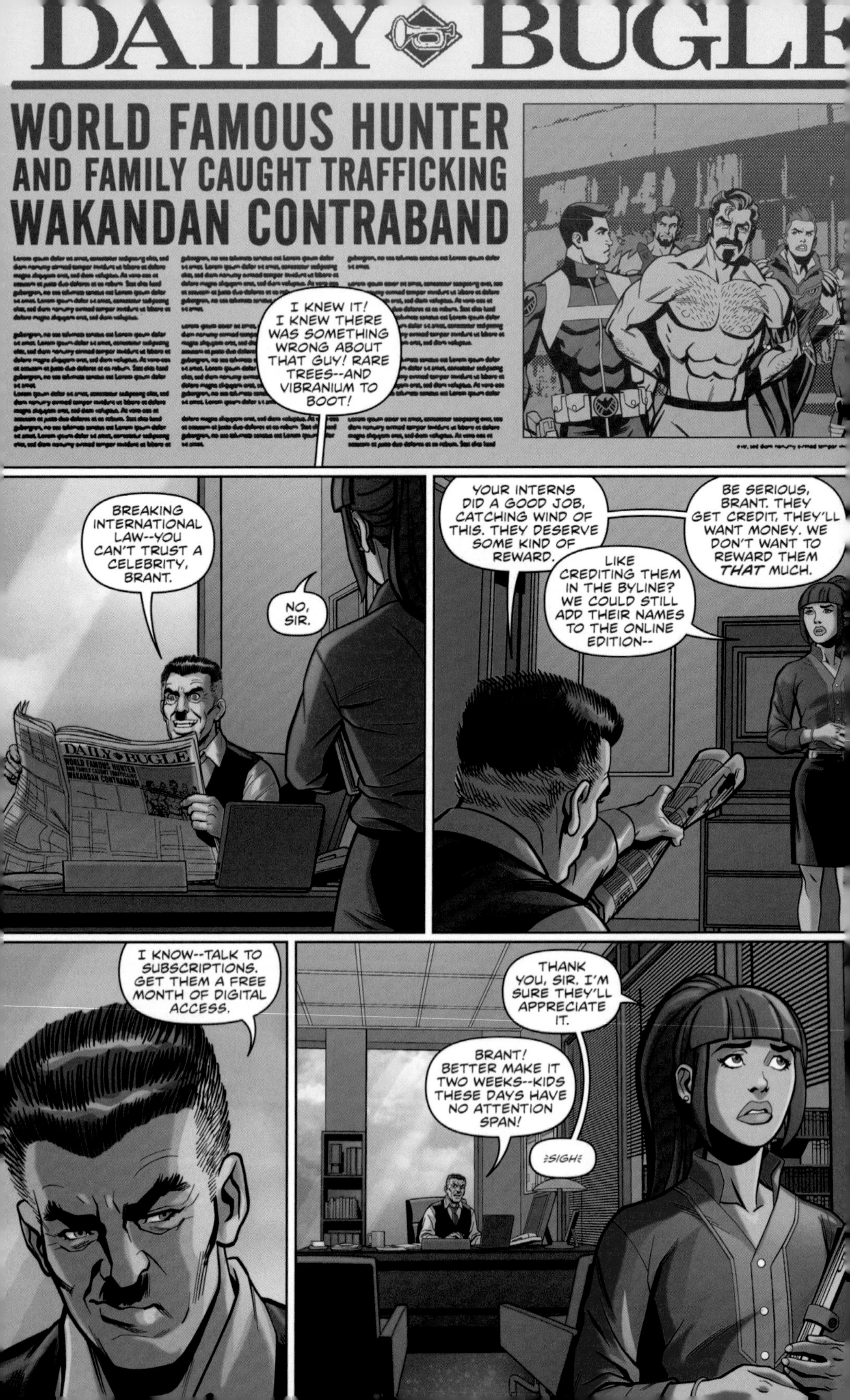
DAILY BUGLE
WORLD FAMOUS HUNTER AND FAMILY CAUGHT TRAFFICKING WAKANDAN CONTRABAND
I KNEW IT! I KNEW THERE WAS SOMETHING WRONG ABOUT THAT GUY! RARE TREES--AND VIBRANIUM TO BOOT!
BREAKING INTERNATIONAL LAW--YOU CAN'T TRUST A CELEBRITY, BRANT.
NO, SIR.
YOUR INTERNS DID A GOOD JOB, CATCHING WIND OF THIS. THEY DESERVE SOME KIND OF REWARD.
LIKE CREDITING THEM IN THE BYLINE? WE COULD STILL ADD THEIR NAMES TO THE ONLINE EDITION--
BE SERIOUS, BRANT. THEY GET CREDIT, THEY'LL WANT MONEY. WE DON'T WANT TO REWARD THEM *THAT* MUCH.
I KNOW--TALK TO SUBSCRIPTIONS. GET THEM A FREE MONTH OF DIGITAL ACCESS.
THANK YOU, SIR. I'M SURE THEY'LL APPRECIATE IT.
BRANT! BETTER MAKE IT TWO WEEKS--KIDS THESE DAYS HAVE NO ATTENTION SPAN!
SIGH

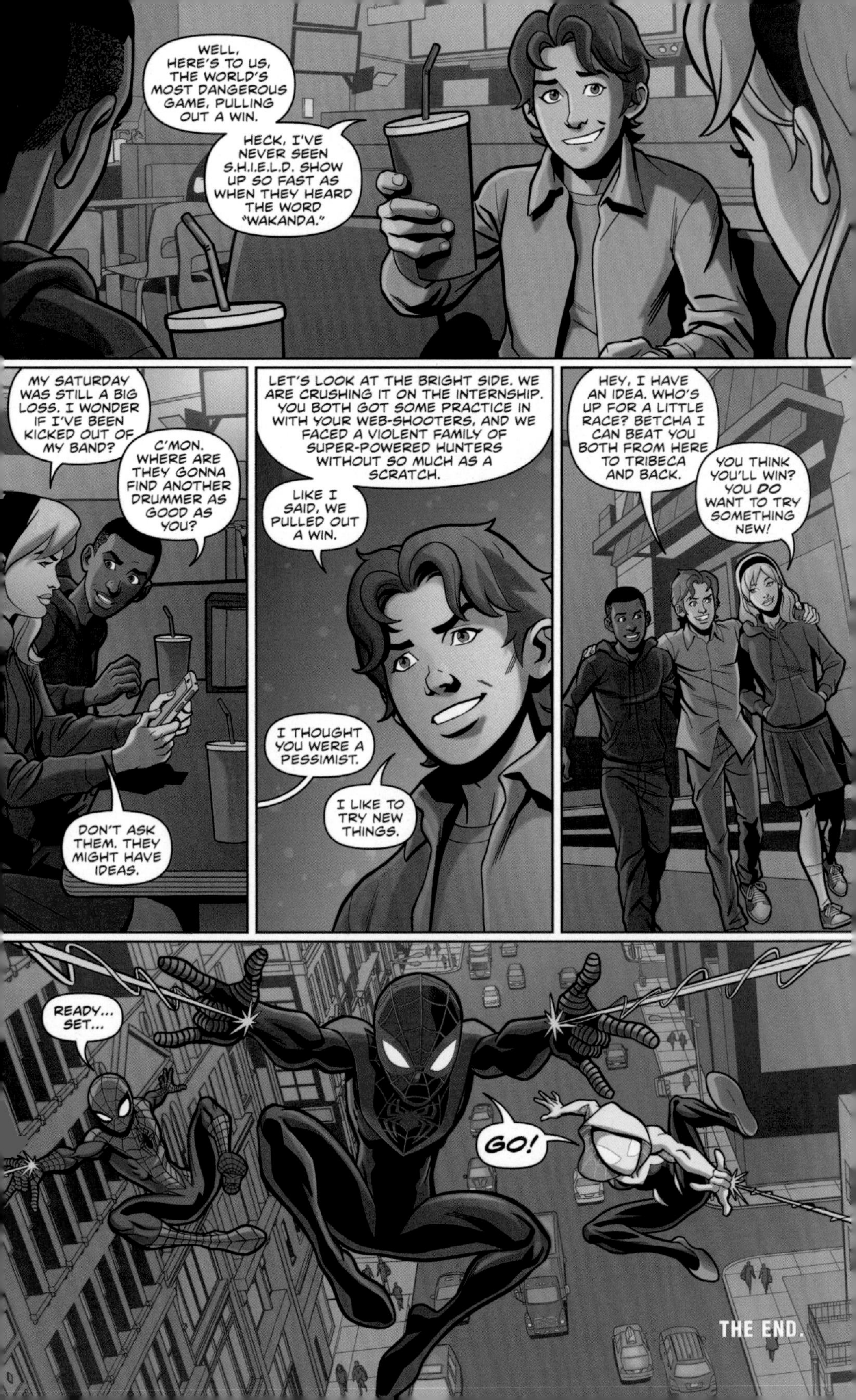
WELL, HERE'S TO US, THE WORLD'S MOST DANGEROUS GAME, PULLING OUT A WIN.
HECK, I'VE NEVER SEEN S.H.I.E.L.D. SHOW UP SO FAST AS WHEN THEY HEARD THE WORD "WAKANDA."
MY SATURDAY WAS STILL A BIG LOSS. I WONDER IF I'VE BEEN KICKED OUT OF MY BAND?
C'MON. WHERE ARE THEY GONNA FIND ANOTHER DRUMMER AS GOOD AS YOU?
DON'T ASK THEM. THEY MIGHT HAVE IDEAS.
LET'S LOOK AT THE BRIGHT SIDE. WE ARE CRUSHING IT ON THE INTERNSHIP. YOU BOTH GOT SOME PRACTICE IN WITH YOUR WEB-SHOOTERS, AND WE FACED A VIOLENT FAMILY OF SUPER-POWERED HUNTERS WITHOUT SO MUCH AS A SCRATCH.
LIKE I SAID, WE PULLED OUT A WIN.
I THOUGHT YOU WERE A PESSIMIST.
I LIKE TO TRY NEW THINGS.
HEY, I HAVE AN IDEA. WHO'S UP FOR A LITTLE RACE? BETCHA I CAN BEAT YOU BOTH FROM HERE TO TRIBECA AND BACK.
YOU THINK YOU'LL WIN? YOU DO WANT TO TRY SOMETHING NEW!
READY... SET...
GO!
THE END.

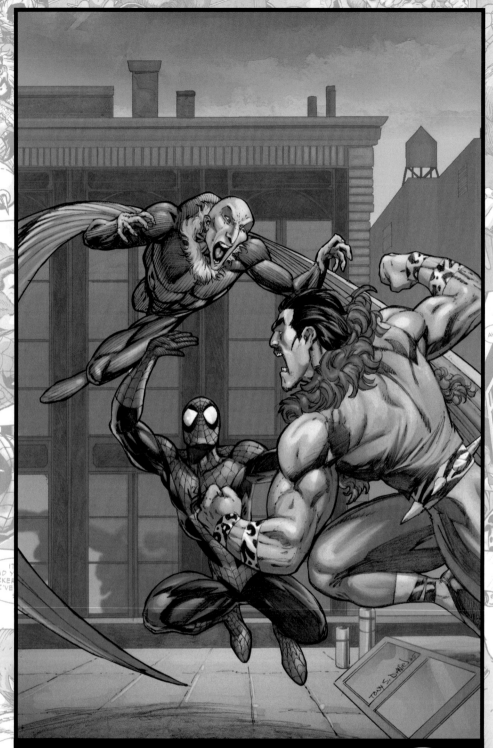

MARVEL ADVENTURES SPIDER-MAN #7

IT'S TIME FOR A SHOCKING TEAM-UP WHEN KRAVEN AND SPIDEY MUST WORK TOGETHER TO TRACK DOWN THE VULTURE!

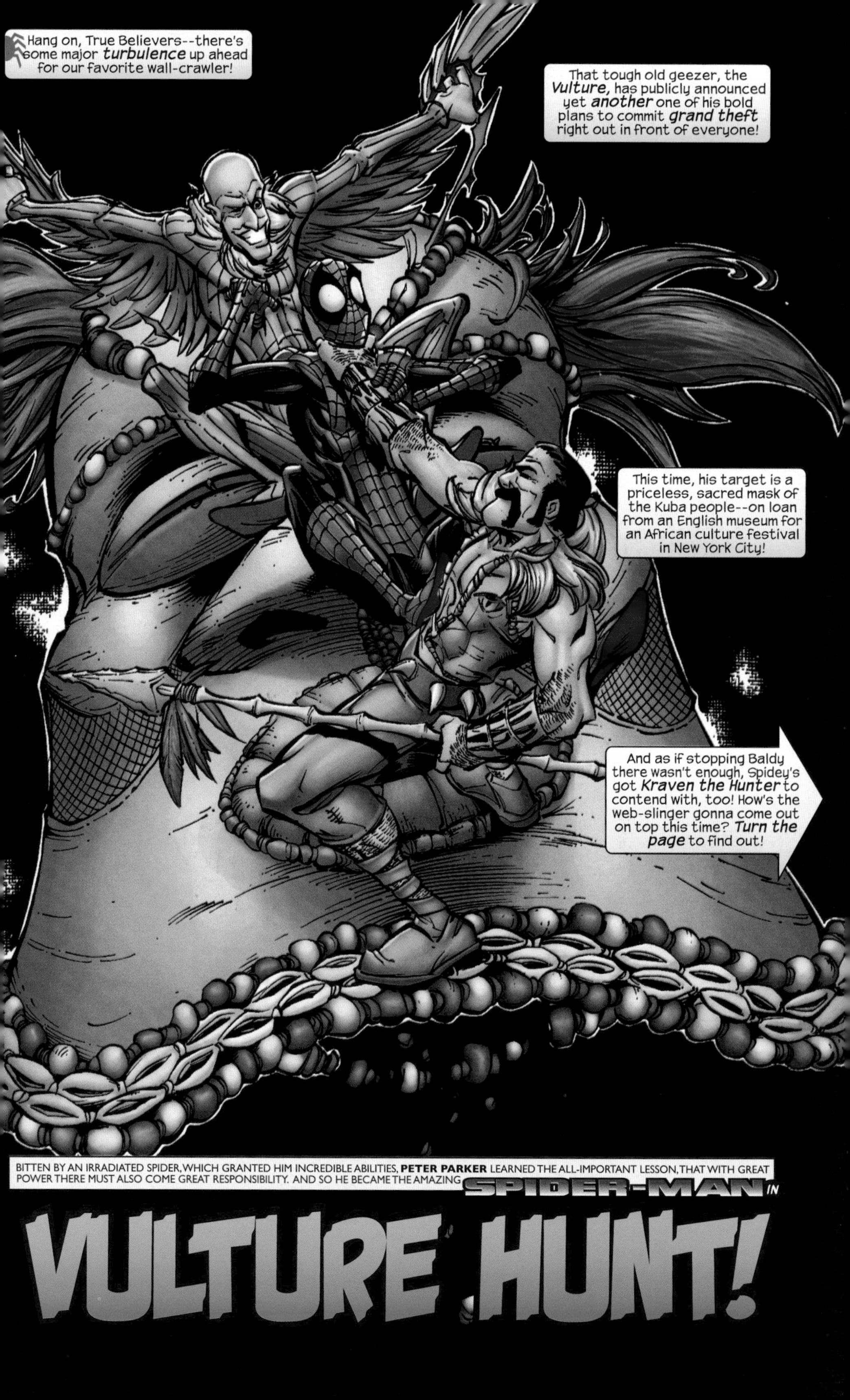
Hang on, True Believers--there's some major *turbulence* up ahead for our favorite wall-crawler!
That tough old geezer, the *Vulture,* has publicly announced yet *another* one of his bold plans to commit *grand theft* right out in front of everyone!
This time, his target is a priceless, sacred mask of the Kuba people--on loan from an English museum for an African culture festival in New York City!
And as if stopping Baldy there wasn't enough, Spidey's got *Kraven the Hunter* to contend with, too! How's the web-slinger gonna come out on top this time? *Turn the page* to find out!
BITTEN BY AN IRRADIATED SPIDER, WHICH GRANTED HIM INCREDIBLE ABILITIES, **PETER PARKER** LEARNED THE ALL-IMPORTANT LESSON, THAT WITH GREAT POWER THERE MUST ALSO COME GREAT RESPONSIBILITY. AND SO HE BECAME THE AMAZING SPIDER-MAN IN
VULTURE HUNT!

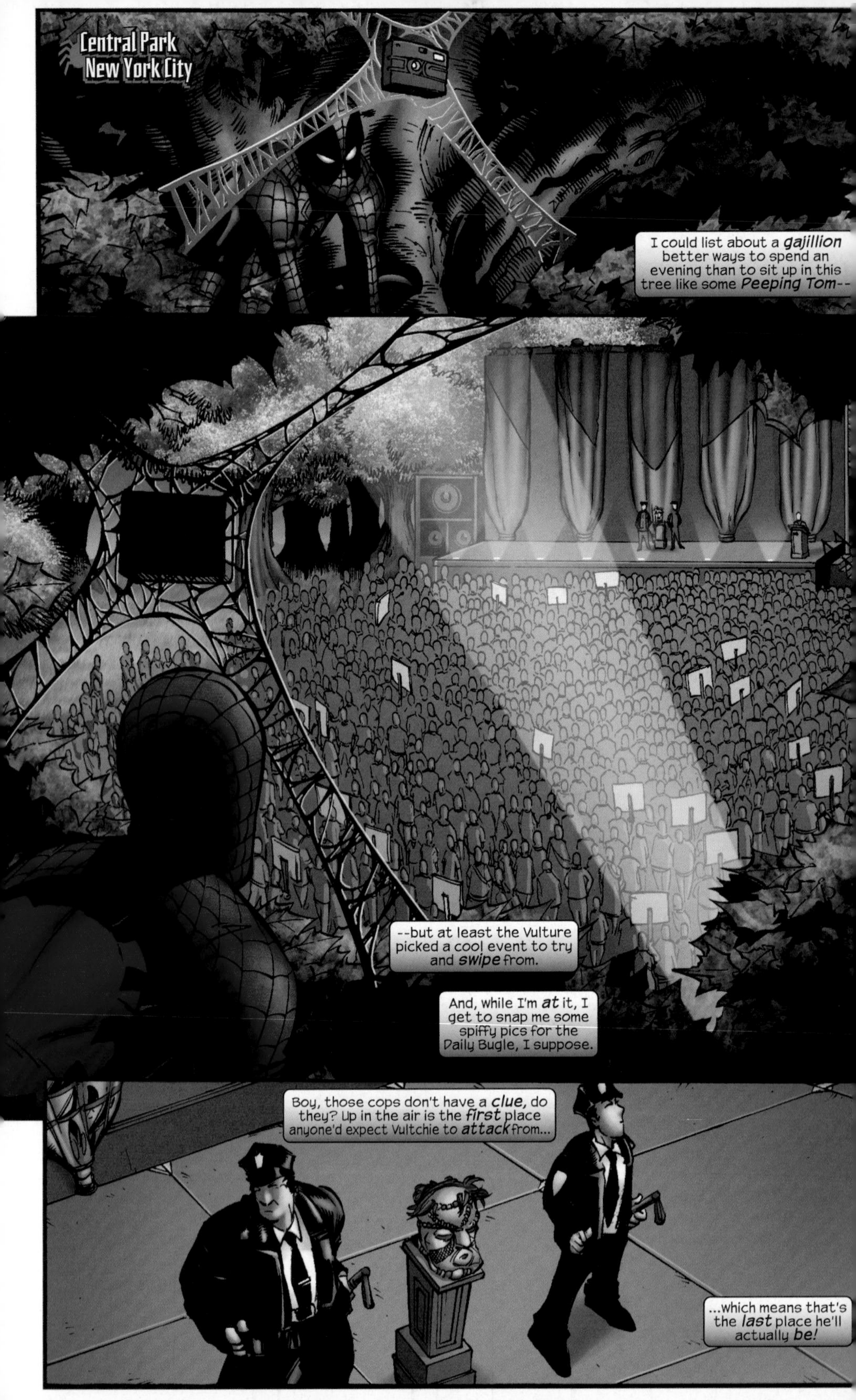
Central Park
New York City
I could list about a *gajillion* better ways to spend an evening than to sit up in this tree like some *Peeping Tom*--
--but at least the Vulture picked a cool event to try and *swipe* from.
And, while I'm *at* it, I get to snap me some spiffy pics for the Daily Bugle, I suppose.
Boy, those cops don't have a *clue*, do they? Up in the air is the *first* place anyone'd expect Vultchie to *attack* from...
...which means that's the *last* place he'll actually *be!*

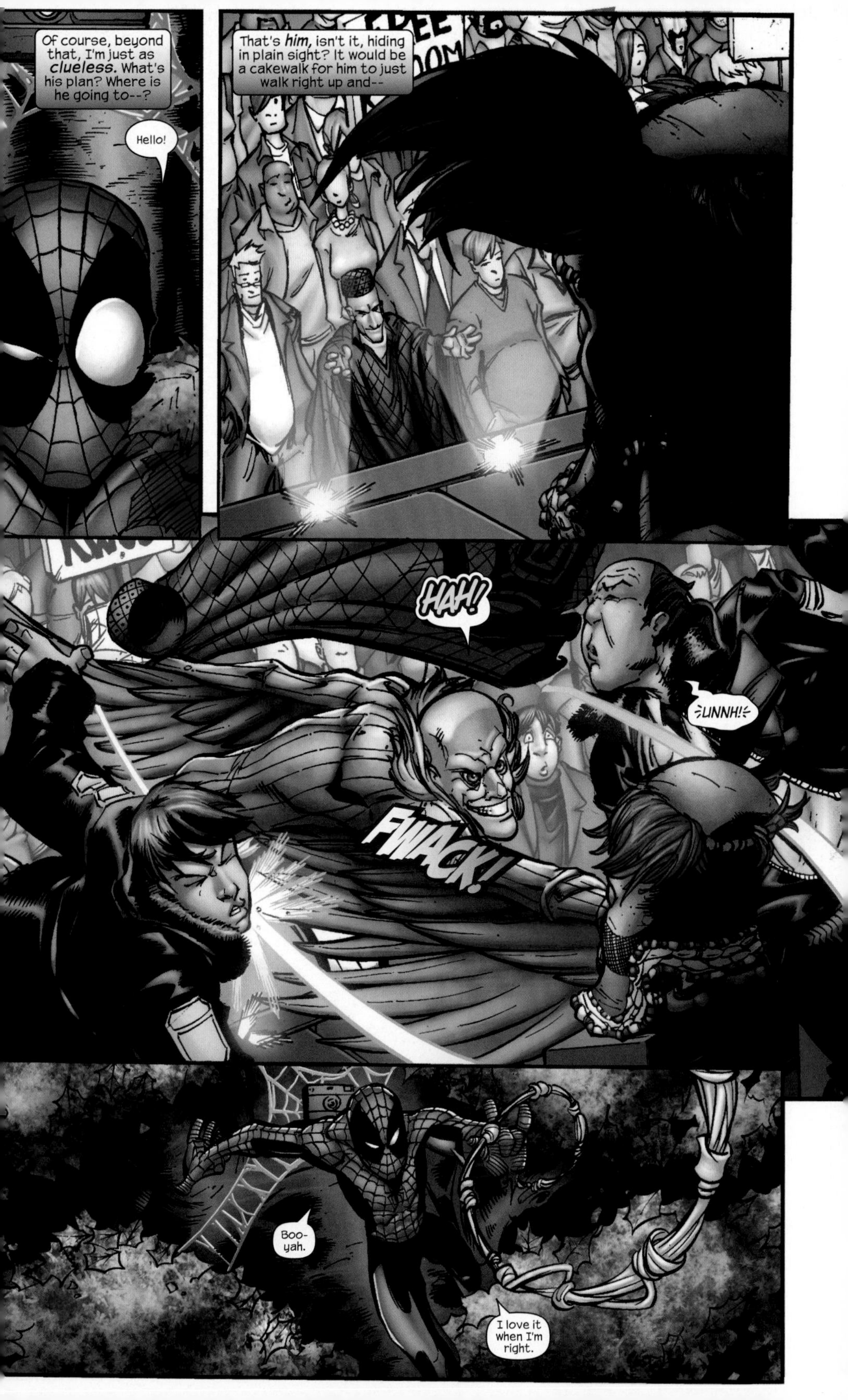
Of course, beyond that, I'm just as *clueless.* What's his plan? Where is he going to--?
Hello!
That's *him,* isn't it, hiding in plain sight? It would be a cakewalk for him to just walk right up and--
HAH!
UNNH!
FWACK!
Boo-yah.
I love it when I'm right.

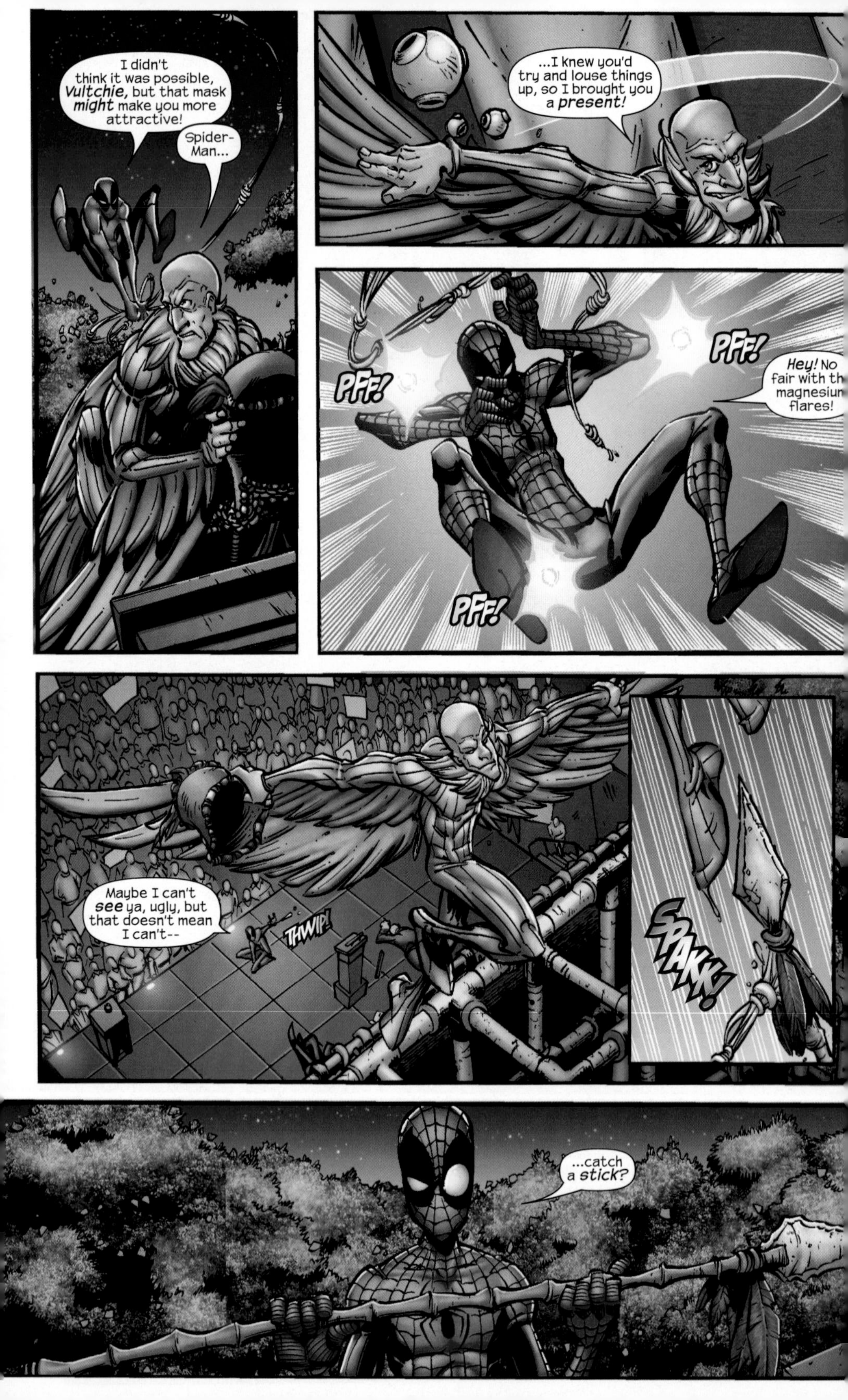

I didn't think it was possible, *Vultchie,* but that mask *might* make you more attractive!
Spider-Man...
...I knew you'd try and louse things up, so I brought you a *present!*
PFF!
PFF!
Hey! No fair with th magnesiun flares!
PFF!
Maybe I can't *see* ya, ugly, but that doesn't mean I can't--
THWIP!
SPAKK!
...catch a *stick?*

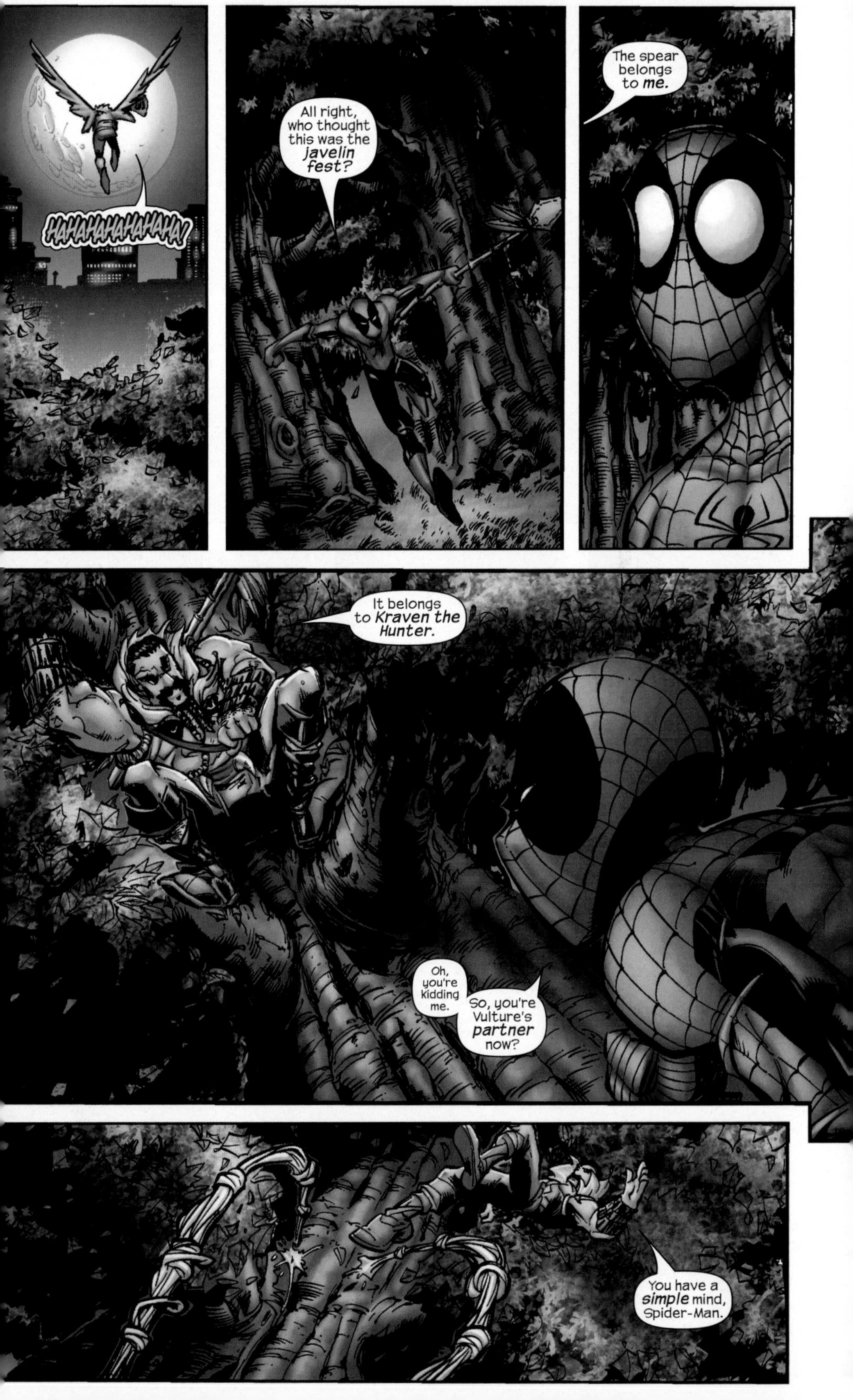
HAHAHAHAHAHAHA!
All right, who thought this was the javelin fest?
The spear belongs to me.
It belongs to Kraven the Hunter.
Oh, you're kidding me.
So, you're Vulture's partner now?
You have a simple mind, Spider-Man.

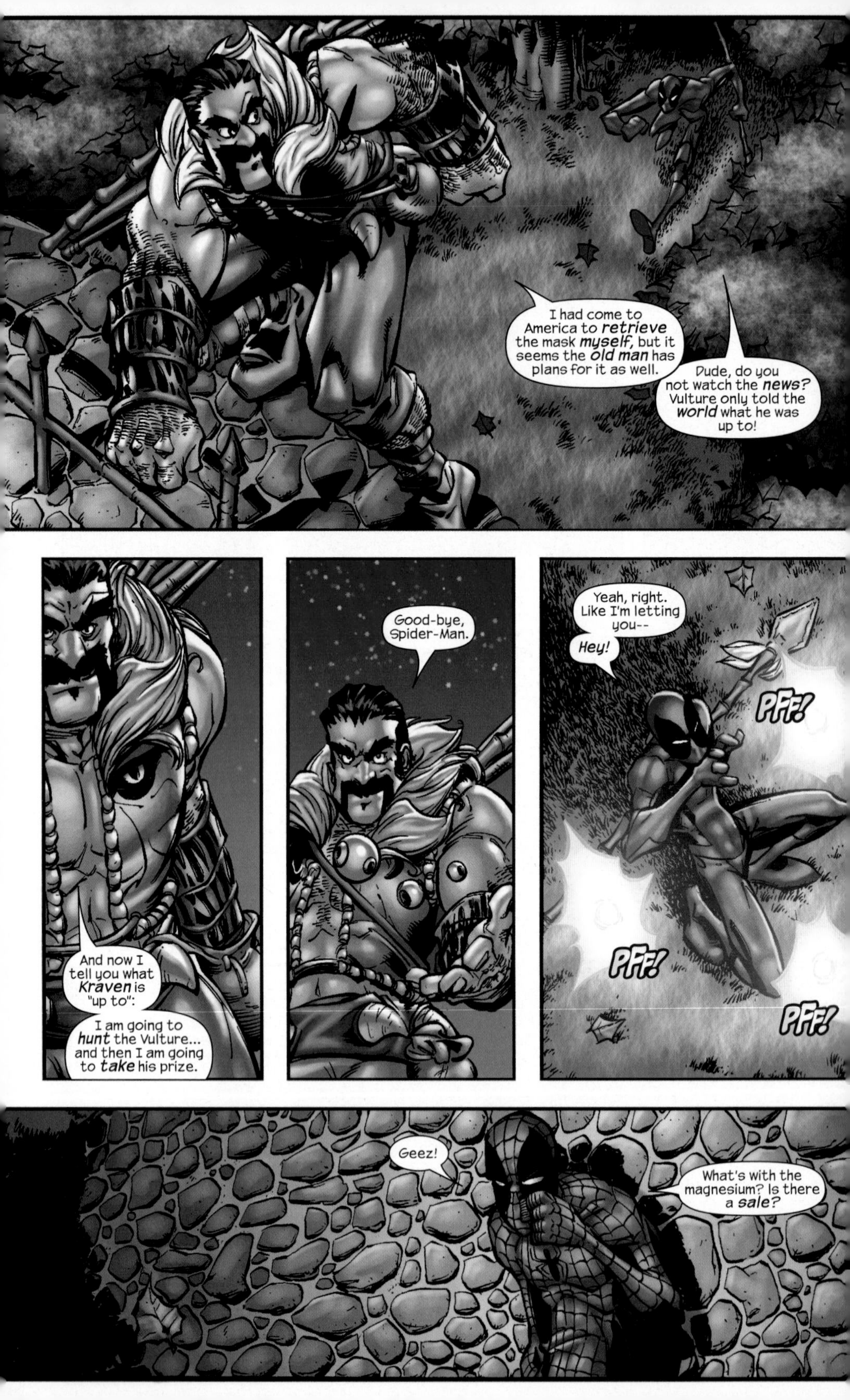
I had come to America to retrieve the mask myself, but it seems the old man has plans for it as well.
Dude, do you not watch the news? Vulture only told the world what he was up to!
And now I tell you what Kraven is "up to":
I am going to hunt the Vulture... and then I am going to take his prize.
Good-bye, Spider-Man.
Yeah, right. Like I'm letting you--
Hey!
PFF!
PFF!
PFF!
Geez!
What's with the magnesium? Is there a sale?

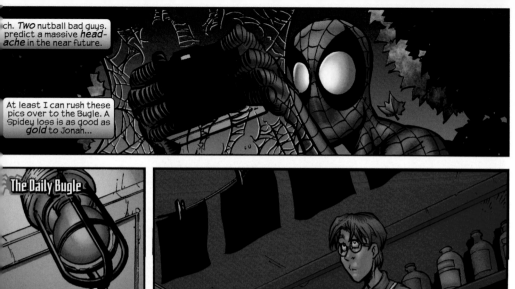

ch. *TWO* nutball bad guys. predict a massive *head-ache* in the near future.

At least I can rush these pics over to the Bugle. A Spidey loss is as good as *gold* to Jonah...

The Daily Bugle

DARK ROOM

Aw, man...!

Is this some kinda *joke*?

These've gotta be the *worst*, most *unprofessional* shots I've ever seen--

--and I've seen 'em *all*!

If you wanna get an *art* degree, Parker, you can do it on your *own* dime! I buy shots that sell papers--*period*!

Speaking of which...

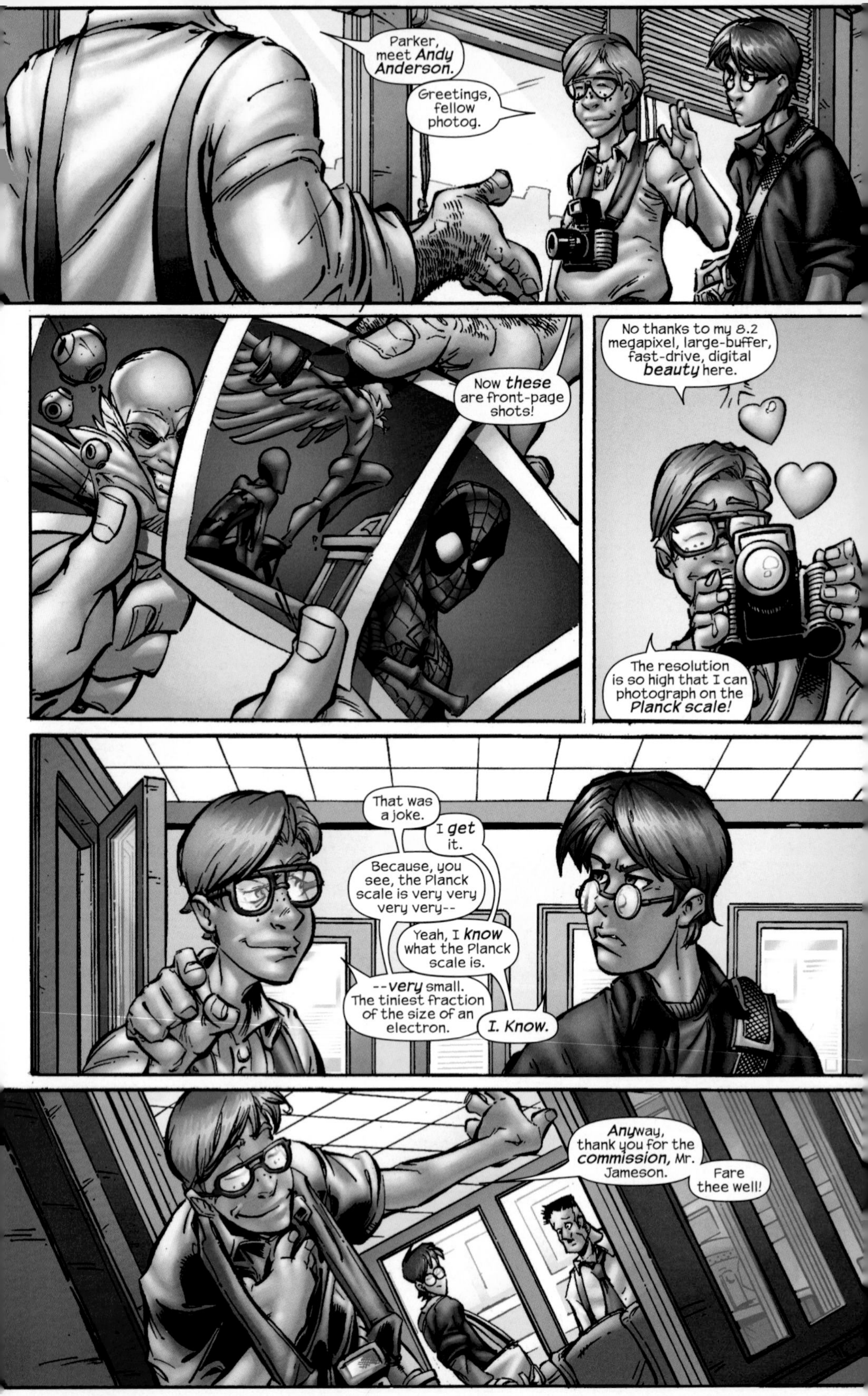
Parker, meet Andy Anderson.
Greetings, fellow photog.
Now these are front-page shots!
No thanks to my 8.2 megapixel, large-buffer, fast-drive, digital beauty here.
The resolution is so high that I can photograph on the Planck scale!
That was a joke.
I get it.
Because, you see, the Planck scale is very very very very--
Yeah, I know what the Planck scale is.
--very small. The tiniest fraction of the size of an electron.
I. Know.
Anyway, thank you for the commission, Mr. Jameson.
Fare thee well!

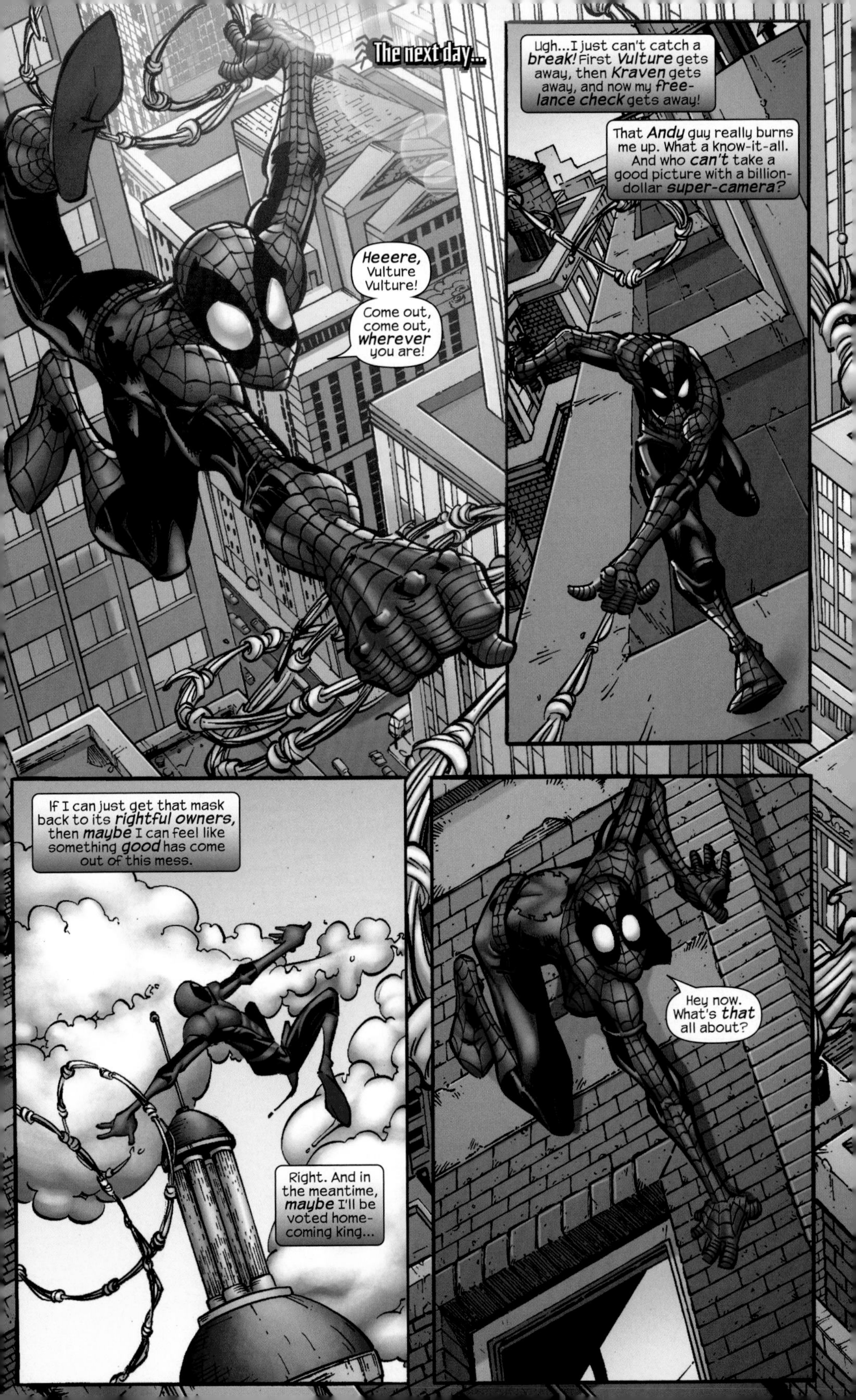
The next day...
Heeere, Vulture Vulture!
Come out, come out, wherever you are!
Ugh...I just can't catch a break! First Vulture gets away, then Kraven gets away, and now my free-lance check gets away!
That Andy guy really burns me up. What a know-it-all. And who can't take a good picture with a billion-dollar super-camera?
If I can just get that mask back to its rightful owners, then maybe I can feel like something good has come out of this mess.
Right. And in the meantime, maybe I'll be voted home-coming king...
Hey now. What's that all about?

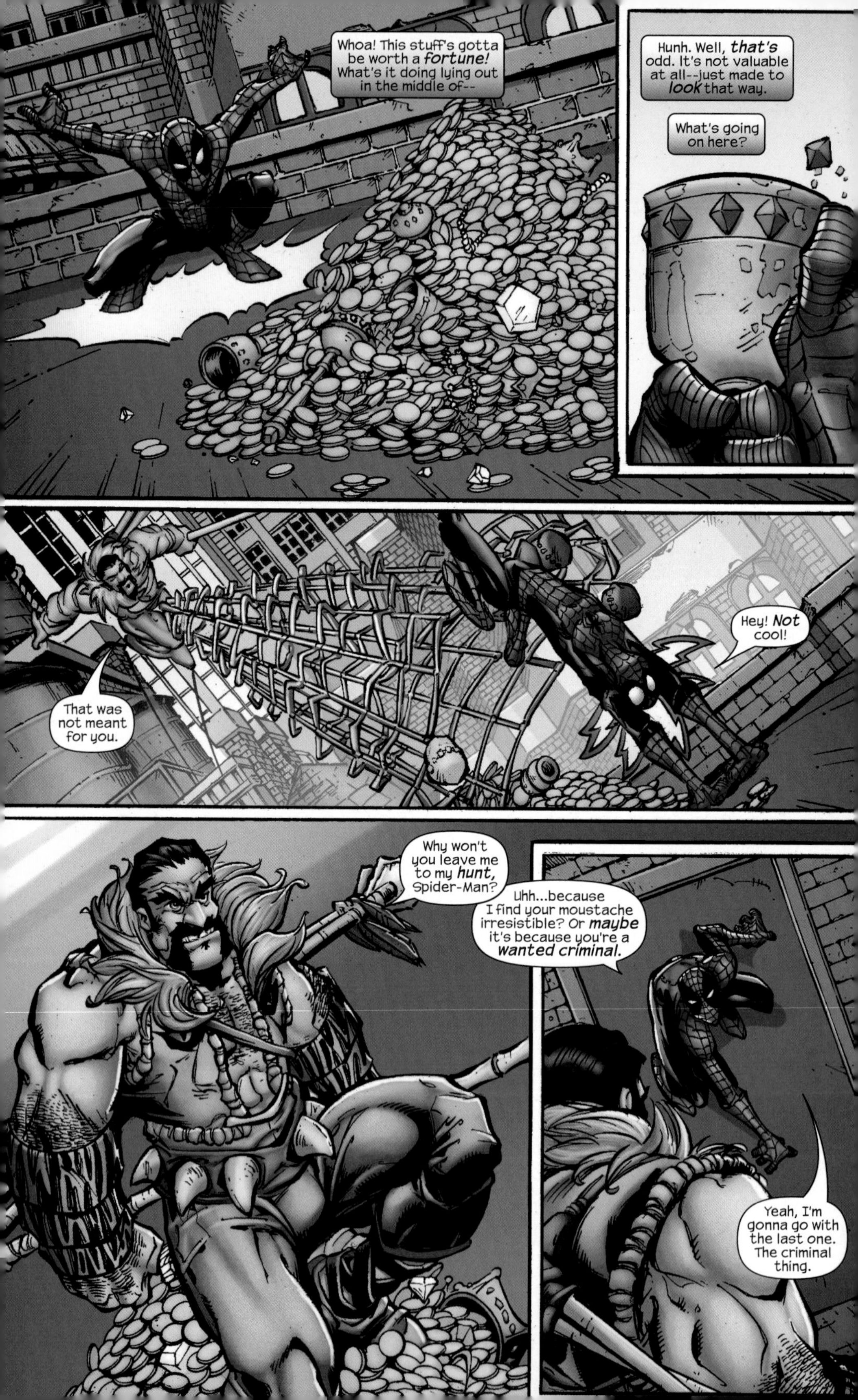
Whoa! This stuff's gotta be worth a *fortune!* What's it doing lying out in the middle of--
Hunh. Well, *that's* odd. It's not valuable at all--just made to *look* that way.
What's going on here?
Hey! *Not* cool!
That was not meant for you.
Why won't you leave me to my *hunt,* Spider-Man?
Uhh...because I find your moustache irresistible? Or *maybe* it's because you're a *wanted criminal.*
Yeah, I'm gonna go with the last one. The criminal thing.

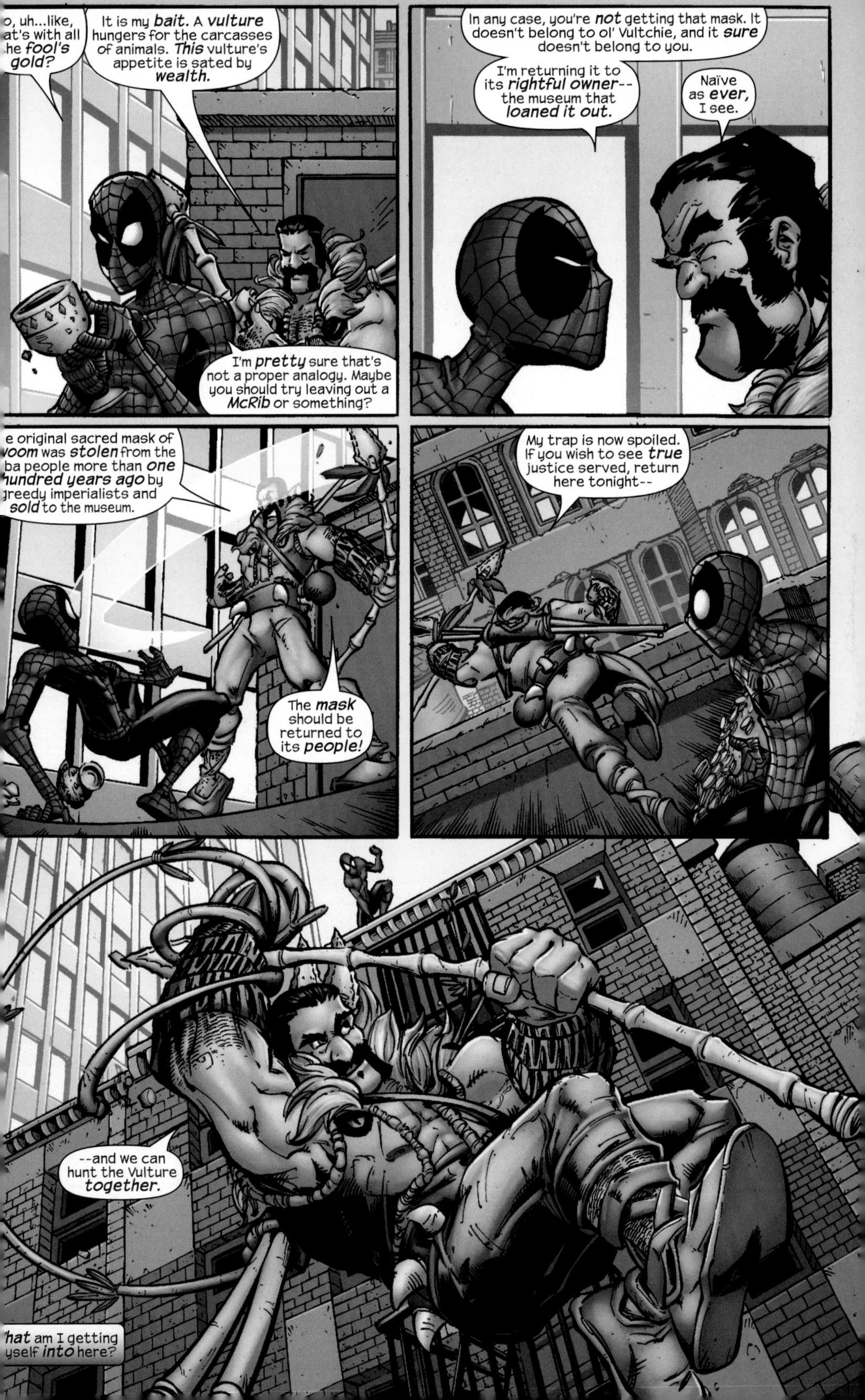

o, uh...like, at's with all he fool's gold?
It is my bait. A vulture hungers for the carcasses of animals. This vulture's appetite is sated by wealth.
I'm pretty sure that's not a proper analogy. Maybe you should try leaving out a McRib or something?
In any case, you're not getting that mask. It doesn't belong to ol' Vultchie, and it sure doesn't belong to you.
I'm returning it to its rightful owner-- the museum that loaned it out.
Naïve as ever, I see.
e original sacred mask of voom was stolen from the ba people more than one hundred years ago by greedy imperialists and sold to the museum.
The mask should be returned to its people!
My trap is now spoiled. If you wish to see true justice served, return here tonight--
--and we can hunt the Vulture together.
hat am I getting yself into here?

DAILY BUGLE

I don't believe it.

BRING BWOOM BACK
500 YEAR OLD MASK OF KUBA LEGEND IN MUSEUM'S HANDS

Kraven was telling the truth. The mask really was stolen from its people. I really hate greeking text...it is so god-awful looking most of the time. Kraven was telling the truth. The mask really was stolen from its people. I really hate greeking text...it is so god-awful looking most of the time. Kraven was telling the truth. The mask really was stolen from its people. I really hate greeking text...it is so god-awful looking most of the time. Kraven was telling the truth. The mask really was stolen from its people. I really hate greeking text...it is so god-awful looking most of the time. Kraven was telling the truth. The mask really was stolen from its people. I really hate greeking text...it is so god-awful looking most of the time.

The mask really *was* stolen from its people. Kraven was telling the truth.

Kraven...

He's a **bad guy.** I can't team up with a bad guy.

Even if I did, and we got the mask back... **then** what? I can't just **hand** it over to the Kuba. Then **I'd** be guilty of stealing.

And what would I do about **Kraven?** "Hey, thanks for helping me do the right thing. Now let me web you up and **turn you in...**"

What's the right thing to **do** here? I just need some sort of **sign...**

Greetings, Peter Parker.

Great. I'm doomed.

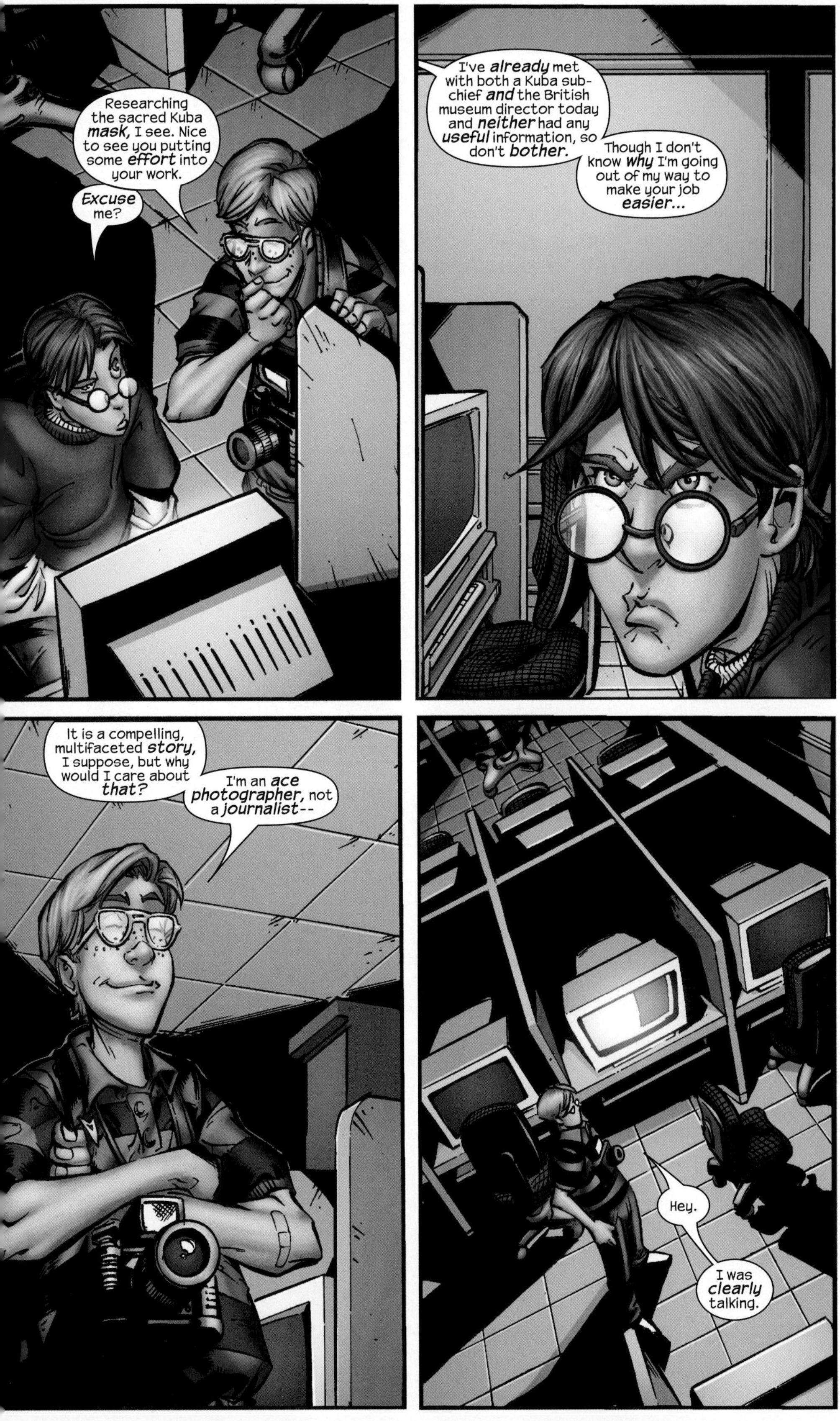

Researching the sacred Kuba mask, I see. Nice to see you putting some effort into your work.
Excuse me?
I've already met with both a Kuba sub-chief and the British museum director today and neither had any useful information, so don't bother.
Though I don't know why I'm going out of my way to make your job easier...
It is a compelling, multifaceted story, I suppose, but why would I care about that?
I'm an ace photographer, not a journalist--
Hey.
I was clearly talking.

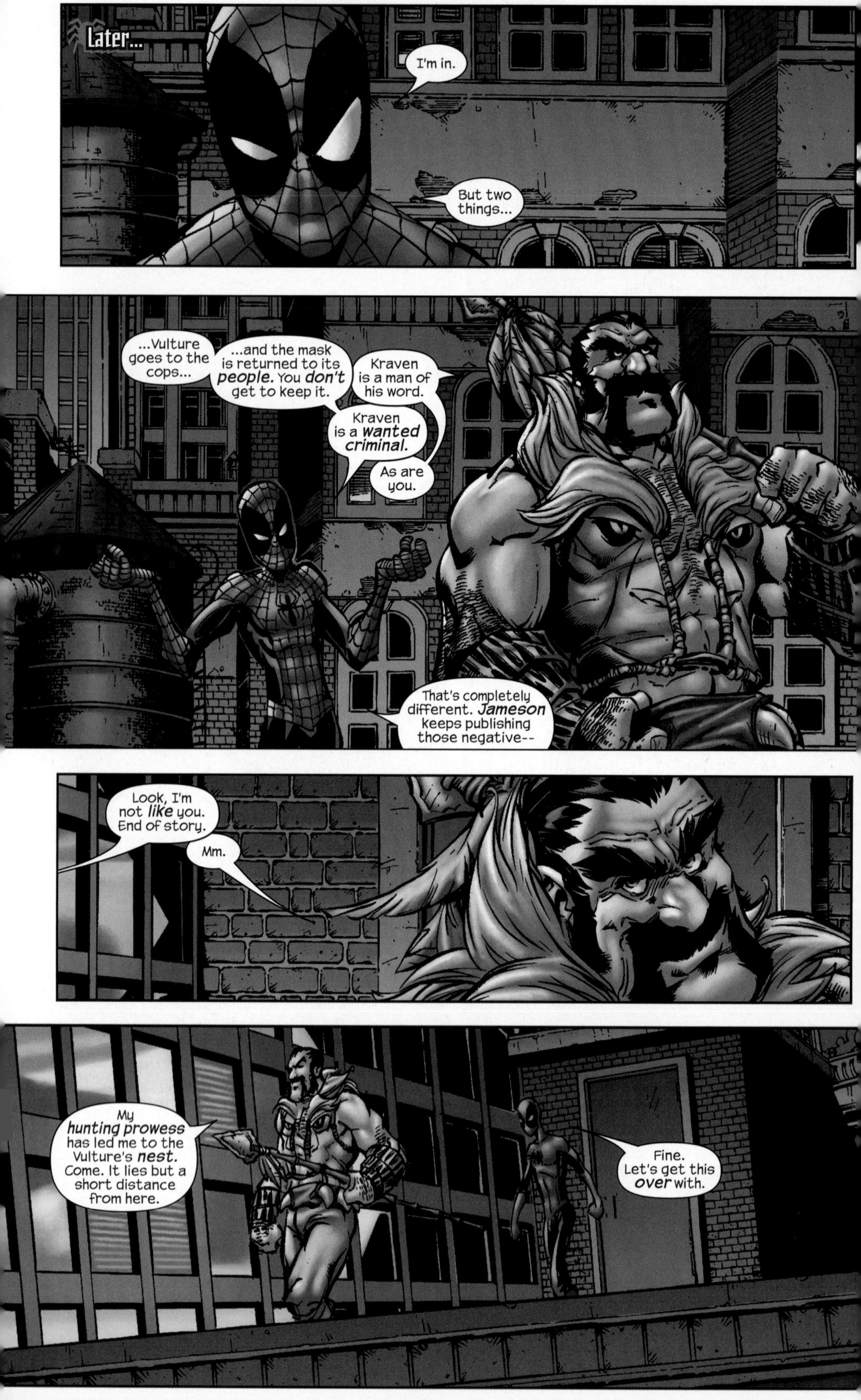
Later...
I'm in.
But two things...
...Vulture goes to the cops...
...and the mask is returned to its people. You don't get to keep it.
Kraven is a man of his word.
Kraven is a wanted criminal.
As are you.
That's completely different. Jameson keeps publishing those negative--
Look, I'm not like you. End of story.
Mm.
My hunting prowess has led me to the Vulture's nest. Come. It lies but a short distance from here.
Fine. Let's get this over with.

Wow. So...

...when you said "nest," you *weren't* just being pretentiously allegorical.

We proceed as planned. I will get into position.

Yeah, you *do* that...

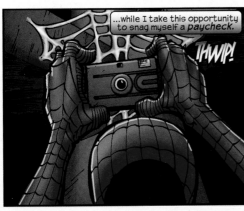

...while I take this opportunity to snag myself a *paycheck*.

THWIP!

Eh? What was that?

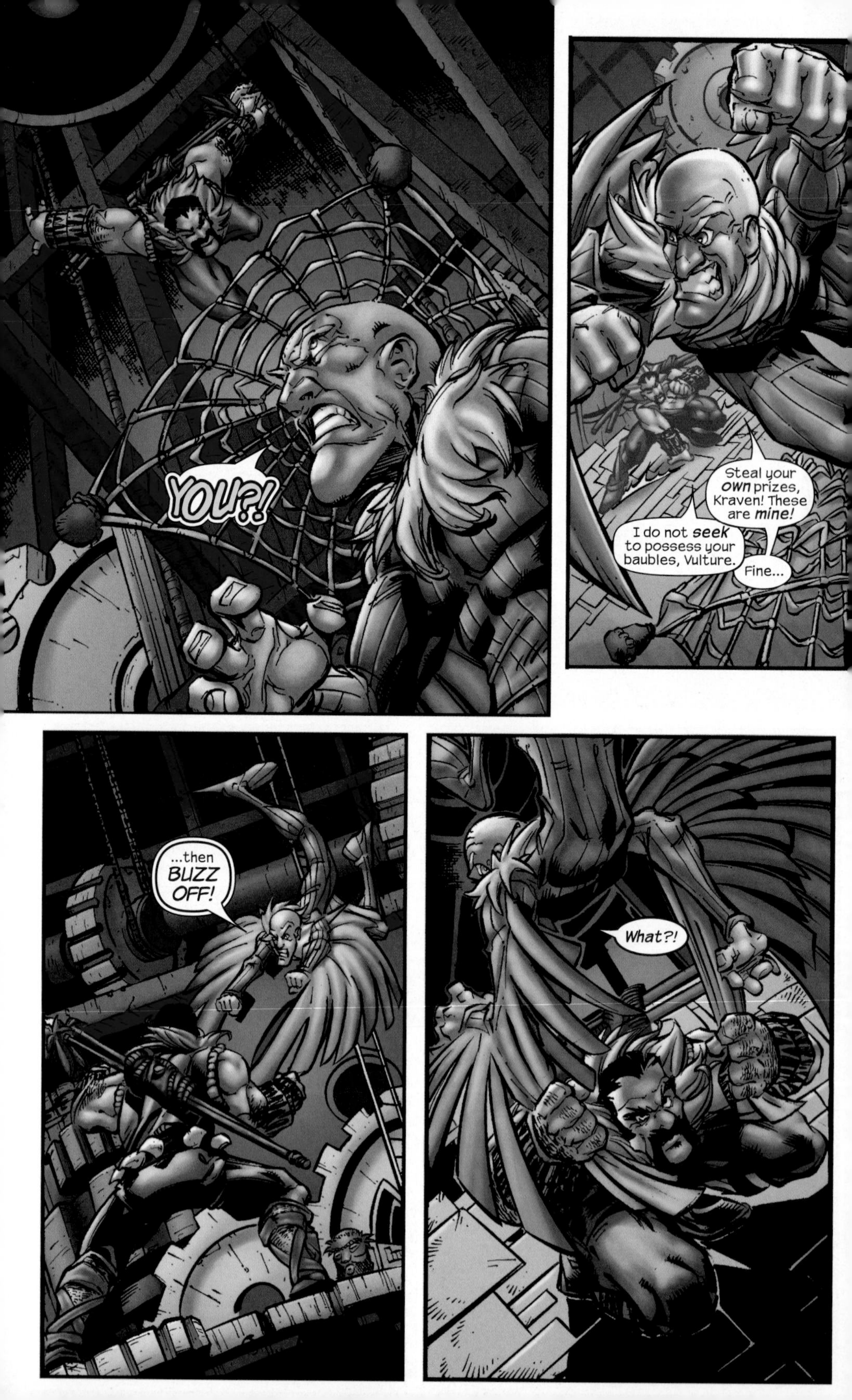
YOU?!
Steal your own prizes, Kraven! These are mine!
I do not seek to possess your baubles, Vulture.
Fine...
...then BUZZ OFF!
What?!

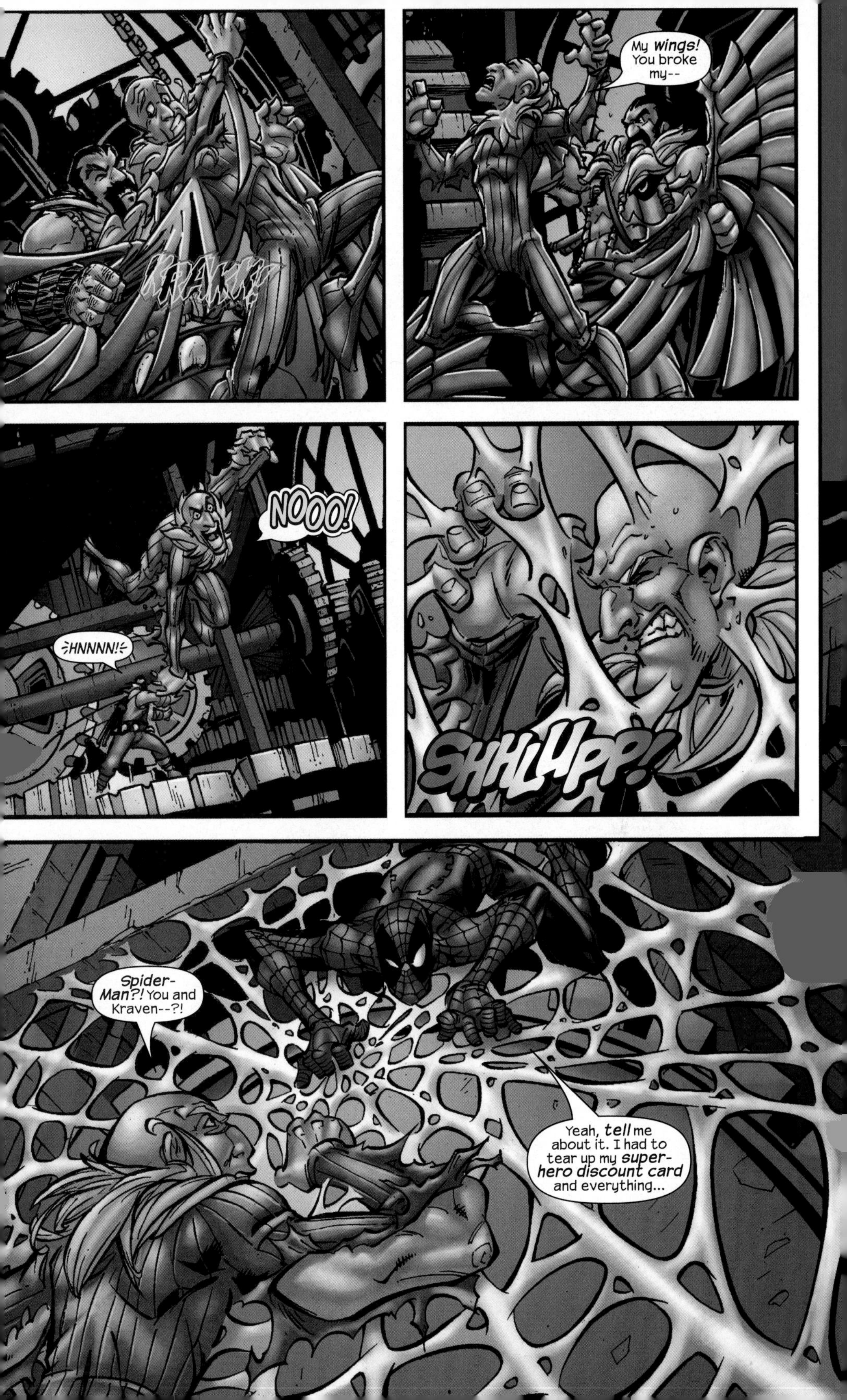
KRAKK!
My wings! You broke my--
NOOO!
HNNNN!
SHHLUPP!
Spider-Man?! You and Kraven--?!
Yeah, tell me about it. I had to tear up my super-hero discount card and everything...

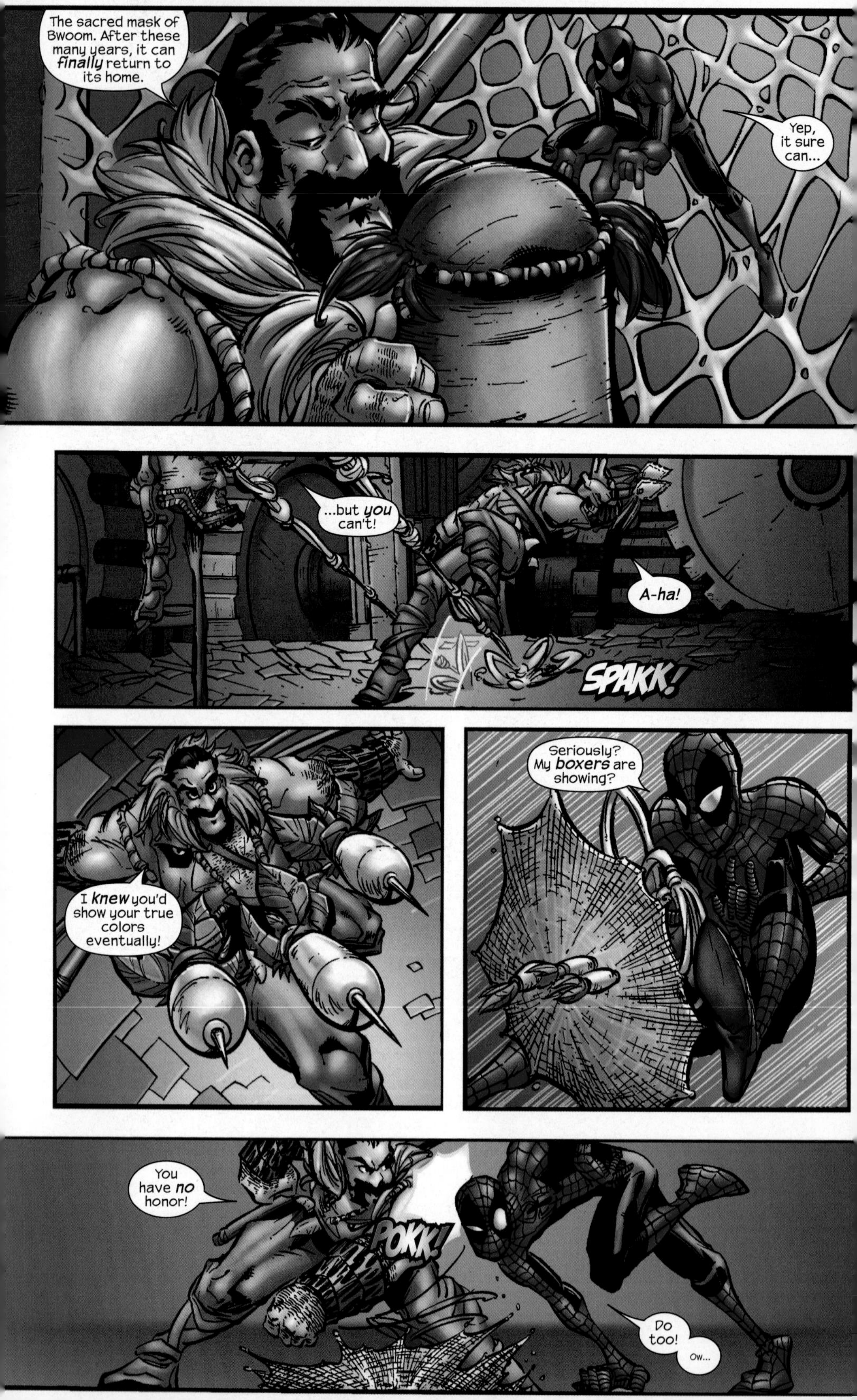
The sacred mask of Bwoom. After these many years, it can *finally* return to its home.
Yep, it sure can...
...but *you* can't!
A-ha!
SPAKK!
I *knew* you'd show your true colors eventually!
Seriously? My *boxers* are showing?
You have *no* honor!
POKK!
Do too!
OW...

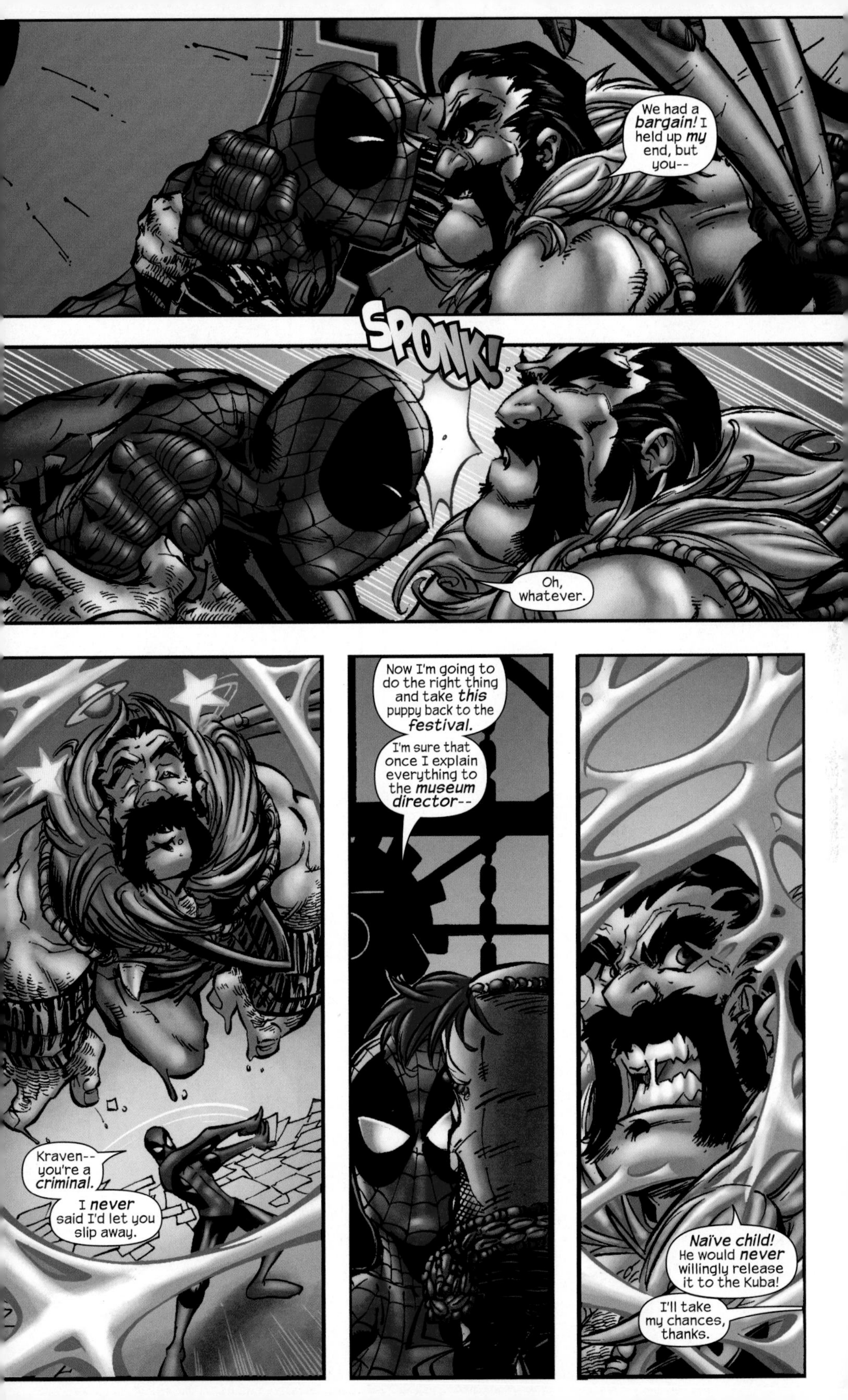
We had a bargain! I held up my end, but you--
SPONK!
Oh, whatever.
Kraven--you're a criminal.
I never said I'd let you slip away.
Now I'm going to do the right thing and take this puppy back to the festival.
I'm sure that once I explain everything to the museum director--
Naïve child! He would never willingly release it to the Kuba!
I'll take my chances, thanks.

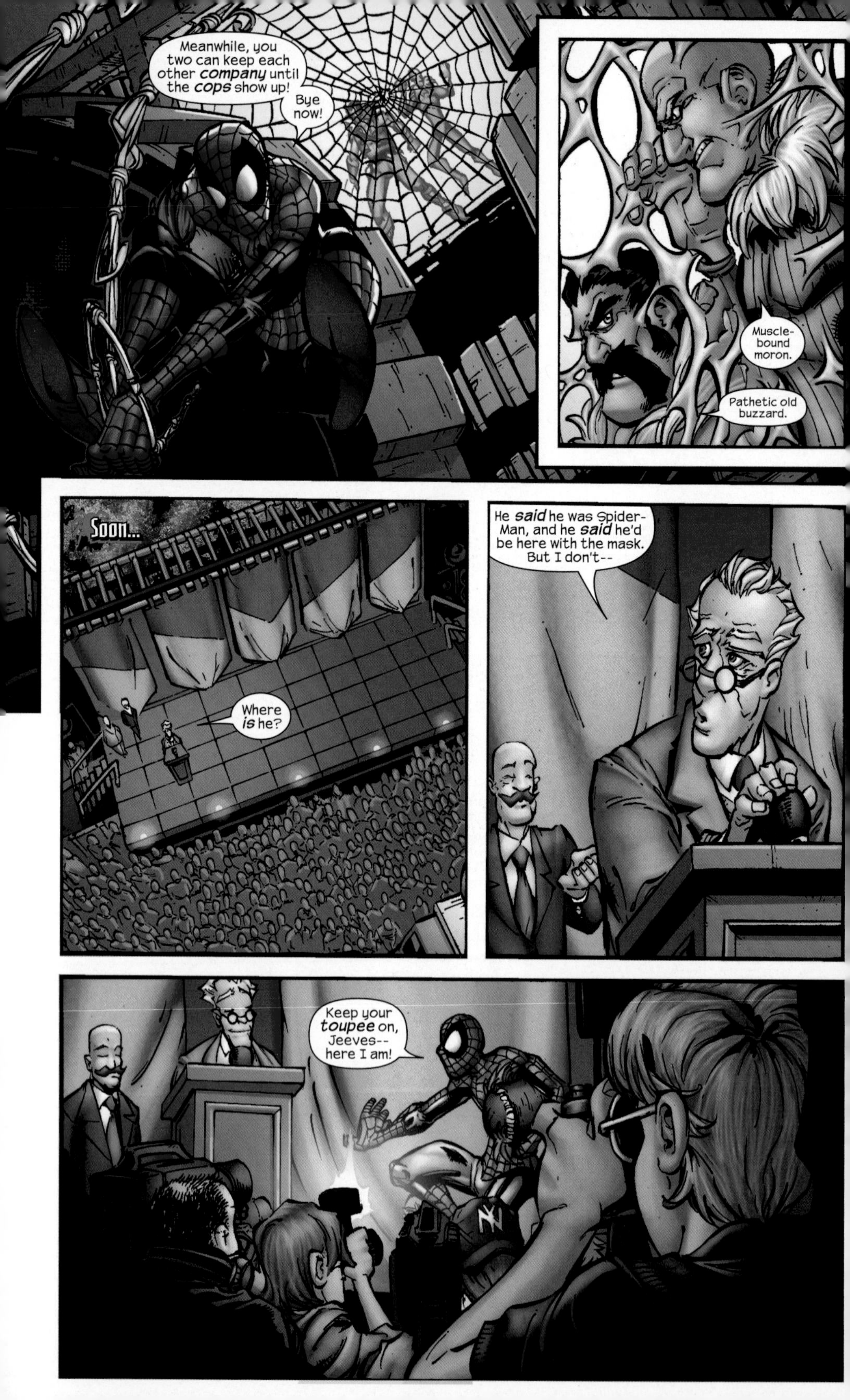
Meanwhile, you two can keep each other *company* until the *cops* show up!
Bye now!
Muscle-bound moron.
Pathetic old buzzard.
Soon...
Where *is* he?
He *said* he was Spider-Man, and he *said* he'd be here with the mask. But I don't--
Keep your *toupee* on, Jeeves-- here I am!

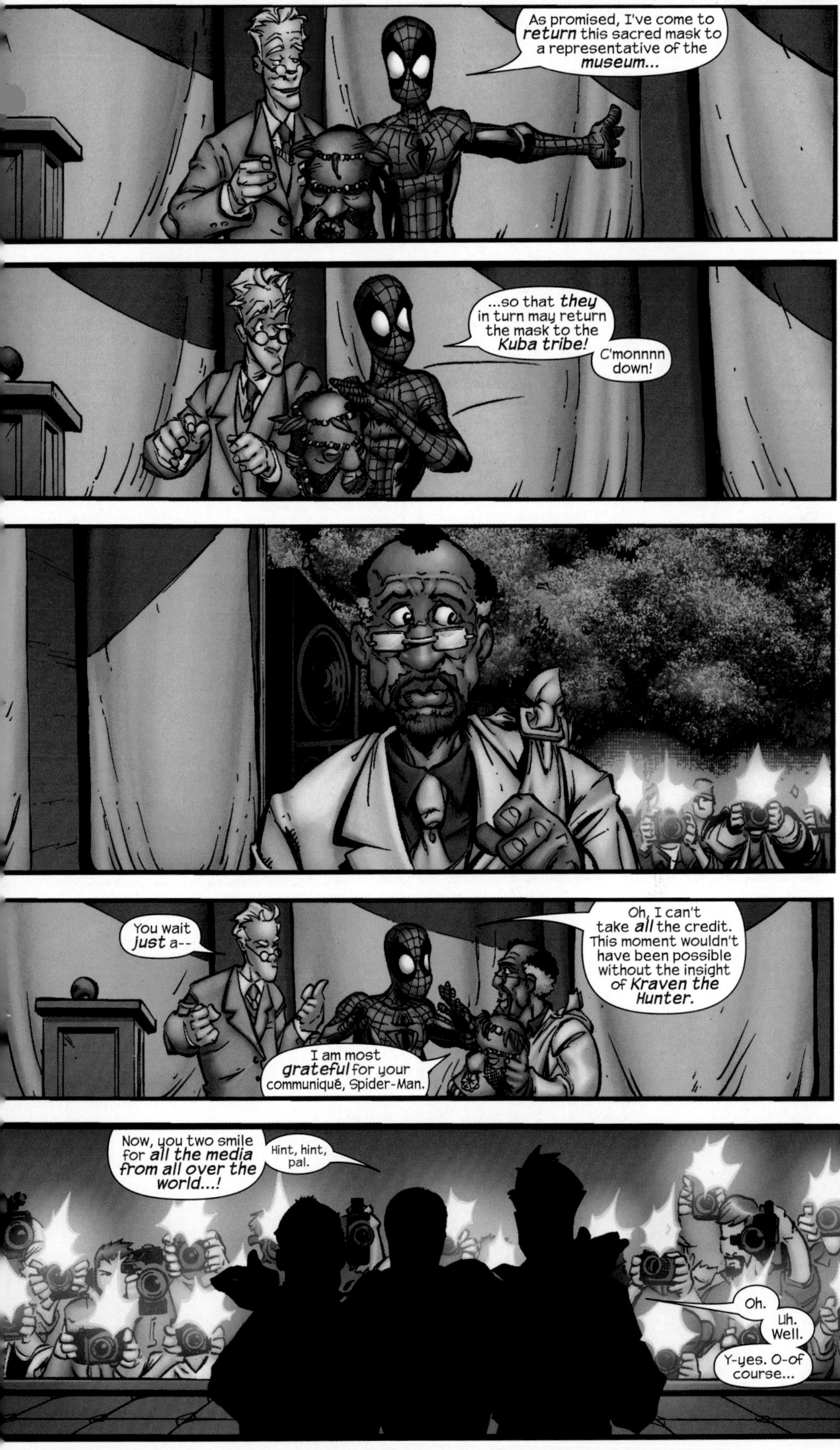
As promised, I've come to *return* this sacred mask to a representative of the *museum...*
...so that *they* in turn may return the mask to the *Kuba tribe!*
C'monnnn down!
You wait *just* a--
Oh, I can't take *all* the credit. This moment wouldn't have been possible without the insight of *Kraven the Hunter.*
I am most *grateful* for your communiqué, Spider-Man.
Now, you two smile for *all the media from all over the world...!*
Hint, hint, pal.
Oh.
Uh. Well.
Y-yes. O-of course...

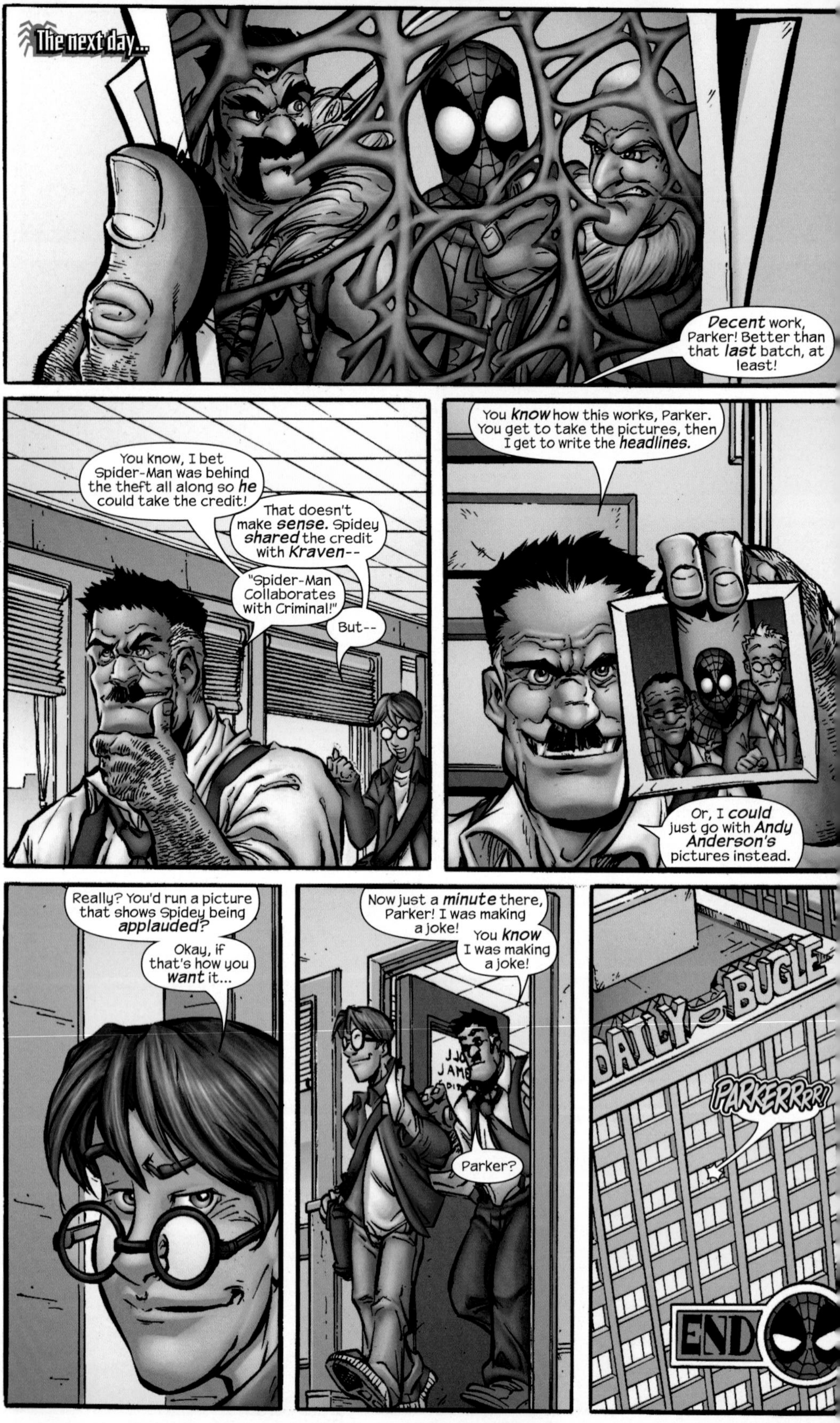
The next day...
Decent work, Parker! Better than that last batch, at least!
You know, I bet Spider-Man was behind the theft all along so he could take the credit!
That doesn't make sense. Spidey shared the credit with Kraven--
"Spider-Man Collaborates with Criminal!"
But--
You know how this works, Parker. You get to take the pictures, then I get to write the headlines.
Or, I could just go with Andy Anderson's pictures instead.
Really? You'd run a picture that shows Spidey being applauded?
Okay, if that's how you want it...
Now just a minute there, Parker! I was making a joke!
You know I was making a joke!
Parker?
DAILY BUGLE
PARKERRrrr!
END

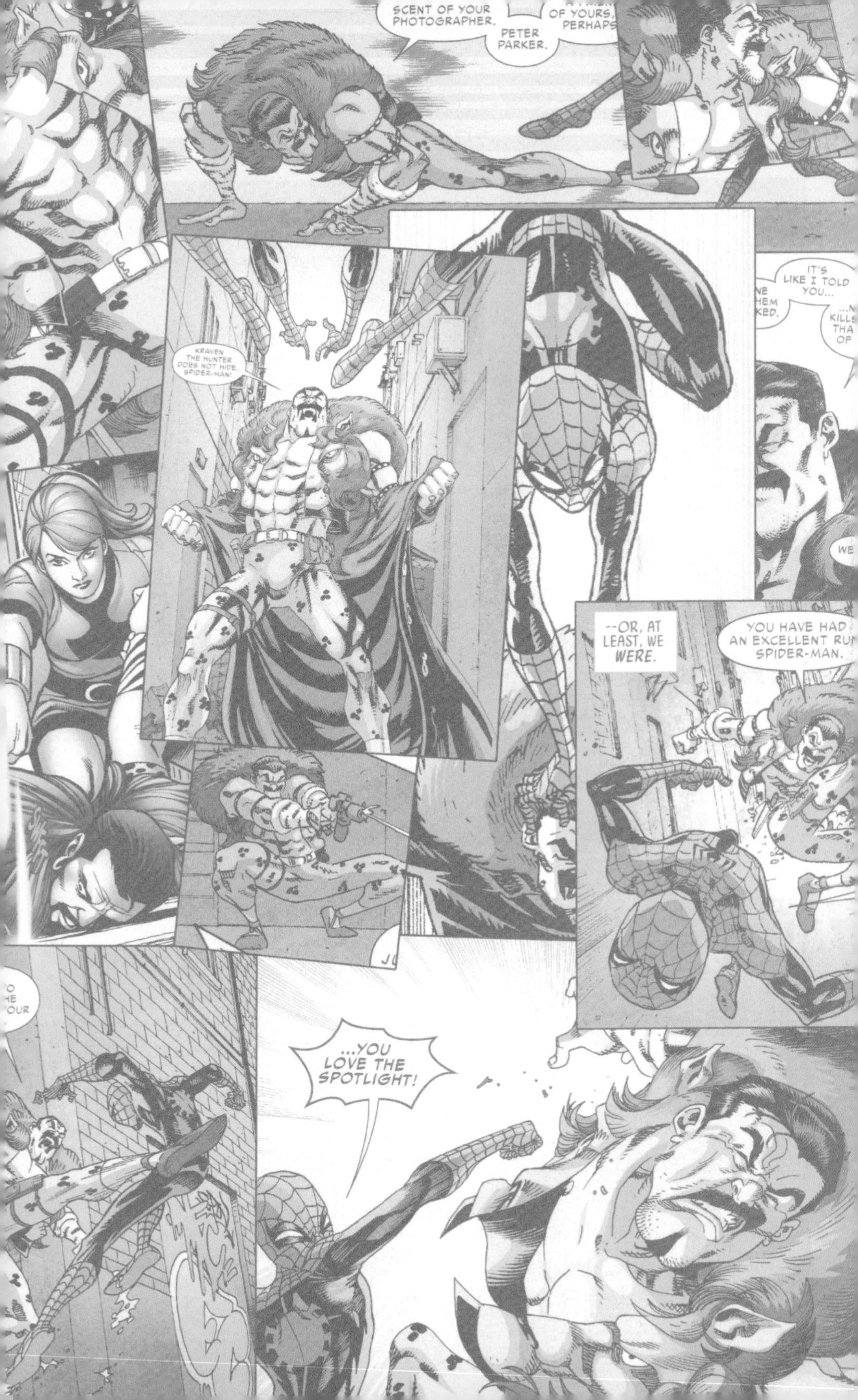
SCENT OF YOUR PHOTOGRAPHER.
PETER PARKER.
OF YOURS, PERHAPS
IT'S LIKE I TOLD YOU...
KRAVEN THE HUNTER DOES NOT HIDE, SPIDER-MAN!
--OR, AT LEAST, WE WERE.
YOU HAVE HAD AN EXCELLENT RU SPIDER-MAN.
...YOU LOVE THE SPOTLIGHT!

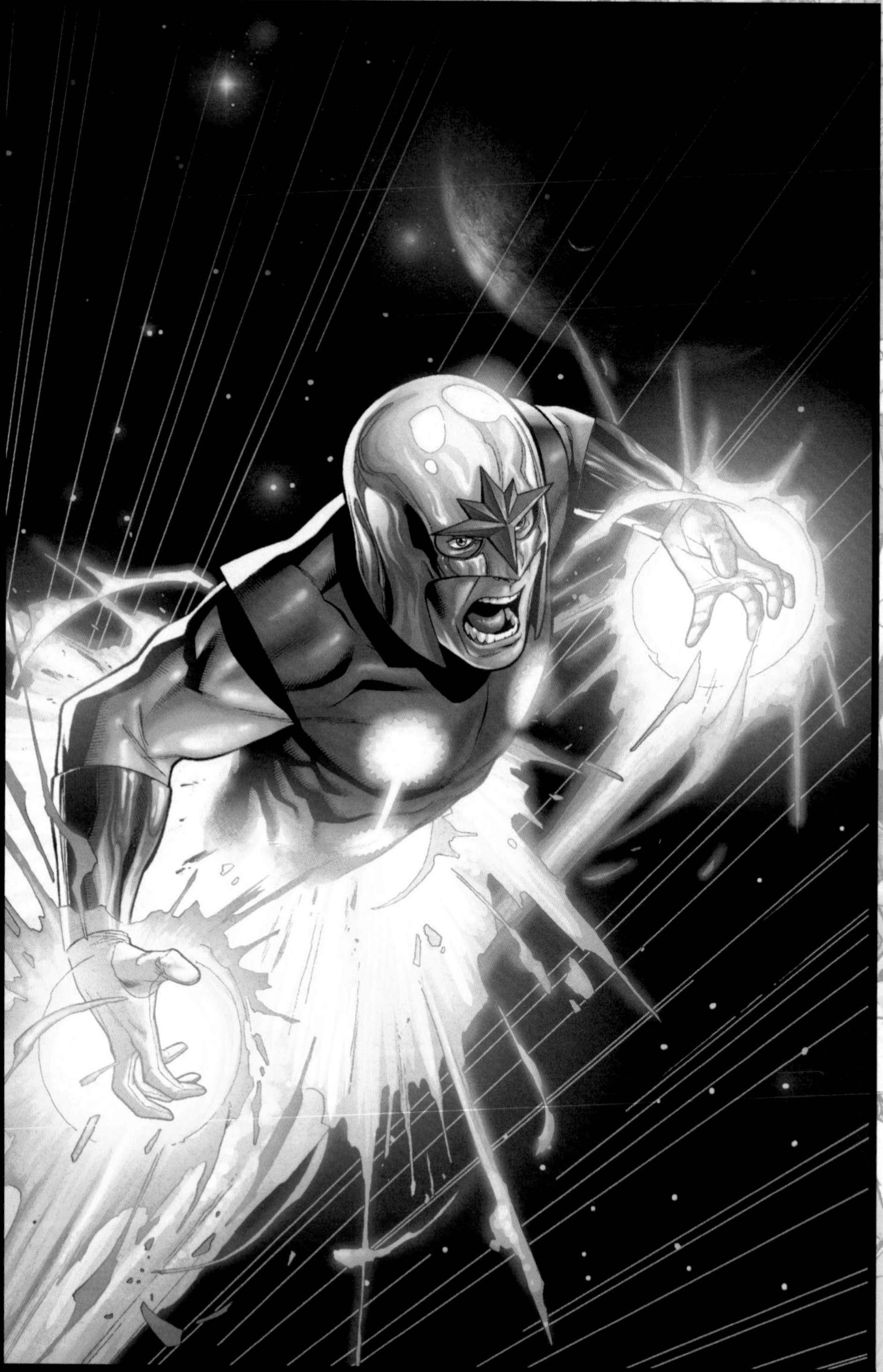

MARVEL ADVENTURES SUPER HEROES #4

KRAVEN IS HUNTING WHAT MIGHT POSSIBLY BE THE WORLD'S MOST DANGEROUS PREY — AND CERTAINLY THE MOST ANNOYING. ENTER: DEADPOOL!

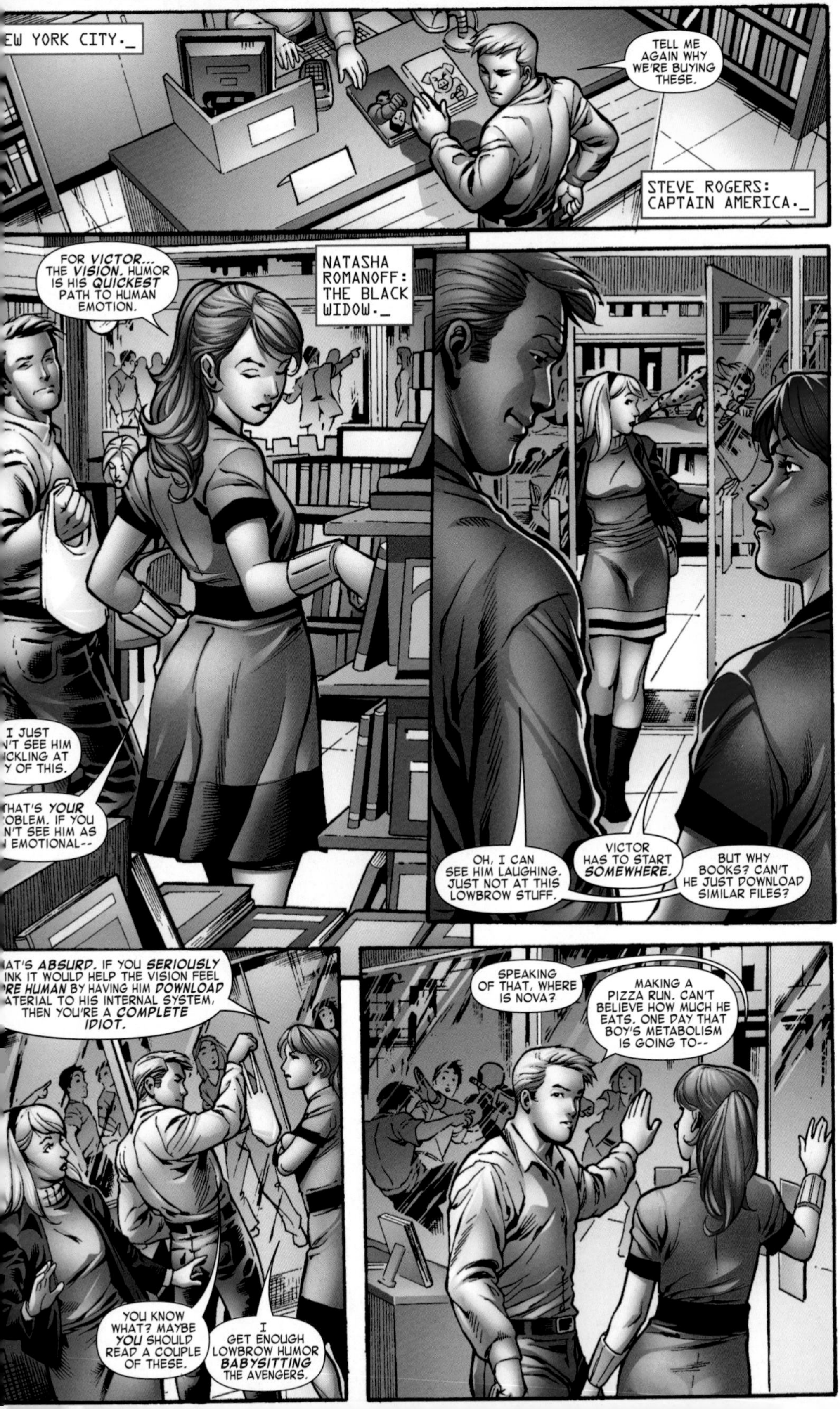
EW YORK CITY._
TELL ME AGAIN WHY WE'RE BUYING THESE.
STEVE ROGERS: CAPTAIN AMERICA._
FOR *VICTOR*... THE *VISION*. HUMOR IS HIS *QUICKEST* PATH TO HUMAN EMOTION.
NATASHA ROMANOFF: THE BLACK WIDOW._
I JUST N'T SEE HIM CKLING AT Y OF THIS.
THAT'S *YOUR* OBLEM. IF YOU N'T SEE HIM AS N EMOTIONAL--
OH, I CAN SEE HIM LAUGHING. JUST NOT AT THIS LOWBROW STUFF.
VICTOR HAS TO START *SOMEWHERE.*
BUT WHY BOOKS? CAN'T HE JUST DOWNLOAD SIMILAR FILES?
AT'S *ABSURD.* IF YOU *SERIOUSLY* INK IT WOULD HELP THE VISION FEEL RE HUMAN BY HAVING HIM *DOWNLOAD* ATERIAL TO HIS INTERNAL SYSTEM, THEN YOU'RE A *COMPLETE IDIOT.*
YOU KNOW WHAT? MAYBE *YOU* SHOULD READ A COUPLE OF THESE.
I GET ENOUGH LOWBROW HUMOR *BABYSITTING* THE AVENGERS.
SPEAKING OF THAT, WHERE IS NOVA?
MAKING A PIZZA RUN. CAN'T BELIEVE HOW MUCH HE EATS. ONE DAY THAT BOY'S METABOLISM IS GOING TO--

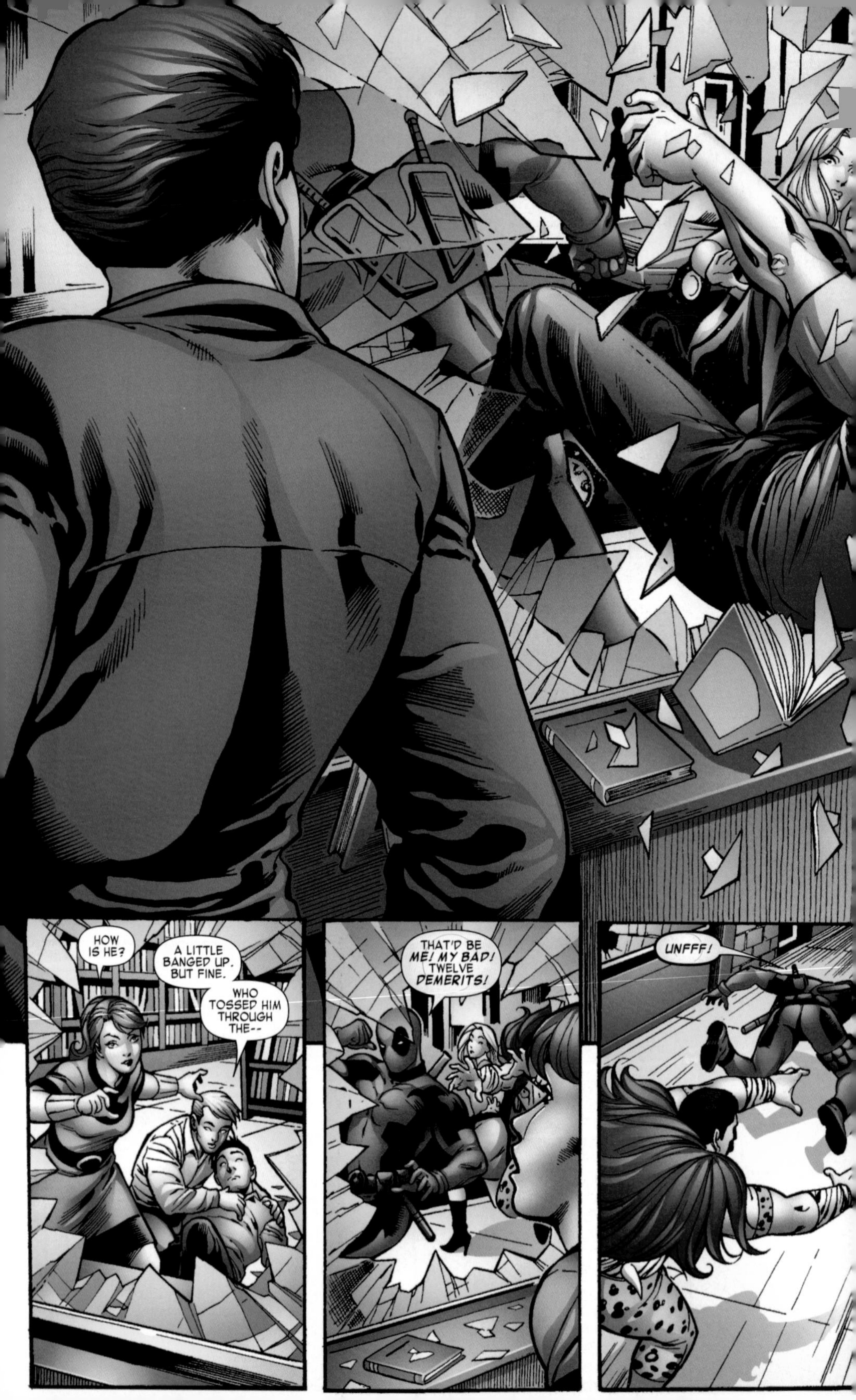
HOW IS HE?
A LITTLE BANGED UP, BUT FINE.
WHO TOSSED HIM THROUGH THE--
THAT'D BE *ME! MY BAD!* TWELVE *DEMERITS!*
UNFFF!

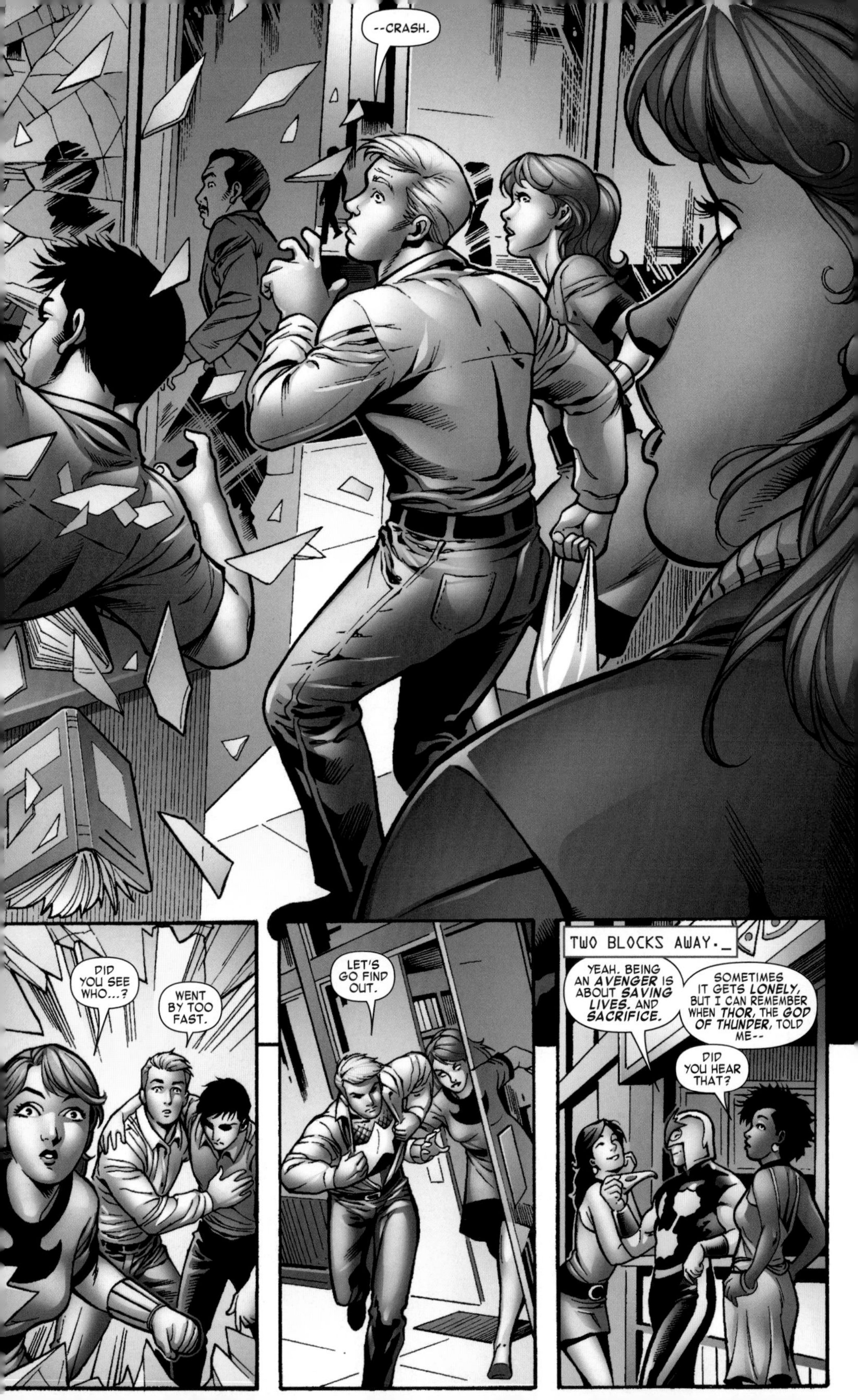
--CRASH.
DID YOU SEE WHO...?
WENT BY TOO FAST.
LET'S GO FIND OUT.
TWO BLOCKS AWAY._
YEAH. BEING AN AVENGER IS ABOUT SAVING LIVES. AND SACRIFICE.
SOMETIMES IT GETS LONELY, BUT I CAN REMEMBER WHEN THOR, THE GOD OF THUNDER, TOLD ME--
DID YOU HEAR THAT?

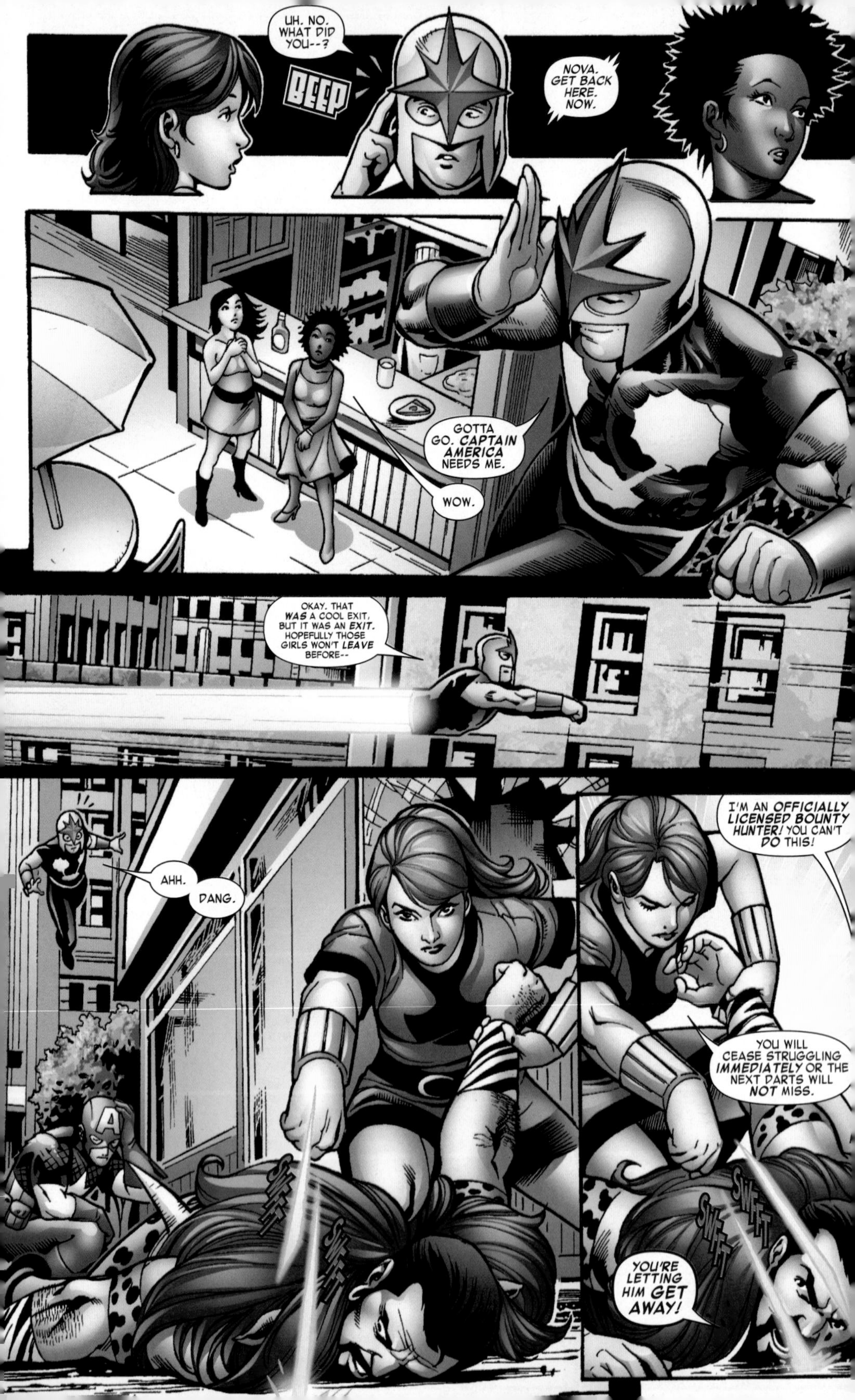
UH. NO. WHAT DID YOU--?
BEEP
NOVA. GET BACK HERE. NOW.
GOTTA GO. CAPTAIN AMERICA NEEDS ME.
WOW.
OKAY. THAT WAS A COOL EXIT, BUT IT WAS AN EXIT. HOPEFULLY THOSE GIRLS WON'T LEAVE BEFORE--
AHH.
DANG.
I'M AN OFFICIALLY LICENSED BOUNTY HUNTER! YOU CAN'T DO THIS!
YOU WILL CEASE STRUGGLING IMMEDIATELY OR THE NEXT DARTS WILL NOT MISS.
SWFFT
SWFFT
YOU'RE LETTING HIM GET AWAY!

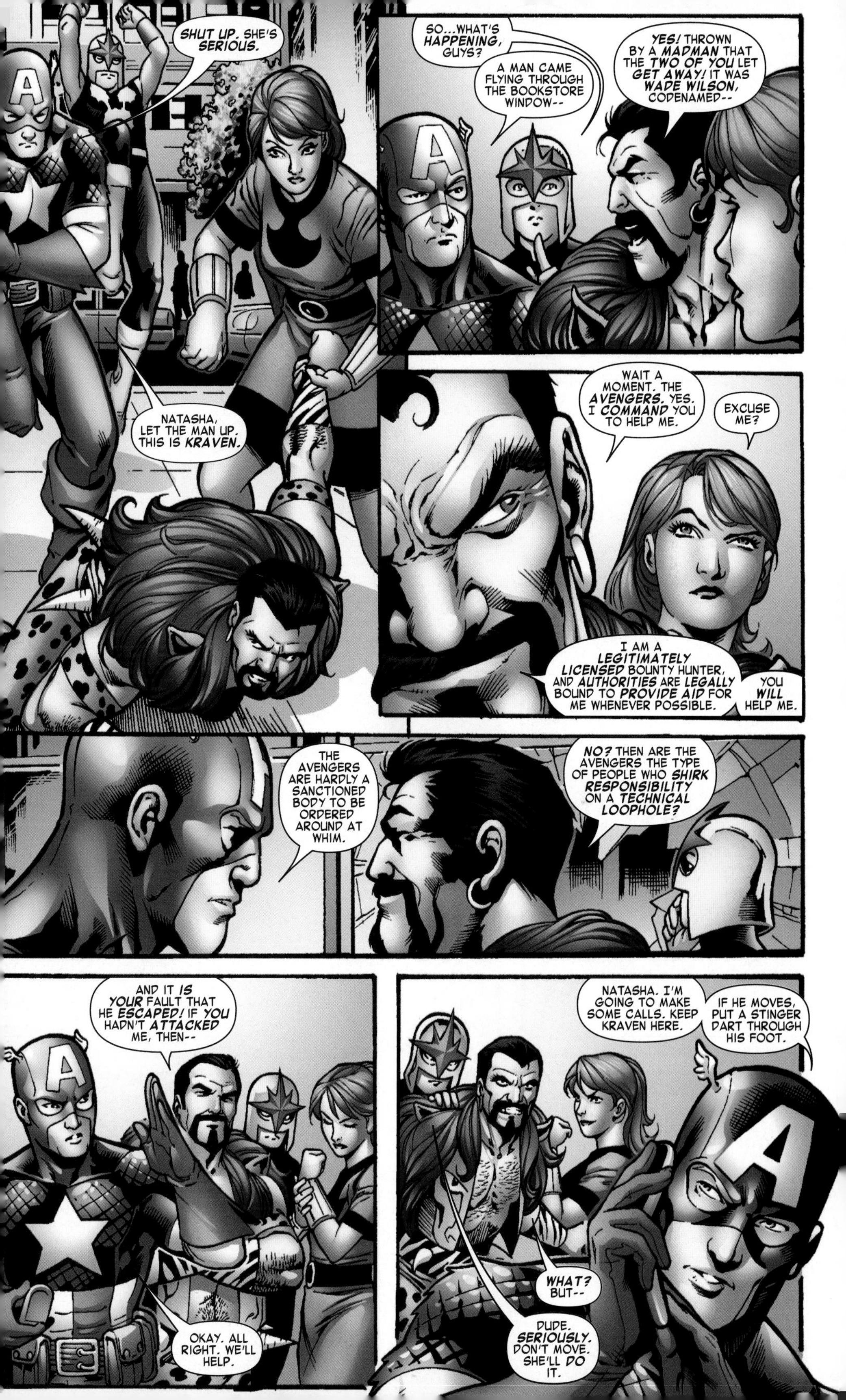
SHUT UP. SHE'S SERIOUS.
NATASHA, LET THE MAN UP. THIS IS KRAVEN.
SO...WHAT'S HAPPENING, GUYS?
A MAN CAME FLYING THROUGH THE BOOKSTORE WINDOW--
YES! THROWN BY A MADMAN THAT THE TWO OF YOU LET GET AWAY! IT WAS WADE WILSON, CODENAMED--
WAIT A MOMENT. THE AVENGERS. YES. I COMMAND YOU TO HELP ME.
EXCUSE ME?
I AM A LEGITIMATELY LICENSED BOUNTY HUNTER, AND AUTHORITIES ARE LEGALLY BOUND TO PROVIDE AID FOR ME WHENEVER POSSIBLE.
YOU WILL HELP ME.
THE AVENGERS ARE HARDLY A SANCTIONED BODY TO BE ORDERED AROUND AT WHIM.
NO? THEN ARE THE AVENGERS THE TYPE OF PEOPLE WHO SHIRK RESPONSIBILITY ON A TECHNICAL LOOPHOLE?
AND IT IS YOUR FAULT THAT HE ESCAPED! IF YOU HADN'T ATTACKED ME, THEN--
OKAY. ALL RIGHT. WE'LL HELP.
NATASHA. I'M GOING TO MAKE SOME CALLS. KEEP KRAVEN HERE.
IF HE MOVES, PUT A STINGER DART THROUGH HIS FOOT.
WHAT? BUT--
DUDE. SERIOUSLY. DON'T MOVE. SHE'LL DO IT.

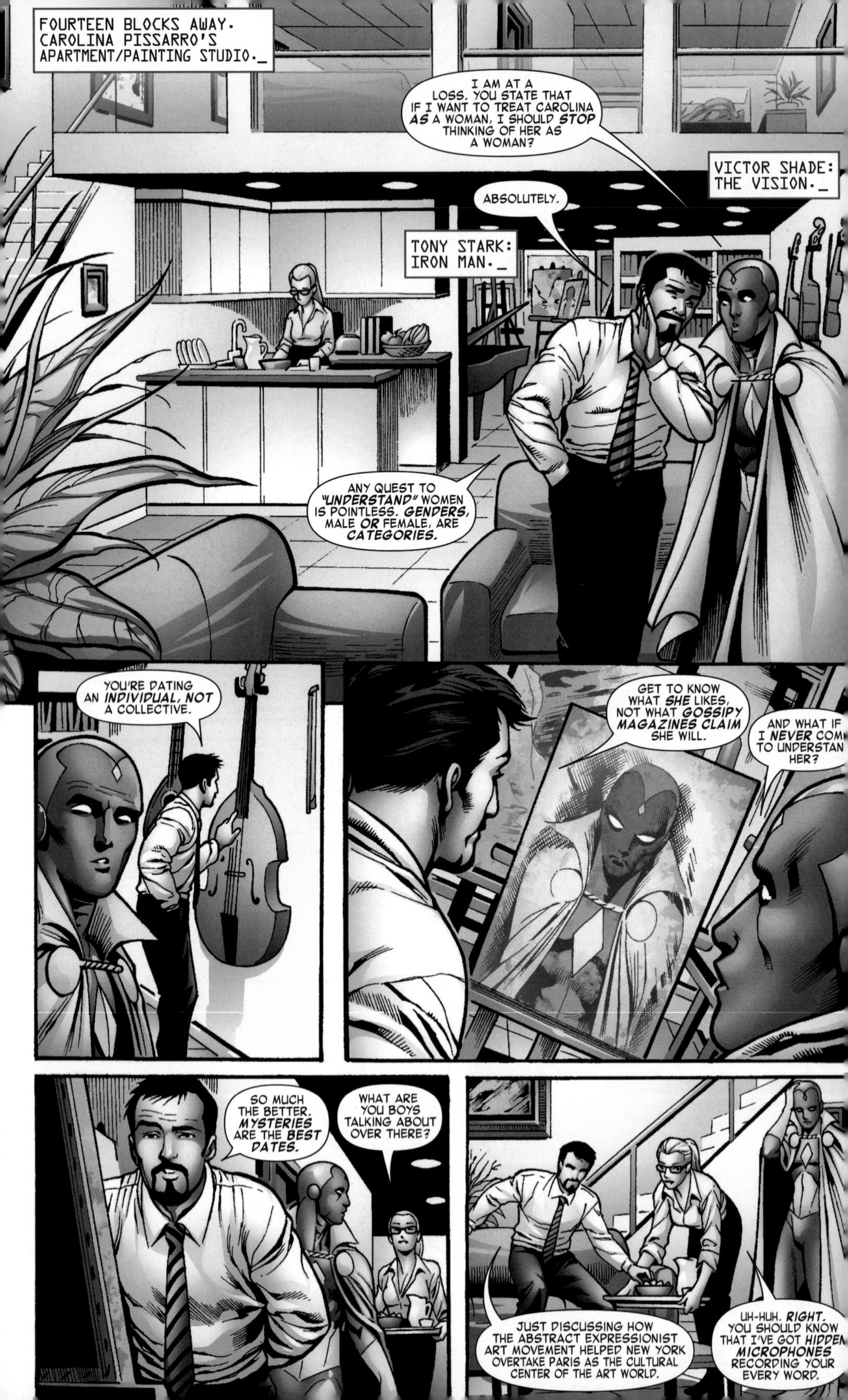
FOURTEEN BLOCKS AWAY. CAROLINA PISSARRO'S APARTMENT/PAINTING STUDIO._
VICTOR SHADE: THE VISION._
I AM AT A LOSS. YOU STATE THAT IF I WANT TO TREAT CAROLINA AS A WOMAN, I SHOULD STOP THINKING OF HER AS A WOMAN?
TONY STARK: IRON MAN._
ABSOLUTELY.
ANY QUEST TO "UNDERSTAND" WOMEN IS POINTLESS. GENDERS, MALE OR FEMALE, ARE CATEGORIES.
YOU'RE DATING AN INDIVIDUAL, NOT A COLLECTIVE.
GET TO KNOW WHAT SHE LIKES, NOT WHAT GOSSIPY MAGAZINES CLAIM SHE WILL.
AND WHAT IF I NEVER COM TO UNDERSTAN HER?
SO MUCH THE BETTER. MYSTERIES ARE THE BEST DATES.
WHAT ARE YOU BOYS TALKING ABOUT OVER THERE?
JUST DISCUSSING HOW THE ABSTRACT EXPRESSIONIST ART MOVEMENT HELPED NEW YORK OVERTAKE PARIS AS THE CULTURAL CENTER OF THE ART WORLD.
UH-HUH. RIGHT. YOU SHOULD KNOW THAT I'VE GOT HIDDEN MICROPHONES RECORDING YOUR EVERY WORD.

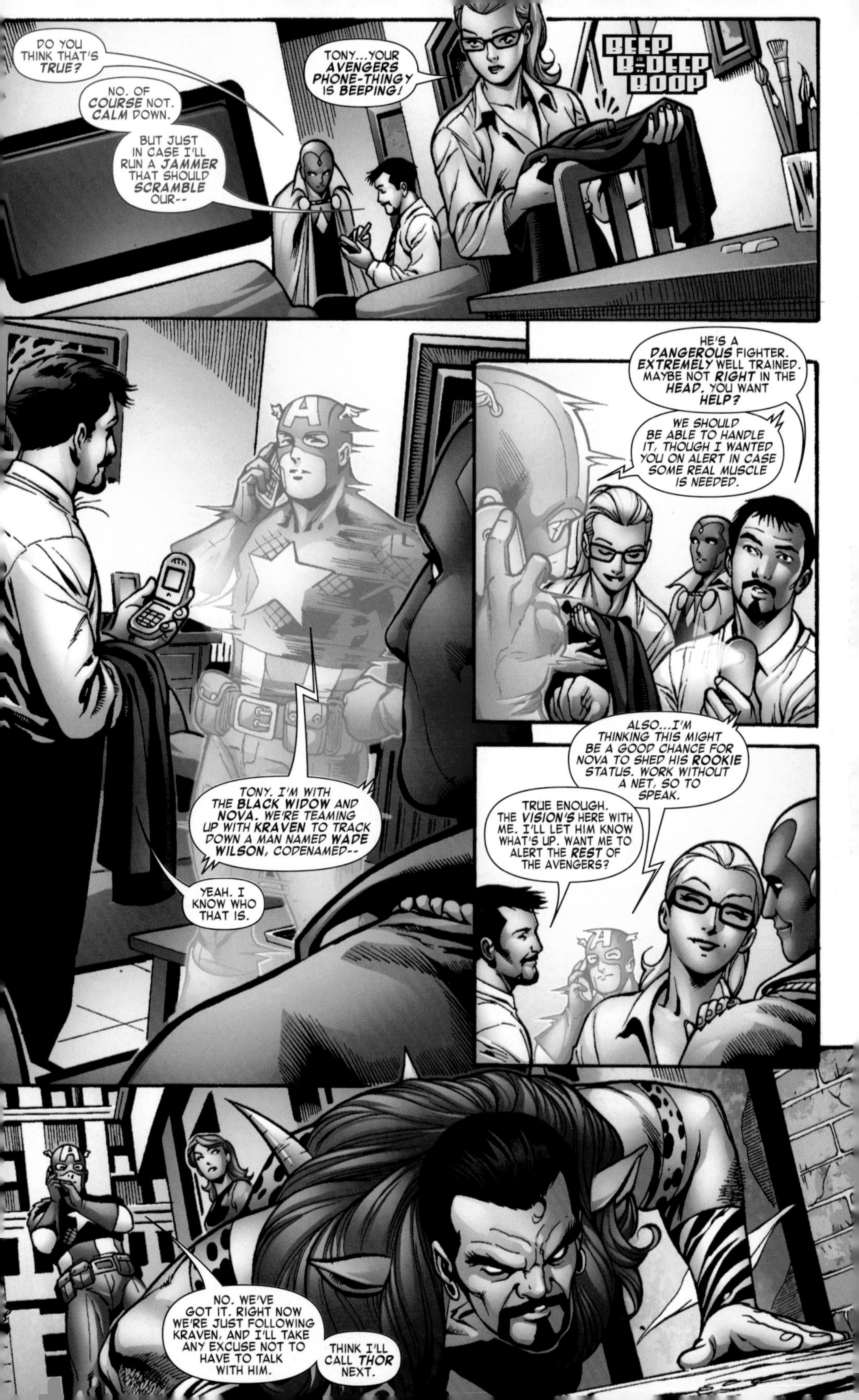
DO YOU THINK THAT'S TRUE?
NO. OF COURSE NOT. CALM DOWN.
BUT JUST IN CASE I'LL RUN A JAMMER THAT SHOULD SCRAMBLE OUR--
TONY...YOUR AVENGERS PHONE-THINGY IS BEEPING!
BEEP B-DEEP BOOP
TONY. I'M WITH THE BLACK WIDOW AND NOVA. WE'RE TEAMING UP WITH KRAVEN TO TRACK DOWN A MAN NAMED WADE WILSON, CODENAMED--
YEAH. I KNOW WHO THAT IS.
HE'S A DANGEROUS FIGHTER. EXTREMELY WELL TRAINED. MAYBE NOT RIGHT IN THE HEAD. YOU WANT HELP?
WE SHOULD BE ABLE TO HANDLE IT, THOUGH I WANTED YOU ON ALERT IN CASE SOME REAL MUSCLE IS NEEDED.
ALSO...I'M THINKING THIS MIGHT BE A GOOD CHANCE FOR NOVA TO SHED HIS ROOKIE STATUS. WORK WITHOUT A NET, SO TO SPEAK.
TRUE ENOUGH. THE VISION'S HERE WITH ME. I'LL LET HIM KNOW WHAT'S UP. WANT ME TO ALERT THE REST OF THE AVENGERS?
NO. WE'VE GOT IT. RIGHT NOW WE'RE JUST FOLLOWING KRAVEN, AND I'LL TAKE ANY EXCUSE NOT TO HAVE TO TALK WITH HIM.
THINK I'LL CALL THOR NEXT.

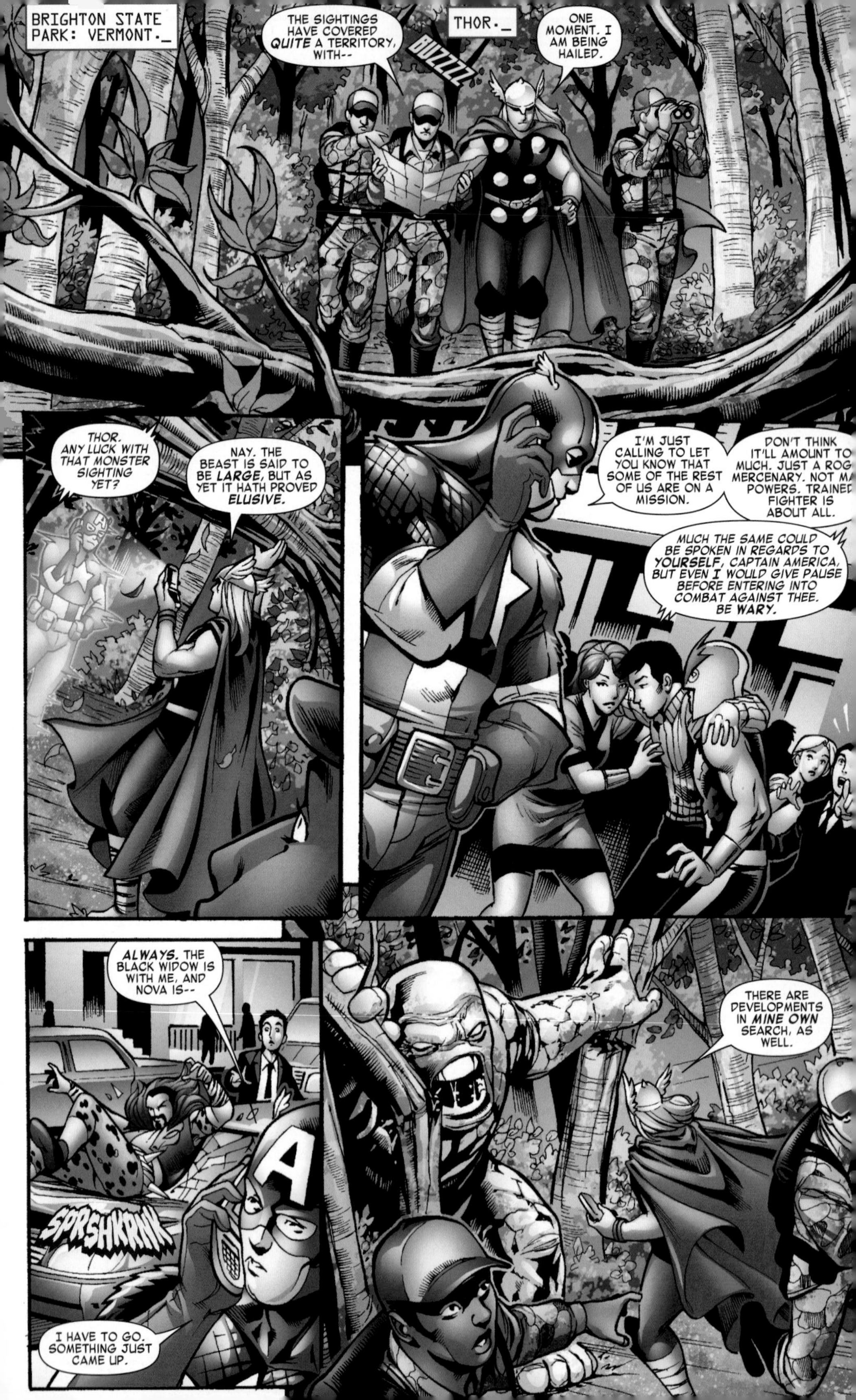
BRIGHTON STATE PARK: VERMONT._
THE SIGHTINGS HAVE COVERED QUITE A TERRITORY, WITH--
BUZZZZ
THOR._
ONE MOMENT. I AM BEING HAILED.
THOR. ANY LUCK WITH THAT MONSTER SIGHTING YET?
NAY. THE BEAST IS SAID TO BE LARGE, BUT AS YET IT HATH PROVED ELUSIVE.
I'M JUST CALLING TO LET YOU KNOW THAT SOME OF THE REST OF US ARE ON A MISSION.
DON'T THINK IT'LL AMOUNT TO MUCH. JUST A ROG MERCENARY. NOT MA POWERS. TRAINED FIGHTER IS ABOUT ALL.
MUCH THE SAME COULD BE SPOKEN IN REGARDS TO YOURSELF, CAPTAIN AMERICA, BUT EVEN I WOULD GIVE PAUSE BEFORE ENTERING INTO COMBAT AGAINST THEE. BE WARY.
ALWAYS. THE BLACK WIDOW IS WITH ME, AND NOVA IS--
SPRSHKRNK
I HAVE TO GO. SOMETHING JUST CAME UP.
THERE ARE DEVELOPMENTS IN MINE OWN SEARCH, AS WELL.

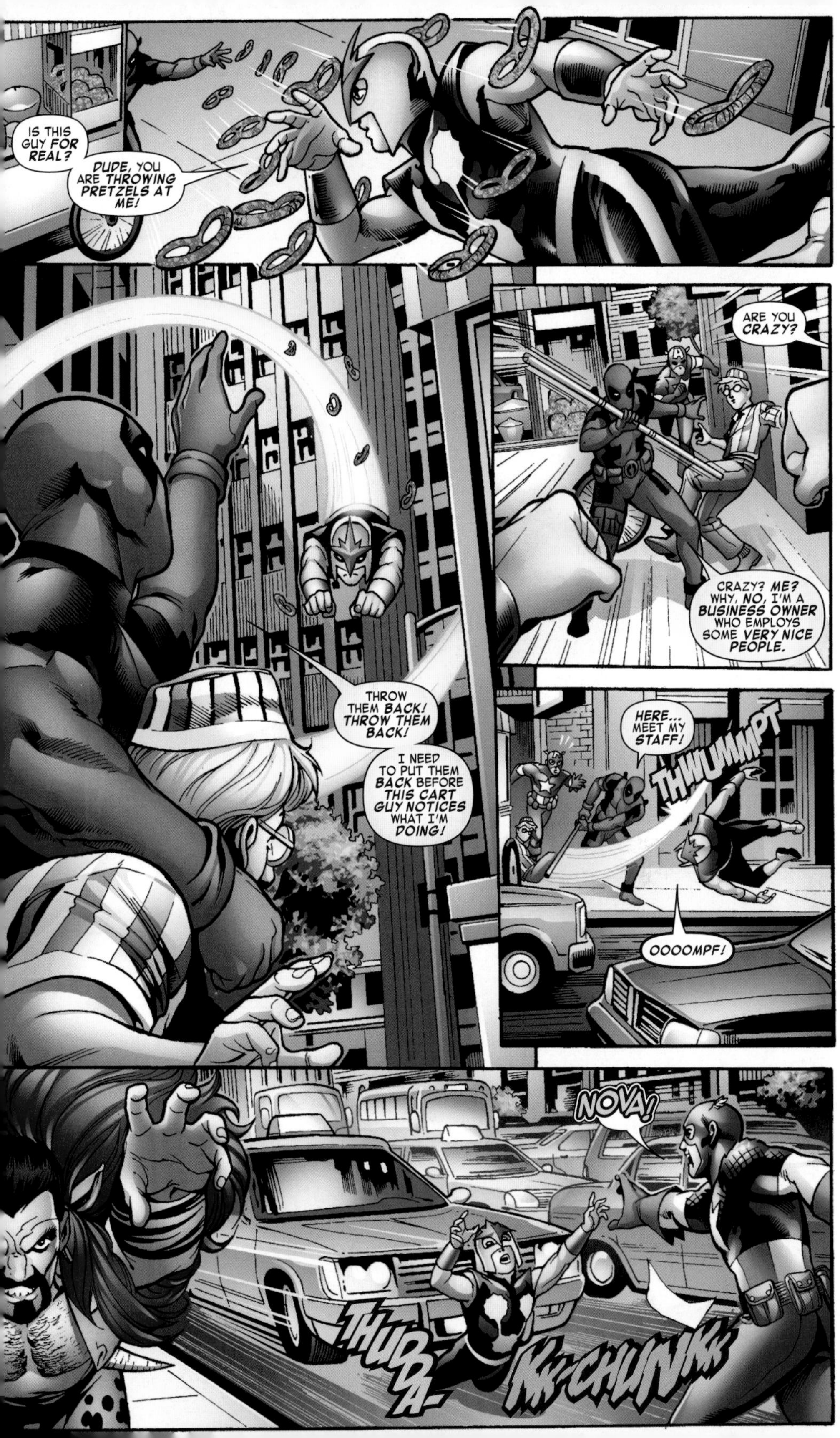
IS THIS GUY FOR REAL?
DUDE, YOU ARE THROWING PRETZELS AT ME!
THROW THEM BACK! THROW THEM BACK!
I NEED TO PUT THEM BACK BEFORE THIS CART GUY NOTICES WHAT I'M DOING!
ARE YOU CRAZY?
CRAZY? ME? WHY, NO, I'M A BUSINESS OWNER WHO EMPLOYS SOME VERY NICE PEOPLE.
HERE... MEET MY STAFF!
THWUMMPT
OOOOMPF!
NOVA!
THUDDA-
KA-CHUNK

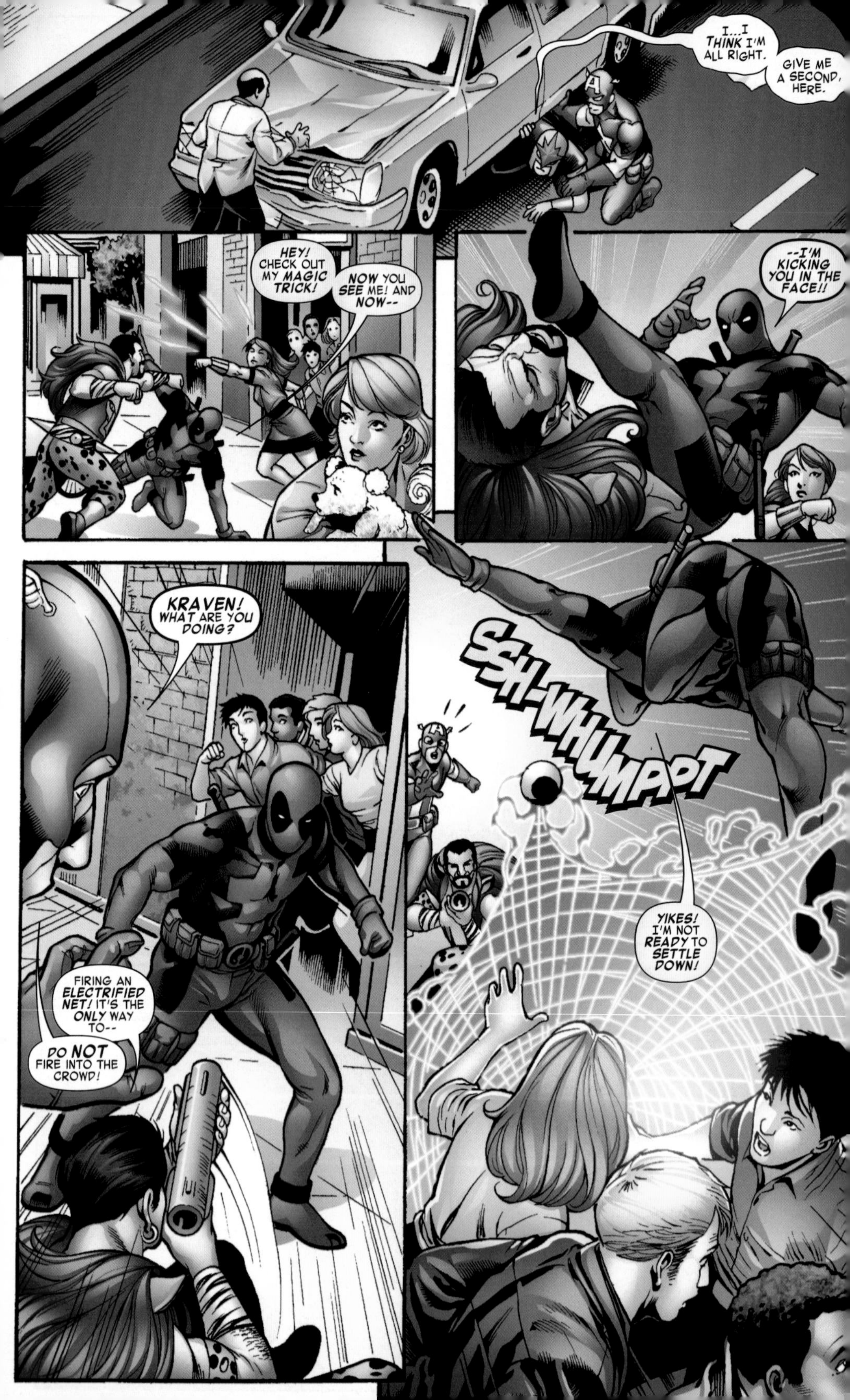
I...I THINK I'M ALL RIGHT.
GIVE ME A SECOND, HERE.
HEY! CHECK OUT MY MAGIC TRICK!
NOW YOU SEE ME! AND NOW--
--I'M KICKING YOU IN THE FACE!!
KRAVEN! WHAT ARE YOU DOING?
FIRING AN ELECTRIFIED NET! IT'S THE ONLY WAY TO--
DO NOT FIRE INTO THE CROWD!
SSH-WHUMPPT
YIKES! I'M NOT READY TO SETTLE DOWN!

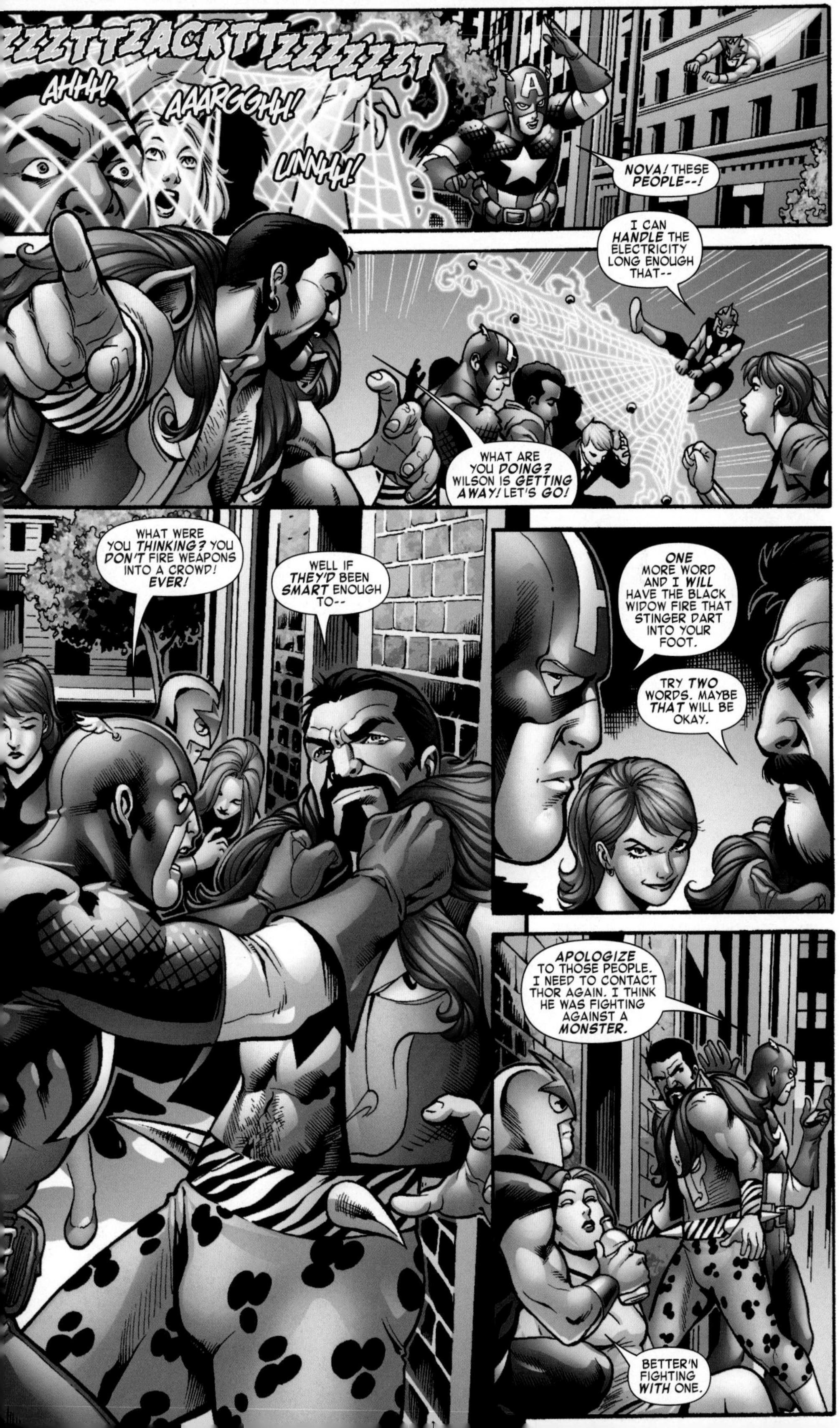
ZZZZTTTZACKTTZZZZZZZT
AHHH!
AAARGGHH!
UNNHH!
NOVA! THESE PEOPLE--!
I CAN HANDLE THE ELECTRICITY LONG ENOUGH THAT--
WHAT ARE YOU DOING? WILSON IS GETTING AWAY! LET'S GO!
WHAT WERE YOU THINKING? YOU DON'T FIRE WEAPONS INTO A CROWD! EVER!
WELL IF THEY'D BEEN SMART ENOUGH TO--
ONE MORE WORD AND I WILL HAVE THE BLACK WIDOW FIRE THAT STINGER DART INTO YOUR FOOT.
TRY TWO WORDS. MAYBE THAT WILL BE OKAY.
APOLOGIZE TO THOSE PEOPLE. I NEED TO CONTACT THOR AGAIN. I THINK HE WAS FIGHTING AGAINST A MONSTER.
BETTER'N FIGHTING WITH ONE.

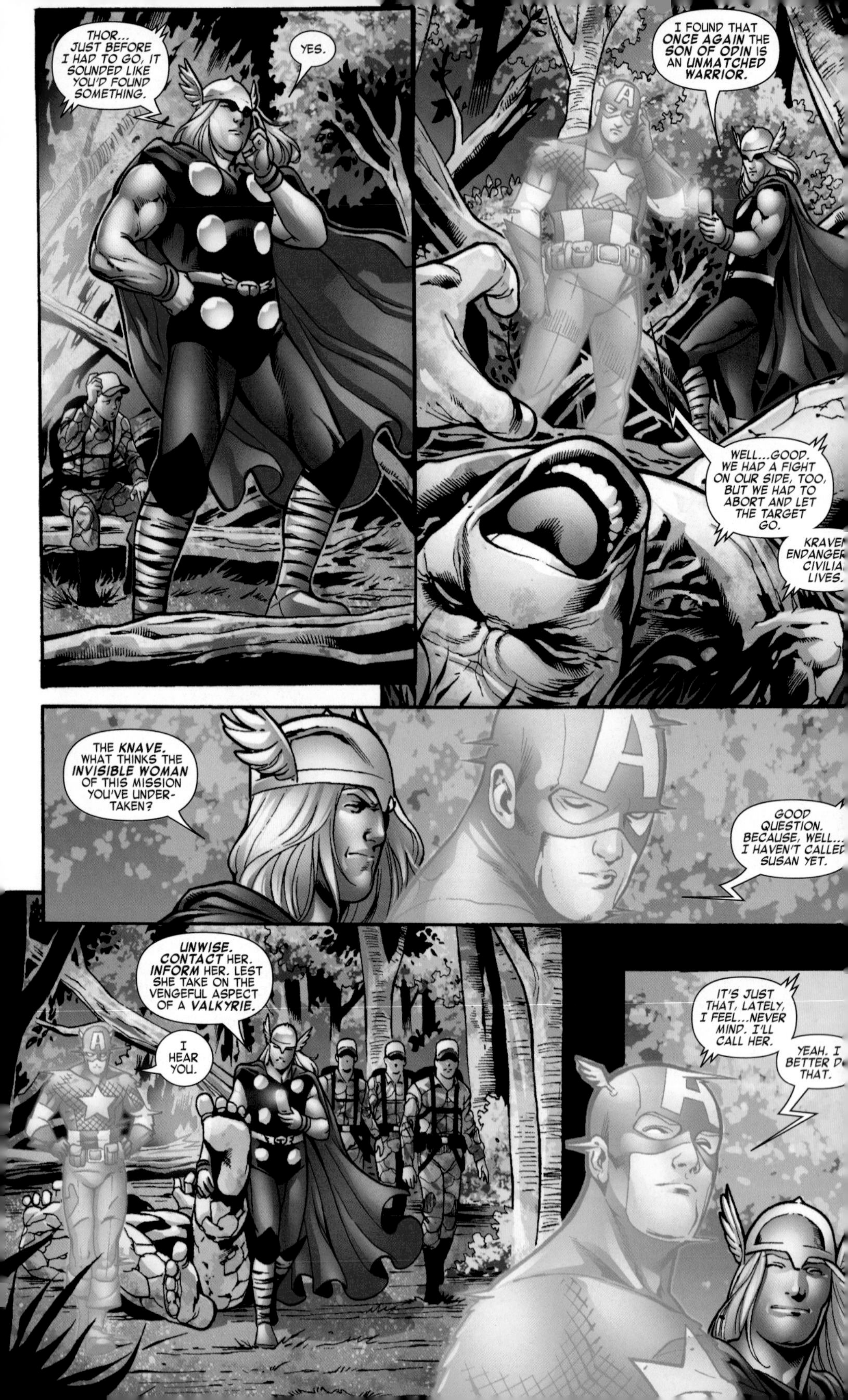
THOR... JUST BEFORE I HAD TO GO, IT SOUNDED LIKE YOU'D FOUND SOMETHING.
YES.
I FOUND THAT ONCE AGAIN THE SON OF ODIN IS AN UNMATCHED WARRIOR.
WELL...GOOD. WE HAD A FIGHT ON OUR SIDE, TOO, BUT WE HAD TO ABORT AND LET THE TARGET GO.
THE KNAVE. WHAT THINKS THE INVISIBLE WOMAN OF THIS MISSION YOU'VE UNDER-TAKEN?
GOOD QUESTION. BECAUSE, WELL... I HAVEN'T CALLED SUSAN YET.
UNWISE. CONTACT HER. INFORM HER. LEST SHE TAKE ON THE VENGEFUL ASPECT OF A VALKYRIE.
I HEAR YOU.
IT'S JUST THAT, LATELY, I FEEL...NEVER MIND. I'LL CALL HER.

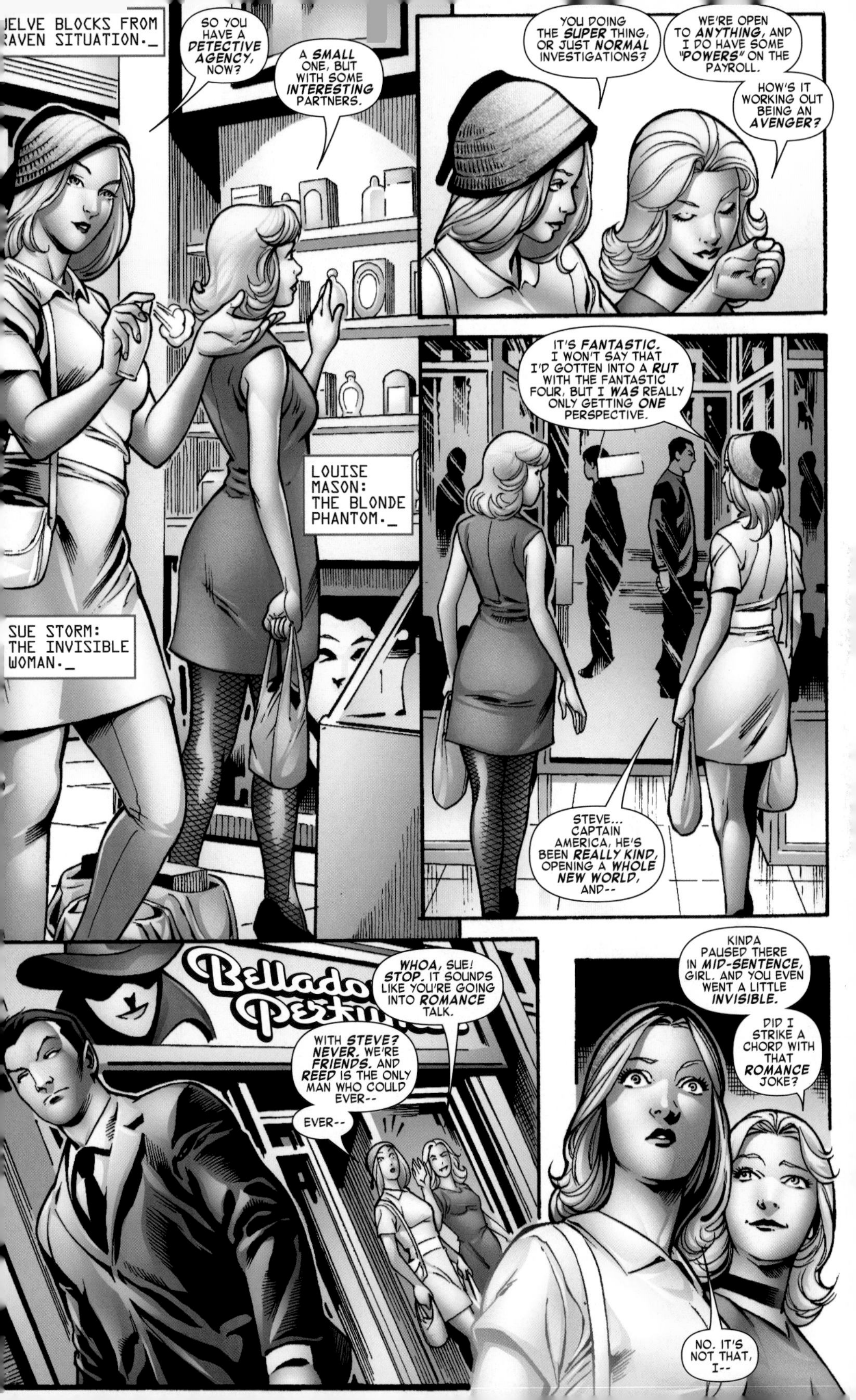

ELVE BLOCKS FROM
RAVEN SITUATION._
SO YOU HAVE A DETECTIVE AGENCY, NOW?
A SMALL ONE, BUT WITH SOME INTERESTING PARTNERS.
LOUISE MASON: THE BLONDE PHANTOM._
SUE STORM: THE INVISIBLE WOMAN._
YOU DOING THE SUPER THING, OR JUST NORMAL INVESTIGATIONS?
WE'RE OPEN TO ANYTHING, AND I DO HAVE SOME "POWERS" ON THE PAYROLL.
HOW'S IT WORKING OUT BEING AN AVENGER?
IT'S FANTASTIC. I WON'T SAY THAT I'D GOTTEN INTO A RUT WITH THE FANTASTIC FOUR, BUT I WAS REALLY ONLY GETTING ONE PERSPECTIVE.
STEVE... CAPTAIN AMERICA, HE'S BEEN REALLY KIND, OPENING A WHOLE NEW WORLD, AND--
Bellado Perfu
WHOA, SUE! STOP. IT SOUNDS LIKE YOU'RE GOING INTO ROMANCE TALK.
WITH STEVE? NEVER. WE'RE FRIENDS. AND REED IS THE ONLY MAN WHO COULD EVER--
EVER--
KINDA PAUSED THERE IN MID-SENTENCE, GIRL. AND YOU EVEN WENT A LITTLE INVISIBLE.
DID I STRIKE A CHORD WITH THAT ROMANCE JOKE?
NO. IT'S NOT THAT, I--

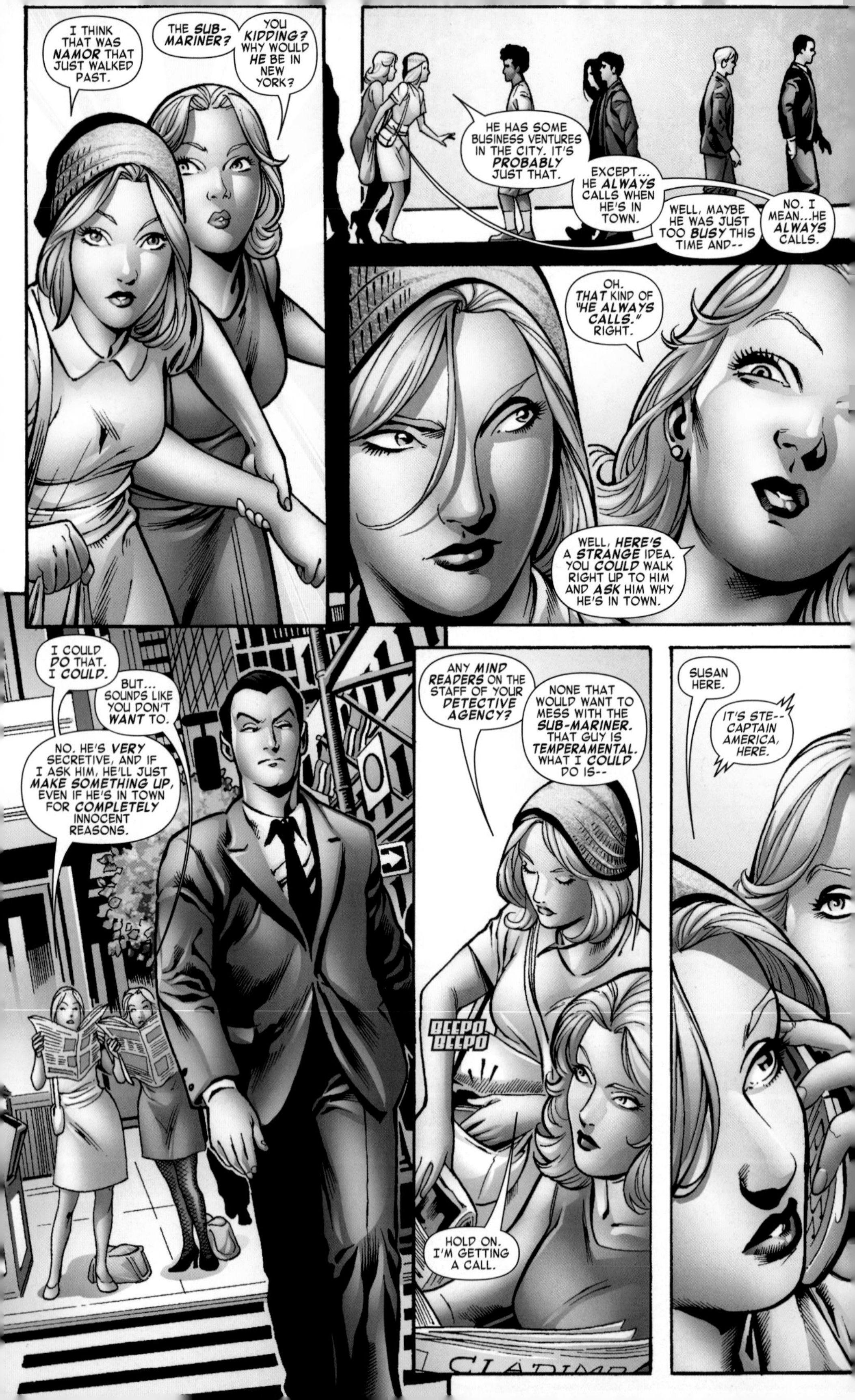

I THINK THAT WAS NAMOR THAT JUST WALKED PAST.
THE SUB-MARINER?
YOU KIDDING? WHY WOULD HE BE IN NEW YORK?
HE HAS SOME BUSINESS VENTURES IN THE CITY. IT'S PROBABLY JUST THAT.
EXCEPT... HE ALWAYS CALLS WHEN HE'S IN TOWN.
WELL, MAYBE HE WAS JUST TOO BUSY THIS TIME AND--
NO. I MEAN...HE ALWAYS CALLS.
OH. THAT KIND OF "HE ALWAYS CALLS." RIGHT.
WELL, HERE'S A STRANGE IDEA. YOU COULD WALK RIGHT UP TO HIM AND ASK HIM WHY HE'S IN TOWN.
I COULD DO THAT. I COULD.
BUT... SOUNDS LIKE YOU DON'T WANT TO.
NO. HE'S VERY SECRETIVE, AND IF I ASK HIM, HE'LL JUST MAKE SOMETHING UP, EVEN IF HE'S IN TOWN FOR COMPLETELY INNOCENT REASONS.
ANY MIND READERS ON THE STAFF OF YOUR DETECTIVE AGENCY?
NONE THAT WOULD WANT TO MESS WITH THE SUB-MARINER. THAT GUY IS TEMPERAMENTAL. WHAT I COULD DO IS--
BEEPO BEEPO
HOLD ON. I'M GETTING A CALL.
SUSAN HERE.
IT'S STE-- CAPTAIN AMERICA, HERE.

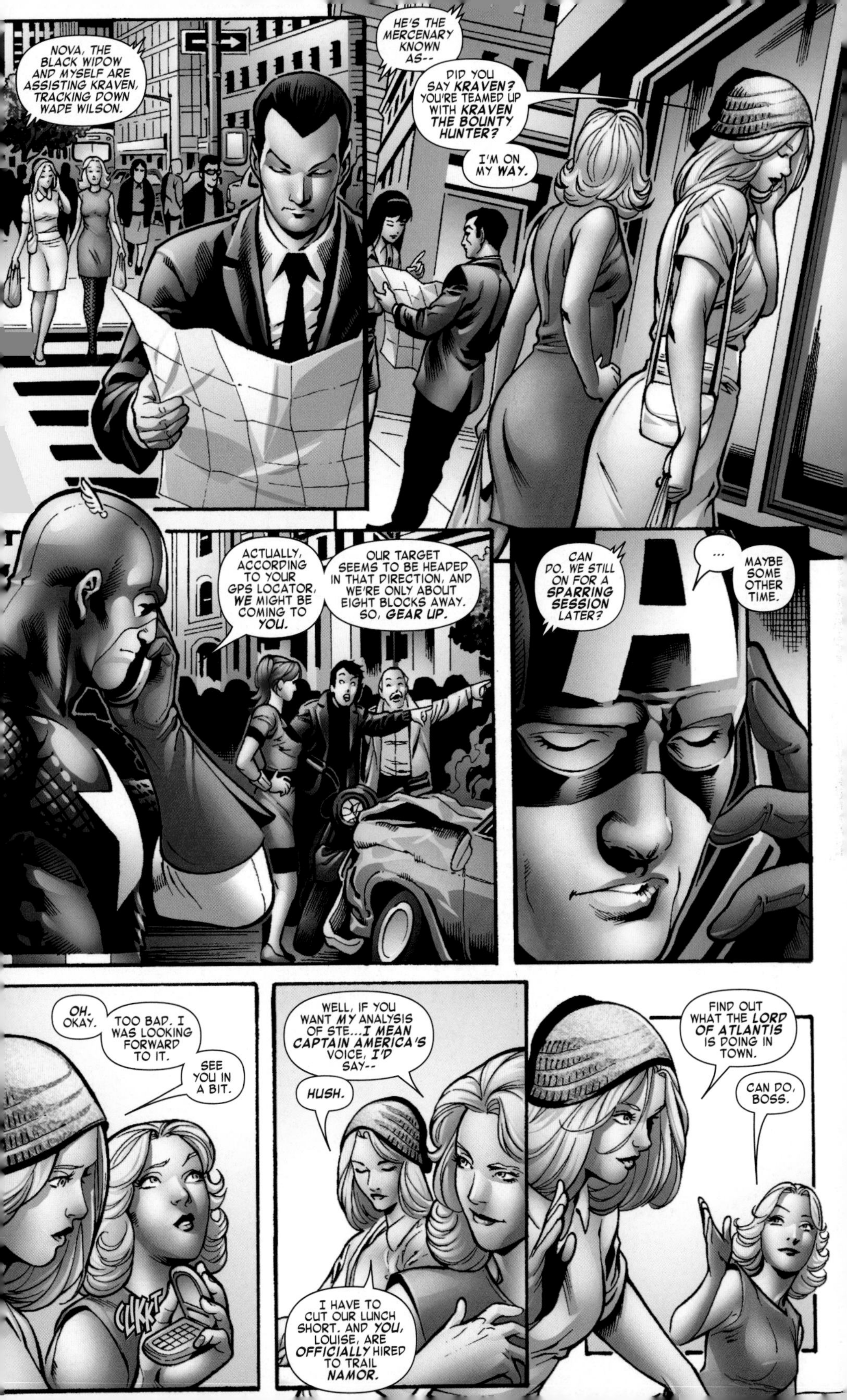
NOVA, THE BLACK WIDOW AND MYSELF ARE ASSISTING KRAVEN, TRACKING DOWN WADE WILSON.
HE'S THE MERCENARY KNOWN AS--
DID YOU SAY KRAVEN? YOU'RE TEAMED UP WITH KRAVEN THE BOUNTY HUNTER?
I'M ON MY WAY.
ACTUALLY, ACCORDING TO YOUR GPS LOCATOR, WE MIGHT BE COMING TO YOU.
OUR TARGET SEEMS TO BE HEADED IN THAT DIRECTION, AND WE'RE ONLY ABOUT EIGHT BLOCKS AWAY. SO, GEAR UP.
CAN DO. WE STILL ON FOR A SPARRING SESSION LATER?
...
MAYBE SOME OTHER TIME.
OH. OKAY.
TOO BAD. I WAS LOOKING FORWARD TO IT.
SEE YOU IN A BIT.
CLIKKT
WELL, IF YOU WANT MY ANALYSIS OF STE...I MEAN CAPTAIN AMERICA'S VOICE, I'D SAY--
HUSH.
I HAVE TO CUT OUR LUNCH SHORT. AND YOU, LOUISE, ARE OFFICIALLY HIRED TO TRAIL NAMOR.
FIND OUT WHAT THE LORD OF ATLANTIS IS DOING IN TOWN.
CAN DO, BOSS.

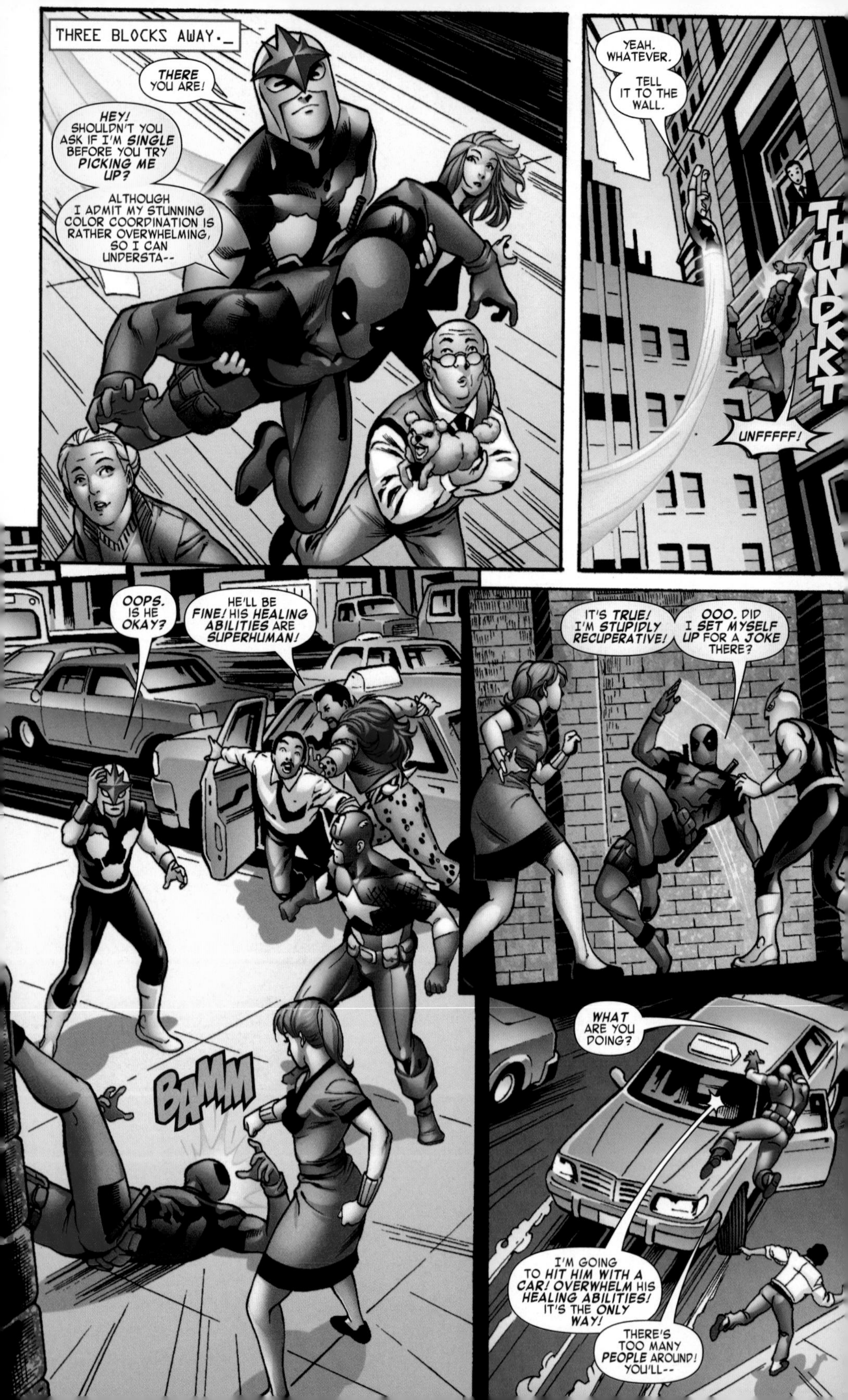
THREE BLOCKS AWAY.
THERE YOU ARE!
HEY! SHOULDN'T YOU ASK IF I'M SINGLE BEFORE YOU TRY PICKING ME UP?
ALTHOUGH I ADMIT MY STUNNING COLOR COORDINATION IS RATHER OVERWHELMING, SO I CAN UNDERSTA--
YEAH. WHATEVER.
TELL IT TO THE WALL.
THUNDKT
UNFFFFF!
OOPS. IS HE OKAY?
HE'LL BE FINE! HIS HEALING ABILITIES ARE SUPERHUMAN!
IT'S TRUE! I'M STUPIDLY RECUPERATIVE!
OOO. DID I SET MYSELF UP FOR A JOKE THERE?
BAMM
WHAT ARE YOU DOING?
I'M GOING TO HIT HIM WITH A CAR! OVERWHELM HIS HEALING ABILITIES! IT'S THE ONLY WAY!
THERE'S TOO MANY PEOPLE AROUND! YOU'LL--

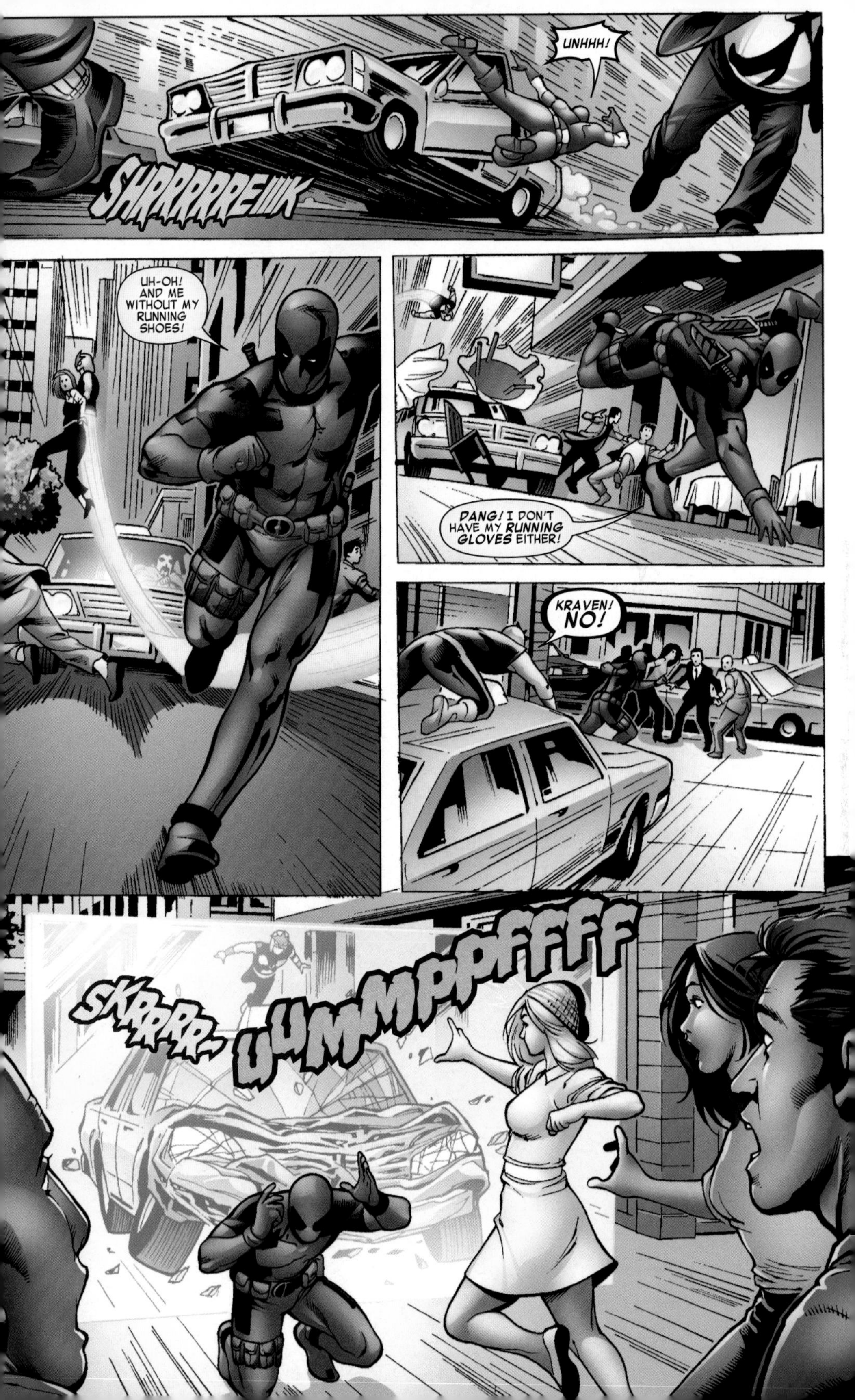
UNHHH!
SHRRRRREIIIK
UH-OH! AND ME WITHOUT MY RUNNING SHOES!
DANG! I DON'T HAVE MY RUNNING GLOVES EITHER!
KRAVEN! NO!
SKRRRR- UUMMPPFFFF

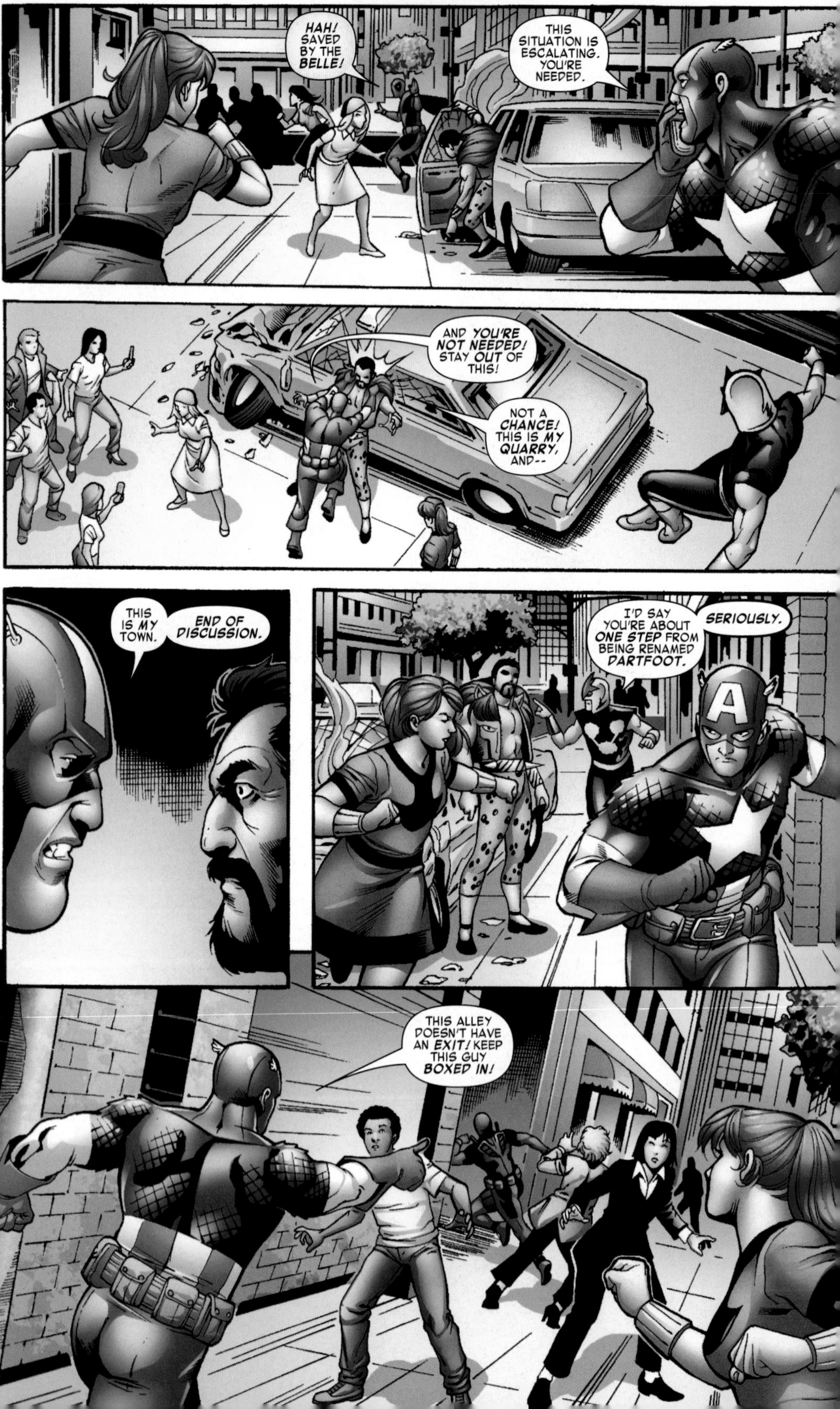
HAH! SAVED BY THE BELLE!
THIS SITUATION IS ESCALATING. YOU'RE NEEDED.
AND YOU'RE NOT NEEDED! STAY OUT OF THIS!
NOT A CHANCE! THIS IS MY QUARRY, AND--
THIS IS MY TOWN.
END OF DISCUSSION.
I'D SAY YOU'RE ABOUT ONE STEP FROM BEING RENAMED DARTFOOT.
SERIOUSLY.
THIS ALLEY DOESN'T HAVE AN EXIT! KEEP THIS GUY BOXED IN!

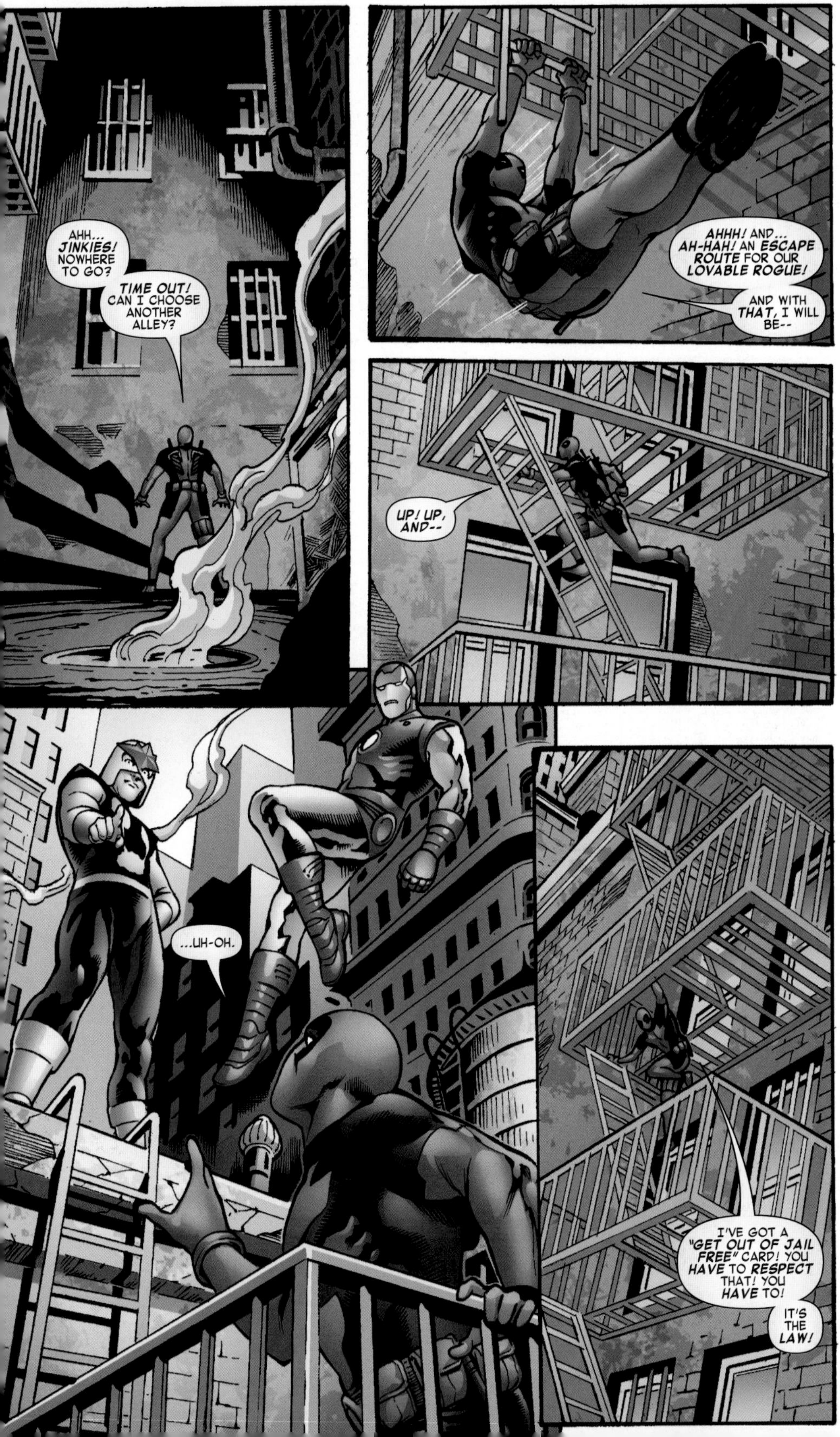
AHH... JINKIES! NOWHERE TO GO?
TIME OUT! CAN I CHOOSE ANOTHER ALLEY?
AHHH! AND... AH-HAH! AN ESCAPE ROUTE FOR OUR LOVABLE ROGUE!
AND WITH THAT, I WILL BE--
UP! UP, AND--
...UH-OH.
I'VE GOT A "GET OUT OF JAIL FREE" CARD! YOU HAVE TO RESPECT THAT! YOU HAVE TO!
IT'S THE LAW!

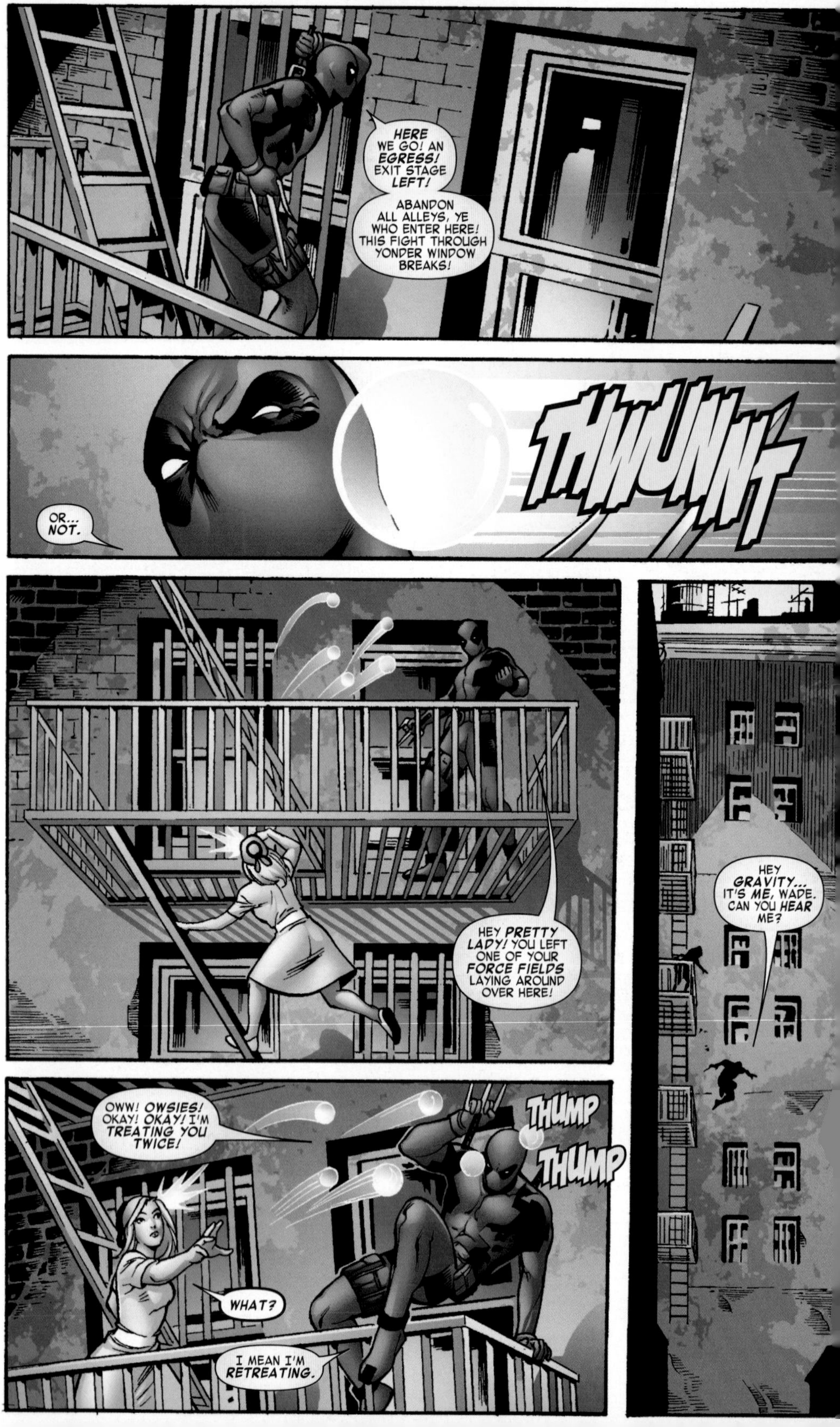
HERE WE GO! AN EGRESS! EXIT STAGE LEFT!
ABANDON ALL ALLEYS, YE WHO ENTER HERE! THIS FIGHT THROUGH YONDER WINDOW BREAKS!
OR... NOT.
THWUNNT
HEY PRETTY LADY! YOU LEFT ONE OF YOUR FORCE FIELDS LAYING AROUND OVER HERE!
OWW! OWSIES! OKAY! OKAY! I'M TREATING YOU TWICE!
THUMP
THUMP
WHAT?
I MEAN I'M RETREATING.
HEY GRAVITY... IT'S ME, WADE. CAN YOU HEAR ME?

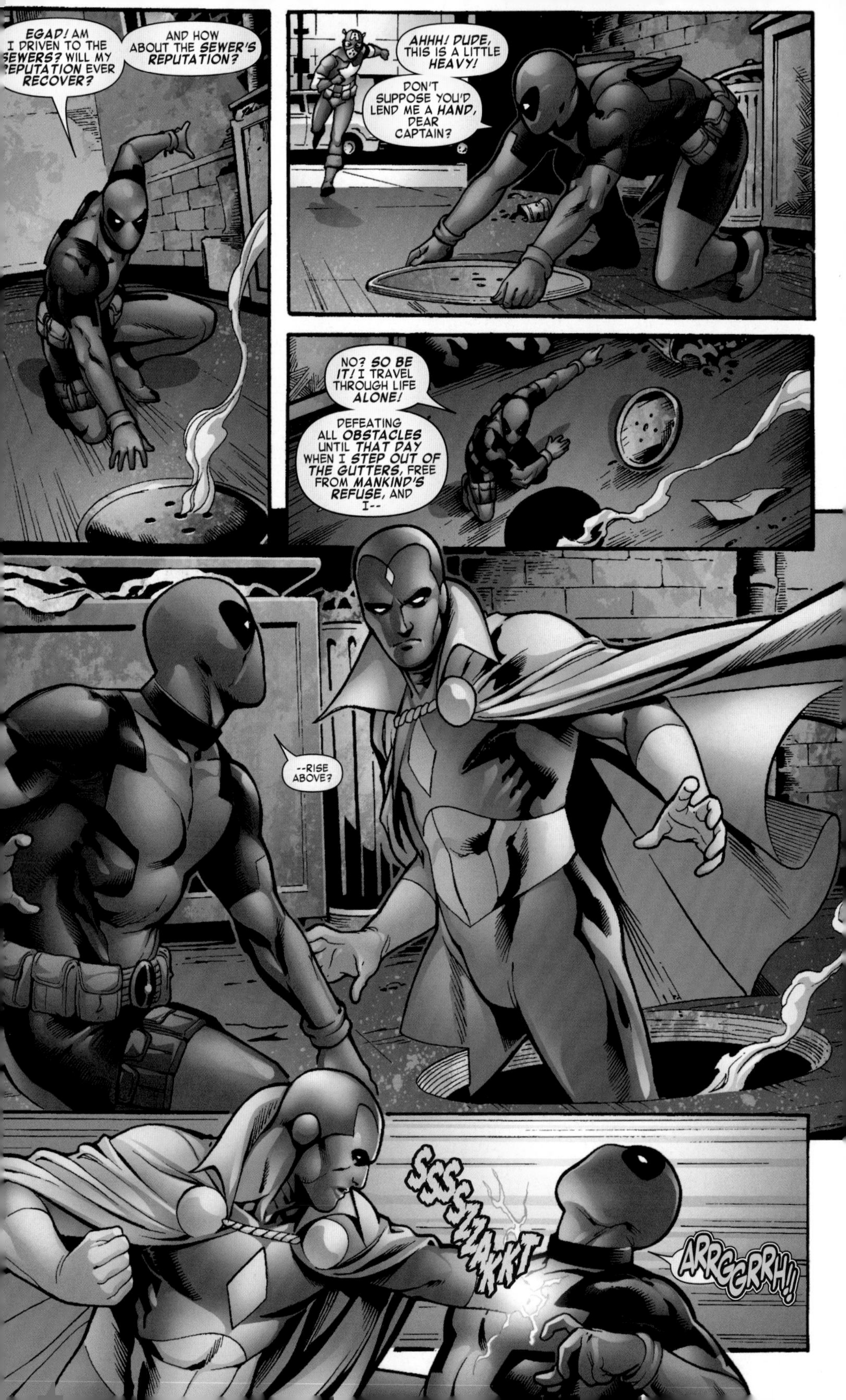
EGAD! AM I DRIVEN TO THE SEWERS? WILL MY REPUTATION EVER RECOVER?
AND HOW ABOUT THE SEWER'S REPUTATION?
AHHH! DUDE, THIS IS A LITTLE HEAVY!
DON'T SUPPOSE YOU'D LEND ME A HAND, DEAR CAPTAIN?
NO? SO BE IT! I TRAVEL THROUGH LIFE ALONE!
DEFEATING ALL OBSTACLES UNTIL THAT DAY WHEN I STEP OUT OF THE GUTTERS, FREE FROM MANKIND'S REFUSE, AND I--
--RISE ABOVE?
SSSSZZAKKT
ARRGGRRH!!

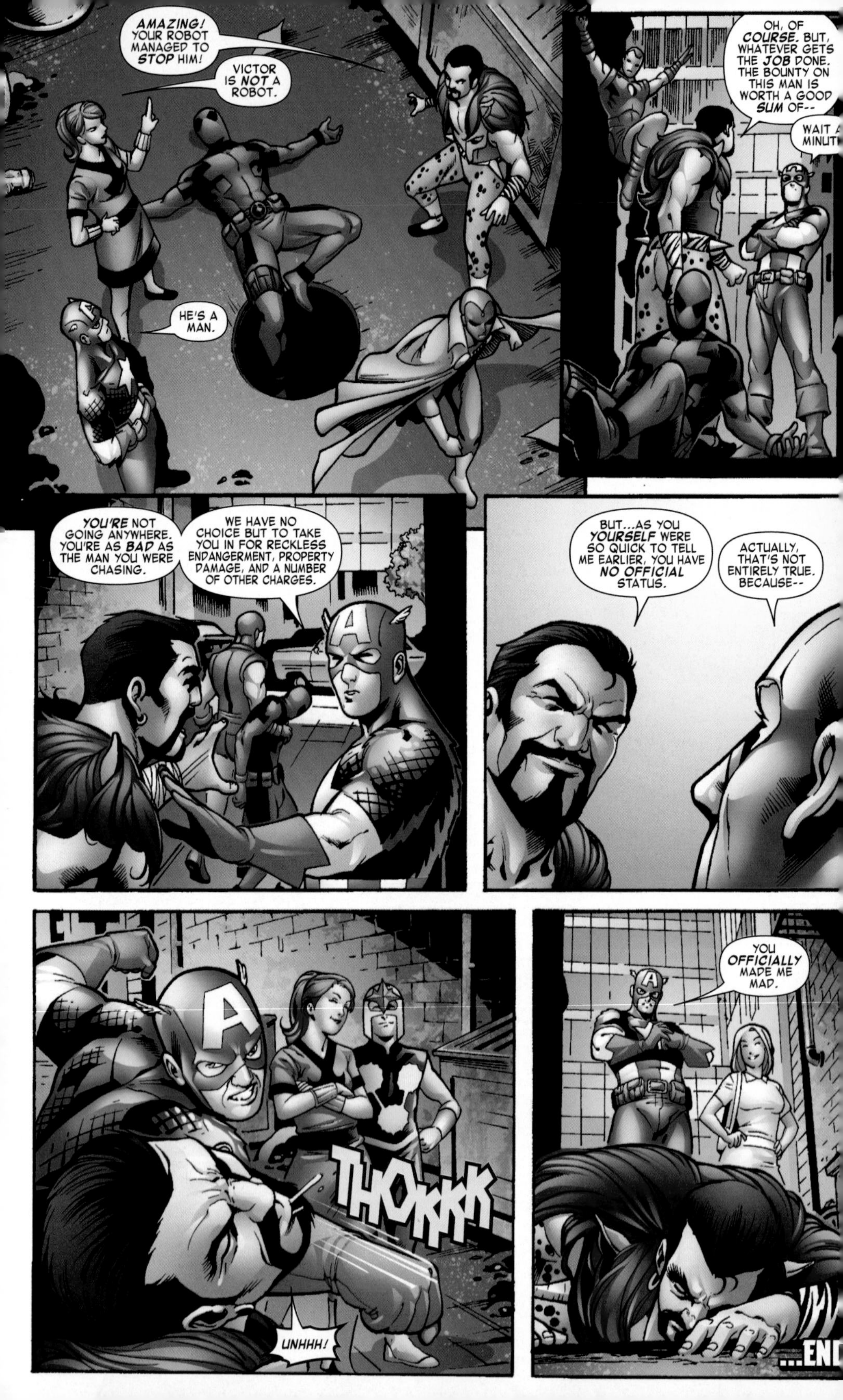

AMAZING! YOUR ROBOT MANAGED TO STOP HIM!
VICTOR IS NOT A ROBOT.
HE'S A MAN.
OH, OF COURSE. BUT, WHATEVER GETS THE JOB DONE. THE BOUNTY ON THIS MAN IS WORTH A GOOD SUM OF--
WAIT A MINUT
YOU'RE NOT GOING ANYWHERE. YOU'RE AS BAD AS THE MAN YOU WERE CHASING.
WE HAVE NO CHOICE BUT TO TAKE YOU IN FOR RECKLESS ENDANGERMENT, PROPERTY DAMAGE, AND A NUMBER OF OTHER CHARGES.
BUT...AS YOU YOURSELF WERE SO QUICK TO TELL ME EARLIER, YOU HAVE NO OFFICIAL STATUS.
ACTUALLY, THAT'S NOT ENTIRELY TRUE. BECAUSE--
THOKKK
UNHHH!
YOU OFFICIALLY MADE ME MAD.
...END

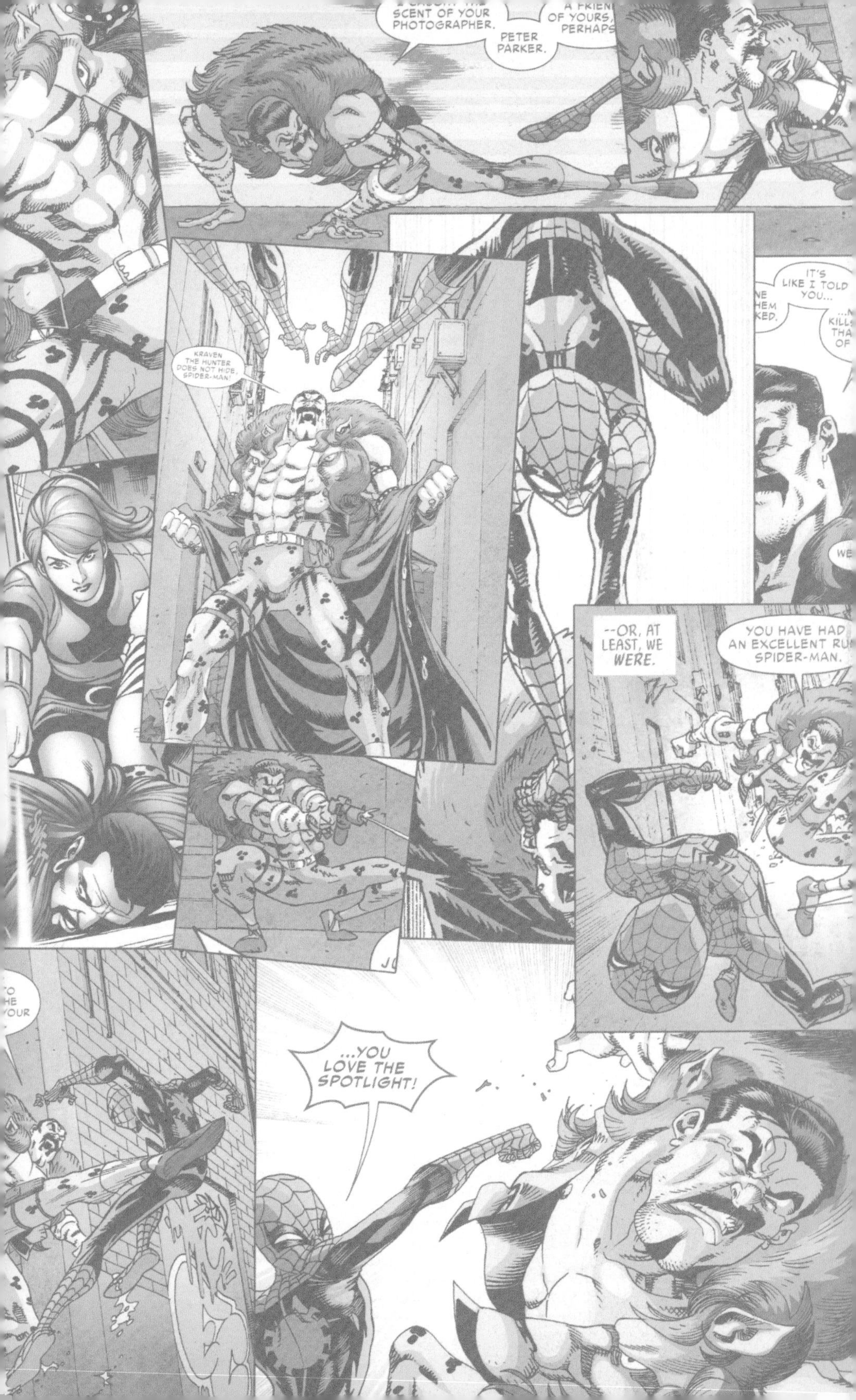

SCENT OF YOUR PHOTOGRAPHER.
PETER PARKER.
OF YOURS, PERHAPS
IT'S LIKE I TOLD YOU...
KRAVEN THE HUNTER DOES NOT HIDE, SPIDER-MAN!
--OR, AT LEAST, WE WERE.
YOU HAVE HAD AN EXCELLENT
SPIDER-MAN.
...YOU LOVE THE SPOTLIGHT!

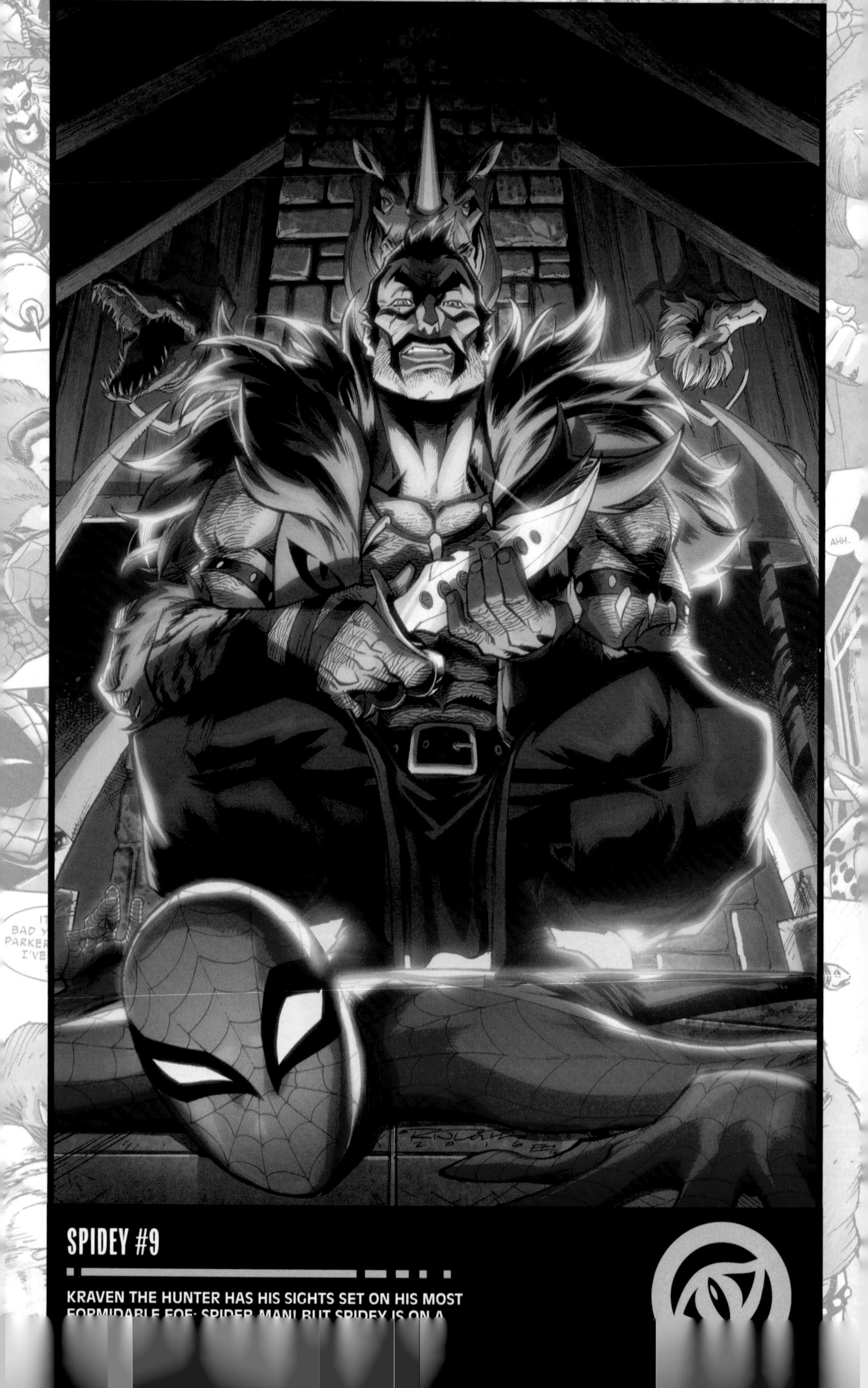

SPIDEY #9

KRAVEN THE HUNTER HAS HIS SIGHTS SET ON HIS MOST
FORMIDABLE FOE: SPIDER-MAN! BUT SPIDEY IS ON A

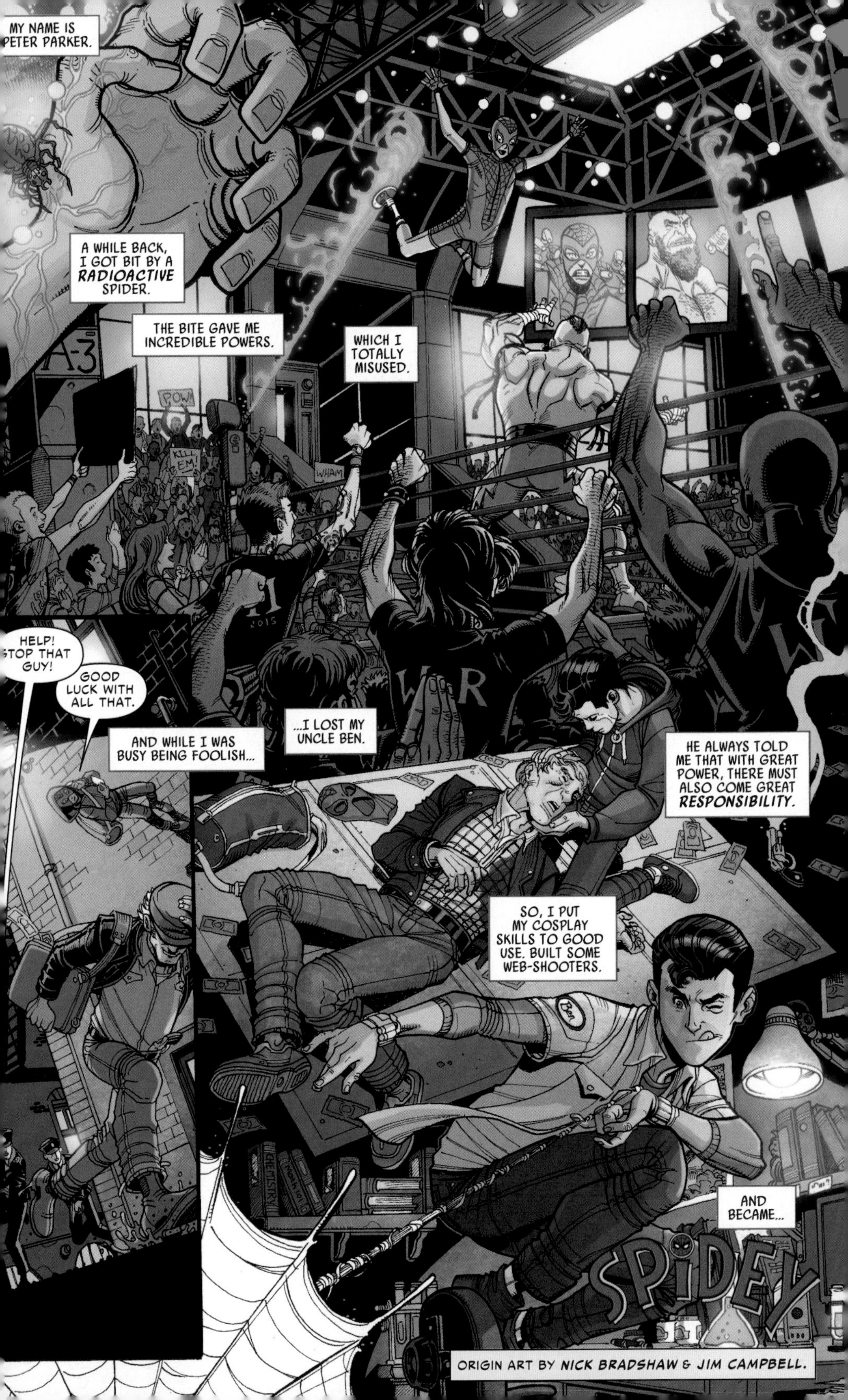
MY NAME IS PETER PARKER.
A WHILE BACK, I GOT BIT BY A RADIOACTIVE SPIDER.
THE BITE GAVE ME INCREDIBLE POWERS.
WHICH I TOTALLY MISUSED.
POW!
KILL EM!
WHAM
HELP! STOP THAT GUY!
GOOD LUCK WITH ALL THAT.
AND WHILE I WAS BUSY BEING FOOLISH...
...I LOST MY UNCLE BEN.
HE ALWAYS TOLD ME THAT WITH GREAT POWER, THERE MUST ALSO COME GREAT RESPONSIBILITY.
SO, I PUT MY COSPLAY SKILLS TO GOOD USE. BUILT SOME WEB-SHOOTERS.
AND BECAME...
SPIDEY
ORIGIN ART BY NICK BRADSHAW & JIM CAMPBELL.

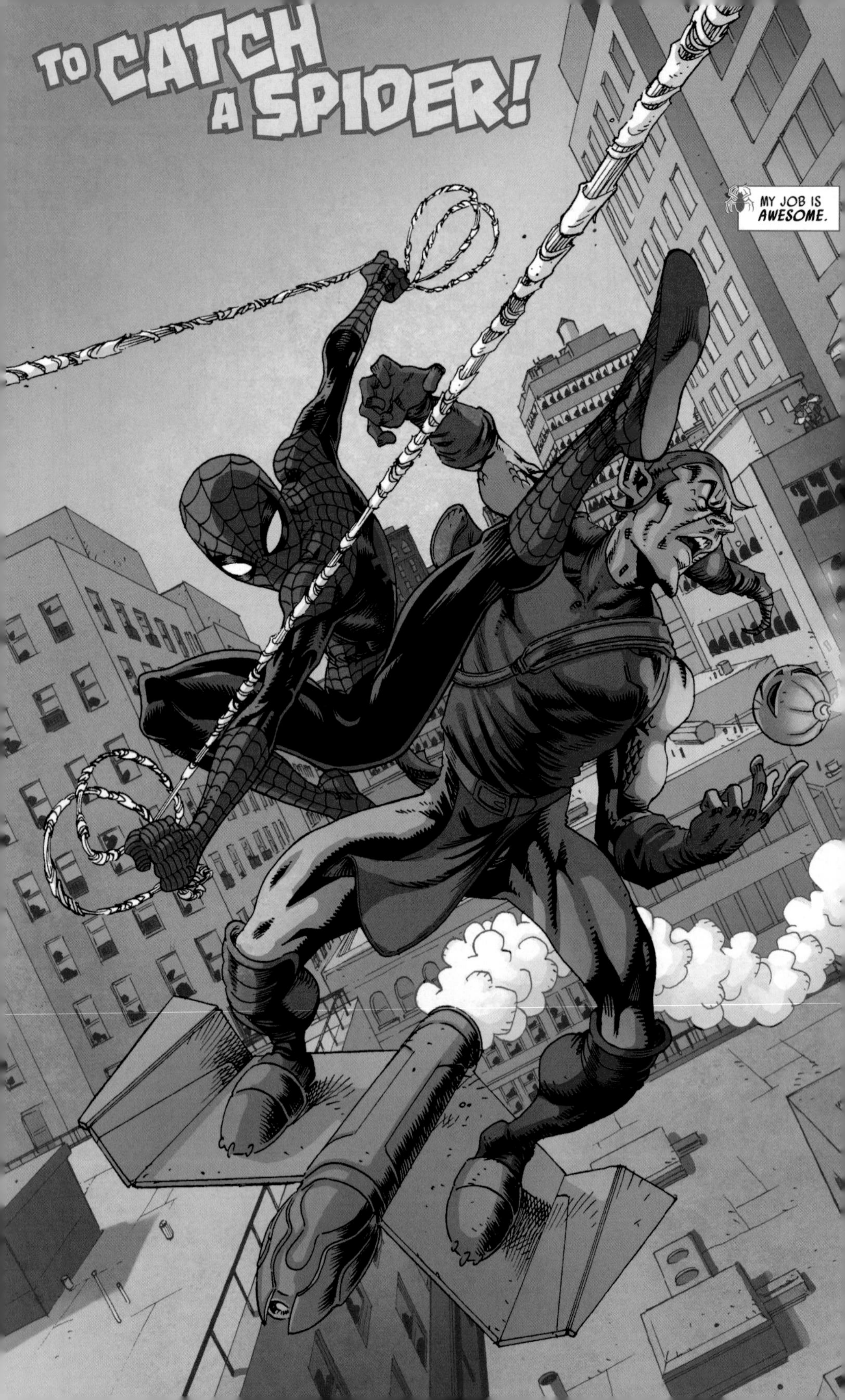
TO CATCH A SPIDER!
MY JOB IS AWESOME.

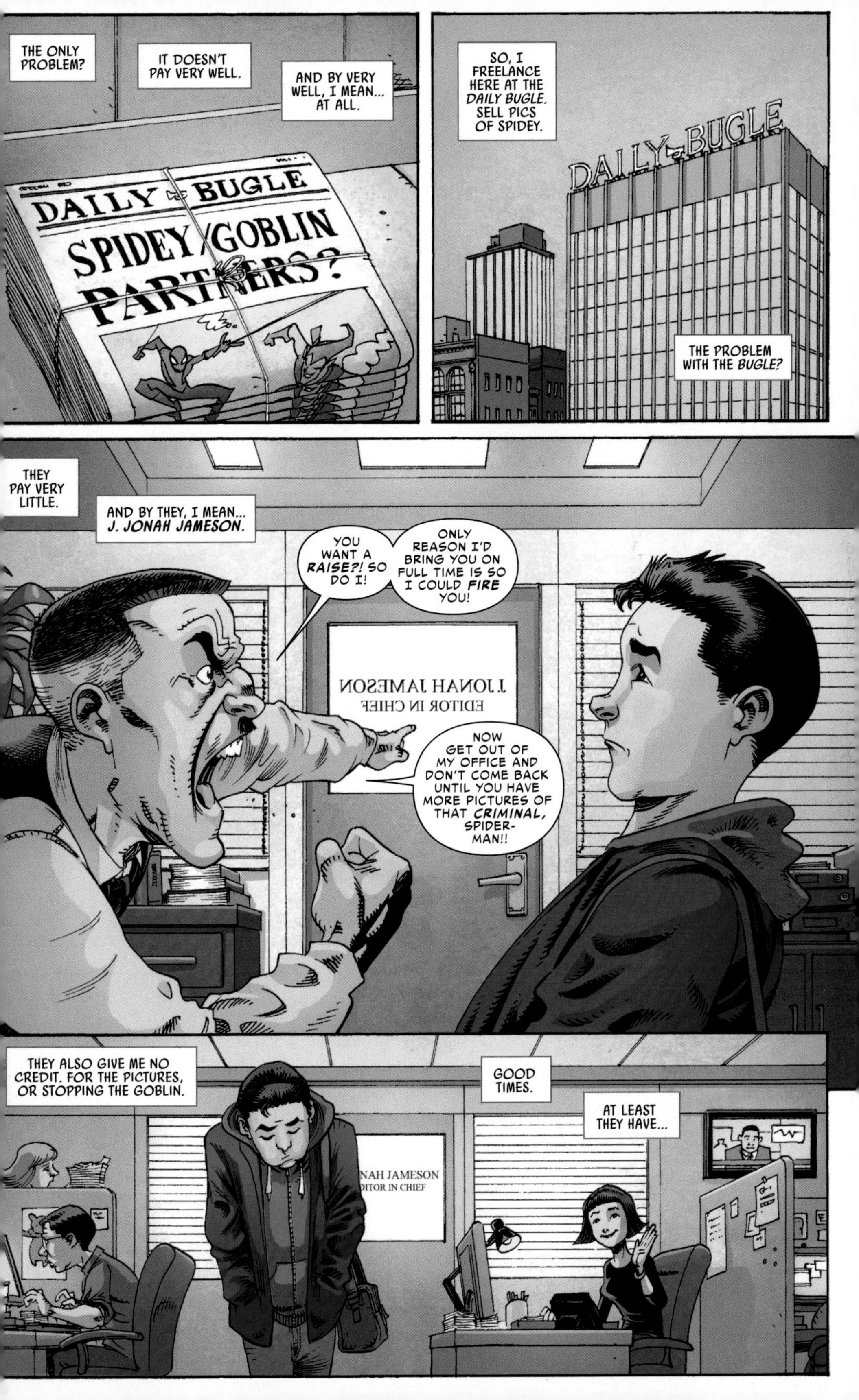

THE ONLY PROBLEM?
IT DOESN'T PAY VERY WELL.
AND BY VERY WELL, I MEAN... AT ALL.
DAILY BUGLE
SPIDEY/GOBLIN PARTNERS?
SO, I FREELANCE HERE AT THE *DAILY BUGLE.* SELL PICS OF SPIDEY.
DAILY BUGLE
THE PROBLEM WITH THE *BUGLE?*
THEY PAY VERY LITTLE.
AND BY THEY, I MEAN... *J. JONAH JAMESON.*
YOU WANT A ***RAISE?!*** SO DO I!
ONLY REASON I'D BRING YOU ON FULL TIME IS SO I COULD ***FIRE*** YOU!
NOW GET OUT OF MY OFFICE AND DON'T COME BACK UNTIL YOU HAVE MORE PICTURES OF THAT ***CRIMINAL,*** SPIDER-MAN!!
THEY ALSO GIVE ME NO CREDIT. FOR THE PICTURES, OR STOPPING THE GOBLIN.
GOOD TIMES.
AT LEAST THEY HAVE...

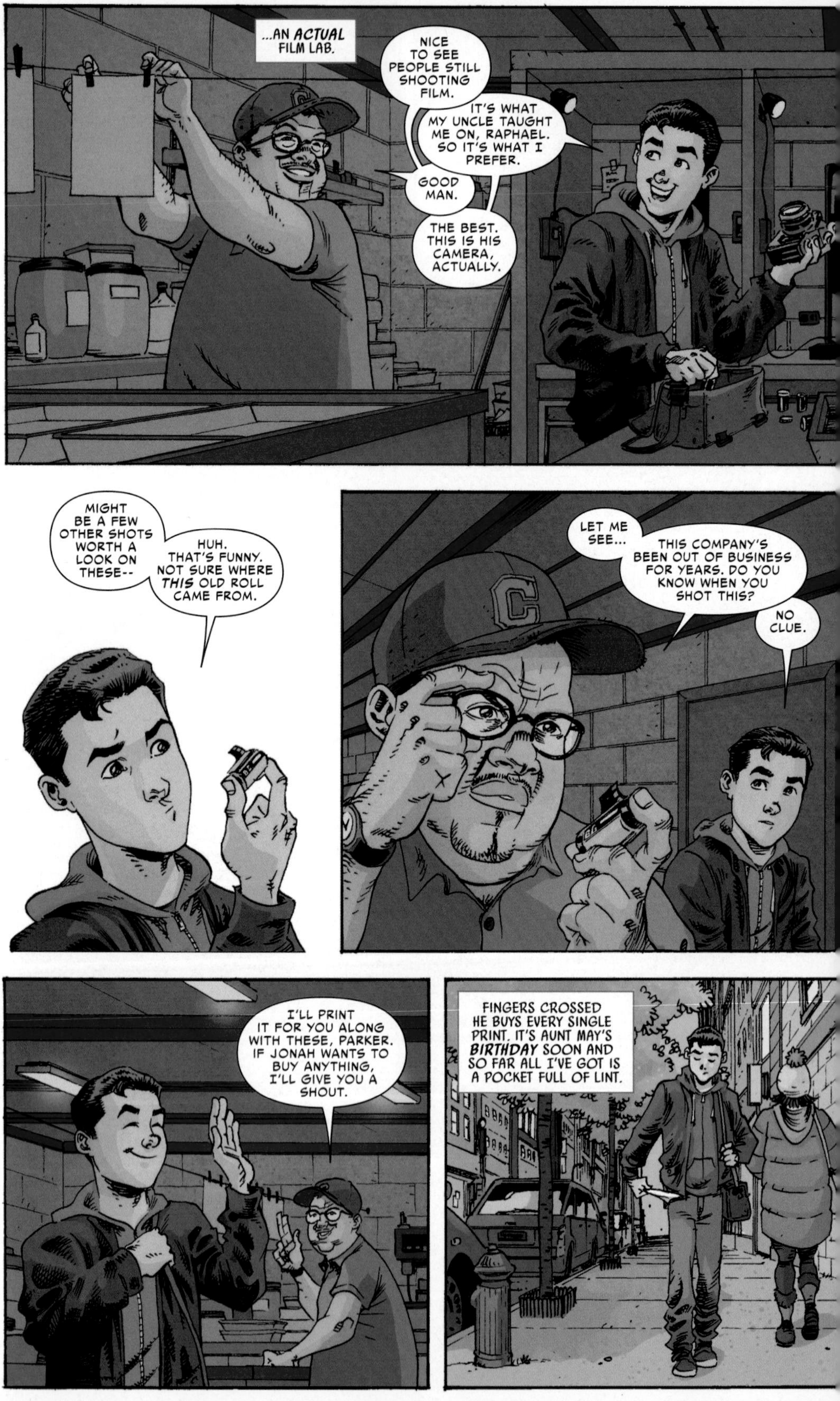
...AN ACTUAL FILM LAB.
NICE TO SEE PEOPLE STILL SHOOTING FILM.
IT'S WHAT MY UNCLE TAUGHT ME ON, RAPHAEL. SO IT'S WHAT I PREFER.
GOOD MAN.
THE BEST. THIS IS HIS CAMERA, ACTUALLY.
MIGHT BE A FEW OTHER SHOTS WORTH A LOOK ON THESE--
HUH. THAT'S FUNNY. NOT SURE WHERE THIS OLD ROLL CAME FROM.
LET ME SEE...
THIS COMPANY'S BEEN OUT OF BUSINESS FOR YEARS. DO YOU KNOW WHEN YOU SHOT THIS?
NO CLUE.
I'LL PRINT IT FOR YOU ALONG WITH THESE, PARKER. IF JONAH WANTS TO BUY ANYTHING, I'LL GIVE YOU A SHOUT.
FINGERS CROSSED HE BUYS EVERY SINGLE PRINT. IT'S AUNT MAY'S BIRTHDAY SOON AND SO FAR ALL I'VE GOT IS A POCKET FULL OF LINT.

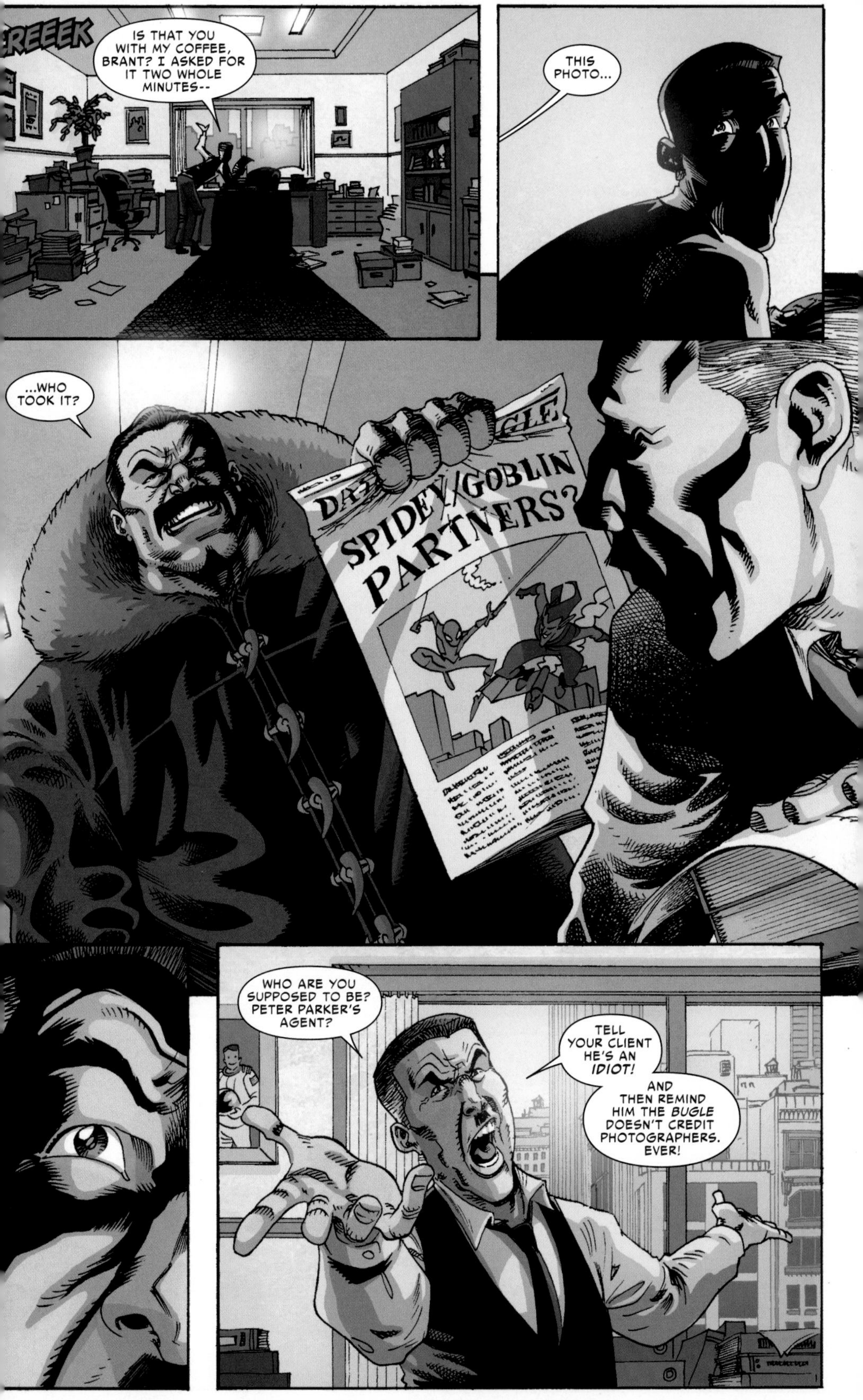

EREEEK
IS THAT YOU WITH MY COFFEE, BRANT? I ASKED FOR IT TWO WHOLE MINUTES--
THIS PHOTO...
...WHO TOOK IT?
SPIDEY/GOBLIN PARTNERS?
WHO ARE YOU SUPPOSED TO BE? PETER PARKER'S AGENT?
TELL YOUR CLIENT HE'S AN *IDIOT!*
AND THEN REMIND HIM THE *BUGLE* DOESN'T CREDIT PHOTOGRAPHERS. EVER!

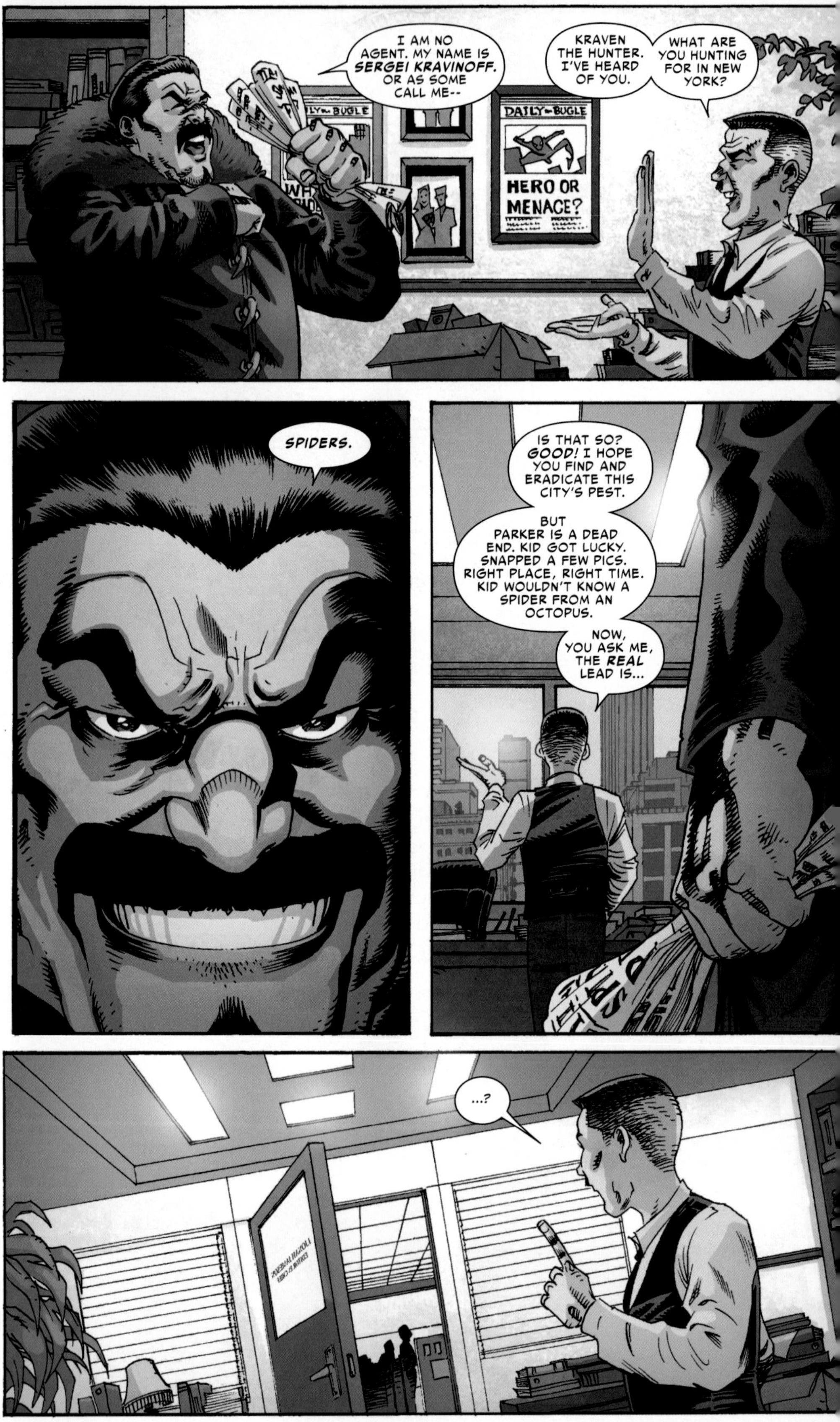
I AM NO AGENT. MY NAME IS SERGEI KRAVINOFF. OR AS SOME CALL ME--
KRAVEN THE HUNTER. I'VE HEARD OF YOU.
WHAT ARE YOU HUNTING FOR IN NEW YORK?
HERO OR MENACE?
SPIDERS.
IS THAT SO? GOOD! I HOPE YOU FIND AND ERADICATE THIS CITY'S PEST.
BUT PARKER IS A DEAD END. KID GOT LUCKY. SNAPPED A FEW PICS. RIGHT PLACE, RIGHT TIME. KID WOULDN'T KNOW A SPIDER FROM AN OCTOPUS.
NOW, YOU ASK ME, THE REAL LEAD IS...
...?

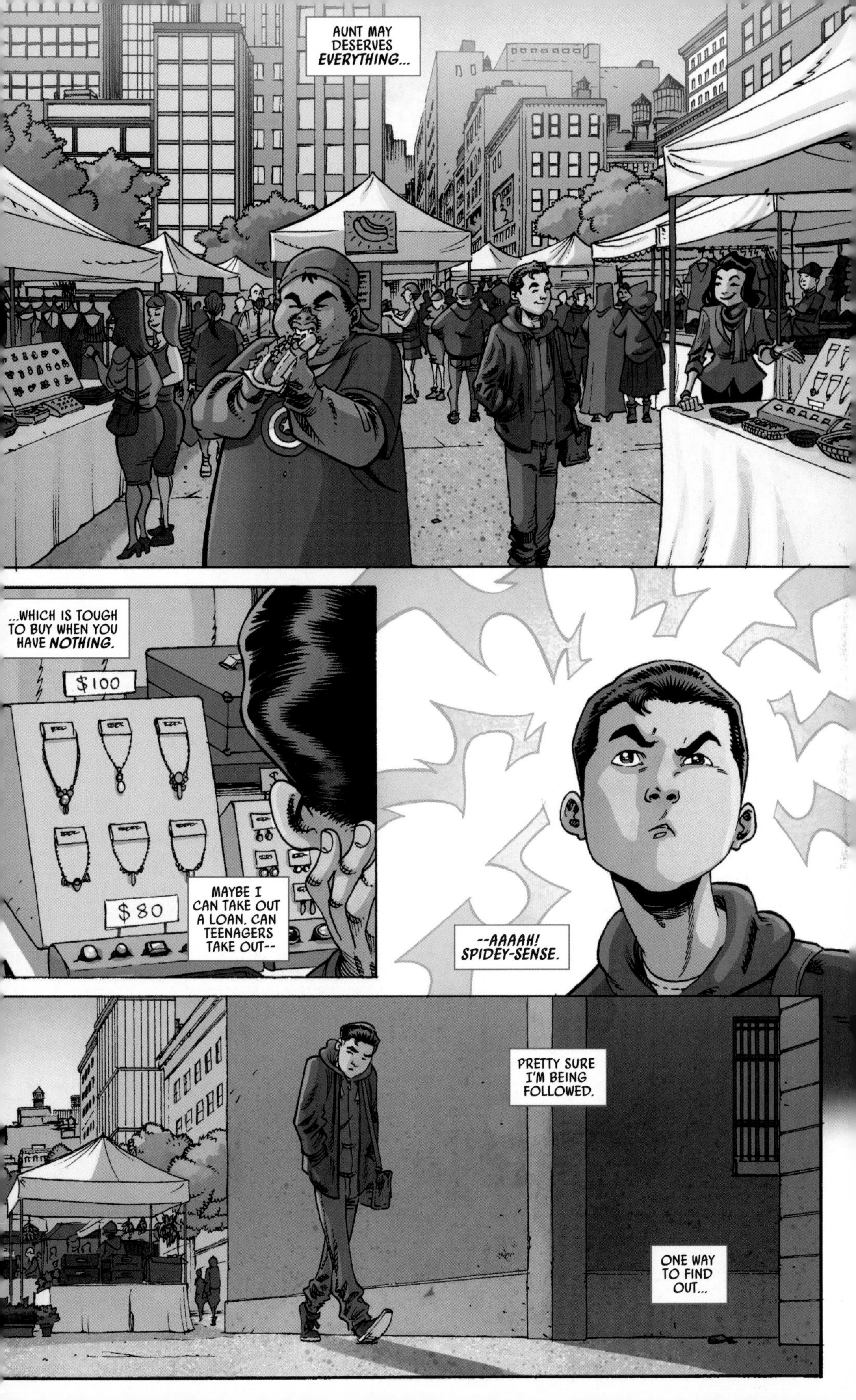
AUNT MAY DESERVES *EVERYTHING...*
...WHICH IS TOUGH TO BUY WHEN YOU HAVE *NOTHING.*
$100
$80
MAYBE I CAN TAKE OUT A LOAN. CAN TEENAGERS TAKE OUT--
--AAAAH! SPIDEY-SENSE.
PRETTY SURE I'M BEING FOLLOWED.
ONE WAY TO FIND OUT...

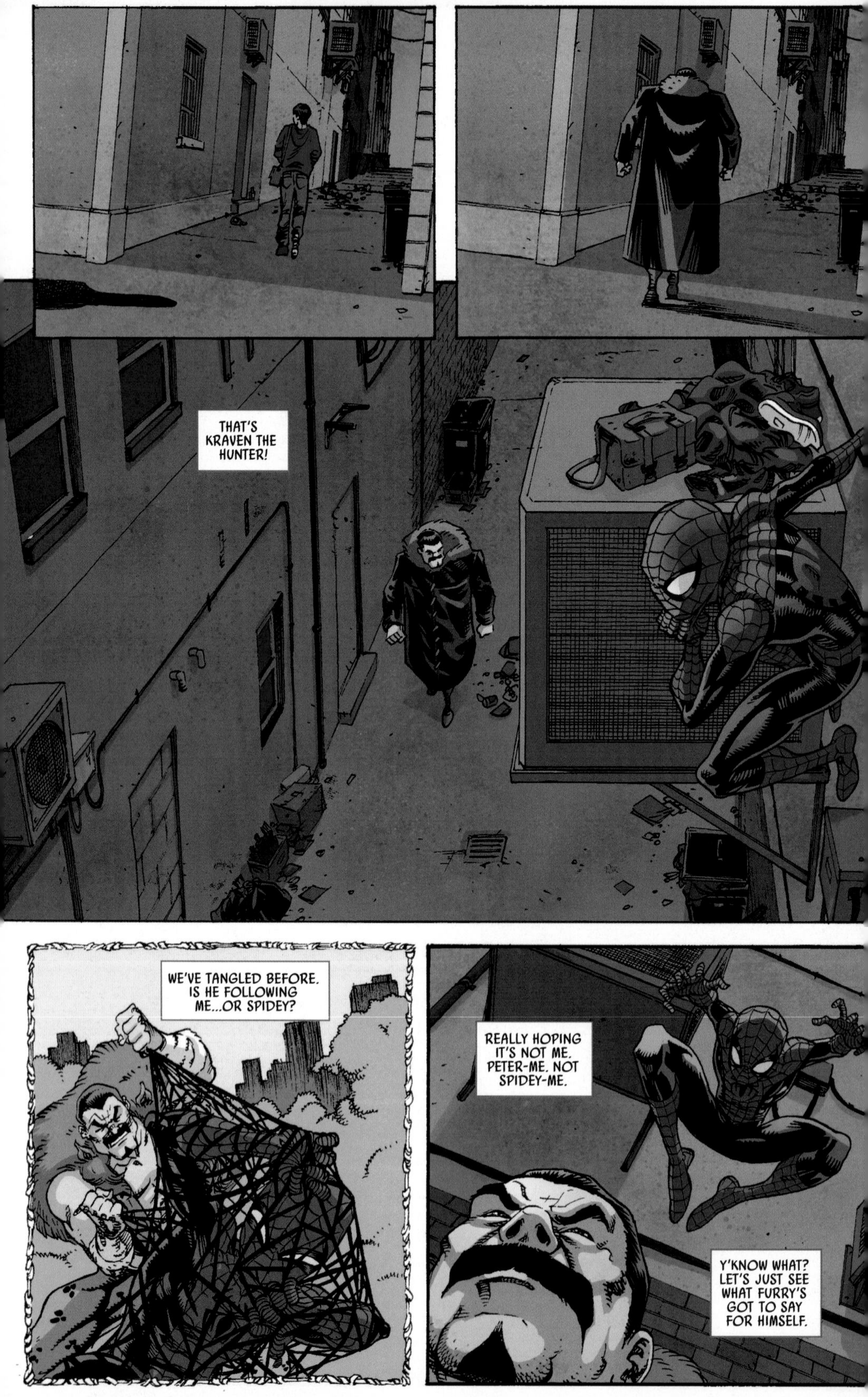
THAT'S KRAVEN THE HUNTER!
WE'VE TANGLED BEFORE. IS HE FOLLOWING ME...OR SPIDEY?
REALLY HOPING IT'S NOT ME. PETER-ME. NOT SPIDEY-ME.
Y'KNOW WHAT? LET'S JUST SEE WHAT FURRY'S GOT TO SAY FOR HIMSELF.

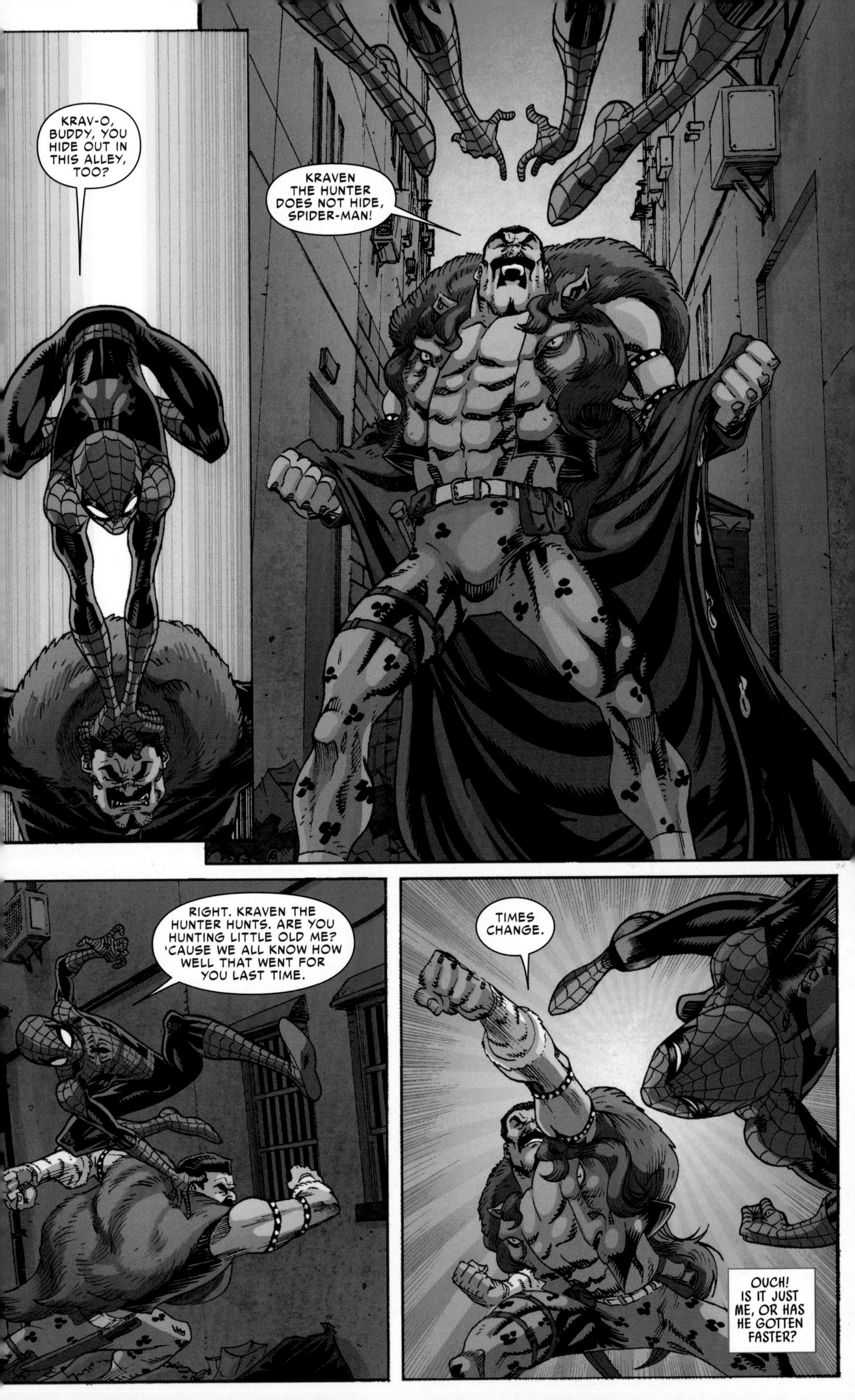
KRAV-O, BUDDY, YOU HIDE OUT IN THIS ALLEY, TOO?
KRAVEN THE HUNTER DOES NOT HIDE, SPIDER-MAN!
RIGHT. KRAVEN THE HUNTER HUNTS. ARE YOU HUNTING LITTLE OLD ME? 'CAUSE WE ALL KNOW HOW WELL THAT WENT FOR YOU LAST TIME.
TIMES CHANGE.
OUCH! IS IT JUST ME, OR HAS HE GOTTEN FASTER?

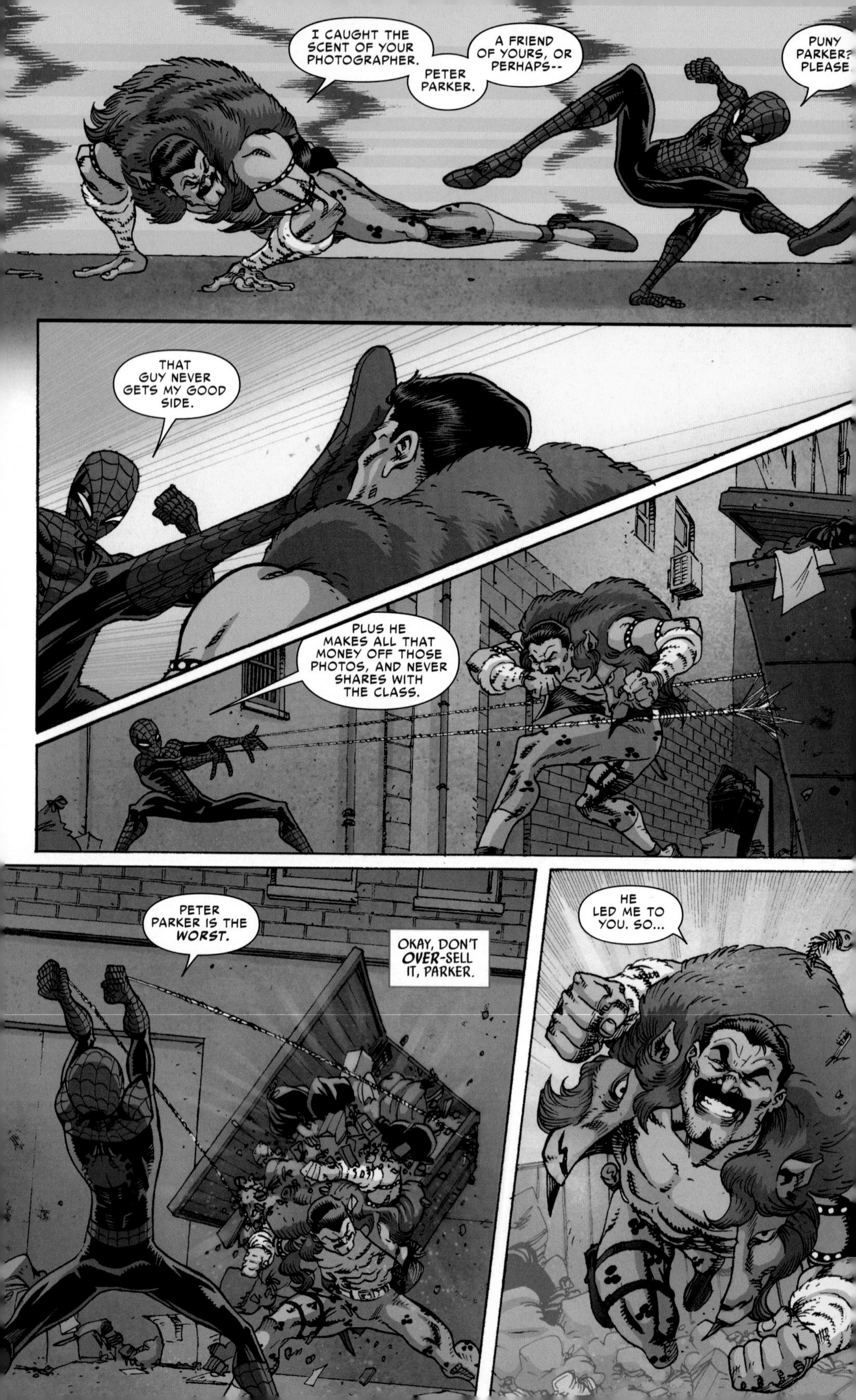
I CAUGHT THE SCENT OF YOUR PHOTOGRAPHER.
PETER PARKER.
A FRIEND OF YOURS, OR PERHAPS--
PUNY PARKER? PLEASE.
THAT GUY NEVER GETS MY GOOD SIDE.
PLUS HE MAKES ALL THAT MONEY OFF THOSE PHOTOS, AND NEVER SHARES WITH THE CLASS.
PETER PARKER IS THE WORST.
OKAY, DON'T OVER-SELL IT, PARKER.
HE LED ME TO YOU. SO...

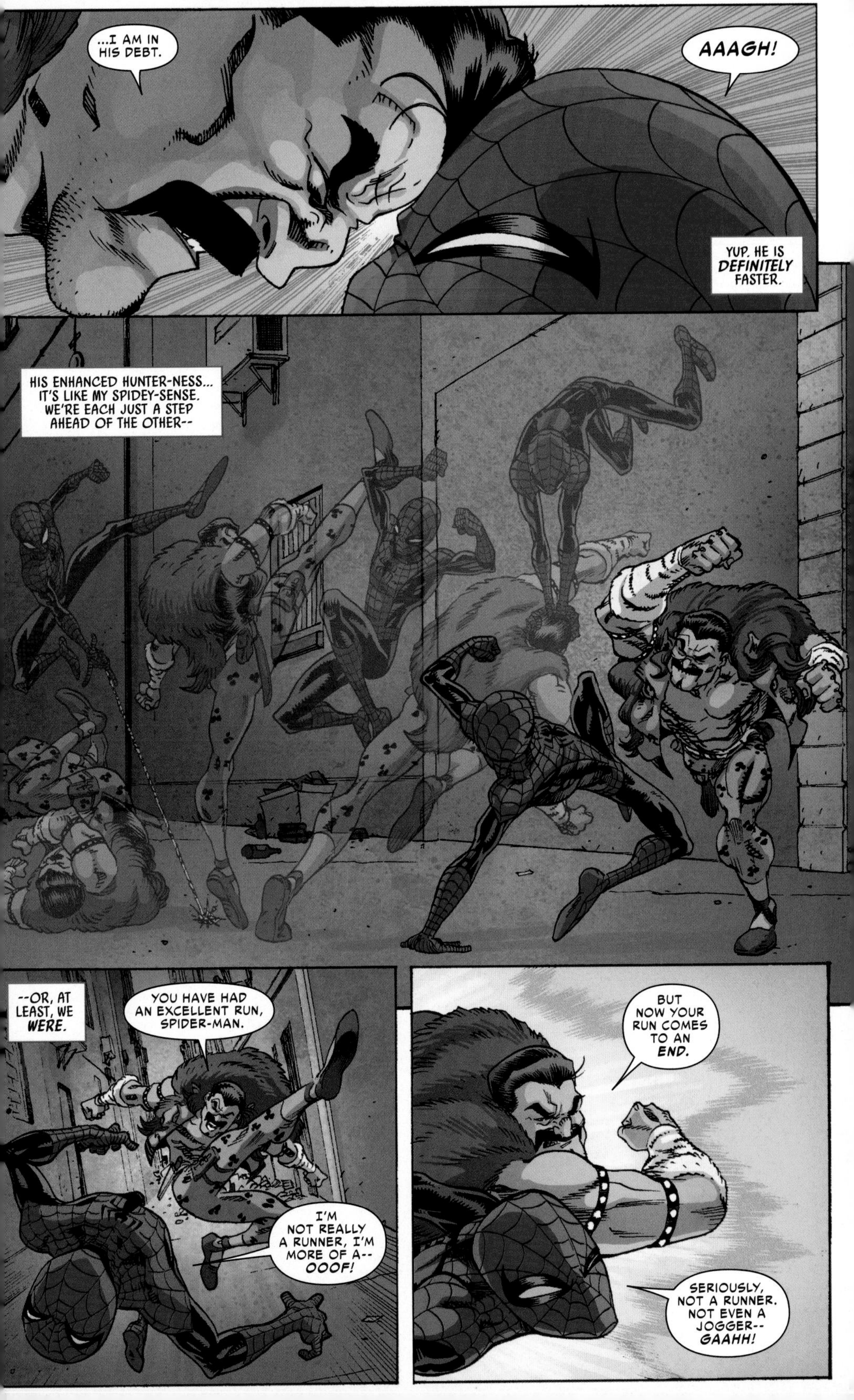
...I AM IN HIS DEBT.
AAAGH!
YUP. HE IS DEFINITELY FASTER.
HIS ENHANCED HUNTER-NESS... IT'S LIKE MY SPIDEY-SENSE. WE'RE EACH JUST A STEP AHEAD OF THE OTHER--
--OR, AT LEAST, WE WERE.
YOU HAVE HAD AN EXCELLENT RUN, SPIDER-MAN.
I'M NOT REALLY A RUNNER, I'M MORE OF A-- OOOF!
BUT NOW YOUR RUN COMES TO AN END.
SERIOUSLY, NOT A RUNNER. NOT EVEN A JOGGER-- GAAHH!

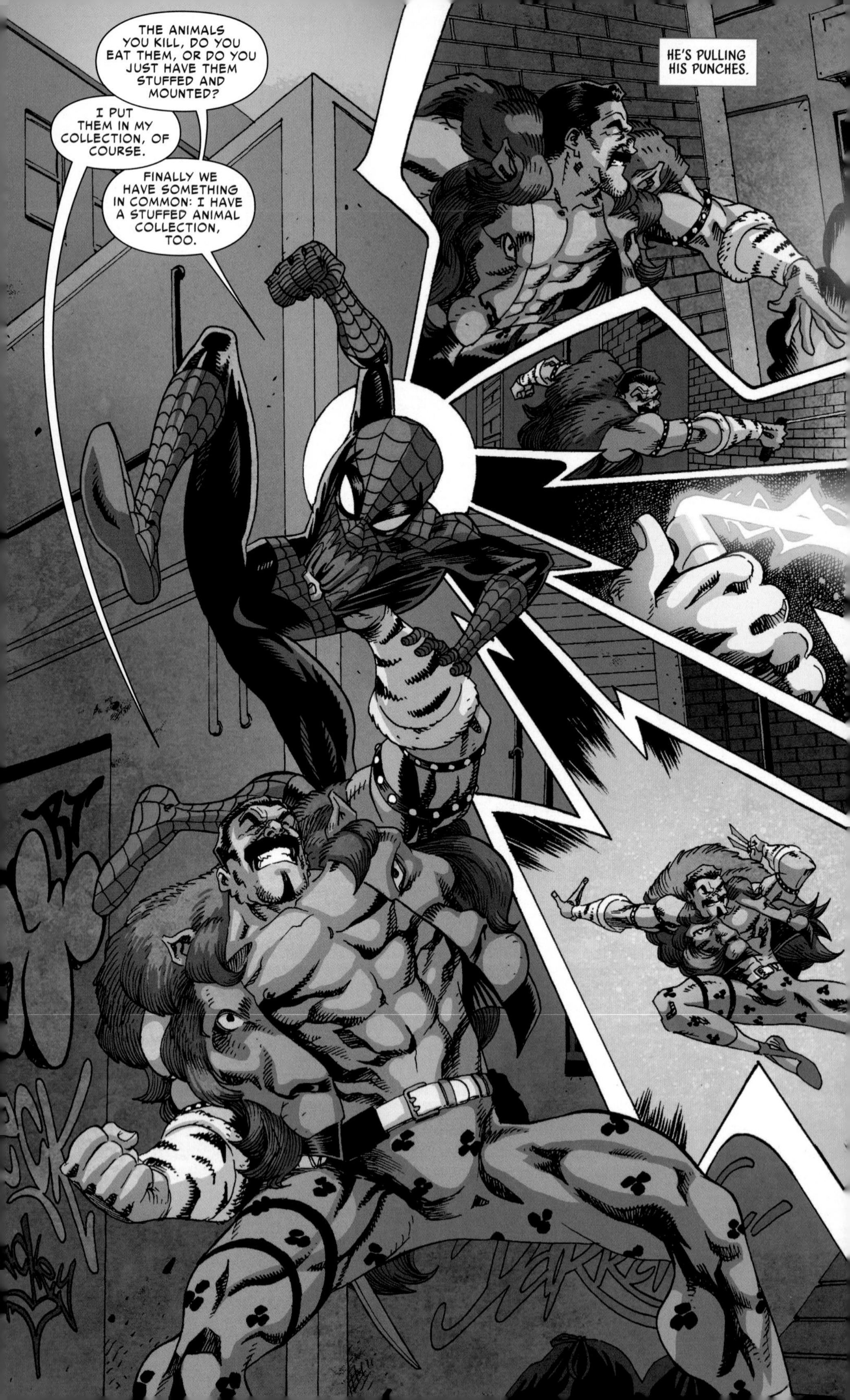
THE ANIMALS YOU KILL, DO YOU EAT THEM, OR DO YOU JUST HAVE THEM STUFFED AND MOUNTED?
I PUT THEM IN MY COLLECTION, OF COURSE.
FINALLY WE HAVE SOMETHING IN COMMON: I HAVE A STUFFED ANIMAL COLLECTION, TOO.
HE'S PULLING HIS PUNCHES.

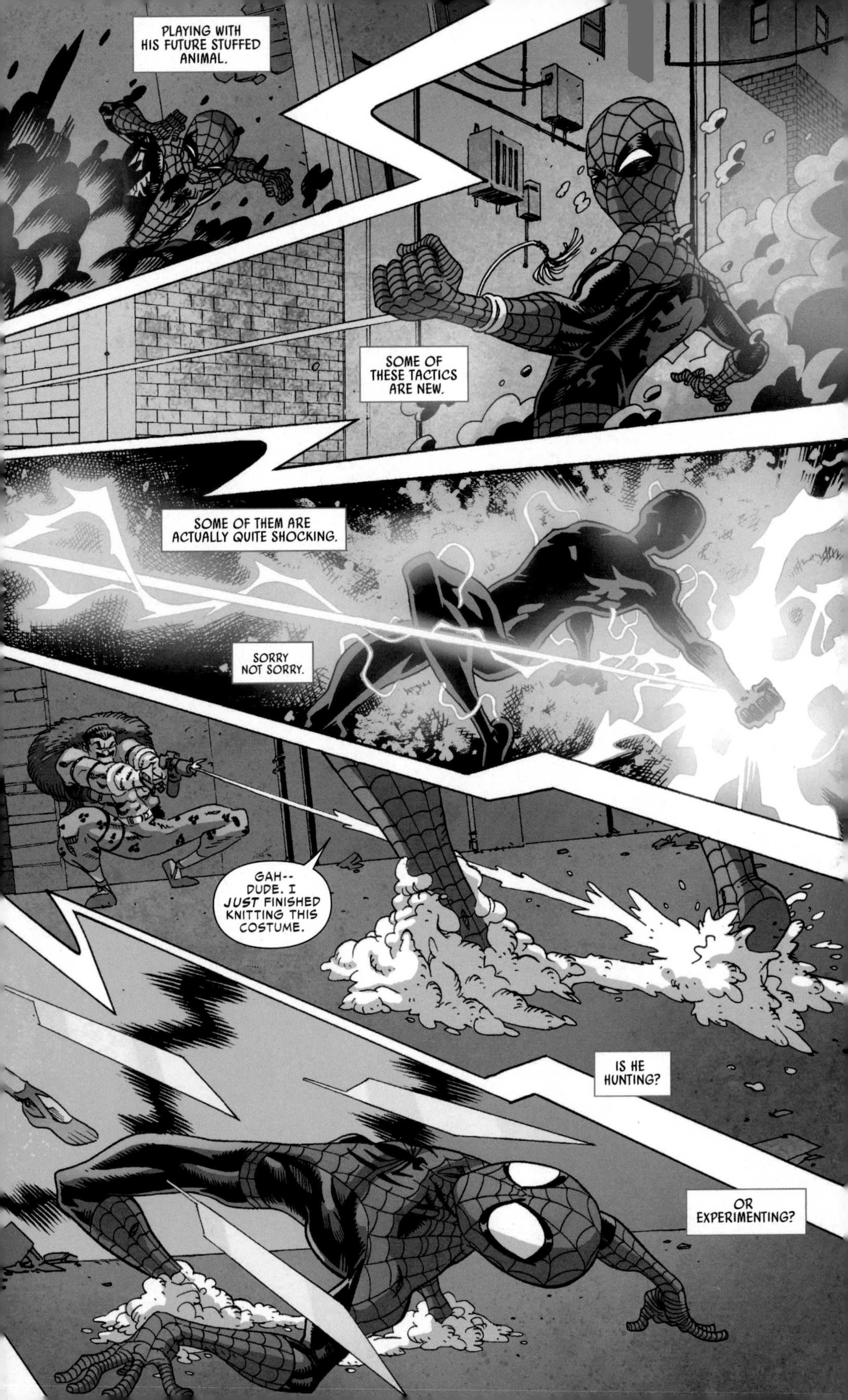
PLAYING WITH HIS FUTURE STUFFED ANIMAL.
SOME OF THESE TACTICS ARE NEW.
SOME OF THEM ARE ACTUALLY QUITE SHOCKING.
SORRY NOT SORRY.
GAH-- DUDE. I JUST FINISHED KNITTING THIS COSTUME.
IS HE HUNTING?
OR EXPERIMENTING?

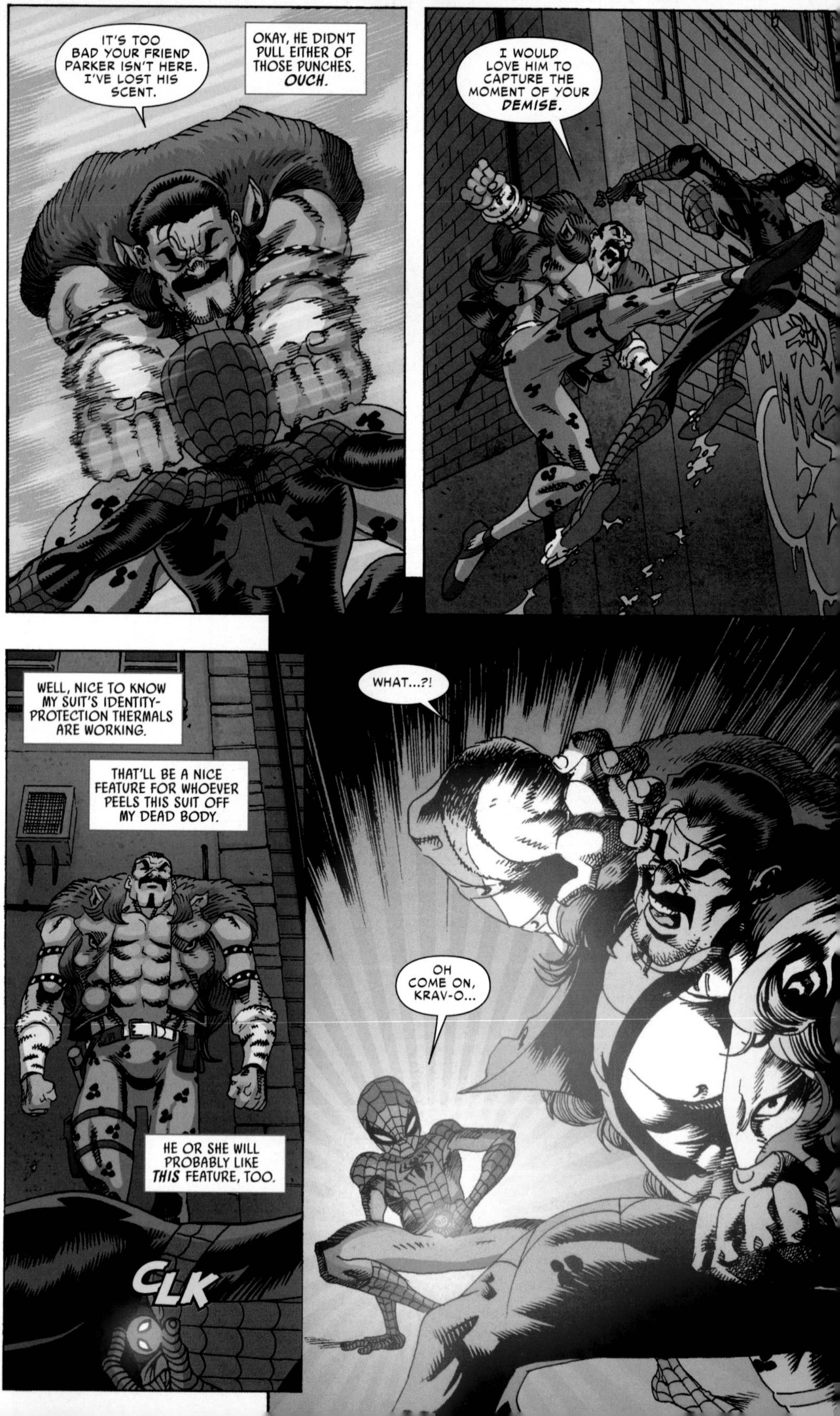
IT'S TOO BAD YOUR FRIEND PARKER ISN'T HERE. I'VE LOST HIS SCENT.
OKAY, HE DIDN'T PULL EITHER OF THOSE PUNCHES. OUCH.
I WOULD LOVE HIM TO CAPTURE THE MOMENT OF YOUR DEMISE.
WELL, NICE TO KNOW MY SUIT'S IDENTITY-PROTECTION THERMALS ARE WORKING.
THAT'LL BE A NICE FEATURE FOR WHOEVER PEELS THIS SUIT OFF MY DEAD BODY.
HE OR SHE WILL PROBABLY LIKE THIS FEATURE, TOO.
CLK
WHAT...?!
OH COME ON, KRAV-O...

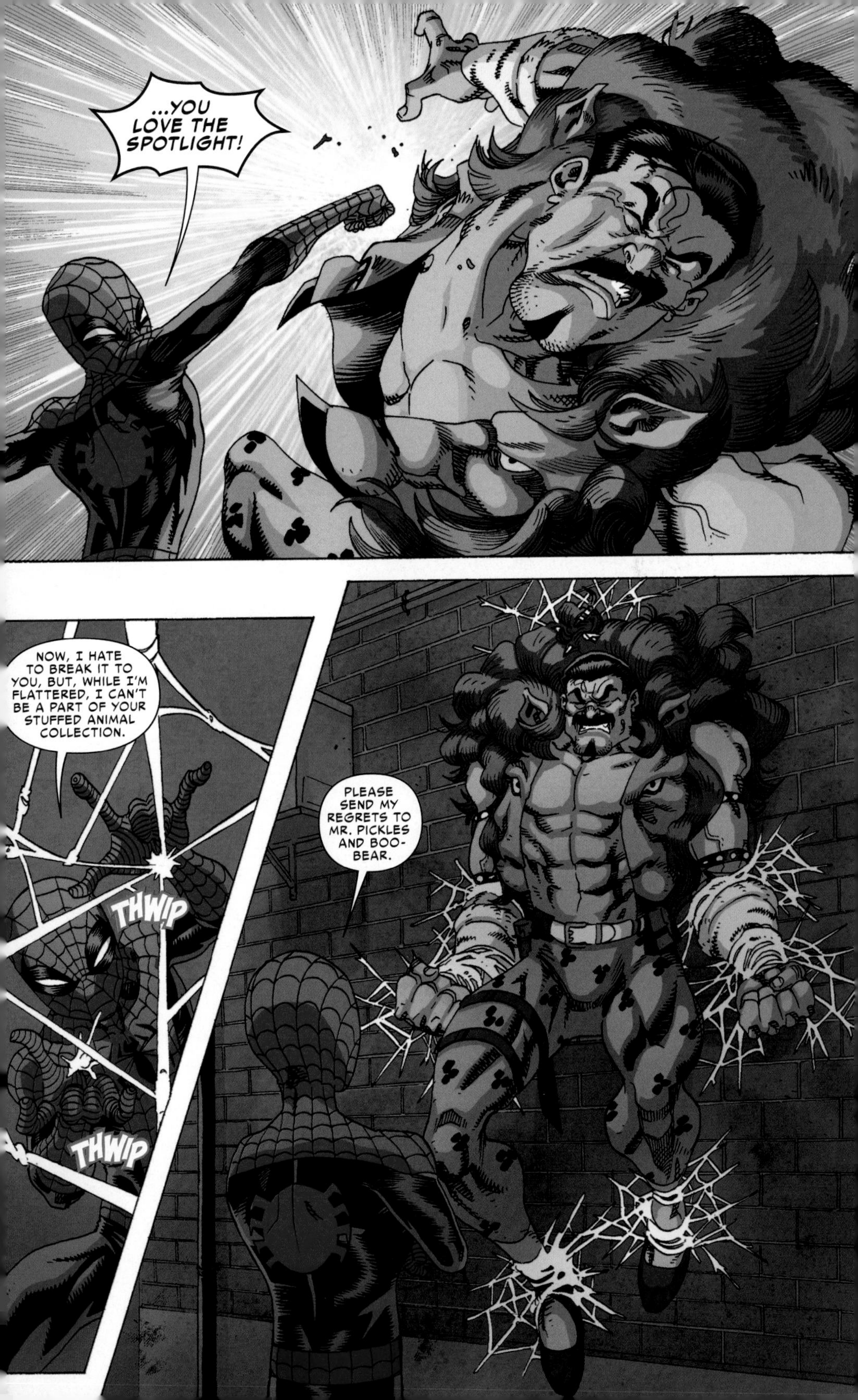
...YOU LOVE THE SPOTLIGHT!
NOW, I HATE TO BREAK IT TO YOU, BUT, WHILE I'M FLATTERED, I CAN'T BE A PART OF YOUR STUFFED ANIMAL COLLECTION.
THWIP
THWIP
PLEASE SEND MY REGRETS TO MR. PICKLES AND BOO-BEAR.

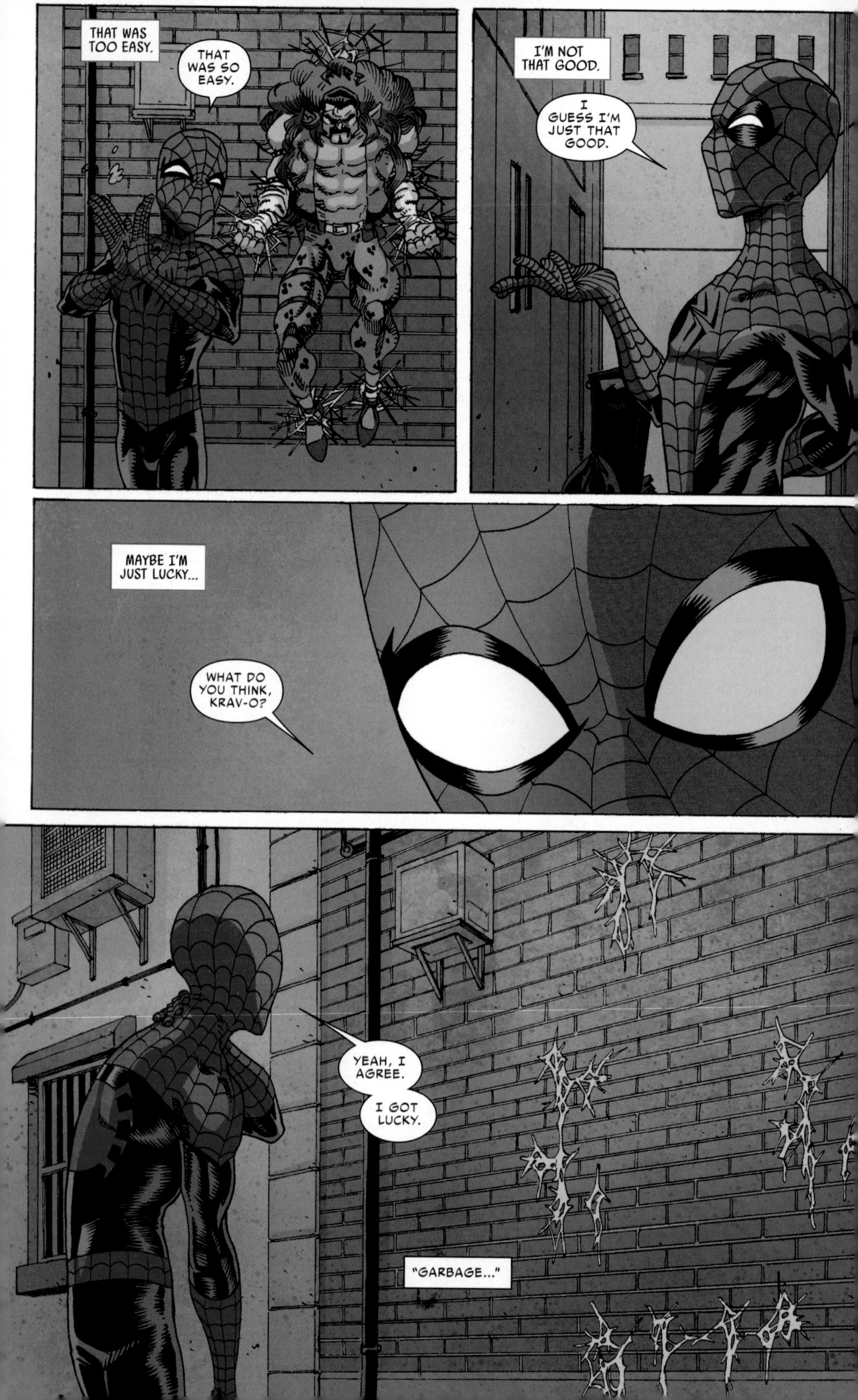
THAT WAS TOO EASY.
THAT WAS SO EASY.
I'M NOT THAT GOOD.
I GUESS I'M JUST THAT GOOD.
MAYBE I'M JUST LUCKY...
WHAT DO YOU THINK, KRAV-O?
YEAH, I AGREE.
I GOT LUCKY.
"GARBAGE..."

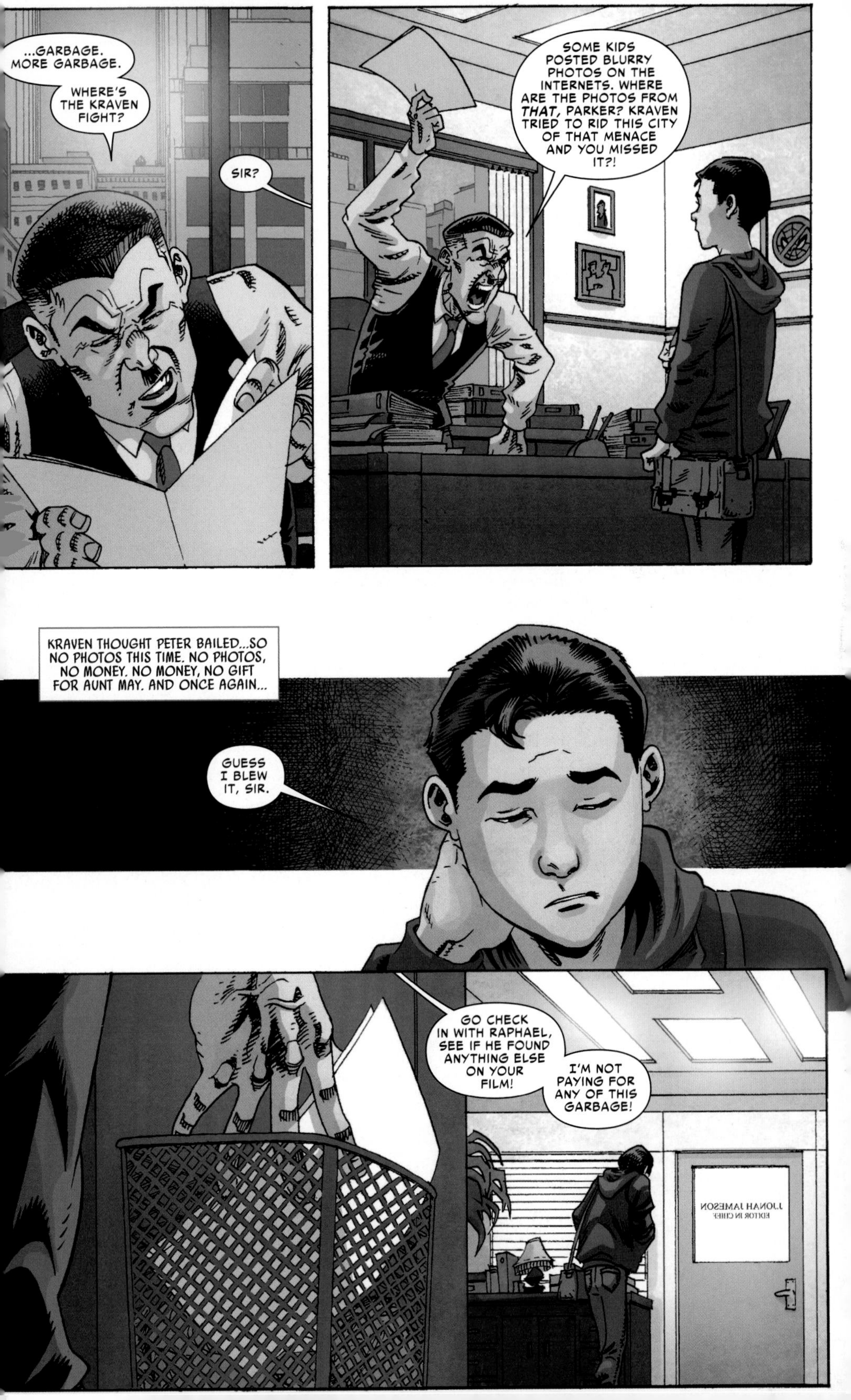
...GARBAGE. MORE GARBAGE.
WHERE'S THE KRAVEN FIGHT?
SIR?
SOME KIDS POSTED BLURRY PHOTOS ON THE INTERNETS. WHERE ARE THE PHOTOS FROM *THAT*, PARKER? KRAVEN TRIED TO RID THIS CITY OF THAT MENACE AND YOU MISSED IT?!
KRAVEN THOUGHT PETER BAILED...SO NO PHOTOS THIS TIME. NO PHOTOS, NO MONEY. NO MONEY, NO GIFT FOR AUNT MAY. AND ONCE AGAIN...
GUESS I BLEW IT, SIR.
GO CHECK IN WITH RAPHAEL, SEE IF HE FOUND ANYTHING ELSE ON YOUR FILM!
I'M NOT PAYING FOR ANY OF THIS GARBAGE!

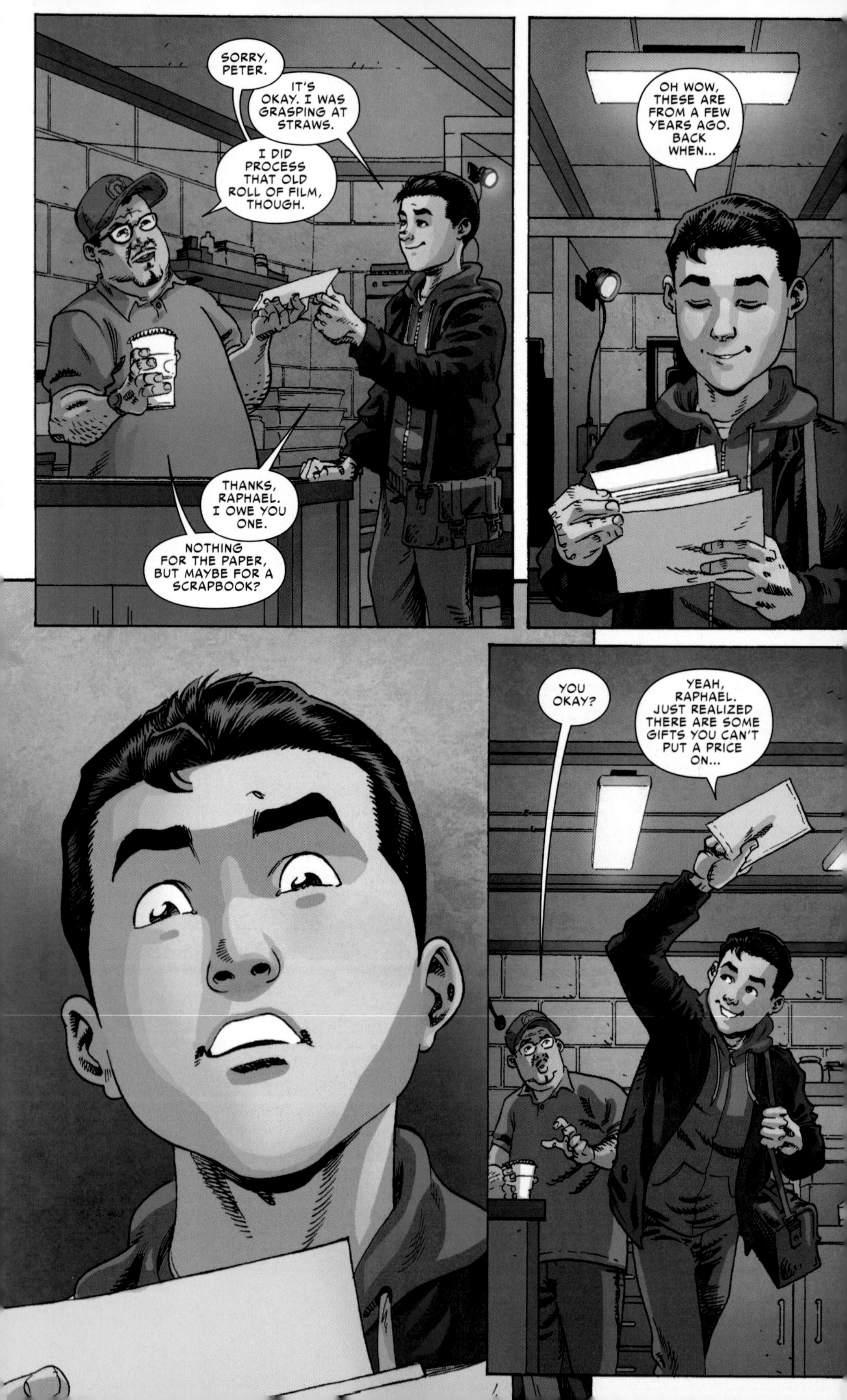
SORRY, PETER.
IT'S OKAY. I WAS GRASPING AT STRAWS.
I DID PROCESS THAT OLD ROLL OF FILM, THOUGH.
NOTHING FOR THE PAPER, BUT MAYBE FOR A SCRAPBOOK?
THANKS, RAPHAEL. I OWE YOU ONE.
OH WOW, THESE ARE FROM A FEW YEARS AGO. BACK WHEN...
YOU OKAY?
YEAH, RAPHAEL. JUST REALIZED THERE ARE SOME GIFTS YOU CAN'T PUT A PRICE ON...

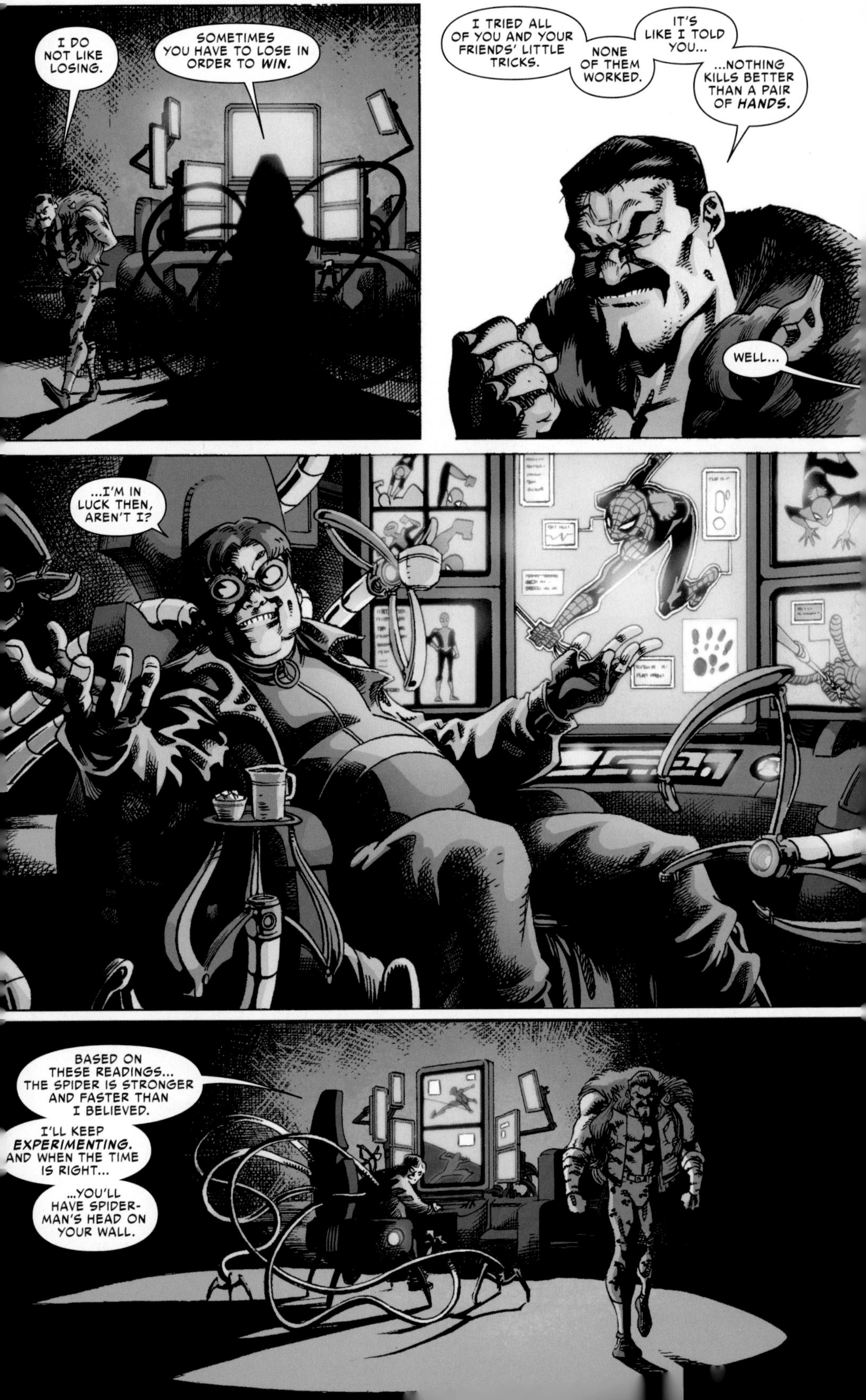
I DO NOT LIKE LOSING.
SOMETIMES YOU HAVE TO LOSE IN ORDER TO *WIN.*
I TRIED ALL OF YOU AND YOUR FRIENDS' LITTLE TRICKS.
NONE OF THEM WORKED.
IT'S LIKE I TOLD YOU...
...NOTHING KILLS BETTER THAN A PAIR OF *HANDS.*
WELL...
...I'M IN LUCK THEN, AREN'T I?
BASED ON THESE READINGS... THE SPIDER IS STRONGER AND FASTER THAN I BELIEVED.
I'LL KEEP *EXPERIMENTING.* AND WHEN THE TIME IS RIGHT...
...YOU'LL HAVE SPIDER-MAN'S HEAD ON YOUR WALL.

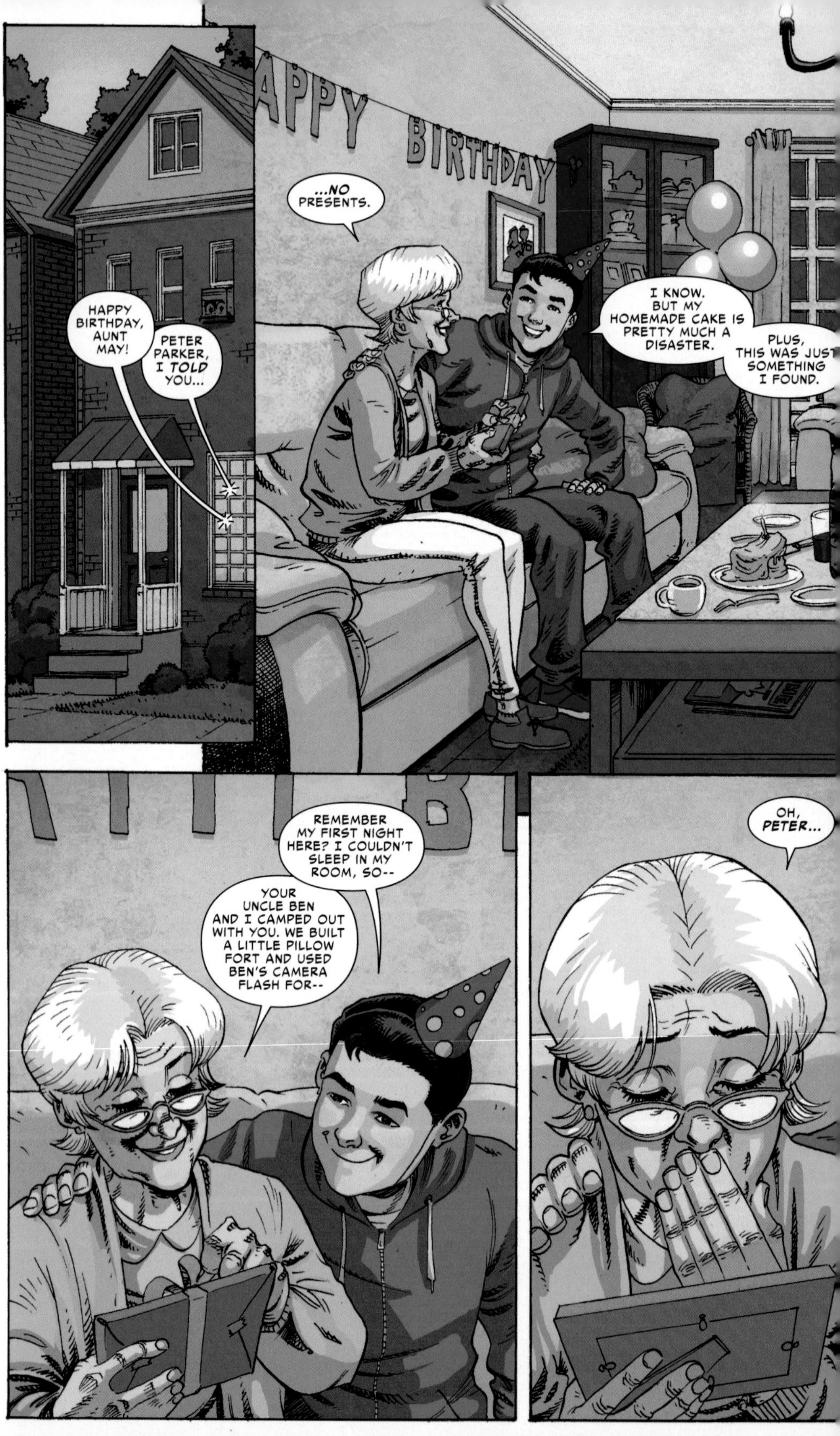
HAPPY BIRTHDAY, AUNT MAY!
PETER PARKER, I TOLD YOU...
...NO PRESENTS.
I KNOW. BUT MY HOMEMADE CAKE IS PRETTY MUCH A DISASTER.
PLUS, THIS WAS JUST SOMETHING I FOUND.
HAPPY BIRTHDAY
REMEMBER MY FIRST NIGHT HERE? I COULDN'T SLEEP IN MY ROOM, SO--
YOUR UNCLE BEN AND I CAMPED OUT WITH YOU. WE BUILT A LITTLE PILLOW FORT AND USED BEN'S CAMERA FLASH FOR--
OH, PETER...

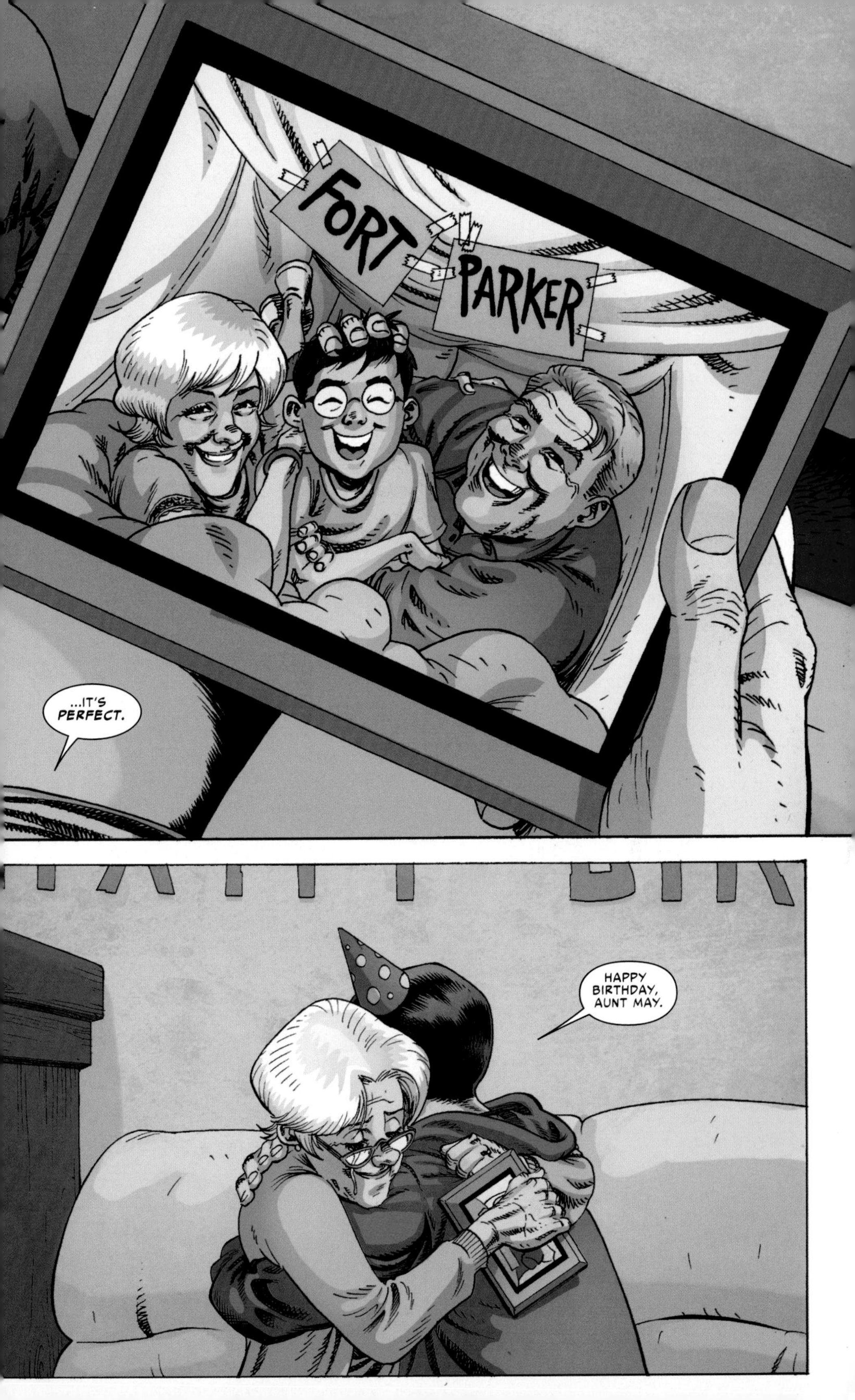
FORT PARKER
...IT'S PERFECT.
HAPPY BIRTHDAY, AUNT MAY.

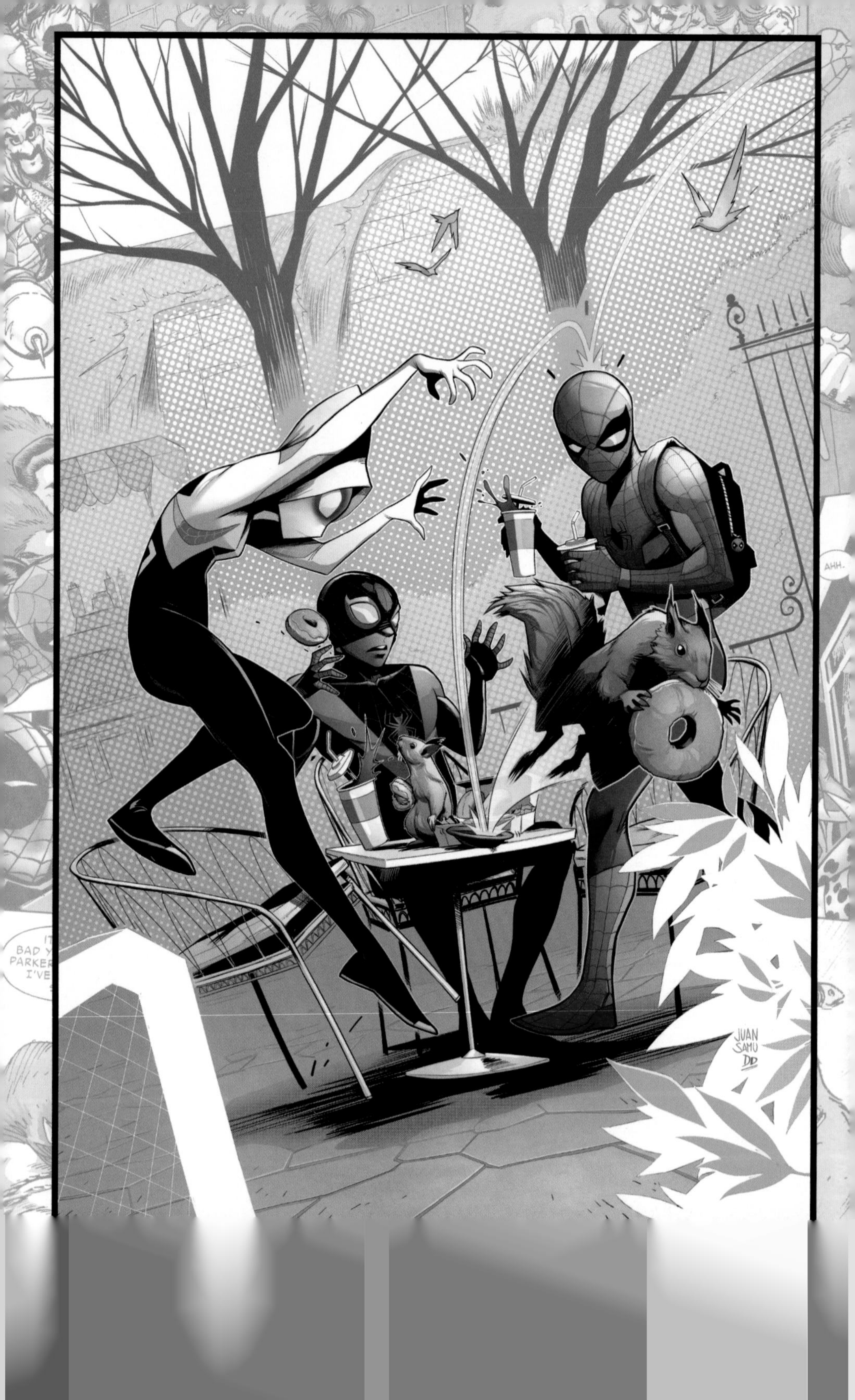
AHH.
JUAN SAMU DD

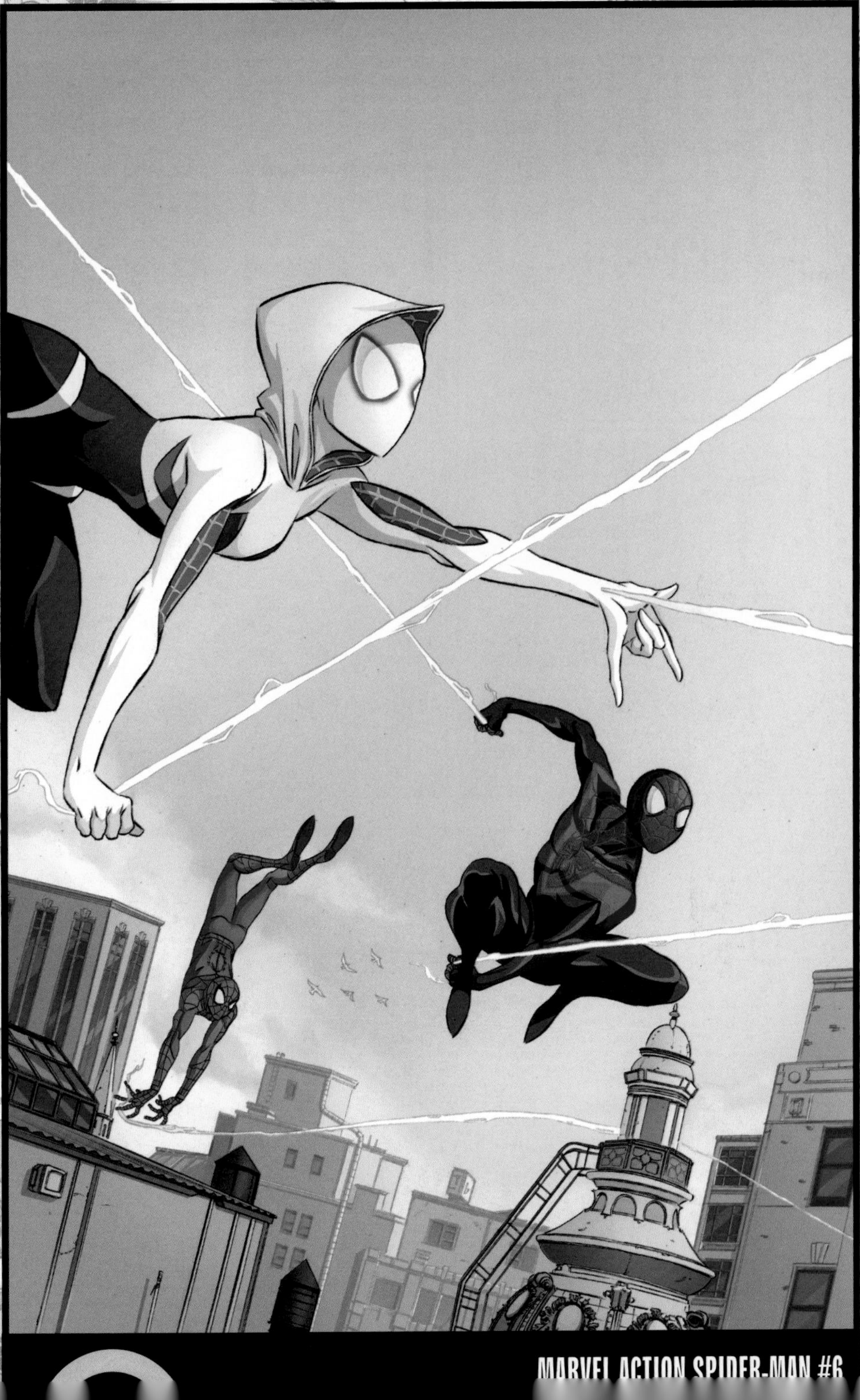

MARVEL ACTION SPIDER-MAN #6

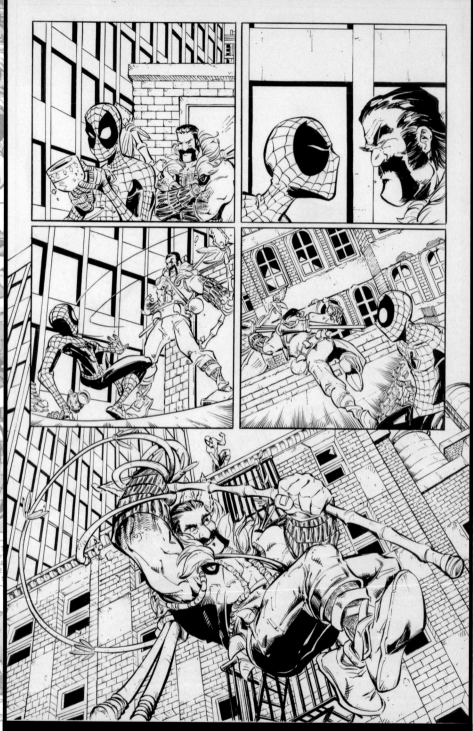

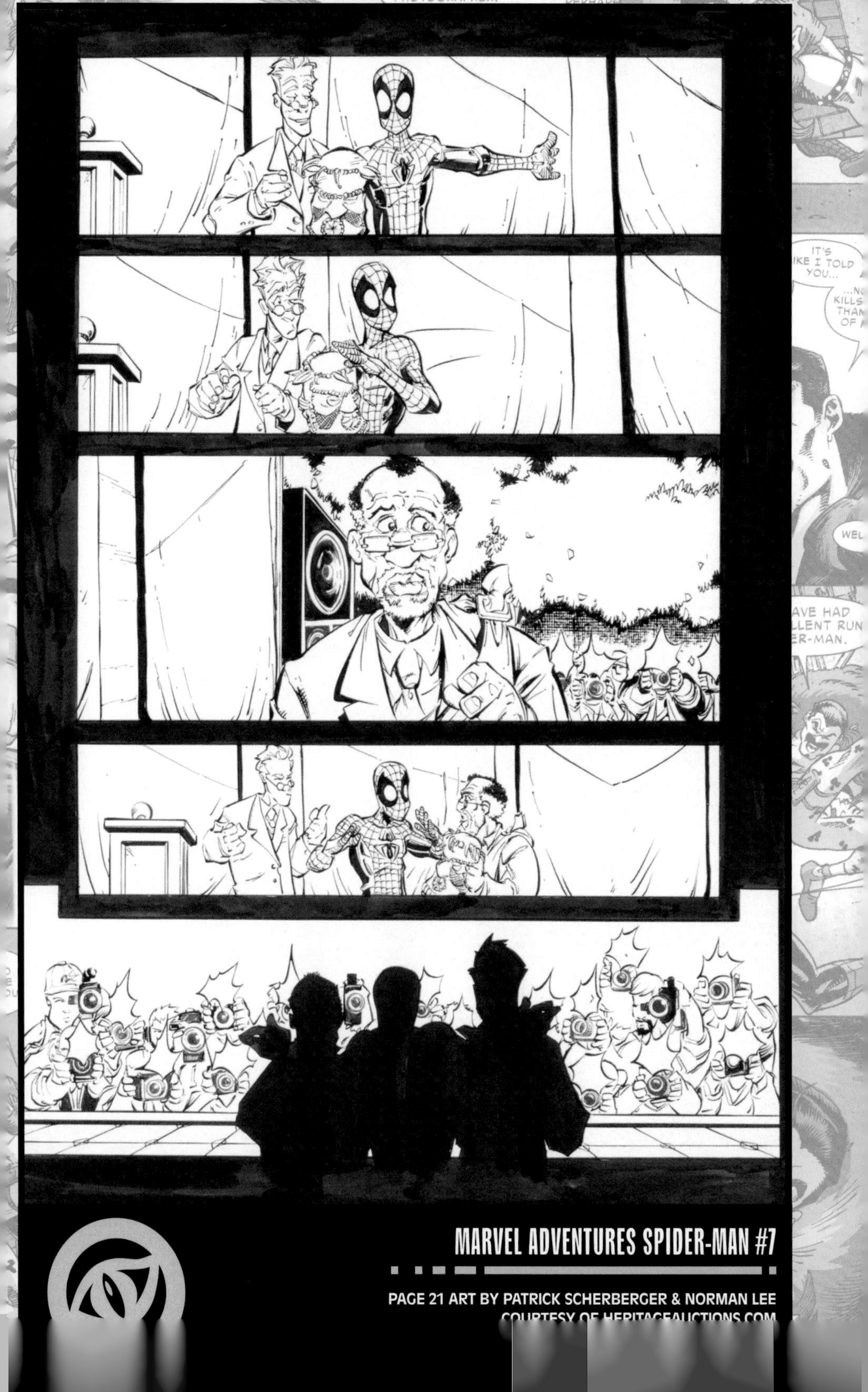

MARVEL ADVENTURES SPIDER-MAN #7

PAGE 21 ART BY PATRICK SCHERBERGER & NORMAN LEE
COURTESY OF HERITAGEAUCTIONS.COM

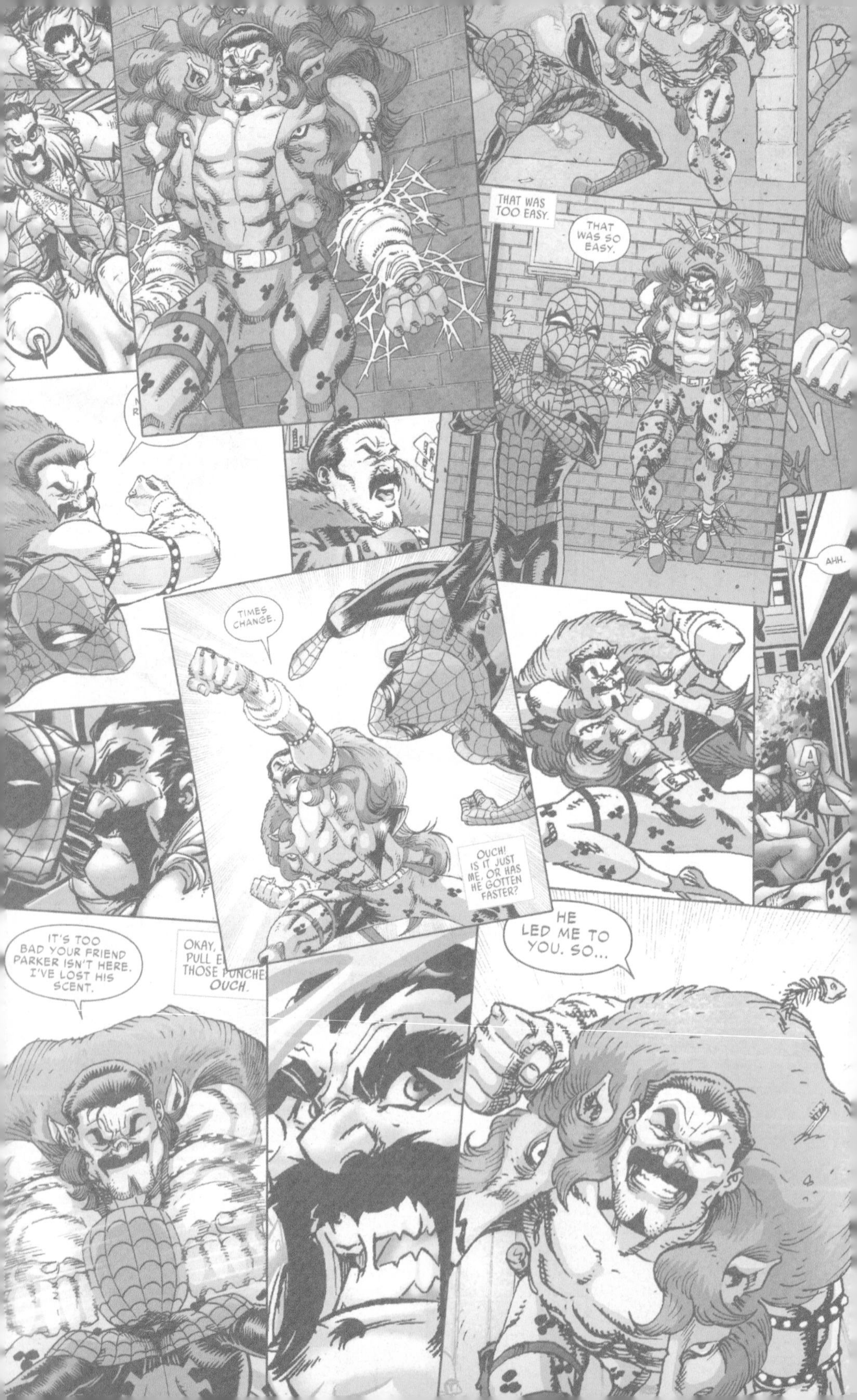
THAT WAS TOO EASY.
THAT WAS SO EASY.
AHH.
TIMES CHANGE.
OUCH! IS IT JUST ME, OR HAS HE GOTTEN FASTER?
IT'S TOO BAD YOUR FRIEND PARKER ISN'T HERE. I'VE LOST HIS SCENT.
OKAY,
OUCH.
HE LED ME TO YOU. SO...